HIGH WARRIOR

A MEDIEVAL ROMANCE

BY KATHRYN LE VEQUE

REIGN OF DE WINTER SERIES
HIGH WARRIORS OF MACROHAN SERIES

KATHRYN LE VEQUE NOVELS

Queen of Lost Stars (House of St. Hever)

**Lords of Thunder: The de Shera
Brotherhood Trilogy**
The Thunder Lord
The Thunder Warrior
The Thunder Knight

The Great Knights of de Moray:
Shield of Kronos
The Gorgon

Highland Warriors of Munro:
The Red Lion
Deep Into Darkness

The House of Ashbourne:
Upon a Midnight Dream

The House of D'Aurilliac:
Valiant Chaos

The House of De Nerra:
The Falls of Erith
Vestiges of Valor
Realm of Angels

The House of De Dere:
Of Love and Legend

St. John and de Gare Clans:
The Warrior Poet

The House of de Garr:
Lord of Light
Realm of Angels

The House of de Bretagne:
The Questing (also related to Swords
and Shields)

The House of Summerlin:
The Legend

The Kingdom of Hendocia:
Kingdom by the Sea

Time Travel Romance: (Saxon Lords of
Hage)
The Crusader
Kingdom Come

Contemporary Romance:

Kathlyn Trent/Marcus Burton Series:
Valley of the Shadow
The Eden Factor
Canyon of the Sphinx

The American Heroes Series:
The Lucius Robe
Fires of Autumn
Evenshade
Sea of Dreams
Purgatory

Other Contemporary Romance:
Lady of Heaven
Darkling, I Listen
In the Dreaming Hour

Sons of Poseidon:
The Immortal Sea

**Pirates of Britannia Series (with Eliza
Knight):**
Savage of the Sea by Eliza Knight
Leader of Titans by Kathryn Le Veque
The Sea Devil by Eliza Knight
Sea Wolfe by Kathryn Le Veque

Note: All Kathryn's novels are designed to be read as stand-alones, although many have cross-over characters or cross-over family groups. Novels that are grouped together have related characters or family groups.

Series are clearly marked. All series contain the same characters or family groups except the

American Heroes Series, which is an anthology with unrelated characters.

There is NO particular chronological order for any of the novels because they can all be read as stand-alones, even the series.

For more information, find it in **A Reader's Guide to the Medieval World of Le Veque**.

TABLE OF CONTENTS

AUTHOR'S NOTE

Welcome to Bric MacRohan's tale, and what a tale it is!

Bric, as we'll see in these pages, is a big Irish knight who is both an invincible and flawed man. There is no one tougher than he is and no one as fearless or fearsome. I've written about a lot of fearsome knights – in fact, all of my heroes are quite fearsome in their own right – but Bric has something special about him that just makes him extraordinarily bad-ass. But when men who have that intense command-and-control personality fall, they fall hard because they have no experience otherwise.

What Bric suffers from, as you will see, is essentially a mild form of PTSD. There are severe forms that affect modern soldiers, but battle fatigue and PTSD have been affecting warriors as long as there have been battles. It was only until modern times that we really came to understand what it was (it was actually diagnosed back in the Regency period), but before that, no one really understood it and considered it cowardice.

It's interesting to note that a 14th century knight named Geoffroi de Charny wrote about the mental instability of knights who have suffered much in battle. But in my research, a Medievalist familiar with de Charny's work made a distinct point between Medieval warriors and today's modern soldier – Medieval knights were born into the warrior life, and modern-day soldiers aren't.

From a very early age, medieval knights were trained as warriors and saw brutality that few did. Therefore, warring was, literally, the only life they knew, so mental fatigue and all that came about differently for them. They'd never known a "civilian" life, only to be thrust into the brutalities of war like today's modern soldier is. So, it's a completely different kind of "battle fatigue" when it comes to the medieval knight and a different mindset for those who observed it.

The House of de Winter features heavily in this book because Bric is the captain of the guard, so I should explain the family tree because he is also related to them – my novel *Lespada* is the main de Winter story. So if you haven't read it, you should. But a little about the de Winter family – Daveigh (pronounced Day-vee) de Winter is head of the House of de Winter at this point. His father, Davyss de Winter the First, is the great-grandson of Denis de Winter (WARWOLFE), descendant of the Visigoths.

Now, here's where it becomes a little complicated – Daveigh is Davyss' eldest son from his first wife. When the first wife passed away, Davyss the First married again and his second wife gave birth to Grayson, who is Davyss de Winter the Second's father. Daveigh married an Irish woman, and that is how Bric came to serve the House of de Winter – as part of her dowry – but Daveigh and his wife never had any children, which is how Davyss II ended up with the de Winter sword, *Lespada*. The eldest de Winter male always carries that sword, and Davyss the Second was the next in line after Daveigh passed on.

Because Davyss the First married a bastard daughter of the Earl of Norfolk, he was given a title upon his marriage – something Hugh Bigod, the earl, had to petition the king for (because barons can only be given lands and titles from the king). A donation to Henry (then-king), and Bigod's bastard daughter received the title of Baroness Cressingham, a title that Hugh de Winter inherited when he married her, becoming Baron Cressingham.

All of these titles were passed down from Daveigh to Grayson (who married Katharine, sister of the Earl of Surrey and Simon de Montfort's lover at the time), and then on to Davyss the Second as the eldest de Winter male. Davyss the Second isn't born until about fourteen years after our story takes place, but it's important to understand where the de Winters fit into the politics of England at this time – they are an extremely important war machine with relations to the Earldom of Norfolk. Kind of like Norfolk's attack dog. And our hero, Bric, is the teeth of that attack dog.

He is the *Ard Trodaí* – the High Warrior.

Since this tale is quite complex (as far as family relations go), there are charts attached, something I don't normally do. But in this case, it was important. Make sure to read them and their notes – it will help clarify the backstory, and how Bric came to serve the House of de Winter, so you can understand how everyone is related.

But lastly, let's not forget about our lady of this tale, the lovely Eiselle (pronounced ee-ZELL). You can see on the family tree how she is related to Dashiell, and the house of du Reims. She's a little lost at the beginning of this book, but she quickly finds her place, and when Bric falls for her, he falls hard. I love how she came to be his rock, the man who was always the rock for others. These two make quite the passionate and bold pair.

Lots going on in this book, so hold on tight, expect a surprise appearance of a former Le Veque hero (Sean de Lara from *Lord of the Shadows* plays a key role in the end), and enjoy the ride!

Hugs,
Kathryn

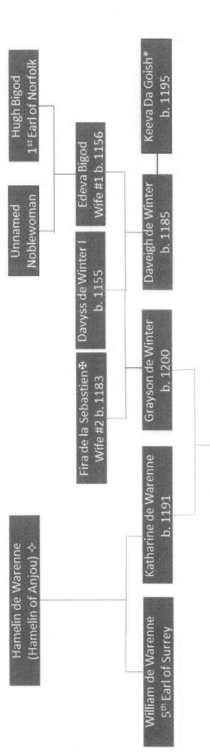

Hugh Bigod
1st Earl of Norfolk

Unnamed
Noblewoman

Edeva Bigod
Wife #1 b. 1156

Davyss de Winter I
b. 1155

Keeva Da Goish*
b. 1195

Daveigh de Winter
b. 1185

Fira de la Sebastien✻
Wife #2 b. 1183

Grayson de Winter
b. 1200

Hamelin de Warenne
(Hamelin of Anjou) ◇

Katharine de Warenne
b. 1191

Davyss de Winter II
b. 1230

William de Warenne
5th Earl of Surrey

Legend

*   Keeva's dowry included Bric MacRohan, Irish knight fostered in England.

✻   Spanish house of San Sebastien, Northern Spain

◇   Hamelin was the illegitimate son of Geoffrey of Anjou, making him part of the House of Plantagenet and a relation to the current king.

House of de Winter c. 1216 A.D.

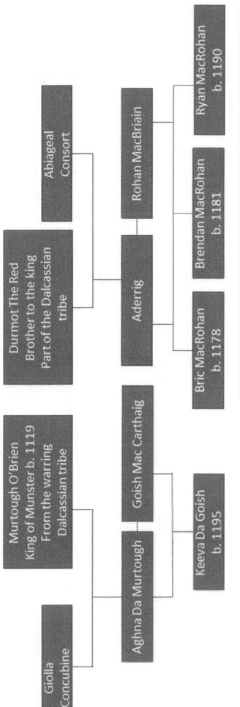

Giolla
Concubine

Murtough O'Brien
King of Munster b. 1119
From the warring
Dalcassian tribe

Durmot The Red
Brother to the king
Part of the Dalcassian
tribe

Abiageal
Consort

Aghna Da Murtough

Goish Mac Carthaig

Keeva Da Goish
b. 1195

Aderrig

Rohan MacBriain

Bric MacRohan
b. 1178

Brendan MacRohan
b. 1181

Ryan MacRohan
b. 1190

The current King of Munster, Domnall O'Brien, pledged his cousin, Keeva, to the House of de Winter, along with lands from Dunvegan from the north, Ardmore to the south, and all the way to the River Blackwater in Munster in exchange for men, money, and the building of castles to protect against the rival Irish kings.

Bric mac Rohan, also a cousin to Keeva, was sent as part of her dowry, but also because he was the best knight Domnall had to offer, a man of great skill who had fostered in both England and France.

Rohan mac Briain is also a descendant of the Dalcassians, the greatest tribe in Ireland, and a direct descendant of High Kings.

House of MacRohan
Sons of High Kings
c. 1216 A.D.

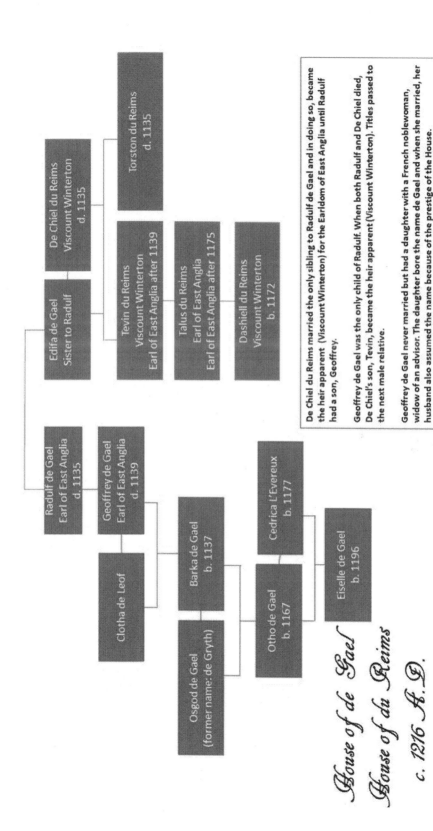

De Chiel du Reims married the only sibling to Radulf de Gael and in doing so, became the heir apparent (Viscount Winterton) for the Earldom of East Anglia until Radulf had a son, Geoffrey.

Geoffrey de Gael was the only child of Radulf. When both Radulf and De Chiel died, De Chiel's son, Tevin, became the heir apparent (Viscount Winterton). Titles passed to the next male relative.

Geoffrey de Gael never married but had a daughter with a French noblewoman, widow of an advisor. The daughter bore the name de Gael and when she married, her husband also assumed the name because of the prestige of the House.

Family tree entries

- De Chiel du Reims, Viscount Winterton, d. 1135
- Torston du Reims, d. 1135
- Edifa de Gael, Sister to Radulf
- Tevin du Reims, Viscount Winterton, Earl of East Anglia after 1139
- Talus du Reims, Earl of East Anglia, Earl of East Anglia after 1175
- Dashiell du Reims, Viscount Winterton, b. 1172
- Radulf de Gael, Earl of East Anglia, d. 1135
- Geoffrey de Gael, Earl of East Anglia, d. 1139
- Clotha de Leof
- Barka de Gael, b. 1137
- Cedrica L'Evereux, b. 1177
- Osgod de Gael (former name: de Gryth)
- Otho de Gael, b. 1167
- Eiselle de Gael, b. 1196

House of de Gael
House of du Reims
c. 1216 A.D.

"Greater love hath no man than this
that he lay down his life for his friends..."
John 13:15

PROLOGUE

20 May, Year of Our Lord 1217
City of Lincoln

I N THE DEAD of night, they moved.

Thousands of men were skirting the great medieval walls of the city of Lincoln, one of the largest and most strategically important cities in all of England. It was held by the rebels against King John, a man who had died seven months earlier.

But the rebels were stubborn. They were fewer in number now, since many had defected to support the new king, nine-year-old Henry, because the church had declared its support for the lad. The pope had gone so far as to say that anyone opposing young Henry was now upon a religious crusade to destroy the church itself, which greatly swung many of the rebel warlords into Henry's fold. No one wanted to be accused of crusading against the church.

Opposing the king was one thing. Opposing God was quite another.

But there were those who had been swayed for other reasons, not necessarily a threat from the pope. The great houses of de Lohr, de Vaston, Burton, Forbes, de Royans, and de Winter returned their support to the crown because it was the right thing to do. The young king had good advisors around him, including the stalwart William Marshal, and it was Marshal who had eventually coerced the great warlords back to their support of the crown.

These were houses that had always supported the crown, and their turn against John had been a difficult decision. The return to Henry, and the hope of a new king, had not been. The decision had been relatively simple.

A united king meant a united kingdom.

But there were some holdouts that still felt Henry would simply be carrying on his father's legacy. It was those stray rebels that were still holding a few cities for the French prince, Louis. And now that Henry was upon the throne, the great warlords who had returned to Henry's support determined it was time to remove the French and the rebels, once and for all.

Lincoln was the first target.

Therefore, in stealth, they moved on a clear night, so clear and bright that the blanket of stars in the sky looked as if they'd been smeared across the heavens. The stars were blending into each other, creating a band of light. An army of thousands marched on Lincoln, staying well out of sight until dawn, when a smaller and heavily-armed group left the main encampment and made their way to the city walls. Payment in gold coins to the rebel sentries on the western gate meant they had entry into the city.

After that, it was chaos.

As the sun rose over the dew-kissed fields surrounding the berg of Lincoln, William Marshall sent battle-seasoned knights in through the western gate, each man leading a crack squad of soldiers. Men like Christopher and David de Lohr went in first, leading their experienced squads as they headed to the north side of the city to clean out the rebels who were in charge of the northern gate.

Other groups led by Gart Forbes, Marcus Burton, and other experienced knights headed straight into the middle of the city to claim the cathedral. The castle, being held by the rebels, would be their last target in the center of the city. They would have to secure the city before they could reclaim the castle.

The south side of the city was the most heavily occupied by the rebels, and a group of men led by Dashiell du Reims, captain to the Duke of Savernake, and the duke himself, Bentley de Vaston, made their way with extreme stealth along the great wall of the city as they headed towards the south gate. Another very heavily-armed group led by Bric MacRohan and Daveigh de Winter, from the respected de Winter family, headed into the heart of the south end of the city to drive the rebels to Savernake so they could crush their enemy between them.

Bric was a man on the move. He had about twenty heavily-armed men with him, while his liege had taken thirty. Fifty of the best men the House of de Winter could provide from their army that numbered in the thousands, encamped about ten miles away with the rest of the loyalist armies. They knew they couldn't breach the city with a massive collective army, for that would only make the people respond with great rebellion. A stealth incursion had been the way to go, catching them off guard and, so far, it had worked.

Catching the rebels unaware was key.

Sneaking up a dark alley that smelled heavily of urine, Bric could see sentries on the main avenue, watching for any signs of trouble. Sheathing his broadsword, Bric kissed the talisman he always kept around his neck for good fortune. Made from steel and in the shape of a cross, it contained Latin words etched into the metal, words that Bric repeated nearly every time he went into battle. They were words that had kept him alive, all this time. He believed in those words, and they had never failed him.

A maiorem caritatum nemo habet.

It was a passage from the bible: *A man hath no greater love.* It was the beginning of a verse that Bric had always kept close to him, something an old Irish warrior had told him when he'd been young. *Keep the word of God with ye, lad, and ye'll always find yer way home.*

And he tried to do just that even though religion had never held much interest for him. Still, the complete verse was from the Book of John. *A man hath no greater love than he lay down his life for his friends.*

It was Bric's magic spell against death, and he believed it implicitly.

He believed it even now as he and another knight, his good and close friend Pearce de Dere, snuck up behind the two sentries and slit their throats before they could scream, dragging them back into the alley for a couple of the de Winter soldiers to stow the bodies while the majority of the squad continued.

There was a thrill to what they were doing, breathing in the familiar stench of danger with every breath. But that was the way Bric liked it. That was the way he functioned best, when his life was on the line every second. It wasn't that he thrived on the risk of death, but more that he was simply focused on a task to complete, and danger was simply part of it. As Bric often said – he didn't focus on the danger of his task, only the task to be done. The man had never failed at anything in his life and, in his estimation, he never would. He was calm, cool, and calculated in everything he did.

And that attitude made him deadlier than most.

Bric and his squad encountered more rebels near the south gate – in fact, perhaps a hundred or more. Unfortunately, the rebels had already spied Daveigh's squad and there was a battle going on. When Bric and his men plunged into the skirmish, it turned into a brutal, bloody brawl – heavy weapons were drawn but Bric was the type that would often strike with a fist first, a sword second. He caught men off guard that way, if he could get close enough to them, and he hammered through them easily.

But their fight had drawn attention, and alarms were going up through the city. Citizens were panicking, barring their doors, shutting out the fight that was going on around them. But some, the men in particular, were taking up arms to reinforce the rebels. Seeing this, William Marshal sent men back to the encamped army, calling them forth because the fighting had also roused the garrison at Lincoln Castle. Now, everyone knew the loyalists were there.

Rebel soldiers were mobilizing.

Still, the Marshal's initial ground work had left the rebel army compartmentalized in pockets of fighting. The loyalists had them in groups, and those groups were being decimated. The fighting went street to street; one street would be secured and then they'd move on to the next.

Rebels were either running, being captured, or being killed, and more than one of them had been chased down by the big Irish warrior with the silver eyes.

But it was more than being chased down by him; they could hear him coming. Bric moved with the greatest stealth when it was necessary. But when he wanted to frighten the enemy, he would howl like a beast. It was a sound that had the rebels in panic mode, because no sooner would they hear the sound than a massive knight would come barreling down on them.

Sometimes he had an ax in his hand, sometimes a sword, but sometimes it was his preferred fists. He'd flattened many a man with those ham-sized fists, and rumors of the crazed knight with the silver eyes was beginning to spread. The rebels lived in fear of that man. Some were saying that he was more animal that human.

The big Irish knight, the High Warrior, lived up to his name on that day.

Bric and his men had just finished cleaning out a small residence of six hiding rebels when Bric emerged from the home, his nostrils still flaring from the excitement of the fight, only to have someone with a scythe jump out at him from an adjoining alley. Bric reacted as he'd been taught – strike first. In battle, there was no time for indecision or second chances. But when the surprise of the ambush settled, Bric looked down at his victim to see it was a boy, perhaps no more than thirteen years of age.

A young boy who just had his guts cut out of him.

For the first time all morning, Bric's command and control mode took a hit. He exhaled sharply, wiping the sweat from his brow at the sight of the child he'd just killed.

"Bloody Christ," he hissed. "Are they fighting with children now? Has their cause become so desperate that they are sending their babes into the streets?"

Daveigh was behind him. His squad of men had joined up with Bric a short time before. Daveigh was younger than Bric by about ten years, but a strong and wise liege, a fine tribute to the House of de Winter. Daveigh Alexandre de Winter, Baron Cressingham and the Earl of Ardmore as part of his wife's Irish dowry, was a broad man with big shoulders, dark hair, and muddy brown eyes. Those eyes were fixed on the tow-headed lad at Bric's feet, bleeding out into the muddy gutters of Lincoln.

"He tried to kill you," he said, slapping Bric on the arm. "There is no shame in protecting yourself, no matter what the age of your opponent. It is the rebels who should be ashamed for sending a child against seasoned soldiers."

Bric shook his head unhappily, having difficulty moving past the dead child. The death of men, and sometimes even women, didn't bother him, but there was a secret about Bric MacRohan – he had a soft spot for children and animals. Therefore, the sight of a dead youth disturbed him greatly.

"I should have looked first," he said regretfully. "I should have punched him in the face. He might have lost teeth, but at least he would have retained his life."

Daveigh eyed him. "Any hesitation on your part and he would have cut your head off," he said pointedly. "Put aside your regrets, MacRohan. There is no time for such things in battle."

Words of wisdom from Daveigh. As the group as a whole moved out, heading towards the castle, they could hear the great horns of de Lohr as the siege engines and battering rams were being brought through the west gate, in pieces, to be reassembled for the siege on the castle. Bric's ears perked up.

"They must have the west side secure," he said to Daveigh. Then, he looked around, as they were still in the south section of the city. "We've secured this portion of the city, my lord. I'll put some men on the gatehouse to the south and when the bulk of the army arrives, I'll staff it with a hundred of our men to ensure it stays in our control."

Daveigh nodded, pleased that their morning of hell was now seeing some relief. "Good enough," he agreed. "If de Lohr is sounding the horns, then he wants every able-bodied man to help him move in the war machines. Mayhap, I should take some of our men and move in their direction."

Bric nodded. "I'll take twenty men with me to the south gatehouse," he said, "but before I do, I shall sweep to the east once more to make sure they don't need our assistance."

"Who is off to the east?"

"Savernake, I believe. They were meeting with heavy resistance, last I saw."

"Then go. I will see you at the castle."

With that, they split off, Daveigh taking his thirty men with him, and Bric taking the remaining twenty. One of those men was Pearce de Dere, with a nasty gash on his shoulder where his mail had been mangled by a club. As they headed east on streets that were now quiet with the dead or the dying, Pearce spoke beside him.

"I've never seen anything like this in my life," he said. "I've never seen a city under siege like this."

Bric's eyes were scanning the streets, the alleys, and the homes, making sure no more children with blades were going to come running out at him.

"It was a bold move for William Marshal to subdue the city like this, but a brilliant move all the same," he said. "In truth, I wasn't sure it was wise with so few men, but it was positively brilliant. We were able to catch them off guard."

Pearce held up his gloved hand, gingerly touching his wounded shoulder. "It was exhilarating," he grinned. "Well worth the injury."

Bric glanced at the mangled shoulder. "You look like a cat has torn you to shreds."

Pearce wriggled his eyebrows. "I've been torn by cats before," he winked, most definitely meaning the human and not the feline variety. "It is well worth the blood they draw."

"You'd better not let your wife hear you say that."

Pearce laughed. He was a glib man in the best of times, a bit of a rogue who'd married a year ago to a woman who had become pregnant. At least, she said she'd been pregnant, but conveniently lost the child before her belly grew. Pearce was convinced she'd tricked him into marriage, so he didn't feel badly about carousing with other females. It was something Bric didn't pay much attention to; a man's life was his own to live as he saw fit, he believed. But watching Pearce's marriage had, in fact, made him more than wary of marriage in general.

"She's heard me say it before," Pearce said. "Moreover, what do I care what she thinks? The little minx is getting what she deserved. She thought she could force my loyalty through marriage? She was wrong. I am like a cloud, Bric. Nothing can hold me down. I am not meant to be tied to an anchor."

Bric grunted. "No man is."

Before Pearce could reply, they rounded a corner and came face to face with a massive brawl involving Savernake and a few de Lohr men. Bric didn't hesitate; he rushed in, throwing punches or lifting his sword when necessary. In fact, he saw his dear friend, Dashiell du Reims, in a brutal fight with at least three men and Bric jumped into the brawl with both feet and both fists. Using his enormous booted feet to kick and disable, and his hands to choke or destroy, he helped Dashiell fight off the ruffians, disabling all three of them until they lay sprawled at their feet.

Breathing heavily, Dashiell tilted his helm back and wiped his forehead. Auburn-haired, handsome, and with a big mustache that was iconic to the man, he grinned at Bric.

"Like old times, eh, Bric?" he said. "This is not the first time you've saved my life."

Like most seasoned men, Dashiell and Bric had a long relationship and had fought many battles together, but the one in particular that Dashiell was referring to had been a nasty skirmish last year when Bric had killed a man who was trying to kill Dashiell.

It had been in the heat of battle, and Dashiell's enemy was hoping it would look as if it had simply been an accident born of battle. But Bric had been there, and he'd prevented a terrible man from killing one of the truly good men in England.

Bric and Dashiell were bonded that way, but Bric didn't like to be reminded of it. What he'd done, he'd done for the love of his friend and nothing more. He was embarrassed at the recognition for saving a friend.

It was the honorable knight in him.

"I think we've saved each other's lives many times over, Dash," he said briskly. "And I'll be thanking you to never say it again."

Dashiell fought off a smile. "You and I always seem to have a great deal of fun when we fight. Why is that?"

Bric snorted. "We are men of fine taste and good breeding," he said. "If we weren't doing this, what else would we do with our time?"

Dashiell patted him on the shoulder, taking a moment to catch his breath as the brawl dwindled around them. "I would not know," he said. "We could take up a hobby, I suppose."

"Fighting *is* a hobby."

"Is it? I hadn't thought of it that way. But I think my wife would like it if I found something else to do with my time. She doesn't like it when I go off like this to enjoy my hobby with friends."

Bric made a face. "Women have no sense of fun."

Dashiell chuckled. "I suppose they have a different idea of fun," he said. "When you marry, you shall see."

"I don't plan to marry."

Dashiell settled his helm back onto his head. "I thought that way, once," he said. "I was wrong."

Bric's silver eyes flashed. "You were weak, Dash," he said. "You let that lovely slip of a woman bewitch you. Now she doesn't like how you spend your time, fighting alongside your friends. 'Tis wrong for a woman to influence a man, I say. And you *let* her."

Dashiell winked at him. "You're bloody right I let her," he said. "When you meet a slip of a woman who bewitches you, you shall understand."

"Bite your tongue, man."

Dashiell couldn't stop the grin now. "I have a cousin who might be perfect for you," he teased. "She is quite pretty. And, her father is wealthy."

Bric rolled his eyes. "I don't care if he owns the bloody royal jewels. My response is still the same."

"Then you are a fool, man."

"And you are an arse's hole, Dash."

Dashiell burst into soft laughter, amused by Bric's animated response. Ever since Dashiell married last year, Bric had been increasingly turning his nose up at the suggestion of a union. With his friends getting married, or already married and having children, Bric MacRohan was quickly becoming something of a rarity in his bachelorhood – the more men married around him, the more devout he became to his bachelor life.

That was why most of Bric's close friends, like Dashiell, found it greatly amusing to taunt the man about marriage because it was nearly the only subject that got a rise out of the usually collected knight.

Knights had to exploit weaknesses where they could find them.

In the distance, they could hear the de Lohr horns blowing again, drawing men to the castle as the siege of Lincoln Castle was about to start in earnest. The gates of the city were being secured and the rebels were either being captured or driven out.

As Dashiell patted Bric affectionately on the cheek and headed off with his men to rendezvous with the rest of the Savernake contingent, Bric headed off to the south gate to secure it with de Winter men. When the southern end of the city was finally secure, Bric moved to join the rest of the de Winter army that arrived from the west gate, taking charge of them as the battle for Lincoln Castle began in earnest.

As the sun set over the city of Lincoln and the siege engines, now reassembled, began to hurl flaming material over the walls of Lincoln Castle, Bric lost himself in the battle, and in his duties, remembering the glory of the day and completely forgetting about his conversation with Dashiell. He especially forgot about the offer from Dashiell about his wealthy cousin, because it meant nothing to him.

In hindsight, it had been a mistake. Those comments by Dashiell would come back to haunt him.

In truth, they would change his life.

CHAPTER ONE

First of June
Narborough Castle, Norfolk

B RIC WAS TRYING to make it to the stables to escape, but he knew
he'd be caught. He knew there was no real escape for him, but he
was going to do it or die trying.

Woe to those who would try and stop him.

I have a gift for you, Bric, Daveigh had said. Only it hadn't been a
gift. It had been a burden. A trap of the most heinous kind. Bric knew
who was behind it; God help him, he knew. A man he considered one
of his closest friends, but a man who was clearly trying to offend him.
When he left Narborough, he was going to ride all the way to Ramsbury
Castle in Wiltshire and shove his fist right into Dashiell du Reims' face.

He was going to flatten the man.

But he had to get out of Narborough first, which would be no simple feat. Narborough was, perhaps, one of the best fortified castles in all
of England, with a massive keep of many rooms, great earthworks
surrounding it, creating something of a maze when it came to actually
entering the inner bailey where the keep was, and then an outer bailey
that was full of men and animals, stables, outbuildings, and even stone-
built residences for the army. Certainly, Bric could make it out to the
bailey – or so he hoped – but making it through that outer bailey and to
the gatehouse without being snared would be the trick.

Men were after him and he wasn't about to surrender.

Now, he was trying to leave the keep without being seen. He had his
own chamber in the keep, right next to the entry. It was simply a place

to sleep, for a man like Bric had no real home or comforts. He could carry everything he owned with him and, at the moment, he was weighted down with heavy saddlebags that literally carried everything he owned. He didn't want to leave anything behind because he was going to ride off and not come back for a very long time, at least until de Winter came to his senses. Bric was prepared to wait it out.

He didn't want to be part of Daveigh, or Dashiell's, political games.

It was dark at this ungodly hour as the night neared the morning. Bric was silently making his way from his chamber towards the keep entry, plastering himself against the cold, stone walls, trying to stay out of any light. He was keeping to the shadows, something he was good at, but the unfortunate part of that plan was that he'd taught every man in his command the same technique. His men were good at it, too. They could remain unseen if they wanted to. As he neared the bolted entry doors, two of his men proved it.

They stepped from the shadows to greet him.

"Where are you going so early, Bric?" Pearce asked, his eyes glittering in the weak light of distant torches. "We thought you might be coming this way."

He gestured to his companion, another knight serving under Bric. Sir Mylo de Chevington was a troll of a man, short and stocky, but as strong as an ox. With his big smile and curly, dark hair, he had an impish look about him, which made Bric want to punch the man in the teeth because he could see a smile playing on his lips.

He glared at the pair.

"Get out of my way," he growled. With his thick Irish accent, the threat sounded most deadly.

Pearce shook his head. "Alas, we cannot," he said. "You know we cannot. De Winter thought you might try to run, so he posted us at these doors. We've been here all night because we knew, at some point, that you would make a break for them."

Bric's eyes narrowed, which was never a good thing. "If you value your life, then you will get out of my way."

Pearce was still smiling as he lifted his sword. Mylo mimicked the movement a split second later.

"I love you, Bric, you know I do," he said, "but de Winter was specific in his orders. We are not to let you leave this keep."

Bric was growing increasingly furious. "You are *my* knights," he said flatly. "You are sworn to obey me, as your commander, and your commander is telling you to get out of his way."

Pearce and Mylo took a defensive stance, swords leveled. They knew what was about to happen and they wanted to be prepared.

"De Winter has ordered us to hold the line," Pearce said, bracing himself. "That is what we shall do, Bric. I am sorry."

Bric's silver eyes were fixed on Pearce. "Nay, you are not," he said. "But you will be if you do not move."

"Bric, have pity," Mylo said. "Would you have de Winter angry with us instead? We took our oath to him, as did you. If you stop to think about this situation, you are disobeying the wishes of your liege by trying to leave Narborough and…"

"And you shall shut your nasty little face, Mylo," Bric snapped, turning his venom on the younger knight. When Mylo's eyes widened with a flash of fear, Bric was pleased. At least he'd get some pleasure out of this event by scaring the fresh young knight. "Now, move aside, de Chevington. Be a good lad."

Mylo was far more pliable to Bric's will than Pearce was but, surprisingly, he didn't move away. He did shift a little, but not enough. That gave Bric the opening he needed to whack the knight's broadsword away and throw a shoulder into him, shoving Mylo right into the wall. As the knight grunted with the force of the blow, Bric made a break for the bolt on the door.

After that, the fight was on.

Somehow, he'd managed to throw the bolt and yank at the door before Pearce and Mylo could stop him, but he couldn't get the door open wide enough to escape before Pearce threw his body at the door to slam it shut again. Swords were up and flying, and Bric had to fend off two good strokes from Mylo, meant to disarm him and nothing more. They weren't trying to hurt him, but they were attempting to disarm him. Bric would die before he let that happen.

The little whelps were going to pay dearly.

The sounds of swords could be heard throughout the keep. On the top floor, Daveigh was roused from a deep sleep by his manservant, who announced that the knights were fighting down in the keep entry. With a smirk, Daveigh tossed off the coverlets and hurried to dress, as did his wife beside him.

Keeva de Winter knew what was happening. This was something that had been building for two days, ever since Bric MacRohan had been informed that he was to be a bridegroom, courtesy of an offer from Dashiell du Reims, heir to East Anglia's earldom. That didn't sit well with the big Irish knight, and he'd locked himself in his chambers for two days. No amount of pleading or shouting from Daveigh could get him to come out. But Daveigh knew, at some point, that Bric would attempt an escape. He'd prepared for that eventuality.

It seemed that he'd been right.

When Daveigh saw that his wife was dressing, he waved her off. "I do not want you downstairs right now," he told her. "If Bric is in battle mode, then you could be injured. You know the man stops for nothing when he is in a fight and I do not want you in his line of sight."

Keeva, pretty and pale, with deep red hair in long spirals down her back, waved him off. "Don't be stupid." Her Irish accent was strong as she pulled on a long, heavy robe that was warm against the cold morning temperatures. "Bric would not turn against me."

"He may not even know it is you until it is too late."

Keeva tied off her robe and headed for the chamber door as her husband hurried to follow, pulling on his boots. She wasn't about to take any foolishness from her husband's premier knight, a man who happened to be her cousin.

"I will stop this right now," she said. "You and your knights have coddled Bric too much. This is ridiculous that you'd let a grown man rebel like this."

Fiery was a word to describe the woman. She was stronger than most men. Keeva charged out of the bedchamber as Daveigh followed, both of them racing for the narrow spiral stairs that led to the level below. Once they entered the darkened first level, where the great hall and several smaller chambers were, they could immediately see the fighting near the massive, double-doored entry.

Instead of two knights against one, several soldiers were now involved, too. They'd been summoned through the kitchens by frightened servants and now a line of armed soldiers stood around the three knights doing battle. There was some shouting going on, mostly shouting encouragement at Bric, who had disarmed Mylo and had the man in a chokehold around the neck, using him as a shield against Pearce, who was genuinely trying not to hurt anyone. All he wanted to do was disarm Bric, but now it had turned into a hostage situation.

But Bric was having no part of Pearce's attempts. As Daveigh and Keeva approached, Bric lashed out a big foot at a soldier who got too close, smashing the man in the knee. As the soldier went down in pain, Keeva's shout brought everything to a halt.

"Bric MacRohan!" she yelled. "If you don't cease your fighting and release Mylo, I will enter the fight and you'll not like it in the least. Do you understand me?"

Odd how one angry woman could stop what dozens of men couldn't. Bric came to an immediate halt at the sound of her voice and released Mylo, shoving the man far away from him. Back against the wall, he stood there with his sword raised as Keeva and Daveigh broke up the ring of soldiers, sending them all back the way they'd came.

But Keeva was genuinely angry. As Pearce and Mylo backed away, she came up to Bric and pointed to his sword.

"Put it away," she grumbled. "How dare you embarrass me. How dare you behave like this."

Bric eyed the woman; she was his cousin, and he had been part of her dowry when she'd come to marry Daveigh de Winter. That was how the bred-and-bled Irish knight had ended up in the service of the English de Winter war machine. But she was also foul-tempered at times, and bold, and she wasn't beyond taking him on in a fight if she was mad enough. Bric wanted to avoid that, but he also wouldn't let himself be pushed around by a slip of a woman.

Even if she was his liege's wife.

"Lady de Winter," he said deliberately. "I am defending myself. It would have done you greater embarrassment had I allowed myself to be captured like a fool."

Keeva scowled. "Go over there and sit down," she said, pointing into the great hall and the nearest table. "Sit yourself down, Bric, and keep your lips shut until I have had my say in all of this."

Bric sighed heavily, eyeing her unhappily before complying. It wouldn't do any good to argue with her if he was attempting to avoid a physical altercation with the woman, so he lumbered over to the table she was indicating and planted himself on the end of the bench. He could see from his periphery that Daveigh, Pearce, and Mylo had followed, hiding behind Keeva because they, too, were fearful of her spitfire Irish temper.

They would let her take the lead. Between two Irish hotheads, that was all they could do.

"Now," Keeva said as she faced off against her cousin. "I have been listening to this foolishness for two days, ever since my husband informed you of your bride. Clearly, you have no understanding of how important this is, so I will explain it to you."

Bric started to open his mouth, but she put up a hand. "Silence!"

He shut his mouth.

Keeva continued. "When I wed my husband, you were part of my dowry," she said. "That meant that you became Daveigh's property. Do you understand that?"

Begrudgingly, Bric nodded.

"Good," Keeva said. "And, as his property, he has the right to do anything he wishes with you. Are we still clear?"

Bric rolled his eyes and looked away. That made Keeva move closer to him to ensure he heard everything she was going to say.

"The House of de Winter is linked by blood to the Earls of Norfolk," she said. "It is a strong alliance. But it is not linked by anything other than an oath to the Earls of East Anglia. Oath alliances can be broken, but alliances by blood or marriage are much harder to break. Dashiell du Reims, your very good and true friend, is the next Earl of East Anglia. Is this a true statement?"

Bric knew where she was going with all of this and he was resisting her with every cell in his body. But he knew he couldn't deny her much longer. In the end, she would have her way, and he was well aware of that.

But he was going to go kicking and screaming all the way.

"It is," he said through clenched teeth.

Keeva was standing over him. "Dash wishes for the Earls of East Anglia, and the House of du Reims, to be joined to the House of de Winter by marriage. His missive to my husband explained this. A marriage to the House of du Reims would make the most powerful alliance in all of eastern England, Bric. Norfolk, de Winter, and East Anglia will be a legendary alliance and you are to be a key part of that by marrying Dash's cousin. *You*, Bric. You play a vital role in all of this. You understand how allegiances work and how important they are. How can you turn your nose up at such an opportunity?"

Bric knew all of this, but when she put it that way, it made him look like a bloody ingrate. "Dash mentioned this alliance two months ago, in Lincoln," he muttered. "We were in the midst of battle when the subject came up about his cousin. But I did not believe he was serious."

"He was," Keeva said. "And I am sure he did not suggest a marriage between you and his cousin simply to make you miserable. I am sure he did it because he loves you."

Bric had nothing to say to that; any man who loved him as a brother would know his views on marriage, as Dashiell did. But Dashiell evidently didn't care. As Bric sat there and fumed, knowing he was on the losing end of this discussion, Daveigh summoned his bravery and stepped forward.

"Bric," he said. Seeing how miserable the man was, he sighed heavily. "I did not agree to Dash's proposal to shame you or punish you. Surely you can see that. I did it because it was important and because I think enough of you to wed you to the cousin of the future Earl of East Anglia. Do you truly think I did this to make you miserable?"

Bric knew he hadn't, but he wasn't ready to concede anything. Everyone knew he was staunchly against marriage, so it wouldn't do any good to reiterate that stance. It didn't matter now, not when Daveigh was determined to make an alliance. Still... he was so damned frustrated.

"But why me?" he finally asked, turning to look at Keeva and Daveigh. "Why must it be me?"

Daveigh sat down on the bench next to him. "Because Dashiell mentioned you by name," he said. "And because I have no sons or daughters to offer. But I do have you, and you are my relation since you are my wife's cousin. *We* are cousins. Bric, I come from one of the ten great ruling families that came to these shores with Gaetan de Wolfe, the Duke of Normandy's Warwolfe, those years ago. My ancestor was so important that he was charged with the security of the great River Ouse and the wash that led to the sea, protecting it from the Northmen invaders, among others. That is why I now hold the Honor of Narborough, and my properties all along the river. You are in command of my army, one of the greatest armies in all of England. You are an important and great man in England – but you remain unmarried."

Bric began to chew his lip, a habit he had when frustrated. "For good reason," he said. "I do not want to be."

"No man does," Daveigh said with a smirk, a smirk that quickly vanished when Keeva shot him a nasty look. "But you are too valuable to remain unmarried. I have no sons to give, so in matters such as these – with marital alliances – I must use other relatives to ensure my empire survives. It is a great honor you have been given, Bric. Not only will your marriage bind de Winter to East Anglia, but you will also be related to the House of du Reims by marriage. Your friend, Dash, becomes your cousin. Is this so unattractive to you that you would shame me by running from it?"

Daveigh was hitting him hard with facts that he could not deny, and Bric could feel himself folding. He was feeling increasingly unsettled and foolish for trying to run from what any sane man would consider a great honor. Bric was more than happy to accept any honor, but he just wished that marriage wasn't involved. With a heavy sigh, he rubbed a hand wearily over his face.

"I am not trying to shame anyone," he said. "But you have many knights under your service. You could use any one of them for a marital contract if an alliance is what you seek."

"True," Daveigh said. "But I only have one knight who is related to my wife, and only one knight who is descended from the O'Briens, the high kings of Ireland. Royal blood runs through your veins, Bric. You are unique and valuable, in so many ways. Do you not understand this?"

Bric did. He was simply trying to find some argument to get him out of this mess, but he realized with sickening certainty that nothing would. He was going to find himself with a wife no matter how badly he didn't want one. In looking at Daveigh, and then to Keeva, he realized that his fight was over.

They'd won.

Bric hadn't lost a battle in his entire life, except the most important battle of all – the battle against having a wife. Grunting miserably, he sat back against the table.

"I understand," he said. "I understand all of it. I understand why you would make such an alliance, but I also understand that you have no consideration for my feelings in this."

"That is because it is a command," Keeva said firmly. "You are a knight, Bric. You have no feelings when your liege gives you a command. You simply do as you are told."

Bric realized that he had to look at it that way, because it was the truth. Keeva was correct. Frustrated, and grossly unhappy, he stood up and sheathed his sword. He'd been holding it in his left hand the entire time.

"I will do as I am told," he agreed. "But in this case, there is something more involved than a simple command. This is a command that will change my life and I do not have to be happy about it. I will do as you wish and marry this girl, but the marriage will be in name only. I draw the line at being ordered how to conduct my marriage, so I will conduct it as I see fit."

It was a defiant statement. "I will respect that," Daveigh said, "but remember this – the woman you are marrying is also Dashiell du Reims' cousin. Offend and hurt the girl, and I have a feeling Dash will not take kindly to that. If you wish to damage your relationship with him then, by all means, be unfeeling and cruel to your wife. If I were you, I would think carefully about that."

Bric looked at him. "I never said I would be cruel and unfeeling towards her," he said. "All I said was that I will conduct my marriage in my own way."

Daveigh still didn't like the sound of that. He looked at Keeva to see if his wife had anything more to say. Her gaze was fixed on Bric.

"I will say this once and I will say no more," she said. "You will behave as a member of the House of de Winter and the House of O'Brien. You will conduct yourself with honor in this marriage, for it is no different than any other task or assignment that has been bestowed upon you. I know you do not wish to be married, but this is beyond your control and you will accept it with dignity. Shame me, or my husband, I will send you back to Ireland with dishonor. Do you understand me, Bric?"

He looked at her. "Have I ever dishonored you?"

"Nay."

"I do not intend to start now. But know this; as you mentioned damaging my relationship to Dash should I be cruel to his cousin, know that forcing me to marry this woman has damaged my relationship with you. Do not expect me to be the loving, kind cousin any longer. If my feelings in the matter are of no concern to you, then I am clear on your regard of me. I understand now that I am only a tool, something to be used, and I will behave accordingly."

With that, he bowed his head slightly, begging his leave, and headed back to the chamber he slept in, just off the entry.

When they heard the chamber door shut, quietly, Keeva and Daveigh turned to each other. Daveigh was more emotional and empathetic than his wife, who tended to be no-nonsense in most things. Keeva was a tough woman but, deep down, she had a tender heart. That's what made Daveigh love her so. Reaching out, he put a gentle hand on her arm.

"He does not mean what he said," he told her quietly. "I would not worry."

Keeva didn't share her husband's opinion. "He means it," she said, turning once more to look at the closed chamber door. "Bric MacRohan never says anything he does not mean. But he must accept that this is his destiny. I cannot help him with that."

Daveigh squeezed her arm and released her. "Then, mayhap, we can only pray that the girl is somewhat attractive," he said. "If we saddle him with a hag, he'll truly never forgive us."

Keeva didn't reply right away. Truly, she didn't know what to say. It was sad to think that her relationship with her favorite cousin hinged on the quality of the bride he didn't want. If the woman was a dog, then the damage would be done. But if she was pretty and accomplished, then at least there might be a chance Bric could be happy in his marriage.

But it was done. None of them could change it. Keeva turned to her husband.

"Tell Dashiell we will send for the lass," she said. "We shall ensure the marriage happens."

Daveigh simply nodded. The marriage would indeed happen, but at what price?

He wondered.

CHAPTER TWO

AYE, SHE'D HEARD tale of the man. Everyone in Norfolk and Suffolk knew of him, and beyond that even. He was famous throughout England.

But she never imagined it would come to this.

It had all happened so fast. But now the time was upon her and there wasn't a thing she could do in protest. Any argument, sage or otherwise, had died long ago and she had approached this day with all of the excitement as one does when anticipating a bloodletting.

A bloodletting, in fact, would have been preferable. She was about to face the man they called the High Warrior, a man soon to be her husband, and the anxiety boiling in her gut was enough to set her to burping in a most unladylike manner.

Unfortunately, she had a nervous stomach that she often couldn't control and, God help her, surrounded by people she did not know made her painfully self-conscious about it. The House of de Winter had sent a carriage to her home, along with a pair of big knights and about twenty men-at-arms. Faced with an armed escort cheerlessly determined to be of service, she'd bid her weeping mother and joyful father a farewell and settled in for the trip to Narborough Castle, seat of the great House of de Winter.

It had been a long and uncomfortable journey. The carriage had rolled and bumped along the way, and she had tried to be discreet as she belched her anxiety away when she thought no one was looking or listening. But when the carriage rolled through a series of sharp ruts about an hour after leaving her home, she burped loud enough to be heard. Though her escort didn't react, she knew they had heard her.

Sweet Jesus, let the earth open up and swallow up my appalling, ill-mannered soul, she prayed silently. *These men are going to think I've been raised by wolves!*

Embarrassment did not quite encompass what she felt but, unfortunately for her, the earth remained closed and she had no reprieve from her embarrassment. The more the miles rolled on, the worse her nervous stomach became until nearly every other breath had some sort of gastric emission to it.

But it was truly a pity that she was focused on her churning stomach and not on the lush Suffolk countryside. Lady Eiselle de Gael had spent her entire life near Thetford, the only daughter of a bastard grandson of a long-dead Earl of East Anglia who made his living importing fine fabrics from France to sell at his business in Bury St. Edmunds. Her mother, being a worrisome woman of ill health, did not like her daughter to stray too far from home, so consequently, Eiselle had spent a good deal of her life sequestered at home or in her father's shop.

The only exception to that rule had been the twelve months she had spent at Framlingham Castle. Being related to the Earls of East Anglia, there was some privilege for her because the earl, Talus du Reims, had been kind to her family. When it came time for Eiselle to foster, he had sent her to the powerful Bigod family to learn something of the world. While the Bigod family had been kind to her, the other wards had been living nightmares. A year was all Eiselle could stand of their nasty behavior before begging to return home.

But it hadn't been a happy return. Her father had been devastated that not one of Bigod's knights had pledged for his daughter's hand. He'd very much hoped for a husband when she'd gone away, but it was not to be. Enraged, he'd put her back to work in his shop, hoping beyond hope that some wealthy man would see her and take her off his hands.

But that's not where her one and only marriage offer had come from.

Eiselle burped into her kerchief as her thoughts moved from her father's shop to the man that all of England knew as the mightiest knight in the de Winter arsenal. She remembered hearing about him whilst at Framlingham but, truthfully, she didn't remember the details. The other wards would whisper and titter about him, and any number of other eligible knights, but Eiselle wasn't usually included in those conversations. What she knew about the man, she'd overheard.

And now he was to be her husband.

Otho de Gael had been thrilled when the missive had come from Dashiell du Reims, their distant cousin and the son of Talus. According to the message, the House of de Winter was looking for a strong alliance to the Earls of East Anglia, and it had been suggested that Eiselle would be an appropriate match for Bric MacRohan, de Winter's most decorated knight. Eiselle remembered with disgust as her father had run around their home shouting *Victory! Victory!*

Finally, the daughter had found a husband.

Eiselle had felt quite cast aside by her father who was so eager to be rid of her. But regrets and reflections had no place in her life now, as her future was set. After a very long day of uncomfortable travel, the future was in sight as they finally neared their destination because a glance from the small windows of the carriage showed a massive curtain wall in the distance.

Eiselle watched with some fascination and fear as the castle loomed closer, its pale gray walls stark against the brilliant green of the summer landscape. To Eiselle, those walls seemed to be hiding something more than protecting those within. She sensed something somber and mysterious from those old walls, which did nothing to ease her nervousness. She drank in the sight, imagining what her life would become from this day forward.

Praying it would be something she could bear.

Eventually, the road evened out and became smoother, and Eiselle began to feel some relief from her nausea. But her relief was short-lived when the thunder of hooves suddenly invaded the air.

"Get the carriage moving," someone roared.

It was a fast and furious command. The cab lurched and Eiselle yelped as she was thrown against the back of the seat. Her knightly escort, so silent for hours on end, suddenly came to life and she could hear their cool, calm chatter.

"Are we under threat, Bric?" a voice asked.

A massive destrier was snorting and kicking up rocks against the side of the carriage as the knight astride it spoke.

"We're not sure, but we may have seen a Nottingham party to the west," the man replied in a very deep, very heavy Irish brogue. "The rebels usually stay well-clear of this area, but it is possible they are scouting to see just how heavily-fortified we are. I am surprised you did not run into them."

One of the men, the one who had stayed so close to the carriage throughout the ride, flipped up his visor to reveal a young and weary face. "We have had a clear journey since leaving the lady's home of Hadleigh House," he said. "We've seen no threat."

The enormous man astride the silver charger waved a big arm at the team, startling the horses into a jerky gallop. "Get them moving! Into the castle!"

Eiselle yelped again as she ended up on the floor of the cab, bounced around like a child's ball in the midst of a frenzied game. She finally got a grip on the seat and pulled herself back onto the bench, holding on for dear life. But her grip on the seat wasn't enough as the carriage charged dangerously over the road and in through the great gatehouse of Narborough. She ended up on her arse, bounced around mercilessly.

A rapid stop came almost as abruptly as the blinding acceleration. Eiselle bumped against the wall of the cab as it lurched to a halt. Ill, and somewhat terrified, she barely had time to collect herself when the carriage door flew open and an enormous figure stood in its place. Jolted by the shock of the door nearly being ripped off its hinges, Eiselle gazed into the open doorway with a mixture of anxiety and outrage.

A man with silver eyes stood there, looking steadily upon her. Dressed in full armor, including a helm that covered most of his face, he looked ready for battle. Sprawled on her bottom in a most unladylike position, Eiselle realized that there was no way to save a very crude introduction. Blowing a stray lock of hair from her eyes, she thought, perhaps, a witty word might salvage the situation. But when she opened her mouth to speak, all that came out was a belch better suited to a drunken barmaid.

Riiiiiiiiiiiipppppppp...

It was a shockingly wet sound. The man with the silver eyes stared at her, his surprise evident. But he did nothing more than lift an eyebrow.

"Greetings to you as well, my lady," he said in his thick Irish accent. "Welcome to Narborough Castle. Are you Lady Eiselle?"

"I am."

"I am Bric MacRohan."

If I had a dagger, I would use it on myself, Eiselle thought, feeling her cheeks flush bright red as she realized who the man was. *MacRohan in the flesh!* Grasping at the last shreds of composure, she pushed her hair out of her eyes and tried to find her footing.

"My apologies, my lord," she said as primly as she could manage. "It has been a rough trip and I... I am afraid that I've not handled it well."

Bric did nothing more than hold a hand out to her. Gathering her skirts, Eiselle put her small hand into his massive one. It was warm and strong. With surprising gentleness, he assisted her from the cab.

The ground was still rolling a bit as Eiselle tried to regain her equilibrium. Bric moved to the back of the cab, snapping orders to the soldiers that were unloading her baggage from the rear. More baggage was on a small wagon that had followed from her home and Bric moved towards the wagon to make sure that it, too, was cleared.

Kerchief to her mouth to prevent any more horrifying gas from escaping, Eiselle was fixed on her future husband, understandably curious about him. He was tall, but more than that, he was just plain big – enormous arms, thick legs, and big hands. All embarrassment aside, he was something to watch; beneath the helm, she could see a square jaw and a hint of a long, straight nose. One of the knights who had accompanied her from her home of Hadleigh House said something to him and she caught a brief flash of a smile with straight, white teeth. But it was all she saw before he closed his lips again and snapped more orders to the men around him.

Eiselle took a deep breath, calming her rolling stomach as she continued to watch the man she had come to marry. He took one of her traveling cases from a soldier on the bed of the wagon and handled it easily. Eiselle knew how much those trunks weighed and it was no easy feat to sling them around as he was. As her stomach calmed and her composure began to return, she could already see that MacRohan was a man who commanded respect.

She wondered seriously what he looked like with his helm removed.

Bric suddenly turned in her direction and his eyes fixed on her. Startled that she was caught staring at him, Eiselle quickly lowered her gaze and looked at her feet. She heard his footfalls as he drew near.

"Forgive me for not tending to you right away," Bric said, his heavy brogue quiet. "I was attempting to unload your baggage, but I suppose I should have unloaded you first. I am sure you would like to rest."

Eiselle dared to look up at him, startled anew when their eyes met. There was an odd jolt to the event; it was the first time she had beheld the man at close range and she felt a strange buzzing sensation in her head. It was rather curious, exciting even. But her embarrassment also returned, so very embarrassed at her ghastly behavior since their introduction.

She could only imagine what he must think of her.

"I do not wish to rest at the moment, my lord," she said, still fixated on his eyes, so blue that they were literally silver. "If you please, I wish to speak with you."

Bric's eyebrows flickered with curiosity, then agreement. "As you wish," he said. Then, he went to take her by the elbow but awkwardly stopped. "Do you wish to speak here?"

He seemed rather ill at ease, as if he wasn't sure how to behave around her. This big, confident knight seemed to be uncomfortable and it made Eiselle feel a little less embarrassed about their rude introduction.

In fact, she found his behavior rather amusing. Her stomach was easing and her composure returning, enough so that she felt inclined to say what had been on her mind since the very beginning of the marriage offer. She would ask the question, sooner or later, so perhaps it was better to establish things now.

She summoned her courage.

"We may speak here," she said, studying his strong, if not slightly angular, features. "There is something I wish to know, if it is not too much trouble."

"I will tell you if I can, my lady."

"I would like to know if you are agreeable to this marriage."

He stared at her. Then, his eyebrows lifted. "If I…?"

"If you are agreeable, aye," she nodded patiently. "Although my father accepted the offer, we are not yet married. And if you are not agreeable, or pleased with the arrangement, then I understand. You've only just now met me, and if I am not to your standard, the contract can be refused."

He blinked and, until the day she died, Eiselle would swear she saw a rush of disbelief followed by a glimmer of amusement. But Bric MacRohan wasn't the amused type, or so she'd been told. The man was as hard as steel and twice as deadly. But he was clearly mulling over her question.

"Are *you* agreeable, my lady?" he finally asked.

"I mean no disrespect, but I asked you first."

He cleared his throat at her bold answer, almost nervously, and averted his gaze. He even shifted on is big legs and glanced at the ground as if he would find the correct answer there. The he gave her a sidelong look.

"Did someone tell you that I was not?"

She shook her head. "Nay," she said. "But this offer was unexpected, and quickly executed, so I simply wanted to know… if you are agreeable or if you were forced into this."

He was looking at her most oddly, as if genuinely perplexed by her question. As if he simply couldn't believe she would ask such a thing. More than once, she thought he wanted to say something about it, but he held his tongue. When he finally spoke, it was with a relatively benign response.

"No one can force me into anything," he said.

She cocked her head curiously, inspecting everything about him. She was looking him up and down, her eyes finally coming to rest on his face again.

"I did not mean to insinuate otherwise," she said. "But do you know what you shall expect from me? As your wife, I mean."

A chuckle escaped his lips. "You're to the point, lass, I'll give you that."

His smile was unexpected and quite attractive. She'd seen it before, briefly, and now she was seeing it again. She liked it; it made her unsettled belly leap in new and strange ways.

"In this situation, I am not sure I can be anything else," she said. "This is all so new and unfamiliar to me. Do you even know what you expect from a wife?"

"I am not sure. I've never had one."

He seemed to have transformed from slightly awkward to slightly amused. His humor made her want to smile although her question was serious. She cocked a well-shaped eyebrow at him.

"When you decide, you'll be sure to let me know?" she said. "I would like to know your expectations so that I do not fall short."

His eyes seemed to have gained something of a twinkle as he gazed at her. After a moment, he held out a mail-covered elbow. "I am coming to think that may not be a possibility."

She was quite curious. "How do you know?"

The twinkle in his eyes grew. "Call it a guess," he said. "May I take you inside now if you are finished interrogating me?"

She regarded him for a moment before accepting his elbow. "I am only finished for the moment."

"I believe that."

Eiselle was positive that he was laughing silently at her the entire trip across the bailey.

CHAPTER THREE

S O MUCH FOR his plans.

Bric had plotted out his introduction to his betrothed ever since he realized he had no recourse in the matter. He had told Keeva that he would not let anyone interfere in his marriage, and he would treat his wife as he saw fit.

Therefore, his plans were to be cool and distant from her, but not impolite. By virtue of the fact that she was his wife and would bear his name, he would show her all due respect, but nothing more than that. He was grossly unhappy with the turn of events and positive that she was not. He was certain that she would be most delighted to be married to de Winter's High Warrior, sinking her claws into him, but he was going to make it clear that he took no delight in being married to her, even if she was Dashiell's cousin.

But the moment he met Eiselle, that opinion changed.

First, her beauty had caught him off guard. She looked like an angel. Then, the first words out of her mouth hadn't been words at all, but a burp that had nearly blown him onto his arse. Most men would have been disgusted by it but, for some strange reason, he hadn't been. In that brief and somewhat shameful moment, the woman had endeared herself to him before she'd even spoken a word. In her embarrassment, he'd seen something that he hadn't expected from her – *grace.*

She'd handled the situation with grace and dignity, at least as much as she was able. No weeping, no fits. Simply acceptance.

He was very surprised to see that.

But, then again, perhaps not so surprised when he remembered who she was related to. Dashiell du Reims was a man of great courage and honor, so it was little surprise that his female cousin was imbued with the same.

An introduction that the lady thought went so terribly wrong, in fact, went well in her favor.

Even now, he'd taken her into the great hall of Narborough and stood aside as Daveigh and Keeva were introduced to her. It gave him time to inspect the woman as she politely fielded their questions; she wasn't very tall, but she wasn't tiny, either. Clad in a pale green shift and surcoat that matched the color of her eyes, her curly dark hair was pulled into a braid, but the natural curl had tendrils escaping, giving her a halo of curls around her sweetly oval face.

And pretty? Bloody Christ, he'd never seen a prettier woman. That had been utterly unexpected. That so lovely a woman wasn't yet spoken for made no sense to him but, then again, if she greeted all suitors the way she'd greeted him – with a burst of noxious fumes shooting from her mouth – then he supposed he wasn't overly surprised. It had been like a dragon's fire breath. Maybe she used it like a shield to chase off the unworthy. But on him, it hadn't worked.

Vast, complete curiosity was all he could feel for her at the moment.

"Please, sit," Keeva told the woman in her heavy Irish accent, indicating the nearest bench. "You must be very tired from your journey. Hadleigh House, isn't it? My husband tells me that it is to the south."

As Bric moved to the opposite side of the table where he could watch her better, Eiselle nodded. "Aye, Lady de Winter," she said as she took her seat. "The house was given to my grandmother many years ago and we have always lived there. It is a lovely place."

Keeva sat down next to her. "Tell me of yourself, Lady Eiselle," she said. "When we received the missive from your cousin, we were quite happy with his offer, but we know so very little of you other than you are Dashiell du Reims' cousin."

Eiselle smiled timidly. "My life has been fairly unspectacular, my lady," she said. "I was born at Hadleigh House in Suffolk and lived there until I was fifteen, whereupon the Earl of East Anglia arranged for me to go to Framlingham Castle to foster. I was there for a year before returning home, and I have worked in my father's stall ever since."

Keeva was very interested. "What is your father's business?"

"He is a merchant, my lady. He imports goods from France and sells them in his stall in Bury St. Edmunds."

"And you have learned much about his business, have you?"

Eiselle nodded. "I can count money and do sums in my head," she said. "My father has taught me how to read and write, also. He felt it was important for me to know."

Keeva looked at Bric, who was studying the lovely young woman quite intently. "Did you hear that?" she asked him. "Your betrothed knows how to do sums and read. She's an accomplished woman, Bric."

Bric didn't like the way Keeva had said it, as if he needed to be convinced that the lovely creature before him was smart and talented and worthy of him. Perhaps that had been true yesterday, but it wasn't true today.

In fact, Bric was becoming increasingly interested in the woman he was betrothed to. She had a soft, delicate voice, something that was quite mesmerizing. She also had a way of wrinkling up that pert little nose when she smiled. He thought it was rather charming. For someone who had been so staunchly against the marriage, he was folding rather easily, and it was a struggle for him to not feel foolish about it.

"She is, indeed," he said. He didn't want to get to know the woman in front of an audience, but he thought he may as well start. Keeva wasn't going to let the woman go any time soon. "You mentioned that you fostered at Framlingham?"

Eiselle turned in his direction. "Aye, my lord."

"You were there for a short amount of time."

"I was there long enough to learn how to run a household, how to paint, and I learned how to sing in Italian. Just a little."

She didn't seem inclined to elaborate on why she'd only spent a year at Framlingham when most young women fostered for several years.

His gaze lingered on her for a moment before simply nodding. He wanted to ask her more, and talk to her more, but he was increasingly resistant to do it in front of his Keeva and Daveigh.

If Eiselle was to be his wife, then he wanted to know her in private, just the two of them. But he suspected Keeva and Daveigh were present for fear that Bric might somehow be rude, considering how he'd made his displeasure with this betrothal known, so he really couldn't blame them. They wanted to make sure he wasn't going to offend or upset the woman. Of that, he had no intention, but he genuinely wanted to be alone with her and was frustrated by the fact that he was not.

"Then I look forward to hearing you sing for me some time," he said, standing up. He was still in his armor and protection, and even still wearing his helm. He hadn't taken it off. "You will forgive me for begging my leave, but I have pressing duties to attend to."

As he stood up, Daveigh stood up and stopped him from moving away from the table. "Where are you going?" he asked, concerned but trying not to look as if he were. "Surely you would like to remain here and speak with the lady."

Bric could see the stress in Daveigh's face. "And I will, in time," he said. "At the moment, you and Lady de Winter have her occupied, so I will leave you to your conversation."

Daveigh was picking up on Bric's frustration, but he was at a loss to understand why the man was upset, other than the fact that his betrothed had arrived. He lifted his eyebrows.

"Would you prefer that we leave?" he asked.

Bric thought he would sound rather ridiculous if he agreed. He'd shown nothing but resistance to this woman, and now he wanted to be alone with her? Confusion joined his frustration, and the more he debated about his response, the more embarrassed he became.

He needed to get out of there.

"I have duties to attend to," he said again. "Nottingham scouts have been sighted in the area and I should be out with my men. I will entrust Lady Eiselle to your care until I return."

With that, he moved around Daveigh and headed out of the hall at a quick pace.

He disappeared swiftly and Eiselle watched him go. She could sense that the man wanted nothing to do with her and her heart sank. She'd asked him what he'd expected in a wife, but it was clear that he wanted no part of the arrangement. She had expressed a fear of falling short of his expectations and he'd alluded to the fact that he didn't think that would be possible but, perhaps, he'd had time to think about it. Perhaps, she was indeed falling short of what he'd expected.

Feeling rather sad and unwanted, she spoke.

"Sir Bric is a very busy and important man," she said, trying to sound as if his rapid departure didn't bother her in the least. "I am sure he has many duties to attend to and idle chatter is not among them. Lady de Winter, if you would be so kind as to show me to my chamber, I would be very grateful. It has been a long trip and I should like to rest before supper."

Keeva thought she heard sadness in the Eiselle's voice and it was all she could do to keep her temper. Bric had succeeded in offending the woman and she was positively livid at the man. But to Eiselle, she was polite and helpful.

"Of course, my lady," she said. "I have a lovely chamber prepared for you on the top floor. It faces south, so there is sun most of the day. I think you will be very pleased with it and… and I want you to know how very glad we are that you are here. In fact, we have already sent for the priest. He should be here this evening. We thought to have the wedding on the morrow."

So soon. Eiselle was surprised to hear that. "As you say, my lady," she said. "I am agreeable to whatever you wish."

Keeva stood up from the bench, taking Eiselle politely by the arm. "Should we send word to your parents? We could delay it a day or two if they wish to attend."

Eiselle shook her head. "The knights that came to collect me offered to escort my parents as well, but they declined," she said. "My father will not leave his business and my mother does not leave the house at all. She has not left the house since I was a young girl."

Keeva looked at her, curiously. "Not even to see their daughter married?"

Eiselle was being forced into an embarrassing admission. She didn't want to tell Lady de Winter how glad her parents were to see her married off, and how happy her father was to be rid of her.

"I am sure Sir Bric will permit me to visit them after we have been married," she said, skirting the issue. "I know my father should like to meet him."

Keeva didn't push, perhaps sensing that the absence of her parents at the wedding was a sore subject. "As I am sure Bric would be happy to return to your home to meet your parents," she said. "But for today, you have come to be married, and on the morrow, married you shall be."

She said it in a tone that left no room for discussion, but there was a reason for that – the lady need not ever know that Keeva and Daveigh believed the sooner the marriage took place, the better. Bric wouldn't have time to run off, or delay it somehow, so they wanted to have the ceremony performed quickly for all concerned.

Eiselle, however, wasn't so stupid that she didn't see that something was afoot between Keeva and Daveigh. Like they had a secret between them. Not knowing these people, and having no idea why they were looking so shrewdly at each other, she simply pretended to be ignorant.

Suspicious, but ignorant.

While Daveigh begged his leave and followed Bric's path from the keep, out into the coming dusk, Keeva took Eiselle companionably by the arm and led her to the spiral stairs built into the thickness of Narborough's keep. The keep itself was a massive structure, with the great hall and several chambers on the first floor and several more chambers, sleeping chambers, on the second and top floor. Truthfully, Eiselle had never seen such a big building, even though Framlingham Castle had been quite massive. But it didn't have the keep that Narborough had.

Eiselle hadn't had much chance to look over Narborough when she arrived, but what she had seen was impressive. The huge keep, in the middle of hill-like earthworks, had a forebuilding around the stone steps that led up into the great hall. The stonework on the exterior, from what she saw, was exquisitely carved, and that same craftsmanship carried into the interior. The door frames and frames around the stairwells also had faces chiseled into the stone. As they headed up to the floor above, she reached out to touch some of the stonework around a very small window.

"This is a beautiful keep, Lady de Winter," she said. "I am sure you and your husband are very proud of it."

Keeva ran her fingers along a face etched into the windowsill as they passed it going up the stairs. "This is a very old keep," she said. "It was built well over one hundred years ago by Sir Denis de Winter, a knight who came ashore with the Duke of Normandy. He was instrumental in helping settle the land, and this keep was built just for him by Savoy artisans. He brought them from France. He built three other castles along the great river, too. I am certain Bric will take you to see those someday. The House of de Winter has an impressive empire."

They had reached the top floor, entering into a large room that had pallets and cots shoved up against the wall. It was where the servants and some retainers slept, but Keeva led her through the straw on the floor, and the scattered bedding, to a small corridor.

"I can see how grand it is already," Eiselle said. "I… I am glad to be here, Lady de Winter. If I have not told you that already, I do apologize. I should have told you that the moment we met."

They came to another elaborately carved doorway with a heavy oak panel set into it, and Keeva paused, facing Eiselle in the weak light.

"And I am very glad you are here," she said, but she had that same expression on her face that Eiselle had seen earlier, as if the woman was keeping secrets from her. "My husband is glad, also, and I am sure that Bric is glad, though he does not show it. My lady… Bric is my cousin and I know him well. He is a man of few words. He does not say what he thinks, and he can be rather quiet when one wishes to have a conversation with him. I tell you this because I do not want you to feel sad or disturbed if he does not express how glad he is to have you here."

It seemed to Eiselle that Lady de Winter was apologizing for the man. "I am not sad nor disturbed, my lady," she assured her. "In fact, he has been quite kind to me. We had a conversation when I arrived, and I asked him if he was agreeable to this arrangement."

Keeva's eyes widened; with fear, Eiselle thought. "You did?" Keeva asked hesitantly. "What… what did he say?"

Eiselle smiled as she thought on their conversation. "He told me that no one forced him into it," she said. "He seemed agreeable."

Keeva let out a muttered hiss. "Thank God."

"What was that?"

Realizing she'd spoken too loudly, Keeva struggled to recover. "I simply meant that… that I am most thankful you and Bric had a chance to speak," she said, quickly opening the door and hastening to change the subject. "Here is your chamber, my lady. I've had the servants bring your trunks up here and you should be quite comfortable."

The room was small, but lavishly furnished. The bed was big, with a great drapey canopy and heavy curtains to keep in the warmth. Her trunks were neatly stacked against the wall, and there was a small table, two chairs, a rather large wardrobe, and a dressing table filling up most of the space. But it was lovely, far more lovely than her room at Hadleigh House had been, and she was quite pleased by it.

"It is delightful," she said sincerely. "Thank you for going to such trouble to make me feel welcome."

The truth was that Keeva was bending over backwards for the lady, compensating for what she was sure was Bric's coldness towards her. But the mention of a conversation with Bric upon the lady's arrival made Keeva very curious, indeed. So he said he was agreeable to the arrangement, did he? She could only hope that somehow, someway, the man had changed his mind.

She intended to find out.

"It is my pleasure, my lady," she said. "I shall have hot water sent up to you so that you may bathe, and I shall send Bric for you when supper is ready. I am looking forward to hearing more about your fostering at Framlingham Castle and more about your life in general. I... I do hope we become friends, my lady. I should like that."

Eiselle thought that was nearly the first genuine and unguarded thing she'd heard from Lady de Winter since they'd met. The lady seemed to have been uneasy since they'd been introduced, with long glances at her husband, and making apologies for Bric as if she felt she needed to. There was something strange going on, but Eiselle couldn't worry about that at the moment. It wasn't as if she could do anything about it, whatever it was. She was forced into this situation as much as any of them and was determined to make the best of it.

"I would be honored to call you my friend, Lady de Winter," she said. "I am looking forward to it."

Keeva smiled at her, a genuine gesture, and shut the door behind her as she quit the room. Eiselle simply stood there, near the window, wondering about the strange atmosphere she had entered into at Narborough. Lady de Winter had made her feel welcome, but Eiselle received a sense of desperation about it, as if Lady de Winter was trying overly hard to make it so.

Strange, she thought.

But then, something occurred to her, something Bric had said. When she had asked him if he was agreeable to the marriage, he'd said something odd –

Did someone tell you I was not?

It hadn't been the response she'd expected, and Lady de Winter's apologies for the man told her that, perhaps, there was something behind it.

Perhaps, he hadn't been agreeable to the marriage, after all.

If he wasn't, then she would surely soon find out.

CHAPTER FOUR

T HEY HAD A priest, and a feast, and a bride, but they had no groom.
Bric, along with Pearce and Mylo, had ridden out just after
sunset when they'd received word that raiders, possibly the Nottingham
rebels, were attacking a nearby village. Concerned that the raid was
meant to draw the army away from Narborough, Daveigh remained
behind with a goodly portion of his army while Bric and the others rode
out to see about the raid.

In Bric's defense, he hadn't a choice about riding away just as the
priest had arrived from King's Lynn to the north. The town in question
was Downham, a few miles south of Narborough, so Bric led a squad of
men from the castle and Daveigh ordered the castle bottled up against a
possible attack.

With all of the men outside, remaining vigilant as a cold and moist
night settled, there were only five people in the hall enjoying a rather
elaborate meal – Keeva, Eiselle, Sir Pearce's wife, Zara, Sir Mylo's wife,
Angela, and the priest who ate more than two men combined. The
priest had introduced himself as Father Manducor, a warrior for God,
and he was a mass of a man who planted himself at the end of the table
and ate like a glutton. In fact, Eiselle was having a difficult time looking
at anything other than the priest, who burped and slurped his way
through Lady de Winter's lovely meal. The dogs who roamed the hall of
Narborough had all congregated around the priest, who was throwing
bones and scraps to the floor at an alarming rate.

Appalled by the priest's behavior, Keeva kept up a running stream
of chatter as the man's ghastly manners could be heard above all. She

had first introduced Zara, Lady de Dere, and Eiselle had been pleased to meet the woman who was very close to her own age. Zara was blonde, rather plain, but she had a bright smile that seemed to be constantly plastered on her face.

Angela, Lady de Chevington, was also introduced, a very young woman who had a two-year-old child she spoke of constantly. Between Angela's chatter and Zara's grinning, Eiselle wondered if she was ever going to fit in with these women. She tended to keep to herself, and she wasn't particularly social because she'd never had much opportunity for such things, so the interaction with new and strange women had her stomach lurching again.

As Angela spoke of her young son and his love of playing in horse dung, Eiselle found herself smiling wanly and drinking far too much wine to settle her belly. At least, she hoped it would. But about an hour into the feast, she started to hiccup uncontrollably.

"My lady, are you ill?" Keeva asked with concern. "May I get you something to ease your affliction?"

Eiselle had her hand to her mouth, struggling to stop the hiccups. "I am not ill, my lady," she said, ripping off a loud hiccup. Mortified, she smiled weakly. "I... I suppose it has simply been a long day and I am weary. My stomach is unsettled and I do apologize for my terrible manners."

Keeva was genuinely concerned. "Your manners are impeccable, my dear," she assured Eiselle. "I am sorry your constitution has been upset. Mayhap you would like to retire for the evening? I am not sure when the men will return, so you may as well retire."

That sounded like a very good idea to Eiselle. She was looking forward to spending some time alone, retreating away from people she didn't know but who were trying to be kind to her. In truth, she was tired of listening to the priest burp and grunt, and he'd deteriorated into farting, so she thought it best to simply return to her chamber.

"I should like to, my lady," she admitted. "I am sorry to retire so early. I am sure you wished to speak long into the night, but I have a feeling there will be many opportunities to do that."

She was looking at the other ladies as she spoke, and Zara smiled that toothy smile at her. "Tomorrow we were planning on going to the stream to the west of Narborough," Zara said. "There are bushes of berries and it is also a very good place to hunt mushrooms. Will you attend us?"

Eiselle knew they were trying to be kind but, before she could answer, Keeva spoke. "Tomorrow is her wedding day," she reminded Zara. "The lass doesn't want to be pawing through the bushes on the day she is to marry. There will be time for that later."

With that, she stood up, indicating for Eiselle to do the same. Eiselle bid a good evening to the ladies at the table as Keeva once again escorted her to the chamber on the upper floor. As they entered the stairwell, Keeva spoke softly.

"Zara and Angela mean well, but I swear to you that I cannot stand their prattle at times," she muttered. "Zara is empty-headed at times and she drinks to excess. Wine is like mother's milk to that lass."

Eiselle looked at her with some shock. "How… terrible," she said, not knowing what else to say. "She seemed kind enough, as did Lady de Chevington."

Keeva snorted. "All Angela can speak of is that little brat who runs wild," she said. "Well, I suppose that is not fair; the lad is very cute, but he has a wild streak in him. She had better learn to tame it before I have to take a stick to him."

She was animated as she spoke, her Irish brogue heavier the more animated she became. Eiselle ended up grinning at her as they ascended the stairs. "A holy terror, is he?"

Keeva looked at her with surprise before bursting out laughing. "A beastly child if there ever was one," she said. "You shall meet little Edward soon enough."

Eiselle lifted her eyebrows. "I am sure I will," she said. "Lady Angela seemed very proud of him."

Keeva rolled her eyes. "God's Blood, the woman lives and breathes that lad. You think she'd birthed the Christ Child."

Eiselle couldn't help the laughter. They reached her chamber and Keeva bid her a good sleep with a kiss to the cheek, leaving Eiselle thinking that she was coming to like Lady de Winter, just a little. She seemed honest, brutally so, and that was a welcome attribute as far as Eiselle was concerned.

Heading into her chamber, she shut the door and bolted it.

Her bower was still and quiet, the only sounds coming from the crackling in the hearth. Someone had stoked the fire, swept the floor, and put an iron pot full of water on the arm that hung over the hearth. Eiselle stuck her finger into it; it was delightfully warm. She was eager to use it to wash with.

Throwing open her trunks, she pulled forth soaps and combs and her sleeping shift. Given that her father was a merchant, she often had access to things most people didn't – she had three bars of hard, white soap that smelled of almond blossoms, and a fourth bar that smelled of lemons. She had skin oils that smelled of flowers, and a salve for her lips that tasted of honey. Every product she had was something she'd simply taken from her father's shop, and he'd simply ignored whatever she did. He father wasn't one to pay much attention to her, anyway.

Unfortunately, there was no tub in which to take a bath in her chamber, and she didn't want to call for one, so she made due with the warmed water from the pot and a bowl on the table. Stripping down, she used a rag and the soap to wash herself, all the while thinking of this momentous day and of the man she'd been pledged to marry.

Bric...

Truthfully, she was disappointed that he'd not been present for the evening meal, but she understood it was unavoidable. Eiselle had spent most of her life at a manor house, with several servants and about twenty men her father hired as protection, and there was never anyone riding out to protect a village or fight a battle. Even when she'd been at Framlingham, she was never directly exposed to the knight who served Bigod. She'd been kept with the other wards, and Lady Bigod made sure her ladies were kept well away from the lustful men. At least, that was the way she'd phrased it.

But that had been Eiselle's only exposure to fighting men, and the military function of a castle, so her experience at Narborough was new and, frankly, disappointing. It was also a little frightening – men riding out to battle, with their sharp weapons and war horses.

It was a very long way from her father's quiet shop.

But it was something Eiselle realized she was going to have to resign herself to. She was to marry the man known as the High Warrior, and she assumed that he would ride to any battle de Winter was involved in. She knew nothing of knights, of their lives, and of how they lived. She hoped her husband would be patient enough to teach her.

If he didn't send her back to her parents first.

Thoughts lingering on her betrothed, and the entire situation, she finished washing and pulled on her sleeping shift that smelled of lavender. Her mother had sprinkled it in her trunks, and everything was infused with the fresh, clean smell. It reminded her of home, and of the garden her mother kept but, oddly enough, she didn't long for what she'd left behind. The only things at home were her indifferent parents, and she wasn't sad for them. As anxious as she had been for coming to Narborough, she actually felt welcome in spite of everything. Now that the excitement of her arrival had died down, she was coming to think she might like it here. At least, she hoped so.

But all of that hinged on Bric MacRohan.

Brushing out her long, dark hair, she re-braided it and stoked the fire once more before climbing into bed. It was quite comfortable and warm, and as she lay back on the pillow, she realized just how exhausted she was. It had been a very eventful day.

Sleep claimed her before she was even aware of it.

BRIC HAD JUST passed beneath the portcullis of Narborough's gatehouse when Daveigh was standing in his path.

"Well?" Daveigh demanded. "What happened?"

Bric pulled his war horse to a halt, climbing off the beast and handing him over to a waiting stable groom, the only man that the horse wouldn't snap at. *Liath* was the horse's name, a massive dappled-gray horse with a nasty temper, but in battle he was invaluable. He could anticipate Bric, so it was like having a shadow. He adored the animal and the feeling was mutual, but it was only Bric that the beast adored.

Anyone else was a potential victim.

"To be truthful, I am not entirely convinced it was Nottingham," Bric said as he pulled off his helm, wiping a weary hand across his forehead. "Rather than engage us, they tried to evade us, so there was more chasing going on than combat. They headed west and we let them go."

"What about the town?"

"The damage wasn't too severe. It seems they were only interested in stealing supplies."

Daveigh frowned. "Foraging," he muttered. "Peterborough is to the west."

Bric nodded. "I know," he said. "John's mercenaries held the city up until a few months ago, but it is possible there are still pockets throughout the area."

"Is that what you believe? These are simply vagrant mercenaries?"

Bric shrugged. "It is as possible as anything else," he said. Then, he looked around the outer bailey and at the massive walls, lit up against the night with fatted torches that billowed black smoke into the sky. "We were not attacked here?"

Daveigh shook his head. "Nay," he replied. "All has been quiet."

Bric pondered that. He'd suspected the attack on the village had been a ruse, as they all had, and was both puzzled and pleased to realize it wasn't. But he wasn't going to ponder it further. He was exhausted, but there was more on his mind than simply sleep.

There was the matter of a certain young woman he'd left behind.

His focus turned towards the inner ward and the keep.

"I saw the priest arrive when I was departing," he said. "I suppose Lady de Winter is furious that the wedding did not take place tonight."

Daveigh looked towards the keep as well. "I do not know," he said. "I have not seen her since you left, but I am sure she is waiting up for me."

"And me."

Daveigh grinned. "She will berate me for letting you ride to battle and avoid the ceremony before she will unleash her anger on you," he said. "If I were you, I would retreat to my chamber and bolt the door. Do not come out until morning, no matter how much she bangs on your door and bellows."

Bric was still looking at the keep. He was thinking on retiring, but not to his chamber. The entire time he'd been away, his thoughts had intermittently lingered on the lovely young woman with the pale green eyes. Was he disappointed he hadn't married the woman that night? In truth, he was, just a little. Other than the initial conversation they'd had, he hadn't really had the opportunity to come to know her. Even so, he couldn't seem to get her out of his mind. So rather than retire to his chamber for the night, he wanted to seek her out and talk to her. He knew it was late, but he didn't much care.

Bric MacRohan rarely thought of anyone else's wants, comforts, or desires other than his own. If the woman was asleep, then he would wake her. He was fearful that if he didn't take the time to speak with her, alone, then he might not have another chance in the near future because Keeva and Daveigh seemed to want to be present whenever he was around her. Therefore, he didn't let Daveigh know what he was thinking. He simply nodded his head.

"Mayhap I shall," he said. "Where is the priest, by the way?"

"I am not entirely sure. I have not seen him come out of the keep, so it is possible he is still in the hall."

"And my intended?"

Daveigh gestured towards the keep. "I am sure that Keeva put her on the high floor, where we put our honored guests. I am sure she has been long asleep by now." He paused. "Bric?"

"My lord?"

Daveigh scratched at his ear, a reluctant gesture. "I hesitate to ask you this, but what do you think of her?"

Bric could see that Daveigh was living in fear of his answer. True to form, he was guarded. "She is pretty enough."

"Quite. I'd say she's damned beautiful."

"I would agree with that."

"Then… you are pleased with her?"

Was he? Bric's first reaction was to the affirmative. Aye, he *was* pleased with her. But he wasn't going to tell Daveigh that. He was too embarrassed to admit it, or anything like it. Instead, he forced a smile.

"Ask me that in a week," he said, turning for the keep. "I will see you on the morrow."

Quickly, he moved across the vast outer bailey of Narborough before Daveigh could stop him, heading through the maze of earthwork and into the inner ward where the keep was situated. Before him, the imposing structure of Narborough's keep loomed against the night sky, and he entered the forebuilding, dimly lit by torches, and made his way up the stone steps into the entry.

It was deathly still in the keep when he entered, and very nearly pitch-dark. But he could see faint light coming from the great hall and as he moved through the darkness and into the cavernous room, he was immediately met with snoring. As he eyes adjusted to the darkness, he could see the priest at the far end of the room, sleeping on a bench before the gently snapping fire.

There were a few others in the great hall, kitchen servants mostly, all of them sleeping near the fire in a group with the dogs nearby, all of them huddling up for warmth. It wasn't unusual for the kitchen and keep servants to sleep in the great hall even though there was another open space on the top floor the servants used as well. In fact, the top floor was really only for sleeping and guest lodging, as it had four rooms that were used for visitors. It was where Daveigh had indicated Eiselle was being housed, so Bric took one of the smoking torches from the iron sconce near the entry and headed for the spiral stairs that led to the upper floor.

The one good thing about the location of the visitors' chambers was that they were well away from the master's chamber where Keeva was sleeping. The master's chamber was on the other side of the great hall, sealed off by two sets of massive doors. It was well protected and well-insulated from the noise of the rest of the keep, and Bric was counting on that. He didn't want Keeva to come running up to Lady Eiselle's chamber and chase him off.

The smell near the top of the stairs told him he had entered the large open area where the servants slept. It smelled like a barnyard with piss buckets in the corner and old straw on the floor. Bric made his way through the snoring servants silently, going to the first door he came to and lifting the latch, only to be faced with an empty chamber.

There was as small corridor to his left and he proceeded to open two more chambers, met with the same inky darkness. But lifting the latch of the forth chamber saw that it was unlocked, and he opened it slightly to reveal a warm room, a fire burning in the hearth, and neatly stacked trunks against the far well. He couldn't quite see the bed with the door cracked open and, in truth, he didn't want to be completely invasive, so he shut the door softly as if he'd never opened it to begin with.

Quietly, he rapped.

He rapped twice more before he received a response, a soft voice whose words were muddled by the heavy door. Assuming she had asked who had come, he tried not to speak too loudly for fear of rousing the servants.

"It is Bric, my lady," he said.

He must have spoken the magic words because the latch lifted and the door cracked open. Looking sleepy, and with her dark hair mussed, Eiselle stood in the doorway, wrapped up in a heavy robe. Her expression was one of both surprise and curiosity.

"Sir Bric," she said, sounding anxious. "Is everything well?"

He nodded, realizing that even sleeping and unkempt, she was still the most beautiful woman he'd ever seen. Probably more so in her mussed state because he found something unerringly charming about it.

"Everything is fine," he said quietly. "I came to make sure you were well-tended after your busy day."

Eiselle nodded. "I am quite well, thank you," she said. "And you? Are you well after riding out to fight off the raiders?"

"There was no fight. It was a waste of time." When she simply stood there, gazing up at him, he thought to press his intention before the situation turned awkward. "I realize it is late, but we have had so little time to speak since your arrival. So if you are agreeable, I thought to only take a few moments of your time."

Eiselle appeared uncertain at first but, after a moment, she stepped back and opened the door wider. "Would you like to come in where it is warmer?"

Considering they were betrothed, it wasn't an improper offer, to seek solitude in the lady's boudoir. Bric took the torch and lodged it into the nearest sconce, lighting up the dim corridor, before entering her chamber. Eiselle shut the door quietly behind him.

"I apologize that I missed the evening meal, but it could not be helped," he said. "I trust the meal was pleasant."

Eiselle nodded, somewhat nervous about his presence. She kept a proper distance. "It was very pleasant," she said. But when that wasn't enough, she added, "Lady de Winter introduced me to Lady de Dere and Lady de Chevington."

"And the priest?"

She appeared hesitant. "Of that, I would not know," she said. "He kept to himself throughout the meal. I… I have never seen one man eat so much."

Bric grunted unhappily. "I would have at least hoped he would speak of plans for our marriage tomorrow," he said. "Did Lady de Winter speak of any such plans?"

Eiselle pulled her robe more tightly around her in the chill of the room. "Nay," she said. "She only said it would be on the morrow, but I do not know anything more than that. Are... are you still certain you wish to go through with it? As I said when I arrived, if the arrangement displeases you, then I may still be sent home."

He just looked at her; petite, curvy, and that face... was he so fortunate that he was actually going to wake up to that face every day for the rest of his life?

"Do you want to go home?" he asked. "You have made this statement more than once and I am coming to think that it is your way of telling me that *you* are not pleased with this arrangement. If that is the case, you need only tell me."

Eiselle shook her head quickly. "I did not mean to imply that," she said. "I simply... that... well, if I may be honest, my lord?"

He fought off a smile. "Please."

Eiselle drew in a long, thoughtful breath and perched herself on the end of her bed. "It is simply that ever since I arrived, I get the feeling that you are not agreeable to this betrothal," she said. "Lady de Winter seemed to apologize for you far too much, as if she thought you were offending me somehow. You even asked me if anyone had told me of your reluctance to the betrothal. In all, I received the impression that this marriage was not a happy circumstance for you. Am I wrong?"

Bric couldn't help it; a smile broke through, tugging at the corners of his mouth. With a heavy sigh, he turned to the nearest chair in the chamber and sat down on it, so heavily that the wood creaked. He'd left his great helm down in the hall when he'd picked up the torch, but he was wearing mail over his entire body along with weapons and a heavy tunic, among other things. He was greatly weighted down and greatly weary, but he didn't feel like retiring in the least.

He had a lady to know, and perhaps there was no better time than now for honesty.

"Since you are being truthful, then I should be as well," he said. "Nay, you are not wrong. Do not misunderstand me, my lady – it is nothing personal against you. While I love your cousin, Dash, and he is like a brother to me, he also knew that I had no desire to marry. I am a busy man, and my vocation is my wife. There is not time for a family. But Dashiell seemed to disregard my personal feelings by proposing this marriage to de Winter, who gladly accepted it to unite the House of de Winter not only to the House of du Reims, but also to the Dukes of Savernake since Dash's wife is the daughter of the former duke. To say that I was resistant to the betrothal is an understatement."

Eiselle was hurt by his words, but not surprised. "I see," she said bravely. "I suppose I suspected all along. The betrothal was so unexpected and sudden, I wondered if you could truly be happy about it. You are a great knight, my lord. Certainly, a merchant's daughter is not the fine marriage you would expect for a man of your station."

He was looking at her, bathed in the firelight. "Normally, that would be true," he said. "But that did not have anything to do with my feelings. I simply do not wish to be married, to anyone."

Eiselle averted her gaze, looking at her lap. "Then I shall pack my trunks and leave on the morrow," she said quietly. "I will not hold you to this betrothal. There is no crime in a man not wanting to be married."

Of all the things Bric thought his future wife would be, a gracious and understanding woman who understood his resistance to a marriage had not been among those thoughts. He'd once thought that any woman fortunate enough to be his betrothed would be most eager to sink her claws into him, eager to bind herself to the High Warrior, but Eiselle was far from it. She seemed not only willing to agree with him, but she wasn't thinking of her own wants in the least.

Or... *was* she?

"You will not pack your trunks," he said. "What you did not let me say was that this was my position before I met you today. I was certain you would ride in here, gloating over the fact that I was to be your husband. You did not do that and, even now, you are willing to do whatever I wish. I must say that I am quite surprised."

She glanced up at him. "Why?" she asked. "I do not wish for you to be miserable, because if you are miserable, I will be miserable. My lord, we do not know each other. Marriage is difficult enough without the added burden of the husband not wanting a wife."

His expression took on a suspicious cast. "You are making this far too easy," he said. "Surely you must have other offers waiting for you, or even a lover."

"None, my lord. Not one."

He could hardly believe that, given her beauty, but he stopped short of telling her so. Instead, he cocked his head curiously. "Then if that is the case, what are your feelings on marriage?" he asked. "I asked you if you were agreeable to this marriage earlier and you did not answer me. Are you agreeable?"

"If you are."

He snorted softly. "Again," he said softly, "that is far too easy an answer. Tell me the truth, my lady, and tell me what you feel and not what you believe I should hear. Are you agreeable to this marriage or not?"

Eiselle lifted her head, looking him in the eye. "As I told you, I have never had a marriage offer," she said. "I will have seen twenty years and one this summer, so I am quite old for a prospective bride. Most girls my age have been married for a few years, but with me… this is the one and only offer I have ever had. It is shameful to say that, and I am sure you are thinking that there must be something wrong with me. But I assure you, there is nothing wrong with me. I have lived with my parents in a relatively isolated life, so there simply has not been the opportunity to seek prospective husbands and my father was not active in such a pursuit, anyway. He seemed to think that men should come to me, not that I should go to them."

Bric shook his head faintly. "I find that astonishing that you have never had a marriage offer," he said. "With your beauty, you could command kings and princes, at the very least. You never even had a marriage offer when you were at Framlingham?"

Eiselle was deeply flattered by his comment, her cheeks flushing. "Nay," she said. "But... well, if we are being honest, it was not a good situation there."

"Why not?"

She averted her gaze again, toying with her hands in her lap. "I went to Framlingham when I was ten years and seven," she said. "I was very old to be a ward, and the girls at Framlingham had all practically grown up together. When I came, they did not like me very much. They weren't very... kind."

Strangely, that statement made him feel rather protective of her. He sat forward, his elbows resting on his knees, his hands hanging.

"Tell me what happened."

She cleared her throat softly. "I would rather not, if you please. I do not wish for you to think that I am complaining or speaking ill of others."

"I would not think that. And I asked because I genuinely want to know. What did those women do?"

Eiselle didn't like to think back to that terrible year, but he was asking a question and she would do him the courtesy of giving him an answer.

"They did not want to be my friend," she said after a moment. "I was an outsider; I understand that. But they were not kind. It was difficult to fit in, so I stopped trying. They began to whisper about me, how I was arrogant and aloof, and one night, one of the girls cut the end of my braid off. Still others stole things from me. One girl stole a necklace from me that belonged to my mother and when I saw her wearing it, she accused me of lying. There was no way I could prove the necklace was mine, of course, unless I sent for my mother, and my mother never leaves the house. My experience at Framlingham was not a good one, my lord. I am glad to forget about it."

The kind of girls she spoke of were the kind of girls Bric had been fearful of – petty, conniving females who would sink their teeth into him and never let go. He'd seen enough of those kinds of women to know he wanted nothing to do with them. Perhaps it was the fear of those women that had truly cemented his resistance to marriage or, at the very least, it had been a contributing factor.

But Eiselle seemed different.

Bric had spent his life priding himself on his judgement of men, often because his life depended on it. He could root out untrustworthy men as if he could see into their very souls and know them for what they were. In truth, for all he knew, Eiselle was telling him a greatly fabricated lie. She could be telling him what she thought he wanted to hear simply to endear herself to him.

But somehow, he didn't think so.

He believed her.

"I am sorry you were faced with that," he said after a moment. "I know what it means to not fit with my peers."

She cocked her head curiously. "How could you know that? You are de Winter's greatest knight and all men greatly respect you."

He wriggled his eyebrows. "It was not always thusly," he said. "Listen to me; I sound as Irish as I look and, in England, that is a crime. I am lower than the pigs in the trough to some. It took years to build up men's faith in me, and with that faith came respect. But it was hard-fought, believe me. It was not a simple thing."

Eiselle smiled timidly. "But you were able to earn it," she said. "You have a great reputation, and I am nothing. That is why I say if you wish to send me home, I will understand completely."

So they were back to that again. Bric knew that he was never going to send her home, not even if she wanted to go. At that moment, he knew that he was going to marry the lass. He might even like it. In fact, he suspected he would if he gave her and marriage in general, a chance and stop being afraid of it. Perhaps the fear of marriage he had was simply the fear of the unknown.

But Eiselle... she was "known". And he liked what he saw.

"Would you be disappointed if I told you that I will not send you home?" he asked. "I will if you want me to. But if you say you will do whatever I decide… I have decided that I do not want to send you home."

Eiselle's smile grew, turning genuine. "It does not bother you that I am not a great lady?"

He snorted softly. "I have a feeling you are greater than you give yourself credit for," he said. "You will let me be the judge of just how great you are."

"Does that mean you have decided what you expect out of a wife? I asked you earlier today and you did not know."

His eyes glimmered at her in the firelight. "Whatever expectations I have, you have already met them."

"But I have done nothing."

"You have been honest. That is the most I can ask from any man, or any woman. As long as you are always honest with me, that exceeds my expectations."

Eiselle was somewhat puzzled by the statement. "I would not know how to be anything else."

"Then that makes you the best wife possible."

She was still confused but, as she looked into his eyes, she swore she saw a flicker of warmth there. She didn't know the man at all. But from what she saw, he was just as honest as he expected her to be. Something told her that she would always know where she stood with him.

"And you?" she asked. "Will you always be honest with me, also?"

"With my dying breath, my lady. Upon my oath, I swear it."

He said it so passionately that she believed him implicitly. "Then our marriage is to your liking?"

"It is."

"I am glad. I… I hope that we shall have a pleasant life together."

That gleam in his eye turned into something else, something curious and intriguing and even… deep. There was definitely something deep there.

"Lass," he said slowly, "I hope it is something more than that."

"What more could it be?"

"I hope we will both find out, together."

Something in his tone gave Eiselle hope that they would, indeed.

CHAPTER FIVE

THE WEDDING DAY was not what Eiselle had expected.
She'd lived a rather isolated and solitary existence, as she'd told Bric. Her mother, ill most of the time, hadn't been overly attentive to her, and other than the servants at Hadleigh House, there weren't other women in her life. Her brief stay at Framlingham hadn't produced any friends, female or otherwise, so Eiselle had always learned to do for herself, and insomuch as that was the life she'd always led, she thought nothing of it. She was very self-sufficient.

But her introduction to Keeva rocked that world.

It started in the morning. Keeva, Zara, and Angela came to her chamber just after dawn with an army of servants bearing a tub, hot water, food, clothing, and a variety of other things. Eiselle was roused from her bed by knocking on her door and once that door opened, she was flooded with an army of do-gooders, all resolute in their quest to help her prepare for her marriage to Bric.

It seemed that it was a community effort.

It had, in truth, been a little disorienting at first as Keeva had gaily charged in with her troops. She had decided that the marriage would be held at midday, in the great hall of Narborough, so there was little time from Keeva's standpoint to prepare the bride. There was much to do and little time to do it.

Keeva was much different from the woman Eiselle had come to know the day before – that woman had been hesitant and, at times, snappish. But this woman was quite happy – ecstatic, in fact – as she had a bath prepared and clothing laid out on the bed.

Eiselle peered at the clothing curiously as Zara and Angela eagerly showed her what Lady de Winter had brought her – a lavish dress made from pale green silk and lined with gray rabbit fur along the cuffs and neckline, with a cutaway layer over the gown that was made from a spectacular brocade. That, too, was lined along the edges with gray fur.

In all, it was a magnificent garment and Eiselle gingerly touched it as Zara and Angela chattered excitedly about it. It was a gift, Zara said, from Lady de Winter, and when Keeva heard the woman spill her surprise, she swatted her on the behind and yanked her over to the tub to help prepare the bath. Scolded, Zara was relegated to pouring rose oil into the water and laying out the sponges.

Truthfully, Eiselle had no say in anything that was going on. She was simply part of the tempest that Keeva was whipping up. It was as if her own son, or daughter, was getting married, and she very happily directed everyone in the room, making sure the dress was brushed off and aired out, the water was hot, the cleansing oils and sponges were at the ready. Soon enough, she chased everyone out of the room but a pair of older female servants, Zara, and Angela, and began stripping Eiselle down for her bath.

That was when she ran into resistance. Eiselle tried to preserve her modesty; God knows, she tried. She tried to hold the shift on her body even as Keeva and Angela tried to pull it off, tugging it down from the shoulders. Her nervous stomach began to act up again and she found herself trying not to belch in Keeva's face. But Keeva was speaking calmly to her, trying to soothe her, yet Eiselle was terribly embarrassed that these women were trying to strip her naked.

Finally, Keeva took pity on her and told her that they would turn their backs as she undressed and climbed into the tub. Eiselle did, swiftly, and plunged into the hot water nearly up to her neck. But once she was in the tub, she was Keeva's captive, with nowhere to go.

That's when the fun began in earnest.

Eiselle was rinsed and scrubbed within an inch of her life. Every inch of skin or hair was rubbed or soaped. Keeva even took a cloth and vigorously rubbed her face with witch hazel, scrubbed and buffing until her pale complexion was rosy. It was more rubbing, scrubbing, and buffing that Eiselle had ever experienced in her life, and certainly more attention than she'd ever known.

Her own mother hadn't been this attentive with her, but Keeva was greatly attentive, cloyingly so, and Eiselle was becoming frustrated with the entire process. She'd been fully capable of preparing herself for her wedding day. But Keeva was Lady de Winter, and Eiselle was to be her subject, so she fought down the annoyance as the woman fussed over her.

But she didn't like it one bit.

When the bath was finished, Keeva had everyone turn their backs to Eiselle as she climbed out of the tub and quickly dried herself with the drying linen that had been put by the hearth to warm. Once she was finished drying her skin, she swiftly pulled on the shift that had been handed to her and as soon as it was over her head, Keeva and her army turned around and resumed their attention in earnest.

Eiselle was placed on a stool in front of the fire and her dark hair was brushed vigorously in the warmth to dry it. Forced onto the stool was more like it as the older serving women took turns with her hair. The brushing and tugging seemed to go on forever, and Eiselle had her hand to her mouth most of the time to prevent gassy emissions but, soon enough, the old women were braiding her hair and carefully pinning it to her scalp in an elaborate dressing that involved golden hair nets and strands of tiny seed pearls.

When her hair was mostly finished, the beautiful pale green dress went on over her shift, and Eiselle was buffeted by women so determined to make her beautiful for her wedding day that she felt like she was being pulled and pushed in every direction. Eiselle knew they meant well, but her annoyance was growing. She simply wasn't used to such attention and found it intrusive, even though she knew Keeva and the others didn't mean it to be. They only meant to help.

But they were like masters working over a slave.

Finally, as the day progressed towards the nooning hour, the pushing, pinning, and primping slowed dramatically. Victory was in reach. Eiselle stood in the middle of the chamber, her arms extended as Keeva and the maids finished the final touches on the dress. Keeva snapped her fingers at one of the old women, who rushed to pick up something that had been left near the door. It looked like a platter but when she held it up, Eiselle could see that it was a mirror. It was highly polished silver, flat in shape, and when the woman held it up to Eiselle, she could see what she had been transformed into.

An elegant, beautiful bride.

Now, the primping and pinning made sense, and her nervous stomach was forgotten. Eiselle gasped softly as the sight of herself in the mirror as Keeva stood next to the mirror, watching the expression on Eiselle's face.

"Do you like what you see, lass?" she asked hopefully.

Eiselle was genuinely speechless; she had no idea she could look so groomed and beautiful, like the fine ladies from the queen's court. She stared at herself, noting the elaborate braids that had been wrapped into buns over each ear, and another braid that skimmed the top of her head, pulling the hair away from her face.

Golden hair nets covered the buns, and the seed pearl strands were woven into the braid across her head and into a long, single braid that trailed down her back all the way to her buttocks. As she stood there, one of the serving women affixed a veil to her head, a sheer pale fabric called *albatross*, and it draped down the back of her, all the way to the floor.

Truthfully, Eiselle could hardly believe she was looking at her own reflection.

"You have made me so… beautiful," she finally said. "I cannot believe it is me that I see."

Keeva smiled proudly. "It *is* you," she said. "Bric will see you and know he is the most fortunate man in all of England."

Eiselle smiled at her, seeing how pleased she was with her handiwork, but she didn't dare mention that Bric had already said such a thing. She didn't want Keeva to know that he'd been in her chamber for several hours the night before. All they did was speak, and speak of many things, but she had a feeling Keeva wouldn't like the fact that they'd spent that time alone before they were married and she didn't want to put Bric in a bad light.

Still, it had been one of the most monumental nights of her young life.

They had spoken mostly about her and her life, as Bric didn't seem to be too inclined to reveal much about himself, but Eiselle didn't mind. He seemed interested in her and that was enough. He knew of her upbringing at Hadleigh House, and of her parents who had wanted a son yet received only a daughter, of the servant children she used to play with, and of the old monk priest who would come from the small village of Thurston to teach her the scripture because her mother did not want to take her into town. She spoke of her love for poetry, something the priest also taught her from the Greek scriptures, and how she had learned to love to sing in the brief time she'd been at Framlingham.

In all, Eiselle thought she presented a rather boring picture of a young woman who had lived a sheltered life, but Bric gave no indication that he thought the same. He'd asked her about her relations at Thunderbey Castle, where the Earls of East Anglia lived, but she didn't know them very well. She only knew Dashiell because he would come to visit her father from time to time, and he always brought her sweets when he came, sweets her mother would steal from her. Bric had snorted about that.

They spoke of the House of du Reims at some length, even as Eiselle grew so sleepy she could barely keep her eyes open. Realizing this, Bric had politely excused himself so that she could return to bed, and he'd done nothing more than smile at her before quitting her chamber. No touching her hand, and certainly no kiss farewell. He'd been strictly polite.

Eiselle had fallen asleep with visions of a silver-eyed knight on her mind.

And now, Keeva had dressed her to please the man. No matter if it had been an annoyance, the end result was worth it. Eiselle was deeply grateful.

"It is I who am the fortunate one, Lady de Winter," she said after a moment's reflection. "I cannot thank you enough for what you have done for me. I am very grateful."

Keeva stepped forward, fussing with the veil so it draped more gracefully. "May I tell you a secret, my lady?"

"Of course. And you may call me Eiselle. I would be honored."

Keeva smiled at her as she continued to fuss with the veil. "Eiselle," she repeated. "Daveigh and I have been married for almost fifteen years and we've yet to have children. I do not think we shall ever be so blessed, and I had been saving this dress for my daughter, should I have had one. It belonged to my younger sister, you see, and it was to be her wedding dress, but she died before she was able to wear it. I have been saving it all of these years and since Bric is my cousin, I think it is most appropriate to give the dress to you. You are my family now, too."

Eiselle was deeply touched. She looked down at the garment, which fit her so beautifully except it was a little too long. That she was wearing a dead woman's dress brought her sorrow.

"What was your sister's name?" she asked softly.

"Maeve," Keeva replied, finally finished with the veil. "It was an illness that took her when she had seen fourteen years. I still miss her, every day, but I believe she would be very happy to see you wear her dress."

Eiselle felt a lump in her throat as she smoothed at the brocade. "Maeve," Eiselle repeated softly. "I will wear her dress with honor. But I will make you this promise – should you ever have a daughter, I will be more than happy to give the dress back. I considered it only borrowed."

Keeva touched her cheek. "You are a sweet lass," she said. "I am very happy to welcome you to our family."

Eiselle smiled bravely. "Thank you, my lady. You do me a very great honor."

Keeva's teary-eyed expression said it all. But she quickly sniffed it away and clapped her hands at the servants, as if she wasn't comfortable being overly emotional or overly sentimental about the dress or about Bric's coming marriage. Emotion embarrassed Keeva, even though she was full of it. It was rare when she let her guard down but, with Eiselle, she felt safe enough.

"Come, now," she said, gathering things like rags and bowls and shoving them at the servants. "Remove these things, swiftly. Zara, you will go to the hall and see if the priest is ready to conduct the marriage. Hurry back, lass, and do not stop to talk to your husband. Run!"

Zara opened the door and rushed off. The servants were right behind her, sending more servants into the chamber to collect the cold water from the bath and the tub itself, removing it all from the chamber.

As much flurry as occurred in beginning the process of transforming Eiselle into a bride that morning, it was with equal flurry that everything involved in the process was removed. Soon enough, the chamber was empty of servants and tubs and grooming implements, and Eiselle stood near the lancet window, feeling the breeze on her face, as Keeva and Angela stood in the open doorway.

Eventually, Angela left because she needed to tend her son and didn't like leaving him with a nurse too long, so Keeva was left waiting for Zara to return with news that the priest was prepared.

Unfortunately, Keeva was impatient and Zara didn't return soon enough. So, excusing herself from Eiselle's chamber, she shut the door and hurried down to the hall. Eiselle grinned when she could hear the woman shouting in the distance. She was full of life, fire, and generosity, and Eiselle liked that. But she was also deeply grateful that the woman left her alone.

Finally, alone.

These were the last few, final moments before her wedding and

Eiselle had a feeling that this would be the last time she would ever truly be alone. From this point forward, she would belong to Bric. And if last night was an indication, she had a feeling they would be spending a good deal of time together. Not that she minded it.

She rather liked him.

It was time for her to be alone no longer.

AFTER BEING INFORMED early that morning that Keeva arranged for the marriage to take place at the nooning hour, something Bric didn't protest in the least, he'd gone to tend his men and do his usual rounds, especially after the raid the night before. He still wasn't entirely convinced that it hadn't been some sort of ruse, so he and Pearce and Mylo had spent time on the battlements as the sun rose, sending out scouts and receiving reports that the area within a five-mile radius of the castle seemed to be free of anything unexpected.

If there were rebels about, they weren't near Narborough. Still, there were three more castles and two manor houses that belonged to the Honor of Narborough, the name of the empire that belonged to the House of de Winter. All of the properties were aligned down the River Ouse, about four or five miles from each other, and Narborough was up at the head of the string of castles. There was Roxham Castle, small but sturdy, and Wissington Castle, which was actually a small village with a keep in the middle, surrounded by enormous walls.

Along with the three castles were two smaller manor houses, Bexwell and Bedingfeld. Keeva liked Bexwell, and preferred it to the cold and often prison-like castles, so that was known as the "other" de Winter home when they weren't in residence at Narborough. Bedingfeld was smaller, a delightful moated manor house with a large garden, but it was further out in the countryside and away from the more heavily traveled areas. It was a paradise unto itself.

But all of these properties could be targets for the rebels, so Bric sent patrols out to check on the locations as the sun began to rise. Each location already had a contingent of men for protection, but Bric wanted to make sure nothing went awry with the rebels on the loose, today of all days.

He didn't want anything upsetting his wedding.

After the time he'd spent with Eiselle last night, Bric was looking forward to their marriage in a way he could have never imagined. It wasn't so much the thrill of taking a wife, a mother for his heirs. If he'd been looking for a mother for his children, he could have picked any woman he wanted. Nay, this was more than that – he'd spent hours last night talking to a woman who had a sly sense of humor and a quiet dignity about her that was rare.

Eiselle had lived a life without affection, without much meaning, but it didn't darken her outlook on the future, nor did it mar her manner. She wasn't bitter or cold; on the contrary, she was kind and thoughtful and compassionate. She was eager to please. Bric had felt an interest in her that he'd never felt with any other woman, and it was an interest he was more than willing to indulge. He was eager for the marriage simply to spend time with her, to find out why she fascinated him so.

Eiselle de Gael intrigued him more than he could control.

Therefore, when his duties were finished and the morning advanced towards noon, he headed into the keep to make sure everything was prepared for the coming ceremony. He knew that Keeva had seen to the arrangements, but he also knew she would be occupied with Eiselle and in helping her prepare, so he simply wanted to see things for himself.

It was a good thing he did. With Pearce beside him, he made his way into the great hall of Narborough only to be confronted by a priest who was eating and drinking to excess at this time of the morning.

As Bric and Pearce approached the table, the priest didn't seem too concerned. The table and floor around him was littered with scraps and hungry dogs, as if there had been a feeding frenzy that was still going on. The priest poured himself more wine and eyed the men as he lifted the cup to his lips. The fact that he didn't even acknowledge them, with a greeting or otherwise, began the slow burn of Bric's temper.

"Well?" Bric said. "We are to have a wedding at the nooning hour. Are you prepared?"

The priest drained the entire cup of wine and burped loudly. "It will be done, my lord," he said, shoveling bread into his mouth. "The couple will stand before me and it will be done. It is no great trouble."

He was slurring his speech. *The pisswit is drunk*, Bric thought with disgust. Not a man of great diplomacy, but a man of quick action, Bric looked at Pearce and jerked his head in the direction of the priest. When Bric grabbed the pitcher of wine and threw it into the hearth, Pearce used his big arm to sweep all of the food in front of the priest off the table and onto the floor.

The dogs, startled by the noise, began barking but quickly settled down when they realized there was more food to be had. As the priest roared in both surprise and anger, Bric grabbed the man by the collar of his brown woolen robes and yanked him to his feet.

"No more food and no more drink for you," he hissed. "You will clean yourself up before you will perform the marriage."

The priest glared at him as much as he could, given the fact that a very big man held him by the neck.

"Release me!" he demanded weakly. "You have no right!"

"I have every right. You shame every priest in England with your gluttonous behavior, and you greatly shame your hosts. No more food, no more drink, until this is over." Still holding on to the priest, Bric turned to Pearce. "Take him out to the well and douse him with cold water until he sobers up. I'll not have a drunkard perform this marriage."

With a grin, Pearce grabbed the priest and began dragging the man out of the hall, ignoring his protests. But as he neared the entry, his wife suddenly appeared and yelped with shock when she saw her husband manhandling the priest.

"What are you doing?" Zara asked, frightened. "Lady de Winter has sent me to make sure he is ready to perform the wedding mass."

Bric came up, motioning to Pearce to continue with the priest, while he dealt with Zara. "The wedding will be performed on schedule," he told her evenly. "Your husband is simply sobering up the priest."

Zara's eyes widened. "He is still drunk?"

"What do you mean 'still'?"

Zara blinked her big, blue eyes fearfully. "He was drunk last night, too," she said. "He sat at the end of the table, drinking and eating and burping all evening. Was he still drinking this morning, then?"

Bric sighed heavily; it did not please him to hear that. "I saw him asleep in the hall last night, so at least he paused drinking long enough to sleep. But he was certainly drinking again this morning."

Zara shook her head sadly. "God forgive him."

Bric snorted rudely. "God forgive him, for certain, I will not," he said. When he saw the shocked expression on Zara's face, he forced himself to calm. He knew he came off as terrifying and irate when his dander was up. "Not to worry, my lady. All will be well. Is my bride ready?"

He was shifting subjects, now bringing up Eiselle, and Zara's fearful expression faded. "Aye," she said. "Lady de Winter has made her look like a goddess. Wait until you see her, Bric. She is more beautiful than anything I have ever seen."

Bric smiled faintly. "I am not sure anything can make her more beautiful," he said. "Will you let her know that the priest will be ready to conduct the ceremony within the hour?"

Zara nodded, but she looked to the entry door with uncertainty. "Are you sure he will be sober?"

Bric's smile vanished and he cocked an unhappy eyebrow. "If I have anything to say about it, he will be," he said. "Is Lady de Winter with my intended?"

"She is."

"Tell her to wait a half-hour before coming to the hall. Your husband and I should have the priest moderately sober by then. If the water doesn't do it, then mayhap I can scare the man into sobriety."

"You might scare him to death, Bric."

He sighed heavily as he headed for the entry. "That," he said, "is a distinct possibility."

As Zara fled back the way she'd come, Bric ended up in the inner bailey, circling around the side of the keep to the secondary well. There was one in the lower level of the keep, in the storage area, protected by the walls of the keep, and then the secondary well used by the soldiers and trades. Bric could see Pearce as the man gleefully dunked the priest's head into a big bucket, and he could hear the priest gasping as he approached.

He watched Pearce dunk the man twice more before he stopped him. He didn't want to drown the man before the wedding could take place, even though it would have been just punishment for his behavior. As the priest sat in the dirt, soaked and sputtering, Bric bent over and slapped the man on the face to bring him around.

"Well?" he demanded. "What did you think was going to happen when you imbibed in too much drink before the wedding? Did you think I would let that go unnoticed?"

The priest yelped when Bric slapped him again, rubbing his stinging cheek as he gazed up at the enormous knight with the heavy Irish brogue.

"I am a man of God," he said, water spraying from his lips. "Hell will welcome you with open arms for striking a man of God."

Bric lifted an eyebrow. "Hell will welcome me with open arms for infractions much worse than that," he said. "I have no fear of God, or of heaven or hell, so think not to threaten me with eternal damnation."

The priest was still wiping water from his eyes, struggling to overcome his drunkenness. "What kind of a man are you that you would not fear God?"

"A man of reason and common sense."

"Such arrogance!"

"Indeed I am, and if I were you, I would tread carefully. And do not act so pious; you will probably make it to hell before I do, so do not imagine that you are better than I am."

The priest mustered a deeply outraged expression. "I did not come here to be insulted by the likes of you," he said, struggling to stand but he was so drunk that it made it difficult. Still, he managed to get to his knees. "Where is Lady de Winter? I demand to speak with her."

Bric shook his head. "I would not do that," he said. "If you think I have been hard on you, that is nothing compared to Lady de Winter. She'll gouge your eyes out and laugh at your misery if she's angry enough. Nay, man, you would do better with me and not the banshee."

The priest was still on his knees, glaring up at him, but it was clear that he was thinking over what he'd been told. Frustrated and tipsy, he held out a hand to Bric.

"Then help me up," he said. "And, for Pity's sake, help me to dry off. Let us get this wretched wedding over with."

Bric took a step back as Pearce took the priest's hand and pulled the man to his unsteady feet. As the priest began to wring out his robes, he glanced up at Bric.

"Who is getting married?" he asked. "You? Or your relation?"

Bric watched the man as he tried to clean himself up. "Me," he said. "What is your name, Priest?"

The man snorted as he brushed the mud off his knees. "Call me Manducor," he said. "And you?"

"Sir Bric MacRohan."

"And you are the husband-to-be?"

"I am."

The priest looked him up and down. "What woman would marry a man as mean as you?"

Bric stared at him. Pearce, having heard the comment, eyed Bric with some apprehension, fearful that he would soon be picking up pieces of the unruly priest after Bric tore him apart. But after a moment, Bric simply broke down into a grin.

"That is a very good question," he said. "If you remain sober, you may yet find out."

"And if I do not remain sober?"

"Then I will tie a rock around your neck and throw you into the river."

"It seems it would be better that I remain sober."

"You are showing true wisdom for the very first time."

Manducor shook off his robes, brushed off his hands, and faced Bric. "Can I at least celebrate with food and drink *after* the marriage?"

He had a rather irreverent way about him, but Bric was coming to think the man was rather sharp and opinionated, certainly not terrible qualities, properly place. He actually thought he might come to like this frank, rude, and mouthy priest. He didn't know why, but there was something unwaveringly brave in the man's eyes. Brave, bold, and rather pathetic, somehow. As if the man had nothing to lose by drinking himself to death and challenging knights twice his size.

Foolish, but brave.

"Aye," he finally said. "You can celebrate when the marriage is completed, but not before. Do you understand?"

"Sadly, I do."

"Good. Then let us return to the hall where you can dry out your robes. You have a marriage ceremony to perform."

Manducor continued to shake out his wet robes as he staggered back towards the keep entry. Bric watched the man go, shaking his head in exasperation as he and Pearce followed at a distance.

"I do not think he gave us his real name," Bric muttered.

Pearce's eyebrows drew together. "Why would you say that?"

"Because *Manducor* is Latin for 'eat'."

Pearce looked at Bric with some shock before breaking down into giggles. Only Bric MacRohan, the man who was so resistant to marriage that he would try to fight his way out of it, would be married by a priest who named himself after his favorite pastime. It was almost too ridiculous to believe.

It was going to be an interesting marriage, indeed.

CHAPTER SIX

F OR EISELLE, THE ceremony and feasting passed in a blur.
    In fact, the entire day had happened so fast that Eiselle felt as if
she were still trying to regain her equilibrium. The grooming in the
morning, then being married by the smelly priest in wet robes at the
nooning hour, and then an entire afternoon and evening of feasting and
song and dance.

Truly, it had been overwhelming.

Keeva had arranged for minstrels local to one of the taverns in the
nearby village to provide music for the feast, and they had played for
many hours as those who had been invited to the wedding feast drank
and danced to excess. All of the guests were senior soldiers and knights,
as Bric hadn't been agreeable to the marriage until the bride actually
arrived so there had been no time to send out invitations.

A few of the soldiers had brought women with them, and Eiselle
had no idea who they were, but they were dressed rather scantily. Since
the soldiers seemed to keep them off in a corner, she assumed they were
women with unsavory reputations brought in from the village. There
were taverns there, and the whores that went with them, so she could
only assume that there were whores in attendance at her wedding.

She didn't mention them to Keeva, however, for fear of upsetting
the woman, but the truth was that Keeva was well aware of their
presence. She wasn't entirely pleased about it, but a few whispered
words from Daveigh had calmed her. She was evidently willing to
overlook it for the sake of the occasion, which was truly a celebration.

Finally, Bric MacRohan had taken a bride and Keeva, more than anyone, didn't want anything to upset that.

Eiselle knew that Keeva had worked very hard to make this moment possible, but the reality was that she didn't know just how hard. Although Bric had confessed his reluctance to marry, she really didn't know the hell he'd put everyone through. All she knew was that she was now Lady MacRohan and that her wedding feast had been full of delicious food, of lively music, and of men and women enjoying themselves.

The musicians were playing a *ductia*, a complex instrumental piece that, in this case, had words to it. Eiselle had heard it before when she had been at Framlingham and she'd even heard Lady Bigod sing it. As she listened to the talented musician play a long, wooden flute, she found herself mouthing the words as she'd heard them.

Bric, who surprisingly hadn't left her side since their marriage ceremony, caught sight of the movement and thought she was speaking to him. Unable to hear her over the noise of the hall, he leaned closer so he could hear her words.

"I did not hear you, my lady," he said. "You were saying something?"

Eiselle's cheeks flushed, embarrassed that he'd caught her singing. "Nay, I did not speak," she said. Weakly, she gestured to the musician. "I was simply reciting the words to this song."

"You know it?"

"I do."

"What is it called?"

"A Lover's Lament," she said. "It is about a woman who longs for a man who has gone off to war."

He lifted an eyebrow in interest. "Is that so?" he said. "I have heard the tune, but I did not know there were words to it. Will you sing it for me?"

The mottle in her cheeks deepened. "Here? In front of everyone?"

A smile tugged at his lips. "You can sing it quietly so only I may hear you."

Eiselle didn't want to deny him, but she was genuinely reluctant to sing to him. Although she loved to sing, it had only been in front of women, or when she was alone in her chamber, so she wasn't entirely sure she was good enough for a public performance. She didn't want to embarrass herself and she could feel the return of the dreaded nervous stomach at the mere thought.

However, Bric was her husband now and she wanted to be the good, obedient wife. If he wanted to hear the song, then she would sing it. When the tune started up again on the chorus, she began to sing.

I have loved, all my life, only thee;

The stars know thy name, the sky weeps at your beauty.

I pray thou will return to my arms,

but if not,

I pray to see thy face every night in my dreams.

Eiselle's pure soprano was crisp and beautiful, and Bric listened to her as if mesmerized. When she finished, she smiled timidly as she hoped for a good response, but all he could do was stare. He was shocked at the beauty that had poured forth from her lips and after a moment, he simply shook his head.

"Astounding," he said sincerely. "You have the voice of an angel, my lady."

Eiselle was deeply flattered, thankful that she hadn't sounded like a squealing piglet. "My thanks," she said. "There are more verses, but I do not remember them all."

"A pity," he said. "I should have you sing to me every night. Do you know more songs?"

She nodded. "A few. But not enough to sing to you every night."

There was a glimmer in his silver eyes. "Then you shall sing to me all of the songs you know, and I shall select my favorites for you to sing over and over."

"You might grow bored if I do that."

"Nothing about you could bore me."

It sounded very much like a compliment and she smiled shyly, turning her attention to her wine and taking a sip. His praise of her singing made her feel quite giddy. In fact, the man in general made her feel quite giddy.

Ever since she presented herself in the hall for their marriage, the look in his eyes had made her breathing come quicker and her heart beat just a little faster. He looked at her as if... as if her presence actually *meant* something to him. Nothing else could have explained that glimmer in his eye, but Eiselle knew this marriage wasn't something he'd been waiting for. He'd already admitted that he hadn't been keen on it.

But she would have never guessed that by the expression on his face.

Even now, he never left her side, sitting next to her even as his knights sat on his right, drinking and talking and laughing. She could hear them. Zara and Angela and Lady de Winter sat across the table from her, and she'd shared a few small, rather bland conversations with them. It was too loud in the hall to do much else other than shout over the tabletop. There was a lot of smiling going on, however, the ladies smiling at her and Eiselle smiling back. It began to get redundant and towards the evening, she stopped looking at them altogether because she was tired of smiling. More food was brought around, which gave her something else to focus on.

As night settled and after several hours of playing, the musicians finally stopped, and the hall seemed quieter, more subdued, as men ate yet another meal at the wedding feast of Bric MacRohan. Most of them were quite drunk by now, and they'd started up pockets of gambling throughout the hall, which was now smoky from the fire that had been burning bright and steady since noon. A blue haze hung in the air that was becoming thicker by the hour.

As Eiselle and Bric delved into a second round of food, which Eiselle mostly picked at because her stomach was still nervous, an old woman wrapped in servant's clothing suddenly appeared with a curly-haired toddler. Angela gasped when she saw the child.

"Come to me, my sweetest darling," she said, taking her son from his nurse. She kissed the child before looking to Eiselle and Bric across the table. "I hope you do not mind that Edward has come to your feast. I promised him that he could kiss the bride, and you know that it is very good luck if a baby kisses the bride. It will ensure your marriage is fruitful."

Across the table, Mylo rolled his eyes at his wife, who cuddled the boy that looked exactly like him. He'd never heard of such a blessing, and Angela couldn't stand spending more than an hour or two away from their son, so he assumed it was his wife's way of permitting the boy to attend the wedding feast. In fact, it seemed that everyone was rolling their eyes at Angela one way or another.

Everyone except Eiselle. She forced a smile at the woman who was trying to bring her baby into an adult gathering, where men were drinking and gambling and cursing. She didn't think it was a good place for the child.

"That is very kind of you, my lady," she said. "I can see that your son is a fine lad."

Angela stood up from the table with the boy in her arms, making her away around the long table and heading towards Eiselle. But the child wasn't too happy with being held; he wanted to get down and run and play with the dogs who were gathered around the tables, waiting for scraps. By the time Angela came alongside Eiselle, little Edward was screaming loudly enough to pierce eardrums.

"Eddie, behave," Angela scolded weakly as the boy kicked and screamed. "Don't you want to kiss the pretty lady? Give her a kiss, Eddie!"

Edward had no desire to kiss Eiselle. He glared at her, barring his teeth, and tried to kick her. Angela finally set her squirming son down on the bench next to Eiselle.

"Eddie, don't be naughty," she said. "This is Lady MacRohan. She just married Sir Bric. You like Sir Bric, don't you? Be kind to Lady MacRohan and give her a kiss for luck."

Edward was whining and squirming, trying to pull away from his mother, but Angela was thrusting the child at Eiselle, who really didn't want to be kissed by such a child. She thought his behavior appalling. When Angela tried to encourage him, he reached up and hit his mother in the face. She calmly told him not to hit her and kept trying to thrust him on Eiselle.

"Angela," Mylo said from the other side of Bric. "Stop trying to force the lad."

He sounded irritated, but Angela was oblivious. "Eddie wants to kiss her," she insisted. "Don't you, Eddie?"

The lad yelled, trying to pull away from his mother, who held him firmly. Mylo sighed with great irritation, hunting down his cup of wine and draining it as his wife wrestled with their son and everyone at the table looked at Angela as if she were a pathetic fool.

Eiselle, however, was trying to be patient about it. She suspected that Angela only meant well, and she knew for a fact that the woman was enamored with her son, as she'd learned on the day of her arrival when that was all Angela would speak of. So, she tried hard to be patient even though little Edward was clearly a beastly child. Angela pushed her son at Eiselle one last time.

"Eddie, please kiss the pretty lady," she said. "It is right and good that you should do so. You honor her."

She'd pushed Edward right up against Eiselle's left arm. Eiselle was smiling politely at the boy, but when he made eye contact with her, he scowled and reached out baby fingers to pinch her right on the top of her hand. It was a hard pinch. Without hesitation, Eiselle pinched him back on his fat baby arm.

Eddie howled.

The table exploded in laughter as Angela snatched her wailing son to her, instantly in tears that her ill-mannered, abusive son had been given a taste of his own medicine. As Edward screamed in her ear, she looked at Eiselle as if she were the most contemptible creature on earth.

"How dare you hurt my baby!" she cried. "My poor, defenseless child!"

Eiselle knew she probably shouldn't have pinched the boy, but she'd never been one to tolerate an ill-mannered child. The servants at Hadleigh House, those who had children, appreciated Eiselle's manner with children in general. She was fair, mostly patient, and kind, but she didn't like ill-mannered or spoiled children, and Edward definitely fell into that category. She was so used to having a free hand with the serving children at Hadleigh House that it didn't occur to her that she shouldn't have punished the terrible child.

But rather than defend herself, her naturally honest nature took hold. She'd never been one to hold back, not when it mattered. And at this moment, she felt as if it mattered. These people were to be her family, weren't they?

She hoped her honesty was appreciated.

"It was hardly a pinch," she said. "If you look at his hand, I doubt you will even see a mark. As for your son being poor and defenseless, you are mistaken, my lady. That child hit you and tried to kick me. So clearly, he is not defenseless at all. He is badly in need of discipline. You believe that only by loving him, you will raise a great son, but I say that if you do not start showing him some discipline now, he will go to foster one day and will be in for a rude awakening when his masters beat him for his bad behavior. You are not doing the lad any favors by coddling him and allowing him to terrorize you."

Angela gasped at the words. But at the other side of the table, Keeva suddenly banged on the tabletop. "Here, here!" she said. "Angela, I have told you that before. You are raising a hellion of a child and unless you do something about it, he will be a beastly boy that no one likes. I do not blame Lady MacRohan for what she did at all. Had it been me, I might have slapped his behind, also."

Angela clutched her son to her as if protecting him against women who wanted to thrash him. Her poor, sweet baby who was as gentle as a lamb! Without another word, she fled the hall in tears, followed by the nurse who was openly weeping. Mylo, who was still on the other side of Bric, watched his wife go. He sighed heavily.

"I should go to her," he said. It was obviously something he was very reluctant to do. When Eiselle turned to look at him, he smiled weakly. "I do apologize that he pinched you. Eddie is a very bright lad, but you are correct – he terrorizes everyone, and Angela will not lift a hand to him. I fear that someday, he will be in for terrible things from men who will not tolerate that behavior."

Eiselle didn't feel any remorse for what she did, but she wasn't defensive about it, either. "I am sorry to have upset Angela," she said, and it was the truth.

But Mylo waved her off. "The shame is mine, Lady MacRohan," he said as he moved away from the table. Then, he glanced at Bric. "You are a fortunate man, Bric. You have a lady with a good head on her shoulders. I envy you."

As he moved away from the table, Eiselle turned to Bric. In fact, he was the only opinion she cared about. When their eyes met, she smiled timidly.

"You told me that as long as I am always honest with you, I shall exceed your expectations," she said. "I hope that is still true. I am honest and I am forthright, and I will not allow a child to maliciously pinch me."

Bric had been fighting off a grin since the incident occurred. But now, he let that smile break through.

"He deserved it," he said. "Better coming from you than from me. If I pinched him, I'd probably twist his skin off."

Eiselle laughed softly because he'd said it so humorously. "I swear that I do not make it a habit of hurting children, but that child is a terror."

"More than you know."

Across the table, Daveigh lifted his cup to the newlyweds. "Then a toast," he said. "May your children be far better behaved than Edward de Chevington. And if they are not, may they be able to run faster than their parents when it comes time to discipline them."

He laughed at his toast as he drank deeply, fairly drunk as his wife shook her head at him. "He does not mean it," she said. "He has wanted to swat Eddie himself, especially when the child runs into his solar and grabs for his quills. He has set the dogs on the boy more than once, although he will not admit it."

Daveigh made a face at her, clearly in dispute, as Keeva grinned at the man. There was a good deal of affection in that expression, and between the two of them. Here, in a relaxed situation, that was easy to see. But soon enough, Keeva returned her focus to Bric.

"You have spent long enough at this feast," she said. "Take your wife and retire for the night. We will see you on the morrow."

Bric didn't need to be told twice. He'd been waiting for quite some time to retire with Eiselle, but she hadn't seemed too eager to leave, so he didn't press her. But he would take Keeva's direction and it would give him the excuse he needed to take his new wife to his chamber where it would just be the two of them. No more kicking Edward, no more drunken Daveigh, and no more soldiers gambling and cursing.

Just him and Eiselle.

He was ready.

"Come, Lady MacRohan," he said as he stood up, politely taking her by the elbow to help her stand. "We have been given permission to leave this frothy gathering, so let us depart."

Eiselle allowed him to help her to her feet, leaning on his arm so she could gather the skirt of her dress so it wouldn't drag in the dirt and the old rushes of the hall.

"Do you have everything well in-hand, Bric?" Pearce asked. He was the only one left sitting near Bric and Eiselle's empty chairs as his wife sat next to Keeva across the table. "We *could* accompany you to your chamber, of course. I have been married for over a year. You may need my advice on things."

Bric snorted rudely. "The day I need your advice, de Dere, is the day

I lose my mind completely," he said. "For what I am about to do, I do not need an audience."

Eiselle heard his words and her cheeks flushed a violent shade of red. She knew what he meant; she knew that everyone looking at her now knew that Bric was about to take her maidenhood and indoctrinate her into the new world of a married life. Fundamentally, she'd known that all along, but now that the moment was upon them, she found she was rather nervous about it.

Now, she was truly to become Lady MacRohan.

As Bric took her through the hall in order to reach his chamber next to the entry, Eiselle could hear Bric's men shouting words of encouragement to him. Bawdy encouragement, in fact. Eiselle kept her head down, holding on to her husband's elbow, praying that the men in the room didn't see how embarrassed she was about all of the attention on them. Truthfully, she hadn't expected it. She had hoped that everything would have been nice and quiet and private, but that wasn't to be.

It was becoming a public spectacle for all to see.

By the time they reached Bric's chamber door, the entire hall was up, shouting encouragement to Bric, who acknowledged them with a simple lift of his hand. Eiselle was fighting down her nerves, but what she didn't realize was that a gang of drunken revelers had crept up behind them. By the time Bric opened the chamber door, the men flooded in, filling the chamber with their loud shouts and lewd laughter.

Somehow in the process, Eiselle was separated from Bric, finding herself over near the bed as two of the men tried to lift her up and put her on the mattress. Frightened, she lashed out at them, slapping one rather violently across the face.

"Do not touch me!" she screamed. "Put me down!"

The men weren't trying to hurt her, but they were so drunk and happy that they didn't pay much attention to the fact that she was genuinely terrified. Then, as it was a custom for men and women to tear a piece of the bride's dress for good luck, they began pulling at her sleeve and at her skirt, trying to tear free a piece of fabric or fur. Eiselle slapped their hands away as fast as she could.

Bric, over near the doorway, saw that Eiselle was struggling with a few of his men as they pawed at her lovely gown. He knew his men didn't mean any harm, but he didn't want them here and he certainly didn't want them upsetting Eiselle. Tossing men aside, he charged through the crowd to Eiselle, putting himself between her and the men who were tearing at her dress.

"Out," he growled, pointing to the door. "Everyone *out*."

Orders from Bric MacRohan weren't meant to be disobeyed, and the men began to funnel out, quickly in some cases. Bric left Eiselle in the corner of the chamber and followed the group out, shoving at them until they were clear of the room. Slamming the door behind him, he threw the bolt.

But it didn't stop the men from pounding on the door, demanding bloodied bedsheets and proof of the bride's virginity. The shouts were loud and the banging on the door even louder. Apologetically, Bric turned to Eiselle, still standing back in the corner, only to see that she was wiping at her face.

She was weeping.

His heart sank.

"I am sorry," he said as he quickly went to her. "They did not mean to upset you."

Eiselle was trying very hard not to sob, but the entire event had her shaken. "They... they tried to tear my dress," she said, her throat tight. "This is such a beautiful dress. It belonged to Lady de Winter's sister. She died young and Lady de Winter gave it to me. And they tried to tear it."

Bric was starting to feel just as bad as he possibly could. With a heavy sigh, he put his hand on her arm, pulling her gently towards the bed.

"I am sorry, Eiselle, truly," he murmured. "They did not know that.

And I know my men; they were not trying to be cruel. They simply did not... think."

She sobbed softly, wiping at the tears that wouldn't stop falling, as he set her carefully on the bed. But she nodded her head, as if to accept his apology, and he took a knee beside her, feeling greatly saddened that she'd been so upset by his thoughtless, careless men. He touched the hem of her gown.

"It does not look damaged at all," he said, his voice soft and low. "It does not look like they tore the gown, but I shall give it to Lady de Winter and she can look it over herself. If there is any damage, she will fix it, I promise. You needn't be upset."

Eiselle was still wiping at her eyes as she looked at him, noticing that his big face was close to hers. She found herself looking into his eyes, such an unusual and pale color. He had a strong jaw, a striking face, one that she found so very handsome.

There wasn't anything about Bric MacRohan that she found unattractive, in any way, and the fact that he was trying to ease her fear and comfort her made him that much more attractive to her. Only a man of great feeling would be able to show such compassion to a woman's silly fears. Given his reputation as a fearless and deadly warrior, she found that aspect of him rather astonishing.

It was a side of him she'd never seen before.

"If you say they did not mean harm, then I believe you," she said, swallowing the last of her tears. "It is just that this dress means a good deal to Lady de Winter. I would be heartbroken if something happened to it."

Bric was smiling at her, pleased to see that her tears were short-lived. "It is an old custom, you know," he said. "A piece of the bride's dress brings good fortune. They were simply seeking good fortune and you cannot blame them for that."

She shook her head. "Nay, I cannot, but they can tear another dress," she said, a smile flickering over her lips. "Just not this one."

He nodded, reaching out to touch her cheek as he stood up. But in that gesture, he realized it was the first time he'd really made the attempt to touch her. It had been so instinctive that the awareness shocked him. Not only was he attracted to her, but it was manifesting itself in gestures he never knew he was capable of – he'd never touched a woman affectionately in his life, at least not with true warmth behind the gesture. Yet, with Eiselle, it had been innate.

As if he'd been doing it all of his life.

It would have been easy to lose himself in that moment, but the banging on the door was distracting him. He realized that he very much wanted to explore his new wife, and he was very curious about his feelings for her, but he couldn't concentrate on any of that with all of the noise going on.

And, God help him, consummating the marriage with all of that upheaval going on was going to be hellish. He'd never bedded a woman he was deeply attracted to and, for the first time in his life, he wanted to figure out what, exactly, he was feeling. Most of all, they needed privacy.

"It was a mistake to come here," he finally said.

Eiselle stood up from the bed, concerned. "Why do you say that?" she said, looking at the bed itself. "Whose chamber is this?"

"Mine," he said. "But, as you can hear, we shall have no peace if we remain here. I did not think on that until now. We would do better up in your chamber. Shall we make a run for it?"

Eiselle could see the glitter of humor in his eye and she grinned. "Will you keep them away from my dress?"

He laughed softly. "My lady, I will beat them off, I swear it. How fast can you run?"

"Faster than you can."

He cocked an eyebrow. "A boast, I see," he said, as if both pleased and skeptical. "We shall soon find out if it is true."

Taking her by the arm, he pulled her over to the door. She was in much better spirits now, and so was he. A quiet chamber awaited them; they simply had to get to it.

"I will open the door and push men out of the way," he said. "Tuck in behind me and when the crowd clears, run for your chamber."

"And you will follow?"

A smile spread across his full lips. "My lady," he said softly, "I will follow you anywhere."

The giddy feeling in Eiselle's chest told her that she believed him, implicitly. He had hold of her as he put his hand on the door.

"Ready?" he asked her.

She nodded firmly. "Ready."

With a wink, he put himself in front of her as he unbolted the door and threw it open. Just as he'd said, a great cheer rose up and he charged out with Eiselle behind him, holding on to his waist. She had her head down, feeling the concussions against his body as he slammed into men, trying to clear a path. Finally, he stepped aside and thrust her forward.

"Go," he commanded quickly. "Run for the stairs!"

Eiselle did. With a yelp, perhaps one of fear and excitement, she began to run, pushing through men who were caught off guard by her swift move. One or two of them reached out, trying to grab her, but she slapped their hands away. Suddenly, she was free of the crowd as she raced for the spiral stairs that led to the upper floor, and she didn't stop or look behind her until she reached her borrowed chamber. Only then did she dare to look back as she rushed through the door and bolted it.

Giggling, and breathing heavily with exertion, she stood by the door nervously, waiting for Bric to come. Fortunately, she didn't have to wait long. He was soon pounding on the door and she opened it, admitting him, before slamming it behind him and throwing the big iron bolt. When he finally came to a halt after the mad dash to the chamber, they looked at each other and burst into laughter.

"A maneuver well-executed, Lady MacRohan," he said. "You are, indeed, quite fast."

Eiselle giggled, still winded from the excitement. "It was fear that brought about my speed," she said. "I did not want to chance having my dress ripped from me by fortune-seekers."

He was still laughing, still smiling, and it took him a moment to realize he probably hadn't laughed or smiled that much in a very long time. In his profession, that wasn't a common occurrence. But with Eiselle, it was becoming the norm. Something about her made him feel light of heart. In fact, the entire day left him feeling light of heart.

Happy.

Of everything he thought his wedding would be, happy was not among them.

"Your dress is intact, my lady," he said. "And I did not have the opportunity to tell you how beautiful you look in it. When I saw you come into the hall for the ceremony, you took my breath away."

She smiled modestly. "Thank you," she said. "May... may I tell you something?"

"Please do."

"I realize that we do not know each other very well, but it seems odd for you to address me so formally. You have my permission to call me Eiselle, should you wish to."

His expression softened, as if he was genuinely touched by her words. "I should like to, very much," he said. "I think I shall call you Lady MacRohan, too, from time to time, because I like the way it sounds. It tells every man that you belong to me, and certainly that is something I never thought I would say, but I am proud of it."

Given their earlier conversations, Eiselle knew that was probably a difficult admission for him. "I hope that I shall always honor you, my lord," he said. "I shall always endeavor to try."

He held up a finger. "If I am to call you Eiselle, then you must call me Bric," he said. "I do not require such formality from my own wife."

She laughed softly. "Bric," she repeated. "It is a very nice name."

"It does not mean what you think it means; that is to say, it does not mean that I am a brick to be stacked with mortar. In Gaelic, it means a bridge, something strong and enduring, for all men to admire."

Her smile remained. "I like that a great deal," she said. "It is a very nice name. Are you an only son, then?"

He shook his head. "Nay. I have two brothers, Brendan and Ryan."

"Are they knights, too?"

"They fight and live in Ireland."

She cocked her head in thought. "Do you miss Ireland, Bric?"

He liked hearing her use his name. It was the first time she'd ever used it, and he found it very pleasant to hear it in her sweet voice. Turning to the hearth where the fire was dying, he knelt down and picked up more wood from the box.

"I used to," he admitted. "You already know that Keeva is my cousin. When she married de Winter, I came as part of her dowry. Daveigh gained Irish lands through Keeva, so I was the exchange – I was to come to England with her and swear fealty to de Winter, thereby swearing fealty to him on behalf of all of his Irish lands. I really had no choice in the matter."

It was true that Eiselle knew he was Keeva's cousin, but she hadn't known the circumstances of his service in England. She watched him as he put more wood on the fire and stoked it.

"But why you?" she asked. "Why not one of your brothers?"

"Because I was the greatest."

Eiselle couldn't argue with that. "Then I am glad it was you," she said. "Otherwise, I would have never found a husband."

He looked at her as if she were mad, but then he ended up breaking down into soft snorts of laughter. "I suspect that is not true," he said. "You would have found one, eventually, but I am glad the one you did find was me, thanks to your cousin. Instead of wringing his neck the next time I see him, I do believe I shall thank him."

Eiselle smiled at him and, for a moment, they simply looked at each other, drinking in the sight of one another and absorbing the situation. They were married now and on this night, certain things were expected of them. Eiselle knew that. Averting her gaze, she moved over to the neat stacks of trunks against the wall and opened up one of the smaller cases. She pulled forth something, something Bric couldn't really see until she came close and held it out to him.

It was a sash of some kind, made from dark brown wool and embroidered from end to end with very beautiful patterns that looked like shields. As he peered at it, she spoke.

"I made this for you," she said. "It is a belt for your tunic. I did not know what to give to you on the event of our wedding, so I made this. If you do not like it, I can make you something else. But I wanted to give you a gift and this was all I could think to do."

Bric stared at it. Then, he reached out and took it from her hands, inspecting the detailed quality of it. After a moment, he simply shook his head, awed.

"It is astonishing," he said in a tone she'd never heard before. "I have never had anyone make anything for me, at least not like this. Thank you, Eiselle. It is beautiful."

"Then you like it?"

"I have never had a finer gift," he said. "I shall carry it with me, always. But that brings me to a very embarrassing admission."

"What?"

He looked at her as if afraid to tell her. "I did not get you anything," he said. "I have not had the time and… nay, that is not entirely true. I told you I was resistant to this marriage and the thought of giving you a gift on our wedding day… I could not bring myself to do it. It was going to be my statement to you of how unhappy I was with this arrangement. Now, I am deeply ashamed that I was so cruel about it. I pray you are not too angry with me."

Smiling faintly, Eiselle shook her head. "We have a pact, you and I," she said. "All we ask is honesty between one another. You have been honest with me about your feelings and I cannot become angry with you about it. But… but I do hope you shall change your mind. I will do all I can to ensure that you do."

Bric was feeling terrible about the fact that he had no gift for her. He was feeling about as cruel and nasty as he possibly could, so very cruel to this beautiful and delicate creature who only wanted to please him.

"You *have* changed my mind," he said quietly. "I told you I was no longer resistant to our marriage, and I meant it. I will make you this promise – I will purchase a gift for you, something wonderful and lovely and deserving of you. It will be the best gift you have ever received."

She smiled bashfully. "That is not necessary," she said. "I did not give you the gift so that you would have to reciprocate. I gave it to you because I wanted to."

"You gave it to a man who did not deserve it."

She looked at him, seeing that he was being very hard on himself. A thought occurred to her.

"There *is* something you can give me," she said.

"Tell me what it is and I shall get it for you, no matter what the cost."

She shook her head. "It costs nothing and you can give it to me right now."

His brow furrowed. "What is this mysterious thing?"

Eiselle felt rather bold with what she was about to say, but something in her wanted very much to say it. He *was* her husband, after all. Perhaps he wouldn't think she was being too bold.

"Since we've met, all has been quite formal between us, as it should be," she said. "Now, we are expected to… to know each other as a husband would know a wife. We've really not even had a chance to know each other more than just a day, and in that time, as I said, all has been quite formal. If you should like to give me a gift, then mayhap… mayhap you can give me a kiss, as a husband would kiss his new wife. It costs nothing and it would mean a great deal."

Bric couldn't believe he'd been so blind. It was, perhaps, one of the better suggestions he'd heard and without a word, he went to her. But he didn't touch her right away. He just stood there, his body up against hers, gazing down into that perfectly angelic face. He'd kissed women before, but never a woman he'd been attracted to. He was ashamed to admit that any physical interaction with women had been with the kind one usually paid when the physicality was finished.

As a man, he had needs, and it was safer to pay for those needs to be taken care of. He'd never wanted any kind of an attachment, and women who accepted money for their services were his preference. No attachment, no emotion. That was how Bric MacRohan had always lived his life when it came to women.

Until now.

Now, he couldn't resist this beautiful woman in front of him, a woman who was now his wife. She belonged to him and he could do anything he wanted to her, and she would forever and always belong only to him. Aye, he was going to kiss her, just as she'd asked.

But he was going to do more than that, too.

Putting his arms around her, Bric pulled Eiselle against his hard chest, acquainting himself with the feel of her. She was soft and warm. Dipping his head down, he kissed her forehead, and her cheek. The fragrances of roses met his nostrils and he inhaled deeply. But that sweet scent was to be his undoing; it was lush and alluring. His embrace tightened and he buried his face against Eiselle's fragrant neck.

Eiselle gripped Bric's shoulders as his mouth moved down her neck, roving over the soft flesh. She was somewhat in shock at his bold actions. Certainly, she'd asked for a kiss, but this wasn't what she had expected. She had been moderately nervous for his kiss, praying her stomach would behave, but that nervousness had vanished. In fact, her momentary shock at his bold action evaporated as her heart began to pound so forcefully that she was positive it was about to burst from her chest.

Bric's tongue, hot and lusty, lapped at the flesh of her shoulder as his fingers pulled aside that beautiful dress. Eiselle could feel his hot breath on her skin, like nothing she'd ever experienced before. She didn't even know such a sensation existed.

She could hardly breathe.

The fire crackled softly in the hearth, sending sparks up the chimney as Bric abruptly swept Eiselle into his arms and deposited her upon her bed. He gently kissed her face, moving to her chin and neck as his fingers went to work on the ties of her gown. Unfortunately, the ties were tight, and didn't come away easily. Bric had to work at it. He managed to get the ones on the left side undone, rolling her onto her left side so he could kiss the exposed flesh. Eiselle groaned softly with awakening pleasure, realizing that she liked this very much. The man's touch lit a fire in her, and she wanted more.

Rolling her onto her back once more, Bric removed the gown slowly, running his tongue over every delectable portion of exposed flesh. Eiselle stared up at the ceiling as the surcoat came off her shoulders, her arms, baring her breasts against the weak light of the chamber. She should have been embarrassed at her nudity, but she wasn't. She wasn't embarrassed in the least, not even when he pulled the surcoat over her hips and slid it the length of her legs.

Is this what it means to have a husband? Eiselle thought as she wallowed in the boneless, lethargic state of her mounting desire. If this was what being married meant, then she was willing to embrace it completely. If Bric could make her feel like this, with her heart racing and her breathing coming in unsteady gasps, then she would happily let the man do whatever he wanted to her, forever and ever.

She was more than willing to let him claim her.

As Eiselle found herself consumed by her first sexual encounter, Bric was having a difficult time pacing himself. Every touch, every kiss, had him wanting to ram his body into hers until he was satisfied. But he couldn't do that. He wanted to go slowly with Eiselle because, for the first time in his life, he was building something with a woman and the only way he could think to do that was to be slow and gentle with her. So far, it was working. But the sight of her nude breasts by the firelight very nearly undid him.

He'd never seen anything so arousing in his entire life.

But he didn't touch her there, at least not yet. He was still trying to acquaint her with his touch and he, in turn, was taking great delight in exploring her body. His hands were on her shoulders, her arms, feeling her silken skin. In fact, he thought he was doing quite well with pacing himself when Eiselle suddenly reached up, took his hands, and put them against her breasts.

"Here, Bric," she whispered breathlessly. "Touch me here."

Bric's control deserted him in an instant. He growled seductively as he descended upon her luscious body. Their lips came together in a cataclysmic clash, his mouth slanting over hers, suckling her lips furiously. Eiselle's cries of passion were muted against his mouth until he moved away from her lips and feasted hungrily at her breasts. As Eiselle writhed beneath him, Bric moved to touch the unfurling flower between her legs.

Eiselle cried out with surprise when his fingers touched the thick outer lips, matted with a fine fluff of black hair. Bric maintained his hold on her nipple as he gently fondled her to allow her to become accustomed to his touch. Eiselle gradually relaxed as she became accustomed to his fingers, and only when her body eased beneath his touch did he attempt to part her lush petals.

She was as slick with moisture, unbelievably hot. Bric stroked the tender folds, his entire body shaking with the force of his need. He'd never known desire like this and he could no longer hold back. It was time to make her his in every sense of the word.

The wife he never wanted.

Bric finally slipped a finger into her sheath, so incredibly tight that he very nearly soiled himself with the pleasure of it. Eiselle's pants of shock quickly turned into cries of pleasure, and Bric could feel her tight passage contracting about his slick finger, pulling at him and demanding him.

He could wait no longer.

Rising to his knees, he ripped off his tunic so aggressively that he tore a sleeve. One boot hit the floor and the other went sailing into the wall. His breeches came off so quickly that he nearly ended up on the floor in his haste to remove them.

All the while, Eiselle watched with wonder as Bric disrobed, finally standing before her, nude and proud and magnificent. His broad shoulders sheltered an exquisitely muscled chest, covered with a matting of graying hair. His flat stomach and narrow waist caught her attention and she was awed by the sight of him. It was the first time she'd ever seen a nude man, and she found it most enthralling. Her gaze came to rest on his enormous arousal, knowing that his hardness was meant for her. Soon enough, it would be buried in her body.

Bric didn't give her time to look at him further, fearful that she might show some apprehension in what they were about to do. So far, she'd been responsive and heated, and he wanted to continue that trend. Climbing into the bed beside her, his big body covered hers, their flesh touching. He could hear himself groaning at the pure delight of it, warm skin against warm skin.

Wedging himself between her legs, he rubbed his manhood against her private core, stroking the outer lips as he had done with his fingers. She was glistening with wet heat, spilling down onto the linens, and he bathed himself in her virginal juices.

Bric wrestled against the natural instinct to ram into her like a rutting bull. He worked carefully, gaining headway bit by bit, feeling her tightness draw him inward. She was so slick that it would have been easy to simply thrust into her, but he refrained. Better to allow her to become accustom to his intrusion before the sting of losing her innocence cast a measure of reality upon their union.

Beneath him, Eiselle was amazingly calm, gripping his muscular arms for support as he forged into virgin territory. Beneath her hands, she could feel his body quivering, straining to maintain control in the face of his desire. She, too, was quivering with anticipation, at pain she knew would soon come.

The moment of possession.

When it happened, it came in a flash. Falling atop her, Bric grasped her breast and descended upon a peaked nipple. Suckling furiously, Eiselle forgot her fears and responded to him in a way she never knew her body was capable of. Her cheeks began to flush with desire as her fingers wound themselves in his thick, blond hair, and Bric knew the time was upon him to act. With Eiselle properly distracted, it was time to take her. Coiling his buttocks, Bric thrust into her harder than he ever thought possible, driving himself the full long length of his throbbing manhood.

Eiselle gasped loudly with surprise at the savage action, a sting of pain rippling through her loins. Bric was seated to the hilt in less than a second and the pain, coupled with his closeness, brought tears to her eyes as she clutched his shoulders with white-knuckled intensity. His swift movement had startled her, and she couldn't help the soft sobs that escaped her lips.

Fully sheathed within her delicious tightness, Bric struggled to remain still as Eiselle writhed beneath him. When he heard the faint sobs, he raised his head from her swollen nipple.

"I am so sorry," he whispered huskily. "I would not have hurt you had there been another way."

Eiselle wiped at her eyes. "It's not... 'tis not the pain, but... but the closeness. I never knew it could be like this."

Bric didn't, either. Wrapping his arms around her, he began to move gently within her. Slowly at first, relishing the feel of his erection embedded within her unbelievably slick folds. She clutched him tightly, wrapping her legs about his hips and clinging to him with an instinctive need.

Bric's pace increased, quickening his thrusts as he was blinded to all else but the feel of her flesh around him. It was the most satisfying thing he had ever experienced. Against him, Eiselle's resumed pants of passion told him that she was beginning to experience the same pleasure that had so easily engulfed him. Now, they were experiencing it together as it was meant to be.

But it was a pleasure that was building to a peak faster than he ever thought possible. In fact, nothing on earth could have prepared Bric for his lightning-quick climax. With a roar, he spilled deep into her womb, feeling every last twitch of his spent desire with the greatest of pleasure. But he continued to move within her, wanting her to experience the same burst of pleasure that would erase the sting of losing her innocence.

He shifted his weight, gazing down at her flushed face as he continued to thrust. Her eyes were closed, her head thrown back, and he found his gaze drawn to her beautiful breasts as they bounced against every thrust he delivered. One hand trailed down her neck, encircling a breast before moving toward the junction where their bodies were joined in passion. That was where the magic of her pleasure pulsed, begging for release.

Seeking her hard nub, he manipulated it fiercely, watching Eiselle's eyes fly open with surprise. In the next moment, she exhaled a loud shriek that echoed against the very walls of the chamber and her entire body bucked and spasmed as she experienced her first release. Over and over the ripples of pleasure rolled over her, and Bric held on to her for fear that she would buck right off the bed. He could feel her entire body quivering and he knew her pleasure had been as good as his, or perhaps even more than that.

The pleasure of a woman, knowing her husband for the very first time.

Enfolded in the warmth of his massive embrace, Eiselle was in a stupor. Her body was limp, her mind a void of satisfaction as she felt the remains of Bric's arousal twitching within her tender folds. It was the most remarkable, private sensation she had ever experienced, and she would have been perfectly content to remain as they were for the rest of eternity.

No words were spoken. After that, no words were necessary. Sleep borne of a deep satisfaction came quickly and when they slept, wrapped up in each other's arms, it was as if they had been doing it since the beginning of time.

CHAPTER SEVEN

H E'D LEFT HER sleeping.

Bric had awoken before dawn with Eiselle wrapped up in his arms, sleeping the sleep of the dead. She was pressed up against him and their legs were entangled as he held her snuggly in his enormous arms. He'd simply lain there, hearing her soft, steady breathing, feeling her warmth against him, and thankful that the day before hadn't been a dream. He knew he could wake up like this every morning for the rest of his life and be quite pleased about it.

In fact, he couldn't ever remember being quite so happy.

From where he lay, he could see the window in the room, and he saw clearly when the sun began to rise as the sky began to turn shades of pink and gold. He had duties awaiting him, but he was loathed to move. He just wanted to soak up the last few minutes with his new wife in his arms. But, eventually, he knew he had to go, so he very carefully disengaged himself from her, tucked her in, and silently proceeded to dress.

The breeches went on and when he went to pull on the tunic, he noticed the sleeve he'd torn in the heat of passion the night before and it made him smile. The tunic went over his head and as he gathered his boots and prepared to leave, he saw the belt Eiselle had made him on the table and he collected it. He was so very touched by her gift and he planned to wear it every day to remind him of her.

With a lingering glance at her dark, sleeping head, he quit the chamber in utter silence.

The keep was beginning to wake as Bric made his way down to his chamber on the near side of the entry. The great hall was strewn with soldiers just beginning to rise, men with aching heads from too much celebration. He even saw the priest sleeping over near the hearth again, thinking that the man had stayed clear of him after performing the marriage ceremony. He suspected that the priest had made a fine display of gluttony throughout the night. That was of no consequence. The man had performed the duty he had come to perform, and Bric intended to pay the man well for his services before he was escorted back to King's Lynn. Given that Bric was so happy about the marriage, he might even thank the man, too.

Heading into his chamber, Bric stripped off his clothing with the intention of washing, but he quickly realized that Eiselle's rose scent was still on his flesh. He found himself smelling his arms, his hands, and he realized that didn't want to wash that scent off. He wanted to bask in it, a scent so subtle yet so powerful that it made him feel lightheaded. Without washing, he simply put on new clothing, including his mail coat and broadsword, and headed out into the dawn of a bright, new day.

As Bric headed into the outer bailey, men were pointing to him and laughing, waving at the new husband. Bric usually ignored that kind of attention but, this morning, he couldn't help but respond with a wave. It was very unlike him to show camaraderie with his men like that, but it was indicative of his mood. He was happy and it was apparent. Making his way to the gatehouse where his knights and senior soldiers were already starting to gather, he ran into a sea of smiling faces.

He knew exactly why they were smiling and he couldn't keep the grin off his face, but he was also quite embarrassed by it. Those bastards were smiling at him because they knew what he'd been up to all night and they further knew he'd gone quietly to his lifelong sentence of marriage in sharp contrast to the man who had tried to fight his way out of it. His grin turned to irritated snorts.

"Stop looking at me as if you are expecting me to say something to ease your curiosity," he snapped, but it was without force. "Give me a report from the night watch."

Pearce, who was nursing a substantially aching head from all of the drink the night before, spoke.

"The night watch reports that all was quiet," he said, putting a hand to his head as if to hold his brains in. "Are you telling me I earned this aching head and you are not going to tell me that it was worth it?"

Bric's eyes narrowed at him. "Nay."

"Not one word?"

Bric turned his attention to the group at large. "Have patrols been sent out for the morning?"

As Bric ignored Pearce, Mylo answered. "They're all away, my lord," he said. "And in case you were wondering, my son survived being pinched by your lady wife, but he now calls her the basty lady."

"What's that?"

"I believe he is trying to say nasty lady."

Bric cocked an eyebrow. "If he tries to pinch her again, he'll find out just how nasty *I* can be," he said. "Next? Any further reports for this morning?"

His question was presented to the group at large, and men shook their heads. Seeing that no one had any comments, he continued.

"I want patrols out for the rest of the day," he told Pearce and Mylo. "I am not convinced the raiders two days ago were an isolated incident, so we must remain vigilant."

"My lord," one of the gatehouse sentries spoke. "We had an old man here yesterday, a farmer delivering grain, who said he might have seen Savernake men in Peterborough. He thought he recognized their orange and yellow standard, but he could not be sure."

That was a curious bit of information. "I wonder what Dash would be doing this far north," Bric muttered. "I suppose we shall soon find out if he is really here. If there is nothing else from any of you, assume your posts."

The group splintered, with men going about their day. Bric turned for the stables because his horse was due to be tended by the farrier this day, and then he intended to walk the inner wall to check posts. He had his day planned out, which also included making a point to see Eiselle, but Pearce and Mylo stopped him before he could get away.

"Well?" Pearce said. "Did your lady wife survive the night?"

Bric knew the question would come. He paused, looking at his two knights with veiled impatience.

"If you think I am going to speak of something indisputably private, think again," he said. "I do not ask you what your experience is when bedding your wife, so why should you ask me?"

Pearce snorted, rather lasciviously. "You do not have to give us the details," he said. "And, if you recall, I did tell you about my wedding night."

Bric threw up his hands. "You told me of your own free will, Pearce," he said. "I did not even ask you."

Pearce looked at Mylo. "It must have been good," he said. "If he was not, he would tell us."

Bric scowled at the pair. "If you two idiots do not leave my presence, you will sorely regret it."

Snickering, Pearce and Mylo wisely headed off to their duties, leaving Bric frowning after them. But even as he turned for the stables again, Bric couldn't help the fact that his frown turned into a silly grin.

Thoughts of Eiselle brought on the gesture, as if he were incapable of doing anything else.

"HE'S *GRINNING!*"

It was Keeva's hissed comment to her husband that had Daveigh rushing to the keep entry to see what she was pointing at.

"Look!" Keeva said excitedly. "He's grinning! God's Teeth, do you think he is actually happy this morning?"

Daveigh could see what had his wife so delighted – Bric was on the battlements of the inner wall, which was perched atop a massive earth berm, and he was speaking to one of the men, an older man who had also come with Keeva as part of her dowry. It was a man they all knew well and, in particular, a man that Bric had served with in Ireland as a young knight. Bric stood on the battlements, his big arms crossed, smiling as he spoke to the old man.

Daveigh watched him with some astonishment. "My God," Daveigh breathed. "He *is* grinning. That is not an expression I thought to see on his face this morning."

"Nor I," Keeva said. She was watching Bric closely. "Look at him; he seems relaxed and... *happy*. I do not think I have ever seen him so happy."

Daveigh sighed heavily. "Thank God," he muttered. "Now the man will not kill us in our sleep for forcing a marriage upon him. Do you suppose he even *likes* it?"

Keeva was genuinely shocked at what she was seeing. She tore her eyes away from Bric long enough to look at her husband.

"I do not know," she said. "But you saw him last night, Daveigh. He never left Eiselle's side, not once, and he seemed quite kind to her. And when they retired for the evening, do you remember how he fended of an entire room of men so she could flee up the stairs? It was very gallant of him, almost as if he were protecting her."

Daveigh was just as surprised as his wife was, over everything. "I saw," he said. "Bric is a chivalrous man, but what I witnessed last night... that was not mere chivalry. That was a man being protective and attentive to his wife."

"Will you ask him if he is happy?"

Daveigh shook his head firmly. "Not me," he said. "I do not want to risk having my eyes gouged out. *You* ask him. He wouldn't dare strike a woman."

As they stood there bickering about who would ask Bric if he was pleased with his marriage, they failed to see Eiselle emerge from the stairwell and approach them from behind.

Clad in a simple, pale-blue shift with a darker blue surcoat over it, which laced up the sides, her braided hair draped gracefully over one shoulder. Having awoken not long before, she looked fresh and radiant nonetheless, and there was a joy in her heart that had never been there before. It made her step light. The same giddy feelings that had swept her the day before now seemed permanently ingrained, and as she came up behind Keeva and Daveigh, she heard their bickering – something about asking someone a question – and peered over their shoulders to see whom they were speaking of. When she didn't immediately see anyone, she spoke gaily.

"Good morning to you," she said.

Startled by her surprising appearance, Keeva and Daveigh turned to see Eiselle standing behind them, noticing immediately that she had the same silly grin on her face that Bric did. Daveigh cleared his throat nervously.

"Lady MacRohan," he said. "You are looking fine this morning. Did you sleep well?"

Eiselle beamed. "I did, my lord, thank you," she said. Then, her focus turned to Keeva. "My lady, I was wondering if you had any chores for me this morning. I feel quite useless with nothing to do, and now that I am a member of this house and hold, I am more than happy to accomplish any task you feel I am capable of. I can sew, or tend the kitchens, or anything else you would have me do."

The woman was asking for work. Keeva could see how giddy the woman was and once the surprise wore off, she realized she was quite thrilled to see it. She was also humored by it.

"I am sure there is much you can help accomplish," she said. "Do you feel… up to it?"

Eiselle nodded firmly. "Anything you wish me to do, my lady, I can do it."

Keeva looked at Daveigh, who had to wipe the smirk off his face. He turned around, heading out of the keep, leaving his wife with the ecstatic new bride.

"I have duties to attend to," he said as he walked away. "Good day to you, Lady MacRohan."

Eiselle watched him go before returning her attention to Keeva. "He is such a nice man," she sighed. "You are a fortunate woman, my lady."

Keeva was having a difficult time to keep from laughing at Eiselle. The woman's joyful mood was too sappy to believe but, in the same breath, it was rather sweet. At least Keeva knew that Eiselle was happy; there was no need to ask her. But she wondered if Daveigh was going to press Bric. She had to admit, she was wildly curious about all of this. It would seem that the morning after the wedding that Bric MacRohan had railed against, all was apparently right in the world with both Bric and his wife.

Truly, it was a miracle.

"Well," Keeva finally said. "I have some fabric I have been saving to have made into a new surcoat. Do you feel up to the challenge, my lady?"

Eiselle nodded eagerly. "Aye, I do," she said. "But… I would like to bid my husband a good morn, if you don't mind. He left before I had awoken, and I have not seen him."

Keeva pointed out into the inner ward. "I saw him on the battlements just a few moments ago," she said. "Go and wave to him, but do not distract him. If there is something you should learn about being the wife of a fighting man, it is to never distract him from his duty. When you have finished, come into my chamber and we shall pull forth the fabric."

Eiselle nodded quickly and raced to the open entry, shielding her eyes from the early morning sun, which was very bright. Pale yellow splashed all along the walls and surfaces of the castle that faced east, and she lifted her eyes to the battlements for a glimpse of her husband. He was right where Keeva had said, standing near the small tower that protected the entry into the inner ward.

But he wasn't looking at her. Bric was in conversation with a soldier and as Eiselle watched, Daveigh joined them on the wall. In truth, Eiselle didn't want to demand Bric's attention – simply seeing the man was enough for her. She could feel her heart race at the mere sight of him, wondering if he felt the same way about their wedding night as she did.

It had truly been a night to remember.

Even thinking about it brought a flush to her cheeks. Eiselle didn't remember any pain at all, only the pleasure and warmth and comfort that his touch brought. She remembered everything about it with great fondness and great excitement, and she realized that she was very much anticipating tonight. She would be alone with him again, exploring this marriage that, so far, had started off so agreeably for both of them. Her gaze lingered on Bric's proud, muscular form before turning away and heading back in to the keep.

It was her first full day as Lady MacRohan and she intended to live it to the fullest.

Already, it was the best day of her life.

BRIC DIDN'T SEE his wife standing at the entry of the keep, looking at him adoringly. He had been speaking to a senior soldier, an old Irishman named Kelly, about the feast the night before. Old Kelly was wise enough not to question Bric on his wedding night as the other nosy men had, but merely spoke of the honor of attending his marriage. The old soldier had fought with Bric's father, Rohan mac Briain, and told Bric that his father would have been proud to see him wed.

Bric lost himself in some revelry with the old man, speaking on their homeland, on Bric's unruly younger brothers, and on things they both remembered. Normally, Bric wouldn't entertain such a frivolous conversation but, this morning, he didn't much feel like focusing on anything serious. He was more than happy to talk about things that had no bearing in his immediate world, simply because his mind really wasn't where it was supposed to be, no matter how much he'd pretended it was. When it should have been focused on his patrols, and the raid from two nights ago, it was on a certain young woman sleeping in the keep. Every so often, he'd lift his hand up, casually, and sniff the inner part of his wrist.

He could still smell roses.

When Daveigh joined him on the wall, he had to stop smelling his wrist because he didn't want Daveigh to notice the odd behavior. As if he was going around sniffing himself in some bizarre fashion. But it was a struggle as he listened to Daveigh talk about the weather, the patrols that were out, and the possibility that Savernake troops were in the area. He finally ended up folding his arms across his chest, tightly, so he wouldn't be tempted to lift one to his nose and sniff it, reminding him of the unforgettable night of passion. He needed to focus on his task at hand and not his bride's delicious body. But his preoccupation of smelling her scent on his arms was cut short when the sentries at the gatehouse began to call out.

Men were approaching.

That was all Daveigh and Bric heard as they quickly descended the narrow steps from the inner wall, heading into the outer bailey just as the sentries at the gatehouse took up the cry to open the portcullis. With the old iron chains groaning, the portcullis was slowly lifted, and Bric could see mounted men on the other side.

All he could see were horses' legs and the distant sight of armed men. Still, he knew the sentries were sharp and wouldn't open the gatehouse to just anyone. Therefore, he knew it was an ally. It took him a few seconds longer to realize exactly *which* ally.

Savernake had arrived.

Quickly, Bric began yelling to the men in the bailey to send for the stable servants to tend the horses of the incoming men. Mylo had come down from the second level of the gatehouse, heading over to meet up with Bric and Daveigh as they watched the influx of soldiers and animals. Bric noticed right away that there weren't very many men, perhaps a dozen or so, and certainly not the big patrol he might have expected from a war machine the size of Savernake.

As Mylo approached, he called out to him.

"Is this all?" he asked. "Or do you see the rest of the army in the distance?"

Mylo shook his head. "This is all," he said. "And they were riding very fast, which is why we opened the portcullis so quickly. Something must be amiss."

Bric opened his mouth to ask him another question when he saw a big knight astride a massive gray war horse approach. Bric recognized the horse; he knew exactly who the knight was. In fact, it was a struggle for him to keep a straight face as the knight dismounted his horse, removed his broadsword from the sheath on his saddle, and wielded the weapon in a defensive stance as he faced Bric.

Dashiell du Reims had arrived.

"If you are going to fight me, then let us get on with it," Dashiell said in a menacing tone. "I've got no time for foolery, so if you are mad enough to kill me, then you may try. I am ready."

Bric just stood there and shook his head, wagging it back and forth. "These are your first words to me? Those of anger and threat?"

"I said I have no time for foolery. If you are going to strike, then do it."

Bric had to bite his lip to keep from laughing at Dashiell's all-out aggressive stance, as if he were prepared to fight for his life. But he understood why.

"God knows, I should be mad enough to kill you," he finally muttered. "I have lived this moment over and over in my mind ever since you went behind my back and proposed a marriage between your cousin and me, wondering what I would say to you when I saw you next. I have planned this out many times."

Dashiell held steady. "I am sure you have," he said. "But before you tell me how much you hate me and how badly you want to kill me, know this: I proposed the marriage to honor you, not to punish you. I know you do not believe it, but my reasoning is thusly – you literally saved my life, Bric. In the battle of Newark Castle last September, you prevented my death and I vowed that I would repay you with the greatest honor I was capable of. *This* was that repayment. Now, you are forever my cousin, my kin, and when I am the Earl of East Anglia, I will greatly elevate you. You shall have lands and wealth. But it starts with the marriage to my cousin, so if you cannot understand that I did this to honor you, then I suppose there is nothing more to say. Attack me if you must; I am ready."

Bric listened to the rather impassioned speech before slowly lifting his eyebrows. With a heavy sigh, he began to make his way towards Dashiell, but he didn't make a move to unsheathe his weapon. In fact, his pace was rather slow and thoughtful, as if he were pondering his response.

But as he came closer to Dashiell, the man backed up, unwilling to let Bric, a notoriously fast knight, get any closer and then unleash his fearsome fists. Dashiell knew full well what Bric was capable of, so he wasn't taking any chances. When Bric saw this, he came to a halt.

"Do you really think that I would hurt you, Dash?" he asked.

"I know what you can do when you are angry enough."

"This is not one of those times."

Dashiell wasn't expecting that answer. In fact, it stumped him, and his brow furrowed in puzzlement. "What do you mean?"

Bric looked at him, a smile playing on his lips. "Your cousin arrived here two days ago."

That brought a measure of surprise from Dashiell. "She did? I was unaware."

"We were married yesterday."

Dashiell's eyes widened. "You were?" He was shocked. "And... and you are not intending to gut me?"

Bric couldn't hold back the smile now. "Nay," he said quietly. "Not to worry, Dash. I am not angry with you."

Dashiell still wasn't convinced. He looked to Daveigh, over Bric's shoulder. "My lord, help me," he said. "Bric is trying to lull me into a false sense of security by telling me he is not angry with me. I have come prepared to fight him, but now he taunts me."

Daveigh started laughing. "He is not taunting you, Dash," he said. "He is serious. The marriage agrees with him."

Dashiell stared at him. Then, he lowered his sword and put his hand over his heart as if it were failing him. "God," he muttered. "I must be already dead. In what world would Bric MacRohan not seek revenge against me for forcing him to wed my cousin?"

Daveigh continued to laugh as he walked past Bric and to Dashiell, planting a hand on Dashiell's shoulder. "Believe me," he said. "No one is more shocked that I am. When I told Bric of your marriage proposal, he literally tried to fight his way out of Narborough and flee. Only my wife's threats against him forced him to remain. The wedding was yesterday and, if I am reading Bric's expressions correctly this morning, he is pleased with it. He seems quite pleased with your cousin."

Dashiell was genuinely astonished. He looked at Bric. "Is this true?"

It was the question everyone had been asking him all morning, trying to force him to confess that he was agreeable to the marriage and to his new wife. He was starting to feel like a fool again, but he fought it, realizing it was his pride that kept him from conceding the point. Only a liar would deny that he was satisfied, and he wasn't a liar. After a moment, he nodded.

"I am."

"Then... then you do not want to kill me?"

"Nay."

"This is not a trick?"

"It is not a trick."

"Swear this to me."

"I swear it upon my oath."

Dashiell stared at him a moment longer before sheathing his sword. "I cannot believe it," he said. "Truly, I am thrilled, but I cannot believe it. Are you *truly* happy about this?"

Bric was growing embarrassed. "What would you have me say?" he said. "I told you I was. Would you feel better if I tried to kill you?"

"Mayhap."

Bric fought off a grin. "Then it will have to be later," he said. "At the moment, I want to know why you are here. We heard rumor that Savernake was in the area."

Dashiell didn't press him any further than he already had about the marriage. He could see that Bric was uncomfortable talking about it and he knew the man well enough to sense that. But he was so stunned about the man's reaction to the forced marriage that it was difficult to focus on anything else. But, he had to – it was necessary because he had come to Narborough for a reason.

Business was at hand.

"We've been with the de Lohr army near Lincoln," he said. "There is a concentration of the remnants from John's French army in the midsection of England, and Lincoln has been hard-hit. That is why I have come; Holdingham Castle is being held by Lord Evedon, who is loyal to Henry. You know the place, Bric – it guards the road that connects Lincoln to Nottingham and also to Newark. It is strategic. Even though John is dead, the French still will not leave England and now there is a buildup near Holdingham. De Lohr believes they will try to cut off the road, essentially separating Lincoln from its allies to the south. I've been sent to summon your army to hold the line at Holdingham."

Daveigh was listening closely. "Holdingham is two days away," he said. "How urgent is the situation?"

Dashiell looked at him. "Dire, my lord," he said. "De Lohr begs you to come immediately to reinforce his ranks."

Daveigh looked at Bric, who was already in motion. If Dashiell said the situation was dire, then Bric wasn't going to ask a lot of questions. He was simply going to do what was necessary to support an ally. Already, he was barking orders to Mylo.

"Bring Pearce off the wall and tell him we are mobilizing the army immediately," he said. "You and Pearce will start with the preparations. I will join you shortly."

The de Winter army didn't mobilize without Bric at the helm, so Mylo rushed off to begin the process while Bric turned to Dashiell.

"We can be ready by sunset," he said, glancing up at the sky as the morning deepened. "We will have a full moon tonight so, barring any cloud cover, we can travel at night. If we only stop once, to rest the horses and the men, we should be at Holdingham by tomorrow at sunset, I should think."

Daveigh agreed with the plan, for the most part. "We must leave at least three hundred men here," he said. "If there are still raiders about, I do not want Narborough unprotected."

Bric nodded. "I will send to Roxham Castle and Wissington Castle for reinforcements for Narborough," he said. Then, he looked at Dashiell. "You shall have around eighteen hundred men by nightfall."

Dashiell was relieved. "Thank you," he said. "I realize you have duties to attend to, but might I trouble you for some food and drink? And may I offer a word of greeting to your wife?"

Bric was back to fighting off a smile at the mere mention of Eiselle. "I think that can be arranged."

Dashiell, finally understanding that Bric truly wasn't going to run him through for the marriage situation, put a big hand on Bric's shoulder.

"Thank you, Cousin," he said.

Bric merely chuckled at the mention of their new familial relationship, which set off Dashiell. The two of them snorted and giggled like a pair of fools the entire walk back to the keep.

All was well between them once again.

CHAPTER EIGHT

EISELLE HADN'T SEEN her cousin, Dashiell, in at least four years. She was very fond of him because he'd always been very kind to her, so the moment Keeva admitted Bric and Dashiell into the enormous master's chamber where Eiselle was sitting by the window, measuring out a pattern on the fabric Keeva had given her, Eiselle jumped to her feet and ran at her cousin, who caught her up in a warm embrace.

"Selly," Dashiell said as he gave her a squeeze. "I did not even know you were at Narborough, yet I hear you are a married woman now. My heartiest congratulations."

Eiselle was thrilled to see her older cousin. "Bric and I were married yesterday," she said. Then, she threw her arms around his neck again and squeezed him as if to choke him. "It is so good to see you. Father told me that you were married last year and I want to hear all about it. You must tell me everything!"

Dashiell smiled warmly at her. "All I can tell you is that I am as happy as you appear to be," he said. "I married Edward de Vaston's youngest daughter, Belladonna."

Eiselle's brow furrowed curiously. "De Vaston," she repeated. "The Duke of Savernake, is he not?"

Dashiell nodded. "He was," he said. "He died last year. Bric knows this. He was there, in fact, when the duke passed away. I married the duke's youngest daughter and she is pregnant with our first child, so I am eager to return to Ramsbury Castle."

Eiselle put her hand on his arm. "I am so happy for you, truly," she said. "You deserve all the happiness in the world, Dash."

He smiled at her. "As do you," he said. Then, he eyed Bric, who had so far been standing aside as the cousins greeted one another. "I am told that marriage agrees with you both."

Eiselle looked at Bric and she flushed a deep red. "Although I cannot speak for my husband, I find it most agreeable."

Now that the attention had shifted to Bric, he found that he only had eyes for his wife. "It is," he said the words she wanted to hear. But then he looked at Dashiell. "We have been married less than a day. What more do you need to hear? I married the woman of your choice and I am not displeased by it."

Dashiell shook his head. "That is truly something I never thought to hear," he said. "I am still astonished."

"Don't be."

Dashiell's amused gaze lingered on him a moment before returning his focus to Eiselle again. "You would not know this, but you are my gift to Bric."

Eiselle looked between the men, curiously. "A gift?"

Dashiell nodded. "He saved my life last year," he said. "Had it not been for Bric, I would not be standing here at this moment. I, therefore, gave him the most precious and honorable gift I could think of – *you*. Treat him well, Selly. He is greater than you know."

Eiselle looked at Bric, appreciation in her eyes. Clearly, she already had a great deal of admiration for the man. Dashiell could see that plainly.

"I am hoping to discover all about him on my own," she said. "We have the rest of our lives, after all. There is no hurry."

As Eiselle looked at him rather dreamily, and Dashiell looked at him rather knowingly, Bric was rather embarrassed by all of the sentiment going around. Touched, but embarrassed. He was greatly warmed by the look in Eiselle's eyes, a look that made his heart flutter as if he were a foolish squire. In truth, he didn't care. He liked it. But he was far too uncomfortable with the situation to say anything remotely flattering or kind to her, especially in front of Dashiell. He was still new to all of this, after all, and he'd had absolutely no practice when it came to an intimate relationship with a woman. Therefore, for lack of a response, he simply forced a somewhat neutral smile at Eiselle before turning to Dashiell.

"Speaking of hurry," he said, "I must see to the preparation for the army. My wife will see to your food and drink. I will be in the bailey when you are finished."

His departure was swift, leaving Eiselle watching him go and feeling somewhat confused by his reaction. It was the first time she'd seen him since their wedding night and it seemed to her that his reaction the morning after was mixed. He'd told Dashiell he was pleased, yet he'd just fled the room as if he were eager to get away from her. Trying not to appear too sad about it, she looked at Dashiell.

"What does he mean by preparing the army?" she asked. "Is the army leaving?"

Dashiell nodded. "It will be soon," he told her. "There is a potential problem, but nothing to worry over."

"What *kind* of a problem?"

"Remnants of John's French army."

"And you will fight them? I mean, Bric will fight them?"

"If it comes to that."

She eyed him doubtfully. "I am not sure I like this."

Dashiell put his big arm around her shoulders, pulling her towards the great double doors that led into the hall beyond. "Selly, you are married to a knight now," he said patiently. "But not just any knight; you are married to de Winter's High Warrior. He is the greatest knight in the realm. You are going to have to become accustomed to the man going to war. It is part of his life and he will not stop it because of you."

Fundamentally, Eiselle knew that, but she still didn't like it. Such a thing didn't matter to her before she'd met Bric, but now that she was coming to know him, the thought of the man in danger had her nervous stomach twitching again.

"I do not expect him to stop," she said. "But... this is something I have never been part of before. I cannot help if I worry."

Dashiell knew that. "My wife is the same way," he said. "She does not like it when I go off to battle, but that is my vocation, too. That is the same life you are to lead now – your husband will go to war and you will patiently wait for him to return. Just know that Bric MacRohan is no ordinary knight; there is a magic about him that most warriors do not have."

They paused as they entered the hall. Eiselle was looking up at Dashiell quite seriously. "I do not care what magic he has, as long as he returns home," she said quietly. "I cannot explain it, Dash, but I have quickly come to like Bric. He is kind and he is patient. In truth, I was terribly nervous when I first came to Narborough. But he put me at ease from the first and that has not changed. I would be devastated if this brief marriage was cut short."

Dashiell grinned, tapping her gently on the cheek. "I would not worry about that if I were you," he said. "Bric MacRohan is like those ancient Irish warriors of legend – there is something immortal about him. He will always return to you, of that I am certain. Now, not to change the subject too drastically, but I could use some food and drink before I depart with the de Winter army. Will you provide me with sustenance, Lady MacRohan?"

Eiselle smiled broadly. "It will be my pleasure, my lord."

Seated at the table and listening to the priest as he continued to sleep off his drinking binge next to the hearth, Dashiell delved into the cold beef and cheese and bread that a kitchen servant had provided. Eiselle sat with him and they spoke of Dashiell's new wife and of the new position as duke. He had assumed the title late last year. Dashiell was very happy with his life, and Eiselle couldn't remember ever seeing the man so joyful or relaxed.

That joy translated into a man who wasn't afraid to show the side of him most people didn't see; the comical side of his personality. He took to throwing bread crusts at the dogs sleeping on the floor, luring them over to the priest who was snoring loudly enough to rattle teeth. The bread crusts would land on the priest and the dogs would lick and bite the man trying to get at the food. The priest would snort in his sleep, batting at the dogs and calling them Satan's children, and Eiselle giggled uncontrollably. It was great fun, all at the expense of the sleeping priest.

That went on for the nearly the duration of the meal, until Dashiell was finally satisfied. Then, their time together was over and Eiselle was sorry to see him go. Dashiell kissed his cousin on the head as he excused himself and headed out to the bailey where men were preparing for war.

Although he'd told Eiselle not to worry, it was inevitable that she did. This was all so new to her, now with her husband heading off to war again. Dashiell told her that she must learn to be brave, but she honestly wasn't sure she could. Still, she didn't want Bric to think she was weak, so whatever she felt, she vowed to keep it to herself. Or, at least *try* to keep it to herself.

But it wasn't going to be easy.

Leaving the priest still snoring away and the table being cleared of the remnants of Dashiell's meal, Eiselle returned to the master's chamber to continue sewing on Keeva's garment.

Keeva wasn't anywhere to be found in the chamber as Eiselle resumed her position over near the windows. The fabric was laid out on top of a coverlet to keep it clean, as it was a deep brownish-red wool, something quite elegant.

Eiselle had been sewing from a young age, so she knew how to create a dress. It was one of the few things her mother had taught her, and she was very good at it. In order to start the pattern for the dress, she'd had Keeva lay on the fabric and then she'd taken chalk to outline the woman's frame. From that, she carefully drew out the drape and basic dimension of the dress.

Eiselle had a sewing kit in her trunks, but she was using Keeva's, and using long, slender iron pins to frame the shape of what she wanted to cut. The cutting would come later with a very sharp knife that was made to cut fabric.

As she pinned, Eiselle could hear the noise from the outer bailey, and more than once she was drawn to the long, very tall lancet windows that faced the west side of the castle. She kept hoping for a glimpse of Bric, but, alas, that was not meant to be. She never saw him, not once.

Saddened, she returned to her sewing and forced herself to focus, losing herself in her project as a way of forgetting about what was to come. This morning when she'd asked Keeva for tasks, it had been because she'd felt happy and energetic, thrilled to be living her first day as Lady MacRohan, but now the task was a way of escaping the reality that her new husband was going off to battle again. The raid two days before and now this... truly, she wasn't sure this was something she could become used to, but better to suffer through it than not be married to Bric at all.

He was worth the anxiety.

The morning dragged on and Keeva finally returned to the chamber to check on the progress of her dress. She'd been spending her time on the inner wall with her husband, who was watching Bric and the knights assemble an army of over a thousand men, wagons, and animals.

Whenever de Winter mobilized, it was always something impressive to behold. Keeva spoke of the times past when the army would mobilize and move out, sometimes for months on end, which brought a bit of a concerned expression from Eiselle. When Keeva realized that she'd frightened the woman, she made every effort to backtrack on her prattle and try not to make it seem as bad as it was.

But the damage had been done.

Was it possible the army would really be gone for months? Eiselle thought gloomily. She was to marry a man and only know him two days before he left for months? It was distressing news, and something she struggled against even as Keeva tried to make it seem that all was not as bad as she'd made it sound. But Eiselle knew better; she knew her husband was leaving and there was nothing Keeva could say to cheer her up.

But she soldiered through the day, working on the dress, something that Keeva praised quite a bit as the hours passed. Eiselle had an eye for a good pattern, and a fashionable dress, and Keeva was thrilled to discover it. It was the years of working in her father's stall that had given Eiselle that eye. She knew what women were wearing and what looked good.

Towards late afternoon, after Eiselle had cut out the dress and was now loosely basting it onto Keeva, Bric abruptly appeared in the master chamber's doorway. When Eiselle caught sight of him, she was so startled that she rammed an iron pin right into Keeva's rump. The woman yelped.

"Oh, my lady!" Eiselle gasped. "I am so terribly sorry! How clumsy of me!"

Keeva rubbed her bum where Eiselle stabbed her. "Not to worry, lass," she said, a grin on her face as she looked at Bric. "I see that your mind was not on your work. Bric, this is *your* fault."

Bric smiled weakly. "I do apologize," he said, but his attention was on Eiselle. "I was wondering if I might borrow Lady MacRohan for a short while."

Keeva didn't have time to reply before Eiselle was rushing in his direction. Seeing this, Keeva simply laughed.

"Go," she waved them off.

Leaving Keeva with the half-basted dress still draped on her body, Eiselle rushed to Bric's side. He wasn't dressed for battle, but simply in a heavy tunic and leather breeches. Eiselle noticed almost immediately that he was wearing the belt she had given him.

"It looks as if my belt fits you," she said.

Bric smiled as he looked down at it, fingering the fabric. "I will never take it off," he told her. Then, he took her by the elbow. "Come with me a moment. I have need of you."

Eiselle went willingly as he took her into the hall where some men were sitting around, eating cold beef and drinking ale. The evening meal was still several hours off, but the servants were stoking the hearth in the hall, building it up into a raging blaze as Bric took Eiselle to one of the long, scrubbed tables and sat her down. He then sent a servant for food and drink as he sat down next to her.

"I do not have much time, but I wanted to see you before I leave," he said quietly.

"To war?"

He nodded. "Dash said he told you."

"He also told me that I must not worry."

Bric lifted his big shoulders. "I cannot tell you how to feel, as I have never had to face this kind of thing before," he said. "Keeva always worries for Daveigh, and I have seen other women throw fits when their men head off to battle. I suppose it is a woman's nature to worry."

Eiselle watched his mouth as he spoke, those full and soft lips that had made her feel so wicked and wanton.

"How would you have me behave, Bric?" she asked softly. "Tell me and I shall do it."

Bric looked at her, feeling those same giddy feelings sweep over him at the mere sight of her. She was so sweet and lovely, and he genuinely didn't want to leave her, which was something of a new sensation for him. He'd spent the past eight hours preparing the army to depart and, all the while, his mind had been lingering on Eiselle and feeling so very regretful that he was going to leave her.

After a moment, he simply shook his head.

"I do not know," he said truthfully. "I have never left anyone behind before, so I do not know. All I know is that for the first time in my life, I would rather stay here than leave to battle. We are only just coming to know each other and I was looking forward to the days to come. Believe me when I say that I am sorry to leave you here."

Eiselle's smile turned warm, genuine. "And I am sorry you are going," she said. "I feel the same way. I would much rather have you remain here with me, where we can feast tonight and speak on foolish things or important things. We can speak on whatever we feel like. But instead, you are departing with your army and I feel... sad. I will admit that I am sad you are leaving."

His gaze was warm upon her. "Good," he said. "I am glad you are sad. That means… well, I am not sure what it means, but I know that I like it. I suppose it means that you are thinking of me."

Eiselle was bold; she reached out and took one of his hands, holding it tightly. He responded by squeezing so hard that he nearly broke her fingers.

"Aye, I am," she said quietly. "I suspect I will always think of you, no matter what. And since you cannot tell me how I should feel, I will be honest and tell you that I am not only sad, but I am afraid for you. I have never known someone I care about leaving for battle."

His smile faded. "Do you?" he asked, shocked. "Care for me, I mean. Do… do you really care for me?"

She nodded, averting her gaze rather bashfully. "You have been kind and understanding and compassionate since I have known you," she said. "How could I not care?"

That was more than Bric expected to hear from her, but he was delighted to the bone. As he sat there and held her hand, he reached into the neck of his tunic and pulled forth a chain looped around his neck that had something affixed to the end of it. He held it up to Eiselle, catching the light of the torches that were now being brought into the hall by servants, illuminating the darkness.

"See this?" he asked. "I have worn this since I was a youth. My former master gave it to me, an Irish warrior who fought well into his seventh decade. His name was Conor and he had no sons, so he gave this to me when I was knighted. Conor told me that this talisman had been passed down through the men in his family and that it had been blessed by St. Patrick himself."

Eiselle was very curious about the talisman; made from steel and in the shape of a cross, it contained Latin words etched into the metal. She ran her fingers along the letters, barely making them out.

A maiorem caritatum nemo habet.

"What do these words mean?" she asked. "I cannot see them very well."

He watched her face as she inspected the pendant. "A man hath no greater love than he lay down his life for his friends," he said. "'Tis from the bible."

She nodded in understanding. "I think I have heard the verse before," she said. "And this brings you good fortune on the battlefield?"

"Aye," he said. "This talisman has protected generations of warriors from death, and it will protect me, so you needn't worry. This will keep me safe."

Eiselle turned it over, inspecting it, before looking up and meeting his eye. "I thought only the superstitious wore talismans."

Bric tried to look serious, but he couldn't quite keep the smile from his lips.

"I am from Ireland, Lady MacRohan," he said. "I have seen many strange things, many things that you would not believe. There are evil spirits in this world, and there are little folk who live beneath the hills. I have personally seen a troll, but that was when I was young. I ran from it when I should have run *to* it and challenged it. You must not scoff at superstition, my lady. It may be more powerful than you know."

Eiselle didn't believe in any of that, frankly, and she wasn't sure how to tell him. "My parents were people of logic," she said hesitantly. "I can only remember going to church a scant few times as a child because my father believed in reason over religion or superstition. His only friend was an alchemist, and he told my father that everything has an explanation. He says there is no magic in the world."

Bric was rather pleased to hear that she was reasonable about life. He'd seen far too many women fall victim to the hysteria of religion and, truth be told, he wasn't particularly religious himself. But he did believe in luck and good fortune, and he believed implicitly in the power of his mighty talisman.

"I suppose our beliefs are our own magic," he said. "I do believe this talisman has power, and I believe the words inscribed on it. I believe it every time I go into battle and it has not failed me yet."

"Then you *should* believe it. You should believe it with all your heart."

"I do. And I want you to, also."

"I will. If you wish it, I will believe it without question."

With a smile on his face, he just sat there and gazed at her. She was such a beautiful creature that he couldn't seem to stop staring at her. But he could still see that she was worried, facing something she had never faced before. Battle was frightening for those who were unaccustomed to it. The longer he looked at her, the more he felt an odd tugging to his heart, a sadness he'd never known before. It took him a moment to realize that, perhaps, he was feeling longing for Eiselle.

He missed her already.

Reaching into his tunic, he pulled the talisman over his head and put it in her hands.

"Here," he said. "I want you to keep this for me. It has brought me fortune and comfort these many years, and now I want it to bring comfort to you."

Eiselle looked at the heavy talisman in her hand. "But," she stammered, "… but this is yours, Bric. You said yourself that you have taken it into every battle and it has never failed you. How can you even think to go into a fight without it?"

His gaze was warm. "Because my faith is in my abilities and my skill," he said. "The fortune my talisman has brought me, even if it is not with me, still lingers. You will keep it safe for me and in doing so, you can ensure my return. I will come back for it… and you."

Eiselle wasn't so sure she should keep his good luck charm. "But it will do more good if you take it into battle, as always. Please, Bric."

He shook his head. "The good it will do me is in knowing you are comforted by keeping it. This is your first battle, after all. You will need the comfort only the talisman can bring."

She smiled wanly. "It *is* my first battle, but I was not going to become hysterical about it, I promise."

He grinned. "I know. But I think my talisman will do more good with you, since this is your very first." Then, he took her hands into his big mitts, kissing them sweetly. "I *will* return. Do you believe me?"

Eiselle was caught up in the expression on his face, how those piercing eyes seemed to reach out and grab her. And the kisses to her hand... she could hardly breathe because of them.

"I do," she murmured.

"Good."

A servant suddenly appeared bearing food, and Bric didn't say anything more. He'd said all he needed to say, and he felt a good deal of comfort in leaving his beloved talisman with his new wife to ease her anxiety, so he let go of Eiselle's hands and he focused on his meal. More people were wandering into the hall, men who would soon be departing and looking for sustenance, so Bric's line of conversation from that point forward was about things that were trivial and had nothing to do with the fact that he felt sad at the thought of leaving his new bride. This woman he never wanted to marry suddenly had him feeling things he'd never felt before.

It was both thrilling and confusing.

He suspected that warfare, from this point on, would not be the same for him. Now, he had a wife to think of, and leaving his talisman with her was his first indication that, perhaps, she meant something more to him than he could begin to comprehend. It was madness, truly, to suspect deep feelings after only a few days, but there was no denying that there was a connection between them, something that went beyond anything he'd ever known before. Leaving his talisman with her was the first indication of that.

Already, he couldn't wait to return to her.

CHAPTER NINE

Holdingham Castle
Forty miles northwest of Narborough

FOUR DAYS SINCE departing Narborough with weather that had been crisp and clear, the day of the actual battle had turned dark and stormy.

De Lohr, de Winter, Lincoln, and Savernake troops found themselves holding the line against an onslaught of French armies that were here simply because the French prince, Louis, had been an ally of the rebels against King John. Almost a year after John's death, Louis wouldn't leave the country because he'd been promised the throne. In light of John's death and Henry's ascension to the crown of England, Louis had no support from the rebels who were now supporting Henry. Cast aside, and angry, he was determined to wreak what havoc he could. With nothing to lose, his recklessness made him quite dangerous.

Even though it was summer, the storm that rolled over Holdingham was severe and within just a few hours of fighting, the ground had turned to ankle-deep sludge. The blood of the wounded was mixing with the rain that puddled of the battlefield, turning everything into a sea of red. The landscape was quite flat, with very little elevation, so everything simply sat and pooled.

The de Winter army was covering the south flank of de Lohr's army, with Savernake covering the north flank, in a line of men and animals that stretched for a half-mile. The Lincoln troops were in Holdingham Castle, a quarter of a mile to the east, shoring up the castle should the French break through the line.

And break, they tried.

The morning had seen vicious fighting with archers, each side launching volley after volley at each other, but the French soon grew weary of the damage they were sustaining. Being that they were ill-supplied these days, they simply didn't have the shields or arrows to withstand a sustained attack from the archers, and when Christopher de Lohr, who was in command of the loyalist army, began to heavily pound them with archers to beat them down, the French broke ranks and began to charge at the long line of English loyalists.

After that, it was chaos.

Bric entered the fray earlier on because the French had tried to hit the flanks to go around de Lohr and on to the castle, so it was up to the de Winter army to hold off the French and prevent them from breaking through. Early on, it was hand-to-hand combat, and Bric spent the hours in the saddle, fighting French knights, dispatching those who were too weak to hold out against him.

The High Warrior was in fine form that day. He blazed through a fight with a French knight who was quite skilled but, in the end, the Frenchman fell to Bric's sword. When the man toppled off his horse, Bric spurred his war horse forward and literally onto the man's body, a massive hoof coming to rest on the back of the knight's head and shoving his face into the mud to drown him. When the knight moved no more, the horse trampled him and dashed off to find more victims.

Once again, whispers of a vicious English knight with silver eyes began to drift among the French lines, and men would run when they saw the black, gray, and red of the House of de Winter, knowing that any man bearing those colors could be the knight with the silver eyes, the one who was killing men as easily as a man could breathe air.

But it was more than that. There also happened to be an abnormal amount of decapitated heads around the battlefield because Bric wasn't one to go for the kill in the chest or belly, as some men did. He preferred the definitive, quick kill of decapitation, and he'd used that technique throughout his career. It was a signature stroke. Unlike some men, Bric wasn't in the battle for the thrill of a fight, for the excitement of proving he was better than anyone else. He was in it for the kill. If a man was his enemy, he was destined to die.

And die, they did.

Towards dusk, the sky was still flooding the fields with rain and men were slogging through mud that was now up to their knees, exhausted as they fought the French who were unwilling to surrender. But the rain had lightened somewhat, and the wind that had whistled through the battlefield all day had eased, so there was hope that the weather would soon clear. Every so often, the clouds would part and bits of blue sky could be seen but, for the most part, it was still a horribly miserable battle.

Several times during the day, Bric had reached for his talisman to kiss it only to remember that he'd left it with Eiselle. *Eiselle.* Such a beautiful name for a woman he was increasingly obsessed over. Truthfully, he didn't regret leaving her his talisman, convinced it was giving her comfort knowing that he would return for it.

But the truth was that he would be returning for her, and her alone.

As the battle wore on and he began to feel his exhaustion, his thoughts turned increasingly to Eiselle and the moment when they would be reunited. He intended to bed her when next he saw her again, perhaps several times, and then he intended to spend all the time he could with her. He'd even been thinking about asking Daveigh if he could take command of one of the lesser castles in the Honor of Narborough, perhaps Roxham Castle, so that Eiselle could be the mistress of her own keep. As it was, Eiselle was secondary to Keeva, and he thought the woman might like her own keep.

As his wife, she was deserving of such a thing.

It would give them time to start their life together, without the chaos of a big castle around them. For the first time in his life, Bric was thinking about easing off from such active duty. He could turn the Narborough duties over to Pearce, who was young and hungry. He was a good commander. And Bric could settle down with his wife at a lesser castle, and they could live a perfectly happy and wonderful little life.

Bric's priorities were changing.

It was rather ironic that he would consider such a thing, coming from de Winter's High Warrior, but he rather thought it sounded wonderful. Just him, and Eiselle, and their life together. If he had to lift his sword now and again, he would do it, but his focus would be on his wife. His family.

His marriage.

But he had to make it home first. Avoiding the arc of an angry Frenchman's broadsword, he brought his own sword around and ended up cutting off the man's arm when his horse suddenly shifted. As the French knight raced off, screaming, Bric noticed Pearce as the man came alongside him.

"How does it look to the north?" he yelled at Pearce. "Is Savernake holding their lines?"

Pearce nodded, trying to hold tight to his excited horse. "Aye," he said. "Dash and Savernake are holding fast. It seems that we've received the brunt of the French attempts to break the lines. I am hearing rumor that we have more dead and wounded than most."

Bric looked around; he could see that he had many wounded and as sunset approached, the French had backed off for the most part. There were pockets of fighting, but not nearly what it had been. He wiped the water and sweat from his eyes.

"I must find Christopher and discover what he has in mind for the conclusion of this skirmish," he said. "The French seem to be fleeing, and we have our own wounded to remove from the field of battle. It seems to me that this battle has come to an end."

Pearce nodded, surveying the field that was full of bodies, beaten and broken. There was so much blood that the mud was red, giving the entire battlefield a macabre and apocalyptic appearance.

"It was a brutal fight, Bric," he said. "Thank God we were victorious. We held the line so the French were unable to make it to

Holdingham. They remain strong."

Bric was thinking the same thing, but he didn't voice it. He rarely bragged in battle, thinking that it was an affront to the gods of war. Oddly enough, the man was always humble in victory, no matter how great or bloody it had been.

"Aye," he said. "We shall live to fight another day. Now, do your duty and sweep the field to ensure the French do not start killing our wounded. We need to have them removed immediately. I will find Christopher and discover what his plans are now that the fighting has died down."

Pearce nodded. "I will," he said. "I will find Mylo and he can assist me. Last I saw him, he was near the de Lohr lines."

"If I see him, I will send him to you."

The knights were preparing to part when they both heard what sounded like a thin wailing. Immediately, they knew what it was because they'd heard it in chorus earlier in the day when the French were lobbing volleys of arrows their direction. It seemed that the French, as a dying beast, weren't ready to give up yet. They were going to inflict what they could until the very end.

Pearce managed to get his shield up, but Bric was a split-second slower. As Pearce's shield was hit with a large, broad-headed arrow, that very same arrowhead hit Bric in the lower left side of his chest.

The noise it made was something Pearce would remember until the day he died.

It was an arrowhead designed to take down horses and other large animals, and the French probably stole it off of another soldier or hunter and reused it. It was such a large arrowhead that it pushed through layers of tunics and Bric's heavy mail coat, carving a hole into the left side of his body and anchoring deep.

Pearce heard a scream, realizing it was his own. But Bric didn't utter a sound; he simply looked down at the enormous arrow spine protruding from his body. In tribute to Bric's strength, he didn't fall from his horse – the High Warrior remained mounted, his left hand going to the spine that was protruding from his body. As Pearce gaped at him in horror, Bric looked at the shaft as if he could hardly believe what had just happened.

For a moment, neither man spoke. They simply looked on in shock. This kind of thing wasn't supposed to happen at the end of a battle, and it certainly wasn't supposed to happen to a man who men had deemed immortal. Finally, Pearce grabbed the reins of Bric's war horse and turned the animal for the encampment to the south.

With tears in his eyes, he escorted Bric back to camp the entire way. Bric never did fall from his horse.

Six days after the army's departure

HE CALLED HIMSELF Manducor, but Eiselle had never met a priest like him.

Truthfully, it wasn't as if she had spent a lot of time around priests. She really hadn't spent time around any. Therefore, Manducor's behavior wasn't something that struck her as particularly strange but, from what she'd heard about priests, the man certainly didn't follow the mold.

Mold...

He smelled like mold. And rot, and any other foul smell that Eiselle had experienced in her lifetime. The man positively reeked. The night Bric and the army had departed, Manducor had wandered into the great hall – God only knows where the man had been – and proceeded to sit across the table from Eiselle and eat until he could eat no more.

Eiselle had never seen anyone eat so much in her entire life. Even Keeva, who had joined her in the hall, had watched the priest slurp up his meal with disgust. No one seemed to know why he was still at Narborough, and why he hadn't returned to his parish in King's Lynn. He seemed quite intent on remaining and even when Keeva told him she would arrange for an escort to return him home, he disappeared and didn't return until the evening meal the next day.

He was a strange, strange man.

But he seemed harmless enough, simply reluctant to return to his church, and when Keeva finally demanded to know why he wouldn't leave Narborough, he proceeded to tell her that his church, St. Margaret's Priory, had suffered through a glut of starving peasants from the countryside due to the unseasonable rains in the spring. The month-long deluge had killed crops as well as people, and Norfolk was a land of swamps and marshes as it was. People were starving, which meant the meager food for the priests had gone to feed the needy.

With that story, the man's ravenous appetite started to make some sense. Keeva talked the man into giving her his robes so they could at least be washed, and taking a bath himself, which he balked at because he couldn't remember the last bath he'd had. It wasn't good for man's soul, he told her, but Keeva was insistent. She wasn't going to have a man who smelled of compost in her hall, so Manducor had no choice but to turn over his robes and wash his dirty body down in the kitchen yard. Keeva gave him a long tunic and an old robe that belonged to Daveigh to wear while his clothing was being washed, but he seemed to like the new clothing so much that he kept it on even when his robes were returned to him.

Eiselle could count on seeing the priest every morning in the hall, breaking his fast, and then every night when the evening meal was produced. Often times, there would be no one else in the hall but them, and the first four days after the army's departure, Manducor sat far away from Eiselle as he ate his meals.

But the past two days, he'd wandered over and sat across the table from her, and their conversation had been awkward and short at times. In fact, their very first real conversation had been about the talisman around Eiselle's neck, something she hadn't removed since Bric had given it to her for safe keeping. The priest seemed fascinated by a charm that had been blessed by St. Patrick himself. But on this sixth night since the departure of the de Winter army, Manducor was more talkative than usual.

The cook had slaughtered a flock of older chickens and had made the most delightful dish of chicken with dumplings and chicken gravy. The smell permeated the far reaches of Narborough, drawing the hungry soldiers who weren't currently on duty as well as Keeva, Zara, Angela, and Eiselle. The great hall had more people in it than usual as a result, and as a storm thundered overhead in a midsummer's shower, a hot and flavorful meal took place in the hall.

Manducor, of course, joined them. He sat at the end of the table, across from Eiselle and Keeva, and slurped, burped, and farted his way through the meal. Zara hadn't been around the man at all, and she'd been happily into her second cup of sweet wine when she noticed his terrible manners. After that, she didn't try to hide her reaction to his burping and farting. Angela sat down the table from him with her rude son, taking no notice of the equally rude priest.

It was the first time Angela had been around Eiselle since the pinching incident, and she was markedly standoffish from Lady MacRohan. Keeva noticed it and thought the woman's behavior was ridiculous, made worse when little Edward didn't want to eat his meal and began to whine as Angela patiently tried to feed him. More than once, he threw food back at his mother, mussing her surcoat. When he threw a spoon at her, clipping her shoulder, Keeva was forced to step in.

"Angela," she said sternly. "I do not mind if you bring Edward to eat with us provided he behaves. If he cannot behave, them he must remain in his chamber. I will not have him upsetting everyone's meal."

Angela looked at her, torn between defiance and feeling wounded. "If you had a child, Lady de Winter, you would understand," she clapped back. "Sometimes children must be allowed to express themselves. If he does not want to eat, I shall not force him."

That was a very hurtful insult as far as Keeva was concerned. Everyone at Narborough knew that in spite of being married for many years, Keeva and Daveigh remained childless even though they wanted children very badly. Upset at the dig, Keeva didn't hold back her ire.

"If I had a child, he would behave a thousand times better than your little monster," she said. "I have warned you before about Edward. If he cannot behave like a polite child, then keep him shut up in his chamber. I do not want to see him, not anywhere in Narborough. Animals like that boy deserve cages."

Angela burst into tears. "He is *not* a monster!"

"I will not argue with you. Get him out of my sight."

Sobbing, Angela stood up from the table and grabbed at Edward, who didn't want his mother to touch him. He pulled away and began to run, but he didn't get very far. Manducor caught the child by the arm and lifted him up, practically tossing him onto the tabletop.

"Let him go!" Angela screamed.

As she rushed to remove her son from the priest's grip, Manducor spoke. "Lady," he said with disdain, "that child is an abomination. I have watched him show you absolutely no respect since you arrived in the hall. How old is he?"

Angela cradled Edward, who wanted to be put down. "He is a baby," she said angrily. "He has only seen two years."

Manducor snorted. "If you do not spank that child, and spank him frequently, you will create a man who knows no discipline," he warned. "When he misbehaves, swat him. You must do this."

Angela was deeply upset. "I think you are horrid," she snapped. "A horrid, smelly man."

Manducor turned back to his wine. "Mayhap," he said, unconcerned. "But at least I am not raising a son who will be a terror. Men will kill him before he is fully grown if you do not do something about him."

Weeping, Angela fled with her screaming son. Eiselle, Keeva, and Zara watched her go before Eiselle turned to Keeva.

"I should feel pity for the woman," she said. "She has a child and no idea how to properly raise him, yet she cannot see it."

Keeva shook her head, irritated with Angela's terrible son. "Mylo is a decent man," she said. "I do not understand why he allows his son to be raised by a woman with no courage."

"She is not doing the lad any favors," Manducor said, shoving more bread in his mouth. "I have seen enough disobedient boys to know that."

Eiselle looked at him. "Oh?" she said. "Do you deal with children as part of your duties at the priory?"

Manducor shook his head. "Nay," he muttered. Then, after a moment: "I had boys of my own, once."

Eiselle sensed something sorrowful in that soft statement. "You *had* children?"

"Aye."

"Then you were married?"

He nodded, but his entire manner seemed to slow. His eyes took on a faraway look, as if divining into a past with too many memories for the weary-hearted.

"Long ago," he said after a moment. "I married young. My wife and children died young."

There was a tragic tale in the making and Eiselle naturally felt pity for him. "I am sorry for you," she said. "Is that why you became a priest? Because your family died?"

He looked at her. Manducor was an older man, perhaps in his fiftieth year or more, with bright blue eyes and shaggy, dark hair. In truth, he wasn't unhandsome, but he was so smelly and unkempt, one would have never noticed his looks. The mention of a long-dead family seemed to bring his eating to a halt and he set his cup down, perhaps mulling over Eiselle's question.

"I became a priest because the priests at St. Margaret's helped me when I needed help," he said, with some regret. "They found me in the gutter, drunk, near death, and nursed me back to health. I could not function, mind you. The death of my family took everything from me. They kept me at St. Margaret's, gave me work and, in time, I took my vows. But I took my vows for my own reasons. I am forever searching for the reasons behind the death of my family. I thought that someday,

God might tell me why."

Both Eiselle and Keeva were gazing at him with some sympathy. "Has He spoken to you yet?" Keeva wanted to know.

For the first time since they'd known the slovenly priest, he actually appeared subdued and downtrodden. The transformation in his expression was astonishing, from a hardened drunk to a man who appeared somewhat resigned to what life had brought him.

"Nay," he said quietly. "He does not speak to me. I hope He will someday, but thus far, He has not. Does He speak to you, Lady de Winter?"

Keeva cocked her head curiously. "About what?"

"About your lack of children. I saw it in your face when the mother of the monster mentioned that you have none. You wish God would speak to you, too."

Keeva had to steel herself against an avalanche of sorrow that threatened with the catalyst of his words. It was such a painful subject, but after fourteen years of marriage, she tried not to think of it. She came from a large family of eleven children and had always hoped to have many herself.

When she married Daveigh, and fell in love with the man, she wanted nothing more than to give him a son. But after several miscarriages in the early years of their marriage, and no more pregnancies in the past six years, she was resigned to the fact that she and Daveigh would never have a son, and it ate at her if she let it.

She tried not to let it.

"It is possible," she said after a moment. "But I have stopped asking Him why women like Angela can bear a child and I've not yet had the honor. It is clear He does not wish for me to have children."

Manducor propped his elbows on the table, folding his hands. "It may be that your life will have other meaning, Lady de Winter," he said. "I have seen enough in my life to know that simply because we do not get what we want, it does not mean we are not needed elsewhere. I was needed at St. Margaret's. Mayhap you will find your needful place, in time."

The words were encouraging, coming from an unexpected source. Eiselle turned to Keeva and smiled, which brought a weak grin to Keeva's lips. Her lack of children wasn't something she openly spoke of, ever, so for it to become the topic of conversation with a priest she didn't have a good impression of, or at least hadn't until this point, was something unique. Oddly enough, his words brought some comfort to an old and sometimes raw wound.

"Mayhap," she said quietly.

Eiselle put her hand over Keeva's and squeezed, and Keeva appreciated the support. But before they could continue the conversation, soldiers at the great hall entry raised a commotion. When Keeva and the rest of the table turned to see what was happening, one of the men ran into the smoky hall, straight for Keeva.

"Lady de Winter." The man sounded breathless. "The army approaches, my lady. We are told to expect many wounded."

Most everyone in the hall heard it. Keeva and Eiselle were on their feet, now with a feeling of panic filling the hall.

"My husband?" Keeva demanded. "Is he among the wounded?"

The soldier shook his head. "Unknown, my lady," he said. "Men were sent ahead of the army to tell us to prepare for wounded. That is all we have been told."

With that, he fled, rushing out into the night beyond. Keeva turned to Eiselle, who had a rather wide-eyed expression.

"We must prepare the hall," she said, surprisingly calm. "We will put the wounded here. Zara, go to the kitchens and ensure they have enough hot water to clean wounds and boil bandages. Then you will find Angela and tell her she is needed. And tell her to bring her sewing kit."

Zara rushed away, leaving Eiselle still standing next to Keeva. "And me?" Eiselle asked, fighting off the fear in her breast. "What would you have me do, my lady?"

It was then that Keeva noticed the apprehension in Eiselle's expression. It occurred to her that Eiselle must not have ever faced anything like this, taking care of the wounded after a battle. The young woman had lived a rather placid life at a manor home in the country, or at her father's stall, so battle and blood and death weren't things she'd been exposed to.

She was about to have a fierce indoctrination into such things.

"You will have the servants move these tables against the walls," she said steadily, keeping her manner calm so that Eiselle would remain calm. "This floor must be cleaned. Have it swept up as much as you can and the rushes burned. Keep the fires blazing; it must be warm in here. You will also have the servants bring every blanket and coverlet they can find in here. Men will need to lay upon something other than the cold floor. Can you do this?"

Eiselle nodded bravely. She wasn't a coward by nature, even if a hall full of wounded did sound like a frightening thing. And Bric? Was he part of the wounded? She couldn't let herself think about that now.

She had a job to do.

"Aye," she said swiftly. "It shall be done."

Keeva patted her hand, seeing that she was trying not to appear as frightened as she perhaps felt. "Not to worry," she said. "You will do a fine job of it. We must make sure the wounded are comfortable. Have... have you tended injured men before?"

Eiselle shook her head. "Never, my lady," she said. She really didn't even know what to expect, and that frightened her a good deal. "But... but I shall do what you tell me to do. I will learn quickly."

Keeva patted her hand one last time and turned away. "Be strong, lass," she said as she turned for the entry. "Remember that they are depending on you, and they need your help. I know you will not fail them."

"Nay, Lady de Winter, I will not."

"Prepare the hall, then. I shall return."

As Keeva rushed out to meet the incoming army, Eiselle took a moment to take a deep breath and prioritize what needed to be done.

Keeva said clear the floor, so she would. But she also needed blankets, so Eiselle caught the attention of a few serving women, huddling fearfully near the door that led out into the kitchen yard.

"You," she said, catching their attention. "Lady de Winter wishes for you to find every blanket and coverlet you can and bring them to the hall. Go into every chamber and strip the beds. Bring it all down here immediately. And hurry!"

As the women rushed off, there were still several soldiers lingering at the other feasting table in the room, having heard the announcement of the incoming wounded. Eiselle turned in their direction, issuing orders like a master sergeant.

"You heard Lady de Winter," she said. "Move these tables to the edges of the room and then we must clear this floor. Find brooms, or use your hands. Do whatever you must to clear this floor. And someone get the dogs out of here!"

The tone of her voice had men moving. She wasn't shouting, but she was firm and loud, and men were more than willing to do her bidding. As the entire room of men began to move and the huge feasting tables began to shift, Eiselle stood back and out of the way, supervising the work. As she did, she caught movement out of the corner of her eye, turning to see Manducor walking up beside her. In Daveigh's borrowed clothes, he at least smelled better than he had when he'd first come to Narborough. When their eyes met, he smiled thinly.

"You will need help when the wounded come," he said. "I can give you such assistance."

She lifted an eyebrow, an almost wary gesture. "You can?" she said. "Do you know much about tending wounded men?"

He sighed faintly, watching the soldiers move the heavy tables. "I told you that I became a priest after my family perished," he said. "Before that, I was a knight for the Earl of Leicester. I have tended many battle wounds, my lady."

Eiselle was quite surprised to hear it. "Then your presence is most welcome."

He grunted. "I thought it would be," he said. Then, he eyed her. "The reason I did not wish to return to my parish right away was not because of a food shortage, as I said. It was because the de Winter army had headed to battle, and I knew you would need help when they returned."

"That is most generous," she said. "But why did you not simply tell us why you had remained? Lady de Winter would have allowed you to stay, so there was no reason to create stories."

He shook his head. "To tell you truthfully why I remained would have forced me to tell you about my past, and that was not something I was willing to speak of." When he saw the glint of humor in her eye, he smiled a crooked smile. "That has since changed, of course. But the night the army left for the battle, I felt strongly that I had to stay and await their return."

"But why?"

"Because I've not felt useful in a very long time, Lady MacRohan. Something told me to remain here."

"Do you think God was speaking to you?"

He smiled, lopsided. "It is entirely possible," he said. "He's never spoken to me about anything else, so it would be ironic if this was the moment He decided to speak. But beyond that, I cannot tell you more."

There was a hint of hope in his voice as he spoke and Eiselle didn't push him. She simply nodded. The drunken, smelly priest was, perhaps, finding a purpose, small as it was. He wanted to feel useful, and he would be badly needed if there were a great deal of wounded. After the conversation they'd shared that night, Eiselle felt as if she were coming to know the odd man, just a little.

"May I ask you another question?"

"You may."

"Is your name really Manducor?"

He chuckled. "If I told you what my name was, you would not believe me, so simply call me Manducor. It is easier that way."

A former knight who was now a priest didn't want to reveal his name. Eiselle thought it was all quite mysterious, but she didn't linger on it. The tables had been moved and now servants were quickly trying to sweep up the floors, and the blankets were beginning to arrive. She had a job to do and she jumped to it with determination.

Not fifteen minutes later, the wounded began to arrive.

CHAPTER TEN

D ASHIELL WAS STANDING in the hall.

When Eiselle looked up from a pallet she was fixing for the wounded, she saw Dashiell just inside the door and it appeared he was looking for something. Or someone. Curious, Eiselle stood up and started heading in his direction. When he caught sight of her, very quickly, he headed in her direction.

"Dash," Eiselle said as she rushed to him. "Are you well?"

Dashiell was exhausted. Every line, every emotion, was showing on his sweaty, grimy face as he looked at Eiselle. Without answering her, he took her by the arm and pulled her away from the servants and the bustle of the great hall.

"Come with me," he said. "I must speak to you."

Eiselle was hesitant. "I cannot leave," she said. "Lady de Winter has put me in charge of the hall. We are to expect many wounded. Was the battle terrible?"

Dashiell couldn't stand it; the woman had no idea of what she was about to face and his heart was breaking into a million pieces for her. What had he told her? That Bric MacRohan always returns from a battle? He'd sworn that to her, and she believed him. It was true that Bric was returning, but not in the same condition as when he left.

God, he felt so very guilty.

"Terrible enough," he said, pulling her along even though she was reluctant. "Selly, Lady de Winter has sent me to you. Bric has been wounded."

Eiselle stared at him a moment as if she didn't quite understand what he was saying. But as she gazed into his eyes and saw the despondency in the depths, it began to occur to her that something was amiss. Something terrible had happened.

To Bric? Was it really true? That which she'd been promised wouldn't happen had apparently happened. Bric had been wounded.

But... it wasn't possible! Hadn't she been given assurances? Hadn't Bric himself promised her that nothing would happen to him and that he would return? Nay... it simply wasn't possible.

... was it?

As Eiselle's knees locked up and her breath caught in her throat, she could only think to ask one thing.

"How badly?"

It was a question Dashiell didn't want to answer. He blinked once, twice, and then tears began to pool in his eyes, tears that he quickly flicked away.

"Badly enough," he said huskily. "Selly, you must listen to what I am to tell you. That will give you an indication of what you are about to face."

That sounded as if he were about to tell her something horrible, indeed, and her composure took a hit. The room began to sway. Eiselle whimpered as she gripped Dashiell with both hands because her legs couldn't seem to support her.

"God, no," she gasped. "What happened? Where is he?"

Dashiell held on to her, fearful of what would happen if he let her go. "He is being brought in from one of the wagons," he said. "Is there somewhere else to put him other than the great hall? He will need peace and quiet if... if..."

"If *what?*" Eiselle practically cried.

Dashiell knew he wasn't doing a very good job of telling Eiselle what had happened, but he was handicapped with his own grief and guilt. He felt as if all of this was his fault; he'd been the one to propose the marriage. He'd been the one to summon the de Winter army for Holdingham. Now, Bric was badly wounded. Mortally, Dashiell thought.

It was a struggle to overcome the remorse he was feeling.

"Listen to me," he said, grasping her by the arms and forcing her to look at him. "I must tell you what happened. Bric was hit by an arrow in the chest. The surgeon managed to remove the arrow and the arrowhead, but what it left in its wake is a sucking chest wound. This happened two days ago and since then, Bric has been in a very bad condition. The surgeon did what he could to pack the wound and sew it up but, earlier today, Bric started showing signs of a fever. If there is poison in his chest, his chances of survival are not good. Sweetheart, you married a warrior and I am so very sorry that this had to happen. Bric MacRohan has never been injured on the field of battle, so for this to happen... everyone is deeply shocked."

Eiselle stared at him and as he watched, the tears began to pop out of her eyes and her face crumpled. *Bric MacRohan has never been injured on the field of battle*, he said. But at Holdingham, he was. It suddenly occurred to Eiselle why.

The talisman!

Bric had given her his talisman, and the one time he'd been without it, an arrow had found its mark. When Eiselle realized that she had been the cause, she couldn't control her anguish. To ease her fear of battle, Bric had given up the one thing that he believed in and the very thing that protected him over all.

Now, she knew what had happened.

She'd left him vulnerable.

"I know why," she whispered. "God help me, I know why. Dash, take me to him. Take me *now*!"

Dashiell didn't think it was a good idea. "Your hysteria will not help him," he said. "Selly, I know this is difficult for you, but you must not be hysterical. If Bric sees that, it will crush him. You must be strong for him, do you hear? Stronger than you have ever been in your life. I know you are capable of it. You *must* be capable of it. For Bric's sake, you must try."

He was right. God help her, he was right. Eiselle struggled to stop her weeping, to stop the panic and grief that was threatening to explode in all directions. Nodding quickly, unsteadily, she wiped at her tears, brushing them away, and took great gulps of air to steady herself.

"I will try," she said breathlessly. "I *will*, I swear it. Dash... *please* take me to him."

He still didn't like the idea. "You are needed much more to prepare a private place for him," he said, hoping to distract her from demanding to go to him again. "Where can we take him?"

Eiselle's thoughts and emotions were scattered, but she managed to focus on his question. "His... his chamber is near the entry," she said, pointing to the door that had been kept closed since the army's departure. "That is his chamber. We can put him there."

Dashiell turned her in the direction of the closed door. "Then go," he said, praying the woman would find the strength he hoped she had. "Go and prepare the bed for him. Clear out the clutter and start a fire so that the chamber warms. They are bringing Bric in now and we will take him right to that chamber where you will be waiting for him. Let your face be the one he sees when he opens his eyes."

Eiselle nodded, still a bit unsteadily, but at least she was standing on her own. Kissing her on the head, Dashiell rushed from the hall as Eiselle headed towards Bric's chamber. There was a great deal of commotion in the hall now as some of the walking wounded began coming in through the entry, but she was completely focused on Bric's chamber, just as Dashiell had asked. She found herself praying to a God she'd never given much notice to that Bric would, indeed, heal. She felt like a hypocrite, but this was a desperate time. She felt as if she had no one else to turn to.

Just as Eiselle put her hand on the door latch, she happened to catch a glimpse of Manducor as the man helped one of the servants seat a wounded soldier against the wall. Remembering what he'd told her about having tended battle wounds, she knew that she needed the man's help. She needed everything he could provide. As she put her hand on the door latch, she called out to him.

"Manducor!"

Hearing his name, he looked up and saw Eiselle over near a half-open door, waving him over. He came, shuffling as quickly as Eiselle had ever seen him move.

"What is it?" he asked.

Eiselle's throat was so tight with emotion that she could barely speak. "My husband," she murmured. "He has been injured. They are bringing him in now and I require your assistance."

With that, she opened the door and Manducor followed. His expression was wrought with concern.

"I am very sorry, Lady MacRohan," he said. "Very sorry, indeed. What would you have me do?"

Eiselle began yanking the linens off the bed; they were in a messy pile, as was the room in general. "You said that you have tended battle wounds," she said. "You will help me tend him."

Manducor saw what she was doing and lent a hand to help her strip the bed. "How badly injured is he?"

The tears threatened; oh, God, how they threatened. "They say he took an arrow to the chest," she said. "He may be with fever. We will know more when we see him, but the truth is that I have no experience tending wounds or illness. My life before I came to Narborough had been a rather isolated one, so I beg you for your assistance. I do not want to lose him."

Manducor knew what it was to lose someone close. He'd watched his wife and two children die of a disease he'd had no power to stop. The physics had tried, but they'd died regardless. Therefore, he was quite sympathetic to Lady MacRohan's request. In truth, he was very sad for her.

Performing the wedding mass several days before, he'd seen how the big Irish knight had looked at his new wife, and he'd seen how she looked at him. There had been interest there; nay, almost affection, even, which was unusual for a couple who had only just met. Clearly, they had been attentive to one another and when Lady MacRohan spoke of her husband, something in her eyes glowed.

Aye, Manducor felt very sorry for the woman. He knew what it was like to lose a loved one.

"I will help," he told her, taking charge because she couldn't seem to. "Quickly; pull the pillows off the mattress. If he has a chest wound, it will probably be better if he lays flat. Is a surgeon with him?"

Eiselle shook her head. "I do not know," she said. "There seem to be many wounded. He will have many men who need his attention, so Bric must have all of mine. And yours; *please*. He will need us both."

Manducor could see the grief in her face and how difficult this was for her. Manducor's heart, something that had been stone-cold for years, began to feel some pity for her.

"MacRohan was cruel to me at the first, but he wasn't wrong," he said. "He tried to drown me when we first met. Did you know that?"

Eiselle looked at him in shock, only to see his old eyes twinkling. "Drown you?" she repeated. "Why?"

Manducor wriggled his bushy eyebrows. "Because I was drunk and he did not want a drunk performing your marriage mass," he said. "Alas, I do not blame the man. At least he was honest about it. I appreciate a man who is honest. Now, Lady MacRohan, we must have hot water brought to us and a fire in the hearth. I will summon the nearest servant for the water and build a fire in the hearth myself. You make sure that bed is clean and ready for your husband."

Eiselle began to tend the bed, smoothing the mattress and shaking out the used linens, simply because it gave her something to do. She was so distraught and nervous that she needed something to do. But her fussing over the bed quickly ended when several men appeared in the doorway, including Dashiell and Pearce and Mylo, all of them carrying a body between them on a makeshift stretcher. Eiselle caught a glimpse of Bric's head and she quickly pointed to the bed.

"Put him on the bed," she said, straining to catch a glimpse of him with all of the men carrying him. "Be gentle with him, please."

More men flooded into the chamber, men who had been following Bric's procession into the great hall. Eiselle didn't know who the men were but it seemed to her, very quickly, that all they wanted to do was stand by and watch Bric as he was tended. Maybe they even wanted to watch him die. But she didn't want an audience for the man, and she quickly rushed to the door to chase them away.

"Please," she said. "He does not need all of you crowding the room. If you are not here to help him, then please go. Your concern is appreciated."

She began to shoo men out. When Pearce and Mylo saw what she was doing, they, too, rushed to help her, pushing men out but being somewhat polite about it. They knew how worried the army was for their High Warrior.

With Pearce and Mylo clearing the room, Eiselle turned for the bed. She could hear Manducor sending for hot water and somewhere over to her left, someone else was building a fire. She didn't know who it was, but she saw the movement in her periphery. There was a great deal of movement as men went to help, doing anything they could. It was a good thing, too; all Eiselle could see in front of her was Bric as they laid him upon the bed.

That was when her entire world came crashing down.

The sight of Bric was, in a word, awful. He wore his leather breeches, no boots, and he was stripped from the waist up. His magnificent chest was bared to the weak light of the chamber, tightly bound from the nipples to the waist with stained, boiled linen. His eyes were closed and he seemed to have a faint sheen on his body and face, as if he were sweating, and an old man with bushy white hair and a face like an old goat bent over him, pulling at the bindings.

Eiselle moved up to the other side of the bed where the men weren't so crowded around. At that moment, all she could see was Bric's ashen face. She then focused on the man as if there was no one else in the room.

"Bric?" she whispered, reaching out to touch his clammy cheek.

"Bric, can you hear me? 'Tis me. 'Tis Eiselle."

"He cannot hear you, my lady," the old man bending over Bric spoke. "He has been unconscious for the past two hours. He does not respond at all."

A sob caught in Eiselle's throat. "He is sleeping," she said hoarsely. "I am sure he is only sleeping."

The old man looked at her. "He is a very sick man," he said. "If he was merely asleep, then he would awake if prodded. He does not waken at all."

Eiselle tore her eyes from Bric's face, glaring at the old man. "And *who* are you?" she demanded. "What do you know of any of this?"

Dashiell was standing next to the old man. "This is Weetley, Eiselle," he said quietly. "He is the de Winter surgeon. He has been with Bric the entire time."

Eiselle backed down, somewhat. "Forgive me. I have not met you yet."

The old man shook his head. "Nor I, you," he replied. "I will assume you are Lady MacRohan."

"I am."

Old Weetley seemed to look her over as if acquainting himself with the lass he'd heard rumor about. She was all anyone at Narborough could speak of since her arrival, and now he could see why. She was a pretty young thing. But Weetley was a man with no tact, living and working with men as he did. In fact, he was something of a hermit when he was not traveling with the army, which was why he and the lady had not become acquainted yet. He had a room full of mysterious potions over in the knights' quarters, and that was where he spent all of his time. After he was finished inspecting Lady MacRohan, he returned his focus to the bandages on Bric's torso.

"Your husband was hit in the chest with an arrowhead meant for a horse," he told her. "It buried itself deep and it was not easy to remove it. First, we had to break the shaft and then I had men hold your husband down as I dug out the head. There was a good deal of damage, my lady, and the arrow took mail and pieces of your husband's tunic into his body when it entered. Some of those pieces are still in his body and that is what is causing his fever, but I could not adequately operate on him in the field. We needed to bring him home for that."

Eiselle thought she was going to vomit. "Will... will you operate now?"

Weetley was oblivious to her pasty face. "Immediately. I must do it while he is unconscious so that he will not feel any pain." With that, he turned to Dashiell. "Have the men bring my medicament bag in. I will also need a fire poker, heated until it is red-hot, to cauterize the wound. And have someone tie his arms and legs to the bed in case he awakens while I am working on him. I cannot have him moving about."

As Eiselle listened, the room began to rock unsteadily. The crass old man was going to be digging into Bric's body, with nothing to dull the pain. *Be strong!* She told herself. *You must be strong!* But it was to no avail; when she heard the old surgeon speak of clean rags and bowls to contain the blood, the spinning world turned to black and Eiselle ended up on the floor.

THE SOUND OF a crackling fire was the first thing she was aware of.

It was dark. Eiselle opened her eyes to a darkened chamber, with only the glow from the fire in the hearth casting light and shadow upon the walls. It took her a moment to recognize her surroundings because it was dark, and because she was somewhat dazed, but the moment she realized where she was, she gasped and sat straight up in bed.

"Bric!" she cried.

Keeva was sitting by the fire. When she heard the gasp, she rose to her feet, rushing to the bed and putting her hands on Eiselle as the woman tried to propel herself off the mattress.

"Easy, lass," Keeva said softly. "Easy, Eiselle. Bric is in his chamber. He is being tended to."

The last thing Eiselle remembered was seeing Bric on the bed, looking as if he were dead already. The tears came.

"I must go to him," she said, trying to struggle against Keeva's grip. "Please let me go to him!"

Keeva knew she was upset, and groggy, but she also knew that the woman couldn't run off in hysterics to see her husband. Tightening her grip, she shook Eiselle hard enough to cause the woman's head to snap.

"Stop yourself here and now," Keeva hissed. "Eiselle, listen to me. Stop your hysterics or I swear I will not let you see him. I'll keep you locked up in this chamber until you come to your senses."

Eiselle looked at the woman in both shock and loathing. "Why would you keep me from him?" she demanded. "He is my husband and it is my right to be with him!"

Keeva didn't ease her grip. "It *is* your right, but I will not let you go to him and act like a fool," she said firmly. "Bric MacRohan is the greatest knight Ireland and England has ever seen, and if you are going to crumble like a foolish little girl, then you are not deserving of such a man. Do you understand me? Swallow your hysteria and be calm for Bric's sake, or I swear I'll lock you in here and throw away the key."

Eiselle was prepared for a fiery retort but it died in her throat as she realized that Keeva was absolutely right – Bric deserved a strong, stoic wife, not a foolish girl. Embarrassment swamped her and her hands flew to her mouth.

"You are right," she said, her eyes glittering with unshed tears. "You are absolutely right. I am so very ashamed."

Keeva breathed a sigh of relief, pleased she wasn't going to have a fight on her hands. "There is nothing to be ashamed of," she said, her grip on Eiselle easing. "This is the first time you've faced such a thing, so no one can blame you for your reaction. But from this moment forward, you must show how strong you are no matter how much you feel like weeping. Tears will not help Bric, but your strength will. Are you worthy of the man, lass?"

Eiselle nodded. "I am," she said. "I swear, I am."

Keeva smiled weakly and let go of her. "Then show us," she said quietly. "Weetley finished surgery on him an hour ago. He cleaned the wound of all the debris he could and stitched him up again, so now all there is to do is wait until Bric decides to awaken."

Eiselle took a long, deep breath, forcing the courage forth that she'd always hoped she had. From this point forward, she wouldn't let herself show her fear or her distress. She couldn't embarrass Bric so. If she was truly worthy of the man, then she needed to show it.

Stiffly, she climbed from the bed, smoothing back her hair which had escaped its braid.

"Is Bric with fever, still?" she asked.

Keeva nodded. "The last I heard," she said, opening the door to the chamber. "Dash has come up to your chamber a few times to inquire on your health. He told me there was no change with Bric about a half-hour ago."

They proceeded out into the short corridor, moving through the open area that smelled like a barnyard where the servants slept. As they reached the spiral stairs, Eiselle reached out and grasped her hand.

"Thank you for all you have done," she said. "I feel terrible that you were sitting with me when I am sure you wanted to sit with Bric. I swear to you that I shall not let you down. I will show you that I am worthy of him, I promise."

Keeva smiled faintly. "I know," she whispered. "Go to him, now. He is in his chamber."

"Will you come?"

Keeva shook her head. "I have other things to attend to, but I will come later."

Eiselle squeezed her hand quickly before letting it go, fleeing down the stairs and to the entry level below. As soon as she came off of the stairs, which were near the hall, she was hit by the stench of men.

It was a horrific smell, of festering wounds mingling with the smoke from the hearth, which had been kept blazing at full capacity to keep the hall warm. Eiselle's last memory was of a hall that only had a few wounded in it, but now as night set in, the cavernous chamber was lit only by torches and the raging hearth, she could see that the floor was lined with the wounded.

Servants and other soldiers, those who hadn't been injured, were making their way amongst the wounded, including Zara. Eiselle could see her, but there was no sign of Angela. Trying not to become ill from the putrid smell, Eiselle headed for Bric's chamber door.

Timidly, she opened the panel, sticking her head in and coming face to face with several men who were either standing at Bric's bedside or lingering against the walls – Dashiell, Pearce, Mylo, the dour old surgeon Weetley, and even Manducor, who was sitting right at Bric's bedside. Dashiell was the first one to greet her.

"Selly," he said, sounding relieved. "How do you feel?"

Eiselle smiled wanly at him. "I feel fine," she said. Then, she looked around the room, at the men standing vigilantly for Bric. "I am ashamed of what happened and I assure you it will not happen again. I... I suppose everyone is entitled to a moment of weakness, and I have had mine. Can someone please tell me how my husband fares?"

It was Dashiell who took her by the hand and pulled her over to Bric's bedside. "Weetley cleaned out the wound," he said quietly. "He rinsed it with wine and herbs, and stitched it tightly. Bric has not awoken yet."

Eiselle looked down at Bric's face, the color of paste. He still had that faint sheen on his skin and as she watched, every so often he would twitch. Her heart began to ache again, stronger than before, and she fought the urge to weep. She swore she wouldn't, but it was so very difficult when she looked at him. Her brave, strong husband, a man she was only just starting to know and care for, was laid out in a most horrific way.

Suddenly, Eiselle remembered the talisman that was still around her neck and she quickly pulled it off. Leaning over Bric's supine form, she put her hand on his chest, up near his neck, pressing the talisman against his clammy flesh.

"It's your talisman," she murmured. "You said you would return for it, and I have kept it safe. Remember that it has kept generations of warriors safe and now… now its magic will help you heal, Bric. I know it will."

He didn't respond to her. In truth, she hadn't expected him to. As she watched him breathe, heavily and laboriously, it was increasingly clear just how ill he was. When she put her hand on his forehead, she could feel the fever in him. It hurt to see him like this, but rather than break down about it, she was determined to play an active role in his healing. She wanted to know how the old surgeon planned to help him, and she turned to the man, who was over near the hearth.

"Now that you have cleaned the wound, what do you intend to do for him?" she asked. "Is there anything I can help you with?"

The surgeon had an iron pot over the hearth, nestled down in the coals as he brewed something that smelled as rotten as the men out in the great hall.

"There is nothing to do now but wait," he said. "But if he awakens, I have a potion for him to drink. The knights from Richard's crusade brought it back from The Holy Land. Some call it Rotten Tea, but it heals miraculously where other medicaments will not."

Eiselle wasn't so sure she liked the thought of the man giving Bric a mysterious potion from lands across the sea. Dubious, glanced up at Dashiell.

"Have you heard of this before?" she asked.

Dashiell nodded. "I have," he said. "Bread is put in warm water until a growth appears. When it turns bright blue, it is steeped with water to become a tea. It is something the men learned from the alchemists in The Holy Land, and I have heard that it is a great cure. It has been known to perform miracles."

Over next to the hearth, Manducor spoke up. "I have heard of this also," he said. "Its use is spreading because it attacks poison that men can die from."

Two men had confirmed the use of the foul-smelling brew, so

Eiselle wasn't dubious any longer. In fact, she was encouraged. "And this will cure his fever?" she asked Weetley, just to make sure.

The old man nodded. "If we can get him to drink it. But he must ingest it for it to have any effect."

Eiselle turned her focus back to Bric, who had stopped twitching and now simply lay still and quiet. Even his breathing had quieted down. She wasn't so sure that was a good thing, but she didn't say so. These men around her knew so much more than she did about wounds and injuries, and she didn't want to sound foolish by asking questions about every little thing.

It was time for her to show a little patience and trust.

Taking the hand that held the talisman, she moved to hold Bric's hand, sandwiching the talisman between her hand and his. She looked down at his hand; it was big and bloodied, the knuckles raw. It reminded her of the battle that may or may not have cost him his life. Surely, he must have been so magnificent in it. She began to caress his hand, thinking of the warrior that all men feared, a warrior now hovering on Death's door.

"Will you tell me about the battle?" she asked, to no one in particular. "Tell me how great he was so I know that this wound was not in vain. Tell me that he made a difference before his time was cut short."

Dashiell could hear both sorrow and pride in her voice, a question asked by a woman who was trying to know her husband in a way that other men did. It was possible that she would never get to know him better than she already did, so he found it a rather sad query.

Begging to know a man she might very well lose.

"You have married a great warrior, Selly," he said softly. "You have never seen anything like Bric MacRohan in battle; he fights with a confidence and skill that can only be heaven-sent. It is like watching Michael the Archangel, fighting against men who have no chance against him. I did not spend much time in battle with him, but Pearce and Mylo did. They can tell you more than I."

Hearing their names, Pearce and Mylo perked up. Mylo looked at

Pearce because he was the one who had spent more time with Bric. It was also Pearce who had been with Bric when he'd been struck down, and there was a huge amount of guilt as a result.

The man had been wrestling with his guilt since it had happened, and it was something that grew worse by the hour. Bric himself had assured him that it had not been his fault, nor was he blameworthy, but Pearce still felt as if he could have done something... *should* have done something... to prevent Bric's injury.

He felt like a failure and, now, he had to face Bric's wife with what he'd done.

He felt sick.

"Lady MacRohan," Pearce said, scratching his forehead in an exhausted gesture, "I have been fighting with Bric for several years. I have never known a man who fights better from one battle to the next. And by that, I mean that his skill and his talents seem to grow sharper and bolder. Our army was to hold the line against the French, who wanted very badly to lay siege to Holdingham Castle. The battle started with the archers, but when the French ran low on ammunition, the hand-to-hand combat started. Bric rushed through the French lines, cutting off heads and arms and... forgive me, my lady. That was probably more than you wanted to hear."

Eiselle looked up at him, seeing that he looked rather mortified, as if he'd told her something that was too much for her delicate ears. But Eiselle smiled at him, letting him know that she wasn't offended.

"It is of no matter," she assured him. "I asked you to tell me what you know of him, through your eyes. What you see is a great warrior. What I see is the kind and lovely man that I married. I find it remarkable that we are speaking of the same man."

Pearce grinned at her, lopsided, looking at Mylo, who also snorted. "We do not think of him as kind and lovely," Pearce said. "Neither do the French."

Eiselle laughed softly, an unexpected moment of humor in the midst of a dreadful situation. After that, she looked at Bric rather adoringly.

"That is what I see in him," she said quietly, gazing upon his pale face. "Mayhap I am the only one."

Dashiell put a hand on her shoulder. "You *should* be the only one to see that," he said. Then, he patted her shoulder and dropped his hand. "Are you comfortable enough that we may leave and find something to eat? We shan't be gone long. Just long enough to find something to eat and check on the wounded."

Eiselle nodded. "I will not leave him," she said. "Take what time you need. I will be here."

Dashiell looked at Pearce and Mylo as he jerked his head in the direction of the chamber door, inviting the men to leave. He suspected Eiselle wanted some time alone with Bric. As the knights filed out, Manducor went to the opposite side of the bed again, passing a critical eye over Bric as the man lay there and sweated.

"He seems quiet now," he said. "We must be ready to administer the tea the moment he awakens."

Eiselle continued to hold his hand, her focus on his face. But after a moment, it trailed down his torso to the stained bandages. It reminded her of the grisly operation performed on him, one that saw a surgeon digging through his innards. The mere thought made her shudder.

"Were you present when the surgeon cleaned his wound?" she asked quietly.

Manducor nodded. "I was."

"He did not awaken, did he? He did not feel... pain?"

"He did not awaken and he did not feel any pain."

Eiselle breathed a sigh of relief. "Thank God," she muttered. Then, she looked up at Manducor as he leaned over Bric and peeled back an eyelid, looking into his right eye. "Is He speaking to you now? God, I mean. You said that He told you not to return to your church because you were needed here. Is God speaking to you about Bric?"

Manducor heard such hope and fear in her voice. The poor lass was desperate for help for her husband, for encouragement that he would recover. The truth was that he couldn't give her such encouragement, not after he saw all of the poison the surgeon cleaned out of MacRohan's chest. Truthfully, it would take a miracle to heal the man, but Manducor wasn't going to tell her that. Right now, she had faith that he would recover.

Manducor wasn't going to destroy that faith.

"He is not speaking to me about MacRohan," he told her. "That does not mean He won't. But I think you should talk to your husband and tell him to get well. He will want to please you, my lady."

"Do you think it will work?"

"It is worth a try."

Eiselle looked at Bric's unconscious face, taking the priest's words to heart. "Bric?" she said softly. "Can you hear me? I hope you can. The surgeon wishes to give you something to help your fever, but you must awaken so that you may drink it. You *must* wake up, Bric. You must get better. I… I cannot lose you. Not when I just found you."

Surprisingly, Eiselle didn't weep with her words, but no words were ever more heartfelt. Even Manducor could feel the sincerity, the utter hope that Bric could hear her in his haze of unconsciousness.

"He will hear you, my lady," he muttered. "Keep speaking to him. He will hear you."

Eiselle did. As Manducor went back over to the hearth where Weetley was stirring the tea that smelled like a horse's arse, they could hear Eiselle speaking sweetly to Bric, soft words from a wife to a husband, deeply personal words that Manducor tried to ignore. It wasn't right that he should hear such things, but the deep affection that the newly married couple had for each other was something that was already strong and true. Manducor had been blessed with such feelings for his wife, so he recognized those sentiments when he saw them.

They were as rare as rubies and twice as precious, but he knew that all he could do for the knight and his lady was pray, so pray he did.

For once, he hoped that God would hear him.

CHAPTER ELEVEN

Two days later

T HE FEVER WAS gone but he still wouldn't awaken.

Eiselle hadn't left Bric's side since the night he'd been brought in to Narborough with his terrible injury. She'd bathed the man, changed his bandages, and sat by his side every single minute of the day and night. She wouldn't even go to bed, not even when Keeva begged her, instead choosing to sleep with her head on the mattress beside Bric as she sat in a chair next to the bed. It was uncomfortable, and she awoke with a stiff neck and back, but she ignored her discomfort. All that mattered was taking care of Bric, and she wanted to be there should he need her.

Manducor had been there most of the time, too, because he had more experience in such things. He would check Bric's pulse and his breathing, freeing Weetley up to tend to the men in the hall. Out of the eighteen hundred men who had gone to Holdingham, seventy-eight had died and they had over three hundred wounded, so Weetley had his hands full with the wounded in the hall and also in the troop house, where they had taken some of the lesser wounded men.

But almost three days after their return, some men were taking a turn for the worse while others were showing signs of healing. They were starting to lose some men to infection, and the dead began to pile up. St. Peter and St. Paul's church was just to the east of Narborough Castle and Daveigh had already spoken to the priests about burying the dead in a mass grave to the east of the church. The priests had agreed, and soldiers had been sent to dig the mass grave. Daveigh wasn't willing to let the stench of the dead to start offending the women at Narborough, so the decision was made to start moving the dead over to the churchyard the following day.

But Eiselle was oblivious to that, and to everything else going on. Dashiell had remained for a couple of days after Bric's injury, for as long as he could, but he had an army waiting for him, an army with wounded that had remained at Holdingham because moving them back to the seat of Savernake would take several days. Dashiell had wounded men he needed to see and plans to make to return to Ramsbury Castle, so after two days of waiting around to see if Bric would live or die, Dashiell was forced to leave.

Eiselle had promised to send him word of Bric's condition, and she'd been driven to tears by Dashiell's painful farewell to his old friend. She'd never seen such camaraderie between men, but in observing Dashiell and Pearce and Mylo, and even Daveigh, she had been given a glimpse of just how much these men meant to one another. It was a loyalty that went beyond politics – it was a loyalty that was in their blood. She'd bid Dashiell a sad farewell as the man returned to his own army.

Now, three days after Bric's return to Narborough, Eiselle was starting to feel the stress of waiting for a man who refused to awaken. As Manducor had instructed her, she'd spoken to the man constantly, keeping up a steady stream of chatter, praying that he would hear her and open his eyes. But on the third day of Bric's unconsciousness, she took to singing to him, singing every song she could think of, including the one she'd sung to him on their wedding night.

"I have loved, all my life, only thee;
The stars know thy name, the sky weeps at your beauty.
I pray thou will return to my arms,
but if not,
I pray to see thy face every night in my dreams."

It was such a bittersweet song, with new meaning these days. Eiselle was too afraid to ask Weetley if Bric was deteriorating, so she simply kept up her singing, her chatter, bathing Bric's face, arms, and chest with cool water, and making sure the hearth was stoked so the room remained warm. She didn't want him to catch a chill.

As the third day began to move into night and the great torches in the hall were lit, Eiselle sat next to Bric's bedside, watching her husband waste away before her very eyes. She'd done so well over the past three days, with no hysterics or tears, but time was wearing on her now. As she looked at the man, feeling the pangs of grief pull at her, she stroked his sticky blond hair and sang softly to him.

O lovely one… my lovely one…
The years will come… the years will go…
But still you'll be… my own true love…
Until the day… we'll meet again…

Her throat was tight with emotion as she finished the song, unable to go any further. She simply wasn't as strong as she thought she was because the anguish she'd been fighting off for three days was now clawing at her, gutting her, begging her to release her emotions as the future she'd hope to have with a man she adored was slipping away. As the fire in the hearth snapped, sending sparks into the room, Eiselle finally lay her exhausted head down on the mattress next to Bric, feeling overwhelmed and despondent.

Is this how it will end, God? She thought, putting her hand on Bric's chest in a protective gesture. *Will I become a widow, with dreams of a life that never was, without a man I know I could have grown to love?*

The tears came as she closed her eyes, with the intention of resting only for a moment.

"Please, Bric," she whispered, her cheek against his big bicep. "Please do not leave me. Please do not let this be over before it begins."

There was no response to a question full of agony. Before Eiselle realized it, she was asleep.

HE'D BEEN DREAMING of angels.

They were singing to him, in a voice so pure and lovely that he wanted to listen to them forever. He'd been dreaming of someplace hot and bright, with a blinding white light, and heat that made him sweat. He'd been a little too young to go on King Richard's crusade to The Holy Land, but he'd heard from others that the heat had been intense. Pale, white knights had returned with skin the color of tanned leather. He'd always imagined what that kind of heat felt like, and now he knew.

He'd been kissed by it.

Gradually, the white light faded and the singing stopped, and then he felt cold and alone. He'd never felt more alone in his life. Where was the singing angel, the one who had kept him company and had given him comfort? Oddly enough, he never saw the angel who had done the singing. He could only hear her, but she sounded familiar. He just couldn't place her. He thought he could remain in that warm, blissful land, but it dissipated, like mist, and then he heard the crackling of a hearth.

His ears began to buzz and when he breathed, he was aware of pain in his torso. He took a breath and he felt as if he were being stabbed on his left side. Bric struggled to open his eyes, but his eyelids felt as if they weighed more than the big stones that comprised Narborough. He could barely get them open, and even then, they were only open a slit. He could see that he was in his chamber off the entry in Narborough's keep and he turned his head slightly, seeing that there was a small arm across the right side of his body, with the hand resting on his chest. Turning his head just a little more and looking down, he could see that Eiselle's face was pressed up against his right bicep, and it was her arm that was draped over him.

"My lord?"

Someone was speaking to him and his eyes, red and swollen, moved off to his left to see the priest standing there. It was the drunken, slovenly man who had performed his marriage mass, only he didn't look drunk or slovenly now. He looked quite lucid and, in truth, quite concerned as he gazed down at him.

Bric tried to speak, but his throat was raw and parched. He could only whisper.

"How... long?" he murmured.

Manducor moved closer so the man wouldn't have to strain himself. "How long have you been unconscious?" he asked. When Bric nodded, barely, Manducor answered. "At least three days, my lord. How do you feel?"

Bric wasn't even sure he could answer that, so he tried to shake his head, but that didn't work out particularly well, either. He could barely move. Manducor sensed that, so he didn't press the man; he simply told him the situation, as he suspected a straightforward man like MacRohan would want.

"You were wounded by an arrow five days ago," he said. "You were brought back to Narborough where the surgeon, Weetley, has cleaned the wound and stitched it. You have been very sick, my lord, and now that you are awake, it is important that you drink a potion the surgeon has brewed for you. I know you are weak, but your lady wife and I will help you."

Manducor reached over him to wake Eiselle, but Bric found his voice. "Nay," he whispered hoarsely. "Let her sleep."

Manducor paused. "She will be angry if we do not wake her," he said. "She has not left your side, my lord. She has been here the entire time, singing to you and speaking to you. She has been quite worried for you."

She has been here the entire time, singing to you. Those words echoed in Bric's groggy mind. The angel singing in his dreams – had that been her? That sweet voice that kept him comforted, that kept him alive? He found himself turning to Eiselle, who was sleeping so heavily

159

against his arm that she was drooling.

"She… she has been here?" he rasped.

Manducor nodded. "She has not left you," he said. Then, he looked down at Bric's left hand and reached down to unwind something from his wrist. He held it up. "She returned your talisman, my lord. She seemed to think it meant something to you."

His talisman. Bric moved his focus away from Eiselle once again to see Manducor hanging the talisman in his face. That great and noble pendant that had been passed down through generations of a great Irish family until it was given to him.

Odd; it hadn't even occurred to him that he hadn't been wearing it when the arrow pierced his chest. Not once did he lament not having worn it, or having left it with his wife. It was something that had been with him since nearly the moment he'd seriously swung a sword, and the battle at Holdingham had been the first time he'd fought a battle without it. It was true that he'd gone to kiss it on more than one occasion during the fight, as that was a habit with him, but he'd never once regretted leaving it with Eiselle.

The woman who hadn't left his side the entire time he'd been ill.

My devoted angel…

"Put it on me," he whispered.

Manducor obliged, helping him lift his head as he put the chain around his neck. But the jostling awoke Eiselle and her head shot up when she realized that Bric was being moved. All she saw was Manducor lifting the man's head and she bolted to her feet, reaching out to slap Manducor's hand away.

"What are you doing?" she hissed groggily. "You will not move him about like that!"

"Eiselle," Bric murmured. "'Tis okay, *mo chroí.* He is putting the talisman on me."

At the sound of his hissing, raspy voice, Eiselle looked at Bric in shock, realizing the man was speaking. He was awake! Her eyes flew open wide at the realization and she cried out, slapping a hand over her mouth in shock.

"Bric!" she said through splayed fingers. "You have awakened!"

He smiled faintly – oh, so faintly – and his eyes glimmered weakly at her. "I had to see your beautiful face again."

Eiselle's shock turned to joy, and a grin of unimaginable brilliance spread over her lips. "How do you feel?"

He didn't answer her right away. He simply gazed at her. Then, his right hand slowly lifted, his hand coming up to cup her face as she looked at him. It was a moment of tremendous sweetness as he touched her soft skin, reacquainting himself with those lovely features. More and more, he was convinced she had been the angel singing to him in his dreams. His heart swelled in ways he couldn't even begin to comprehend, overwhelmed with her dedication.

"I understand you have been with me the entire time," he said.

She put her hand over his as he touched her face. It was the most magnificent touch imaginable and her heart, so frightened by his wound and illness, began to beat again, just a little. There was hope in his touch; hope that he might actually survive.

Hope that he would heal.

"Nearly the entire time," she said. "I will admit that I have not been around an injured man before, and the night they brought you in, I... I became a little sick over it. But I recovered quickly and I've not left you since. I wanted to be here when you awoke."

His big, rough fingers caressed her cheek, her jaw. "Sick? What do you mean?"

She looked embarrassed. "I... well, I fainted. I've never seen such a wound before and... it overwhelmed me, I suppose."

The corners of his lips twitched. "And you shall never see one like it again, God willing," he said. "In answer to your question, I feel a good deal of pain. Will I live?"

Her smile faded. "You will," she said firmly. "I will not permit you to do anything else. Weetley has cleaned your wound, and Manducor and I have been doing all we can to ensure there is no poison."

"Manducor?" he asked, turning slightly to see the priest. "Are you a healer?"

Manducor shook his head. "A former knight, my lord," he said quietly. "I have tended many a battle wound."

That statement caused Bric to look at Manducor through new eyes, perhaps with a little more respect now. *A former knight.* He briefly wondered why the man had turned to the priesthood, but it was only a fleeting thought. In truth, he was surprised the priest had been so attentive to him, considering he'd been fairly rough with the man. But now, the priest's presence made more sense – perhaps the former knight in Manducor had understood Bric's manner.

"Then you have my thanks," Bric said quietly. "And I am sure Lady MacRohan is thankful, as well."

Eiselle nodded. "He has been quite helpful," she said. "In fact, your fever is gone but Weetley made a terrible-smelling tea for you to drink. He wanted you to drink the moment you awakened, so I am sorry to say that you must take it."

The smile on his lips grew as he looked at her. "You sound as if you are giving me orders, Lady MacRohan."

"I am."

Eiselle held her ground, hoping he wouldn't rebel against such a statement. Instead, he emitted a noise that sounded like a chuckle.

"Aye, madam," he said. "Give me a kiss and I shall take whatever potion you wish."

Eiselle kissed him, gladly. Manducor turned away as the married couple shared a private moment, a sweet kiss that was as pure and fresh and new as the earth on the day that God had created it. It was a kiss full of the promise of hope and affection, a sign that something deep was brewing between the pair, something a stolen French arrow couldn't destroy.

There was hope for a new future on the horizon now.

In the end, Bric drank the Rotten Tea that tasted as foul as anything he'd ever tasted in his life. He drank it twice every day, for the next week, until his wound showed signs of adequate healing and his health began to return. Weetley permitted him to eat beef broth but little else, and Eiselle sat by his side and fed him for the first few days until he was strong enough to sit up and feed himself. Then, it was beef broth with pieces of bread soaked in it. He ate it ravenously.

Little by little, Bric MacRohan began to heal.

As the days passed, and finally the weeks passed, it was clear that Bric was going to recover. Within ten days of his injury, he was able to stand, and then he began taking short walks around the great hall with his wife, who held on to him tightly as if she could keep a man of his size stabilized. Manducor, or even Pearce or Mylo or Daveigh, would usually follow around behind them, making sure Lady MacRohan didn't get into any trouble she couldn't handle. But Bric remained rock solid, demonstrating the sheer resilience of the man.

Everything seemed fine, and there was a sense of relief and joy around Narborough as de Winter's High Warrior recovered both his strength and his health. Physically, the man was rapidly healing. Mentally, however, was another story.

The worst was yet to come.

CHAPTER TWELVE

Mid-August

"**H**AVE YOU NOTICED anything different about Bric?"

The question came from Daveigh, directed at Pearce, on the cusp of a fine August day. A storm had blown through the night before, leaving the following day bright and blustery. In the outer bailey of Narborough Castle, in the area near the troop house where the men would train or stage, Bric was running some new recruits to the de Winter war machine through a series of drills.

But it wasn't the Bric they'd known in the past.

The High Warrior that had made a name for himself was a man of great skill and talent when it came to training men, but he was also a man of little patience. He'd been known to go head-to-head with a soldier or even a knight who was too timid or too hardheaded to understand what he was being taught, and the pupil would always lose. Bric wasn't beyond punching men in the face, or slicing them with his broadsword simply to teach them a lesson. That was simply his way, and the men would learn very quickly as a result.

But the Bric nowadays didn't seem willing to push the men that hard. In fact, he almost seemed pleasant in his training these days, which wasn't like Bric at all. The knights had noticed it, as had Daveigh, but no one was willing to say anything about it, hoping that Bric would regain whatever confidence he'd lost as a result of that terrible wound, but as the weeks passed and nothing seemed to change, it was Daveigh who said something to Pearce about it.

Those fateful words, what they'd all been thinking, had finally been uttered.

"Different?" Pearce turned to his liege as they both stood on the edge of the training area watching Bric and the newer recruits. "What do you mean, my lord?"

Daveigh was feeling greatly depressed by the Bric he was witnessing these days, meaning he had no patience for Pearce's ambiguity. He eyed the man unhappily.

"You know exactly what I mean," he said quietly. "Be honest, Pearce – we've been watching Bric with the men for the past several weeks and things are... different. I was hoping it was simply because of his brush with death, the fact that he was physically still recovering, but his entire manner is different these days. This is not the Bric MacRohan we knew before that arrow hit him in the chest."

Pearce was fiercely loyal to Bric. He knew what Daveigh was driving at, but he wasn't going to agree with the man.

"Give him time," he said. "He nearly lost his life two months ago. Tasting death is going to change a man, but he will come around. It is not as if we are talking about an unseasoned weakling. We are speaking of Bric MacRohan."

Daveigh sighed heavily, watching as Bric grabbed a sword out of a soldier's hand, pushed the man back, and then swung the sword in a controlled fashion as he explained something to him. Two months ago, Bric probably would have drawn his own sword against a man who was having trouble learning a technique and engage him in swordplay that would have eventually drawn blood. As he watched Bric explain something rather than demonstrate it, he shook his head.

"I know," Daveigh muttered. "Mayhap you are correct; mayhap he simply needs time. I suppose almost losing his life is bound to shake him up, because Bric has never faced such a thing. He has never even come close. But this... it looks as if he is nursemaiding the men rather than being the master he needs to be."

Pearce wasn't going to agree with him, even if it was true. "If it is bothering you so much, have you spoken with him?"

Daveigh shook his head. "Nay," he said. "Truthfully, I am simply glad to have him back. If his dance with death has changed him somewhat, I suppose it is a small price to pay. But this is not the man I have known all of these years. I am not sure I like it."

Pearce watched Bric as he handed the sword back over to the soldier so the man could try what he'd been shown.

"It is still Bric," he said quietly. "I simply think you should give him time. He will come around."

Daveigh looked at him. "And what if he does not?" he asked. "What if we are summoned by another ally and Bric must lead the army? Will he lead with the same fearless bloodlust we are used to, or will he shepherd the men like a dog herding sheep, fearful they are going to be injured?"

Pearce looked at him. "I have every faith in Bric MacRohan, my lord," he said. "I have heard of injuries changing men and their outlook. Bric has much to consider these days, mostly a wife he adores. He has much to live for and it was something he nearly lost two months ago. Everything changed for him, all at once, so I do not believe we should judge him so harshly right now. Give him time to become accustomed to everything that has happened to him and I am sure we will see the old Bric make a return."

Daveigh knew that what Pearce said was very true; much had changed for Bric in a short amount of time. Drawing in a deep breath, he exhaled thoughtfully.

"I suppose I simply miss the man who called everyone a pisswit," he said. "Bric's insults were the only fun we ever have around here. Why does he not insult men anymore? I miss that."

Pearce grinned. "I am sure that will come again, with time."

Daveigh eyed the young knight. "You are wiser than you look, de Dere."

"Thank you, my lord."

With a smirk, Daveigh wandered away, heading off to the stables to see to a new horse he'd purchased recently and leaving Pearce to watch

Bric instruct men with a kindness unlike him. In truth, Pearce missed the old Bric, too.

As Pearce pondered the situation, Eiselle had just exited the keep with Zara. Over the past few weeks, the women had become friends. As Keeva had once told Eiselle, Zara was a little dim-witted, and liked to drink excessively, but she was quite humorous and Eiselle found her to be honest, sometimes brutally so. Bric had told her the story about Pearce and how the man believed Zara had tricked him into marrying her, but Eiselle didn't believe it. Zara didn't seem manipulative, certainly not like Angela was.

Angela, in fact, had increasingly isolated herself against the other woman, hiding out with her naughty son, but she would make an appearance at the evening meal on occasion, complaining or trying to guilt her husband into doing something she wanted him to do. It didn't matter what it was – dancing, a new pony for their son, or any number of things she felt were important. She would whine, Mylo would mostly ignore her, and eventually she would leave the meal in tears. Edward no longer made an appearance at any of the meals where the adults were present, but Angela would take him outside daily so the child could run about and get into trouble.

Even now, Eiselle and Zara could see Angela and Edward in the inner bailey as Edward chased the waterfowl that were basking in the sun on the banks of the moat. Ducks were flying in all directions as Edward ran through them, kicking at them. Eiselle and Zara watched from a distance.

"I do not suppose he could fall into the moat, could he?" Eiselle muttered.

Zara couldn't hold back the laughter. "I have often hoped for that myself," she said. "Somehow, Angela always seems to grab him before he can fall in."

"Pity."

The two chuckled as they made their way to the small gatehouse that opened up into the outer bailey beyond.

"Edward was a cute babe," Zara said. "In fairness to Angela, she had a difficult pregnancy with him. Weetley made her stay in her bed for months on end, so when Eddie was born, one would have thought Angela was the only woman in the world to have ever given birth to a child. Lady de Winter requested that I attend the birth and I swear I never want to have children after watching Angela go through her dramatics. It was harrowing."

Eiselle grinned. "I understand that childbirth *can* be very painful."

Zara nodded. "That is true, but I would expect that some women bear the pain with some dignity. She had no dignity at all."

Eiselle chuckled. "I shall remind you of that should I ever attend a birth of your child."

Zara rolled her eyes. "If I behave as Angela did, slap me."

"I shall remind you of *that*, too."

It was Zara's turn to chuckle. But quickly, her smile faded. "I pray that someday you will have the opportunity," she said. "I wish I knew what God had planned for me. I know that Pearce would like a son. I was pregnant when we married, you know, but I lost the child shortly thereafter. Pearce has never believed that, but it is true. He thinks that I tricked him into marriage."

The subject of the mysterious pregnancy came to light, quite unexpectedly. Eiselle pretended that she'd heard nothing about it. "Why would he believe such a thing?" she asked. "Surely you would not lie about something like that."

Zara lifted her shoulders. "Nay, I would not," she said. "But he did not want to marry me. Pearce did not want to marry anyone; he simply wanted to love women and leave them. I lived in King's Lynn with my parents when we met; my father is a tanner and Pearce purchased boots from him. He was quite taken with me, as I was with him, and I will admit that I allowed him to take... liberties. But I could not help it; I loved him so. When I became pregnant, I told him and he did not believe it was his child. He refused to marry me but I told him I would tell my father if he did not, so he did. Still, he has not let it stop him from seducing other women. He thinks I do not know that, but I do."

Eiselle was looking at Zara quite seriously. "Oh... Zara," she breathed. "I am so sorry to hear that. I do not understand how he could do such a thing to you."

Zara shrugged. "It is my fault," she said. "I wanted the man to marry me. I did not care that I was trying to curb his nature in order to do it. He likes women and does not see his marriage to me as an obstacle to that."

Eiselle frowned. "Well, I do not like it. Does Bric know?"

"They all know."

Eiselle was quite unhappy by the sad tale. "Then I cannot imagine he approves of it. What a terrible thing for Pearce to do."

Zara put her hand on Eiselle's arm. "Please, do not tell Bric that I told you," she said. "I do not want him to know because it might get back to Pearce, and I do not want my husband to know that it bothers me. That would make me ashamed."

"What do you mean?"

Zara glanced up, seeing the training field off to their right, where her husband was standing on the fringes, watching Bric train some newer recruits.

"It is that dignity I spoke of," she said quietly. "Angela had none in childbirth, and she continues to have none. For me, it is different – dignity is all that I have. As long as Pearce does not know his behavior bothers me, then I retain my dignity. But the moment he knows I am distressed by his behavior, it is as if I lose any semblance of pride. I lose my dignity. Therefore, I have to pretend his behavior does not bother me because only then can I live with it. I do not know if that makes any sense, but it is the way I feel."

She was right – it didn't make much sense to Eiselle, but she didn't argue with her friend. "I cannot pretend to know how you feel," she said. "All I know is that if Bric did such things to me, I could not stand it. It would destroy me."

Zara looked at her. "That is because you love him," she said. "Everyone knows that. We can all see it. And Bric loves you; he would never do anything to hurt you. It is different with Pearce and me – there is much love lost between us. I wish I could fix it, but I cannot."

"Then you do not love him any longer?"

"I do. I always will. But everything that fed that love is gone until my feelings are but fragile shells of what once were. They are hollow. But that does not mean they are gone."

Eiselle simply patted her on the arm, unsure what to say to her. Zara's relationship with Pearce was complicated, at best. But Zara was right about one thing – Eiselle loved Bric. *Mo chroí*, he called her. *My heart.* It was the sweetest thing she could imagine, and even thinking of her husband made her heart flutter and her spirit soar. She felt as if she were walking on clouds, every moment of every day. This had been her life for the past several weeks and it was as if she couldn't remember her life before Bric. Now, all she cared about, or looked forward to, was her husband.

He had become her entire life.

They were nearing the training field now and they could see the men crowded up around it. These were new recruits, from what Bric had said, men that had been gleaned from the surrounding countryside, farmers and laborers who were looking for something better in life.

De Winter had a great reputation for being fair, and schooling men, and Bric was a huge part of that reputation. She knew that he trained the men because he spoke of them every night when he was finished with his duties. Sometimes they would sit with Pearce and Mylo and Daveigh, eating their evening meal and speaking of the new recruits, but sometimes she and Bric would sit off on their own and talk quietly. Sometimes they would even take their meal in their chamber so they could be alone, and those meals always ended up with making love in their cozy bed.

It was those meals that Eiselle liked best.

Life at Narborough went on after the battle at Holdingham, with Bric returning to duty and Eiselle finding her own place at the castle.

Usually, she stayed to the keep and went about her duties for Keeva, which mostly consisted of sewing or overseeing the servants in their duties, as Eiselle had a kind but firm hand when it came to dealing with the servants. But today, Eiselle had come to see her husband because she had been repairing some clothing for the man and needed to have him try them on so she could finish them.

It was true that she could wait until he was finished for the day, but he was usually so exhausted that she didn't want to bother him with such things. Moreover, she didn't usually see him during the day and today, she was missing him just a little. Even just a glimpse of the man or a few words from him would mean the world to her.

So, she wandered out into the outer bailey and, even now, stood well away from the group of men who were in training. Zara stood with her for a few moments, but Pearce was also watching Bric and her gaze lingered on her husband before she muttered an excuse and headed off. When Eiselle last saw her, she was heading in the direction of the kitchens. She thought it rather sad that Zara didn't feel the excitement for her husband that Eiselle felt for hers, but given the state of their marriage, Eiselle didn't blame her. But she also refused to let the woman bring down her mood, in any fashion, so she remained in place as she watched Bric demonstrate a few hand-to-hand combat skills.

Even just a few weeks ago, no one knew if Bric would be capable of continuing his duties at Narborough as he had. No one knew what the future would hold but, these days, the future was bright and beautiful as far as Eiselle was concerned.

Bric was back, as strong as he ever was, and she loved watching him work with the men. It made her heart swell with pride. She was so fixated on Bric that she hardly noticed Mylo as he walked in front of her, heading towards the troop house. He said something to her but she didn't respond, so he stopped and said it again. Only then did Eiselle realize he was speaking to her and she grinned, embarrassed that he'd caught her daydreaming.

"I am sorry," she said. "I did not hear you, Mylo."

Mylo smiled. "I know," he said. "Bric often has that same look when it comes to you."

Eiselle thought that was a sweet observation. "And he does not hear you, either?"

"Sometimes, he does not. I am coming to think it does no good to speak to either of you these days."

Eiselle giggled. "Again, my apologies," she said. "I did hear your voice, but not your words. If you greeted me, then I shall say good morn to you, but if you did not greet me, then give me a moment to pretend I know what you said. I will figure something out."

It was Mylo's turn to laugh. "Not to worry, Lady MacRohan," he said. "I know that you are watching Bric and that is exactly where your attention should be. I simply wished you a good day."

Eiselle dipped her head politely, smiling at the man as he walked away. She liked Mylo; he was easy-going, and very humorous when the mood struck him, and she honestly couldn't see a man like that married to a woman like Angela, but she'd never asked why he married her. As she pondered Mylo being married to a very odd woman, a voice suddenly caught her off guard.

"Greetings, Lady MacRohan."

She yelped, startled that Bric had snuck up beside her while she hadn't been paying attention. As soon as she saw who it was, she giggled uncontrollably.

"You startled me," she gasped, hand on her chest as if to still her frazzled heart. "I did not see you approach."

Bric stood next to her, his eyes twinkling. "I know," he said. "You were too busy looking at Mylo, whom I shall now have to kill because he has your attention."

Eiselle wrapped her hands around his big forearm in an affectionate gesture. "He does *not* have my attention," she said. "If you must know, I was wondering how a nice man like Mylo is married to a woman like Angela. That marriage puzzles me."

Bric's gaze flicked over to Mylo, who was still walking away. "There is no great mystery," he said. "It was arranged. And Angela seemed like a nice enough lass when she first came to Narborough. It was after she gave birth to that brat that her manner changed."

Eiselle nodded in understanding. But she didn't want to talk about Mylo and Angela. She was far more interested in her husband and her grip on him tightened as she smiled up at him.

In public for all to see, this was the most affection they would display. No hugging, no kissing, because as Bric explained it once, that was something only for the two of them to experience. He didn't want to share his happiness with everyone at Narborough. But Eiselle couldn't keep her hands off him, making it very difficult for Bric not to reciprocate.

"Then I feel sorry for Mylo," she said. "But I do not wish to speak of him. I would like to speak of you; has your day been pleasant so far?"

He smiled down at her. God, it was so incredibly easy to swallow her up in his arms and kiss her until she swooned, and he found himself fighting off the urge. His arms fairly ached to hold her.

"It has been uneventful," he said. "Some of the new recruits are as stupid as tree stumps, so progress has been slow. With all of the men who were put out of commission at Holdingham, we desperately need healthy men to fill their positions, so it is going to take some work to make these men battle-ready."

Eiselle's smile faded. "And you?" she asked quietly. "Do you feel battle-ready?"

He lifted his big shoulders, averting his gaze. "I am always battle-ready," he said. "I was born with a sword in my hand. That has not changed."

Eiselle hoped that was the truth. She, too, had heard the whispers around Narborough, that MacRohan didn't seem himself after his devastating injury, and some men were even saying that the fearless knight was no longer fearless. But she had never repeated what she'd heard to Bric because she honestly didn't believe it. The High Warrior had not lost his fearlessness; she would stake her life on it. But not having been around Bric very much before his injury, she didn't really know the man and his manner prior to that event, so all she could go on was his reputation and what she saw these days.

What she saw was a man who went about his duties, a man who was, and ever would be, de Winter's greatest knight.

She believed in him.

"I simply meant that you have had some pain in your torso when you swing a sword," she reminded him. "Does it still pain you?"

He seemed resolute. "The pain will fade. It will not stop me from doing as I must."

"Do you fear that de Winter will be called to fight again?" she asked. "I heard the servants saying that the French rebels have been moving south, to London. They say that is where Prince Louis is now, waiting for a fleet of ships from France. Is this true?"

Bric looked at her a moment without reacting. Then, he smiled weakly. "There are many rumors flying about, Lady MacRohan. I would not take what the servants say too seriously. The weak minded have vivid imaginations."

"Then it is not true?"

"I did not say that. I simply said there are many such rumors flying about, but nothing has yet been confirmed. Until it is, you should not worry about it. When the time comes, I will tell you the truth about things."

Eiselle sensed that he simply didn't want to speak on the subject, so she didn't press him. Instead, she shifted the focus to the reason why she'd come.

"As you say, Husband," she said. "I apologize if I sounded foolish with my questions."

"You did not."

"Then that would be a first," she teased. "My father used to say that everything out of my mouth was foolishness."

Bric couldn't help it; he reached up to gently stroke her cheek. "Not everything," he said quietly. "When you tell me you love me, that is not foolish."

Her cheeks flushed sweetly. "Nay, it is not."

"Tell me again."

"That I love you? You know that I do."

"I know. But I want to hear it every day."

"Then I shall tell you every day if you tell me that you love me, too."

His eyes glimmered warmly at her. "I love you," he whispered.

"And I love you. I love you madly."

They were words that fortified his heart in ways he could have never imagined. He never knew that three little words could make him feel such joy, such contentment. He very much wanted to kiss her, but his natural restraint railed against it. But he knew that if he stood here with her much longer, he wouldn't be able to resist the urge, so it was best to remove himself from temptation.

"Now that I have heard the words that will carry me through my day, I am content," he said. "But if there isn't something else you wish to discuss with me, I must return to the men. Still, it has been a welcome respite to see you."

Eiselle was touched. Bric wasn't the great flatterer other than to tell her of his love for her, but the compliments he did pay her were simple and sweet. She adored that about him. The past several weeks had been a learning experience for them both, and they were improving in their communication.

The man who never wanted to be married had learned a valuable lesson when the arrow almost ended his life – he learned that life was worth living, in all circumstances, but most especially with the right woman by his side. And Eiselle was learning about a life she could have never imagined, something romantic and sweet that she'd heard of but never believed she would experience.

For both of them, the unexpected and, in one case, unwanted marriage had become the most important thing in the world.

"Do you think I just came here to gaze adoringly at you, then?" she jested. "I really did come here for a reason and it was not to distract you from your duties. It was to ask you if you have time to try on the clothing I am repairing for you. I believe I have it right, but it would help if you would try the pieces on so I that can make any necessary adjustments."

He glanced at the group of men about twenty feet away. "I do not have the time at the moment," he said. "But, mayhap, in an hour or so. Will that be acceptable?"

She nodded. "It will."

He winked at her. "Thank you, *mo chroí.*"

Eiselle simply smiled as he turned once again and headed back to the training area where the men were practicing with wooden swords they had fashioned. Pearce had entered the activities and he broke off a group of men and took them over to the south side of the field for instruction in archery. There were targets set up on piles of hay for the men to practice on. But Eiselle paid little attention to Pearce as she turned back for the keep; her attention was on Bric until the very last moment. She wanted him to be her last memory before she turned her attention to something else.

Bric saw when his wife had headed back towards the keep, her dark hair blowing in the breeze. Even though he was reclaiming his broadsword to continue his instruction to the men, his thoughts were lingering on her. Such a lovely, sweet creature who was turning into a woman that was quite eager in his bed. She seemed to crave sexual contact as much as he did, and she needed absolutely no prompting to respond to his will. Even thinking about that made his loins feel warm, so he quickly diverted his attention. It would do no good to feel a need for his wife when he still had work to do.

But knowing what was waiting for him this night made him want to complete his work just a little faster.

With that thought on his mind, he bellowed orders to his recruits, demanding they give him their attention, and they did. He had an eager audience of both young and old men, and he resumed the lesson where he'd left off. He was teaching the men defensive tactics which, in the past, he'd taught them by physically demonstrating – and in some cases, violently – what happens when an enemy tries to kill them and how to counteract their attacks.

But today, Bric was being a little less violent about it and a little more explanatory. In truth, what Eiselle said was correct – his torso still pained him to swing a sword, and sometimes he felt he was tearing up all of the healing he'd done, which had forced him to be somewhat cautious when engaging in physical activity.

At least, that's what he told himself. The truth that he kept buried was that he didn't want to reinjure himself. For the first time in his life, he was concerned about his physical state.

It was an unusual concern, indeed.

But it was something he tried to push through, alien feelings that he'd never experienced before. As the men gathered around him once again, he pulled one young man out of the crowd and spoke to the men about the proper way of using a sword for defense rather than offense. He had the recruit properly positioned as he explained what needed to happen in the heat of battle, while over in the crowd of men who were learning how to properly hold a bow, Pearce had given one of the recruits an arrow to see if the man could properly handle it. Unfortunately, the recruit accidentally let the arrow fly and it sailed into the air, landing about two feet from Bric as he was instructing his men.

Bric didn't remember running into the keep after that.

All he remembered was something unfamiliar – the powerful sense of panic.

CHAPTER THIRTEEN

ISELLE HAD JUST sat down with one of Bric's tunics in the chamber near the keep entry that was Bric's former sleeping chamber. Bric decided to occupy Eiselle's chamber, and that was where the newlyweds spent their time, but his former chamber had been converted into a solar for the ladies.

That was where the women now spent their time, sewing or drawing or reading aloud. When the noise of the hall grew too much, they could close the doors and shut themselves in, and Keeva had moved furs and rugs and chairs and even a couch into the solar so that she and her ladies could be comfortable.

It was also an Eddie-free zone, meaning Angela was welcome but her son was not. Consequently, Angela had barely spent any time in it at all, but that was normal as of late for her. Meanwhile, Keeva and Eiselle and Zara enjoyed it as a place to call their own.

It was into this room that Eiselle was settling when she heard someone come in through the keep entry. The great doors were usually closed and when they swung back on their old iron hinges, they made a great deal of noise no matter how much the servants greased them up. Therefore, she heard the doors opening and the rapid boot falls of someone. She didn't think too much of it until she heard someone wretch, and the sound of liquid splashing on the floor of the entry.

Curious, not to mention concerned, Eiselle rose from her chair and stuck her head out of the solar just in time to see Bric rush towards the spiral stairs that led to their chamber, pause once again to vomit onto the stairs, and then disappear up the stairwell.

Throwing her sewing onto the nearest chair, Eiselle raced after him. She ran past two big puddles of vomit, up the stairs, and nearly stepped into a third puddle at the top of the stairwell. There were servants on that level and they'd already come out of their alcoves to see what the fuss was about, and Eiselle quickly instructed them to clean up the mess. She didn't mention who had left it, but the servants heard the door to her chamber slam, so they could probably guess. Still, Eiselle didn't say anything more as she rushed to her closed chamber door and lifted the latch.

The room was illuminated only by the light coming in through the lancet windows as she entered, as the fire in the hearth had long died and now there was only ash. Immediately, she spied Bric in the corner, leaning against the stone, with his hands over his face.

Greatly concerned, Eiselle came around the side of the bed, wondering why her husband was cowering in the corner and breathing as if he were about to explode.

"Bric?" she said softly. "What is wrong? Are you ill?"

His hands came away from his face and he looked at her with an expression Eiselle had never seen before. Bric not only had an unusual eye color, but the shape of his eyes was somewhat unusual as well – almond-shaped, some would call it. They were both unique and beautiful, but they were eyes that could narrow down in a slit in a flash-second, a particularly terrifying trait the man had.

At the moment, however, Eiselle didn't recognize them. They were as wide as she had ever seen them, as if Bric had been deeply shocked by something. He didn't answer her right away; he simply stared at her. Eiselle took a timid step towards him.

"Bric?" she said again, her brow furrowed in concern. "What is the matter? Are you ill?"

His mouth worked as if he wanted to say something. Then, it was as if he simply went boneless – his entire body collapsed until he was sitting on his rump in the corner, his back pressed against the wall. He couldn't even answer her, and Eiselle sank to her knees where she was standing so that she could be on his level.

Now, he was starting to frighten her.

"Please, Bric," she whispered. "What is wrong?"

He took a couple of short, panting breaths followed by one long, deep one. "I do not know," he finally said. "I was standing with the men, with a sword in my hand, and an arrow landed in the dirt a few feet away. And, suddenly, I'm running. I'm running blindly and the next I realize, I'm at the top of the stairs. Then, I'm in this room. I... I do not know what happened, only that I am here and I feel... I feel..."

Eiselle crept closer to him as he trailed off. "*What* do you feel?" she asked softly.

He was looking at her as if he couldn't breathe. "My God," he muttered. "All I could think was that I did not want to die. That arrow... I heard it... and then all I could think was that I did not want to die. I did not want to leave you."

Eiselle moved in closer, reaching out a timid hand to him. "You will not leave me," she said. "And I will not leave you. I will always be here, Bric."

She was close enough that Bric could touch her, and he did. He pulled her into a crushing embrace, burying his face against her belly as his arms went around her torso. It was almost like he was attempting to hide or, at the very least, block out whatever was troubling him so. Eiselle ended up with the man practically laying in her lap as she tried to put her arms around him to comfort him.

"I am here," she said soothingly. "I am not leaving you, I promise."

Bric was trembling in her arms; she could feel it. He was shaking all over. She tried to hold him tighter, trying to comfort him, but he simply remained where he was, his head in her lap and his muscular arms around her body. Eiselle thought the man might shake apart right in her arms, and she could feel his breathing – it was irregular, sometimes slower, sometimes faster. Eiselle simply held him tightly, not knowing what else to do.

Time passed, but Eiselle was uncertain as to how much. It could have been seconds, or it could have been hours. It seemed like forever. She could hear noise from the bailey wafting through the windows of their chamber, her grip on Bric very tight as she wondered why the man was so shaken. She's never seen anything like it in her life other than from her mother, who panicked on a regular basis and imagined she was sick or dying. It began to occur to Eiselle that Bric was panicking over something, something he couldn't explain, and it puzzled her greatly. The most powerful knight in England didn't panic. He didn't fall.

... did he?

As she sat there in the dim light, the chamber door quietly opened. She could see the panel moving very slowly, opening further and further, until Manducor's head suddenly appeared. He had an expression of concern on his face as he looked at Bric, crumpled up in his wife's arms.

The priest had been in the kitchen yard, his favorite place when he wasn't in the hall. But in this case, he'd been arguing with the beer wife about the flavor of her brew. The woman was very old, married to one of the house servants, and she liked to swap in seasonal ingredients into her brews to alter the taste. Her last batch of brew had contained elderberries in it, and Manducor was grossly opposed to the use of it in ale. They'd been bickering back and forth when he'd seen Bric bolt from the training area, strange behavior from the normally calm man, so he'd come into the keep to see if Lady MacRohan knew what had her husband on the run.

Now, he found MacRohan laying on the floor, his head and shoulders in his wife's lap. It was shocking to say the least. He took a few uneasy steps into the chamber.

"My lady," he whispered. "Is... is everything all right?"

Eiselle simply shook her head. "I do not know."

Bric heard them. He'd been half-dozing, anything to escape this crippling panic he felt, but at the sound of Manducor's voice, he suddenly sat up. It was one thing for Eiselle to see him like this, but quite another for someone else.

"Nothing is amiss," he said, his voice a growl.

Manducor was wary of his tone. "I did not mean to suggest there was," he said. "I saw you run and thought to help. I thought that mayhap there was something amiss with Lady MacRohan, so I only came to make sure there was nothing wrong."

Bric was suddenly on his feet, pulling Eiselle to stand. "I told you nothing was wrong," Bric said, although he wouldn't look Manducor in the eye. "And the next time you enter our chamber, you will knock. Is that clear?"

"It is, my lord."

Bric was clearly uncomfortable and edgy. He took Eiselle's hand, kissed it twice, before letting it go and quitting the room. He simply blew out of the chamber without another word. Eiselle stood there a moment, both confused and shocked with what had happened. She looked at Manducor, lifting her shoulders weakly.

"I do not know what is wrong," she said. "He could not tell me. All he said was that he was working with the men, saw an arrow hit the ground, and then he ran up here."

Since Manducor had been a knight for years before joining the priesthood, he'd fought in many battles and he had an inkling as to what might be the problem. He'd seen it before, with some, but he couldn't really believe that a man of Bric MacRohan's strength would suffer from such a thing. *A weakness of the heart*, they'd called it. *A Man of Dishonor* was another term. There were a few names for it, none of them particularly kind.

Like most of the inhabitants of Narborough, he had heard the rumors about MacRohan, about how he seemed less aggressive than he had been before his injury. Men were whispering that he'd lost his edge, that the injury had damaged his unwavering courage, but the whispers were those of concern and not condemnation. Nothing Manducor had heard was condemnation for the beloved High Warrior of Narborough.

Therefore, he tried to be tactful when he spoke.

"Sometimes, an injury can affect a man's mind," he said. "I have seen men cower from swords once they were cut by them. MacRohan said that he fled when he heard an arrow?"

Eiselle nodded. "He said he heard the arrow and he ran."

"Then it is possible the sound of an arrow brings back memories of that terrible wound, something that frightens him."

Eiselle frowned. "Not Bric," she said firmly. "He is the greatest knight in the realm. He is not afraid of anything."

Manducor could hear her staunch belief in her husband's greatness. "My lady, sometimes men are afraid of things they cannot comprehend," he said. "Battle will do strange things to a man's mind. It is possible that MacRohan's brush with death has made him fearful of things he would not normally be afraid of."

"Nay," she said strongly. "Bric MacRohan is the High Warrior. He does not know fear and I resent you for saying so."

Manducor cocked an eyebrow at her. "It is that attitude that will sink him," he said. "Do not tell him how strong he is. Do not shame him with talk of being de Winter's High Warrior. If your husband is suddenly feeling some panic over his brush with death, then those things will not help him. They will only hurt him."

Eiselle was deeply upset by his words, but she was also upset at herself because she'd been thinking nearly the same thing, only Manducor had been brave enough to speak of it. Bric was invincible and she didn't like the fact that Manducor had seen him in a moment of weakness. She didn't want anyone to see Bric in his moments of weakness, regardless of the cause, and she didn't want any further gossip spread about it.

Whatever was happening with Bric, she was certain he could overcome it.

"Listen to me," she said, pointing a finger at the priest. "You will not speak of this. You will not tell anyone what you saw, do you hear me? I will not have you planting doubt in men's minds as to the greatness of my husband. He has a formidable reputation, and if you ruin that, I will kill you."

Manducor believed her. He was touched by her fierce defense of her husband, but he was also concerned with the fact that she didn't realize her husband may be suffering from mental anguish that only another fighting man would understand. Denying it wasn't going to make it go away. Putting his hands up, he backed down.

"I would never ruin his reputation," he said. "I think you know better than that. But I am telling you that you must be vigilant with him, my lady. He may have inner demons that he cannot control, so you must take great care with him."

Eiselle was angry, confused, and concerned. Manducor's words made sense to her, which was the most frightening thing of all. Without another word, she rushed from the chamber, leaving Manducor to wonder if the arrow that had carved into MacRohan's body had not only damaged his flesh, but his mind. He'd seen such things in his lifetime. With Bric, only time would tell.

Regardless, de Winter needed to know, if he didn't already.

"MY LORD, YOU wished to see me?"

Bric asked the question, standing in the door of Daveigh's solar. The lord of Narborough had a big chamber with one wall that was shaped like a half-circle, with windows that faced out over the inner bailey. Sunlight streamed in from the openings, bathing the room in a bright glow.

Daveigh looked up when he heard Bric's question. He was seated at the massive table that held maps, missives, and any number of documents or utensils that helped him manage his great empire. There was also a gaggle of dogs beneath the table, big Irish wolfhounds that had been sent to him from his properties in Ireland, and dogs that, on occasion, had been sicced on young Edward de Chevington when the lad wandered into Daveigh's solar. The dogs' heads came up, curiously, when Bric entered.

"Come," Daveigh waved him over to the table. He set aside a missive he had been reading to focus on Bric. "How goes the training this day?"

Bric knew immediately what Daveigh meant. In fact, he'd suspected from the beginning why he'd been summoned; he and Daveigh had served together for a very long time and there wasn't much they kept from each other. Such was the nature of their relationship. He knew Daveigh had been out in the training area earlier, but he wasn't sure he'd been there when Bric had panicked at the arrow strike. Even if he hadn't been present, other men were. Surely someone had told him what had happened. Therefore, Bric was preemptive in his reply.

"I am sorry for what happened earlier, my lord," he said frankly. "I did not mean to run off like that, but I... I was ill. Ask the servants. I managed to expel the contents of my stomach inside the keep, but I am better now. It must have been something I ate."

It was typical for Bric to be straightforward and, in truth, Daveigh was indeed going to ask him about the situation earlier, when Bric had run from an entire troop of new recruits who had seen the High Warrior bolt into the keep. Pearce had seen it, too, and he'd been able to cover for Bric, but Daveigh was concerned about what the new recruits would think. Rumors were being whispered throughout Narborough these days, rumors that Daveigh had mentioned to Pearce, and surely the new recruits were hearing them.

Given Bric's latest behavior, those rumors couldn't be ignored any longer. It was time to address them.

In an effort to protect Bric, and to help the man, Daveigh needed to know what was going on and he didn't believe Bric's explanation in the least. He knew better.

"Do you remember when you first came to Narborough?" he asked, leaning back in his chair. "When you first came here with Keeva? Do you recall that after you swore your oath to me, I put you in charge of a troop of men?"

Bric nodded, but he wasn't giving in to the pleasant mood that Daveigh was trying to create. He was on his guard. "I remember."

"Do you recall that your accent was so thick, no one could understand you?"

"I do, indeed, recall."

"You called the men motley malcontents, as I recall, and it came out as 'markley malkents', or something to that effect. Then you became even more angry when they couldn't understand you."

"Those were difficult times, my lord."

Daveigh grinned. "For all of us," he said. "But you eventually won their respect. It just took time."

"Indeed."

Daveigh's smile faded. "I will ask you a question, Bric, and you will give me an honest answer."

"I would not lie to you, my lord, not ever."

"You just did."

Bric cocked his head curiously. "When did I do this disgraceful thing?"

"When you told me that you'd eaten something that had made you ill. That was not the truth, was it?"

Bric stared at him a moment before clearing his throat softly, trying to maintain eye contact with the man but having difficulty doing it.

"It was my way of saying you should not worry," he said after a moment. "Whatever is happening with me, it will pass."

Daveigh drew in a long, thoughtful breath. Then, he stood up from his chair, wandering over to the lancet windows that overlooked the inner bailey. His movements were slow, and pensive, as he pondered the world outside his windows.

"When I was very young, my father went on crusade with King Richard," he said. "I was so young when he left, I do not even remember, but I do remember when he returned. He'd taken the land route back and by the time he came home, he was a shell of his former self. In fact, I did not know him when he came back. He looked as if he'd been starving and destitute for the last four years of his life. Did I ever tell you that story, Bric?"

"Some of it."

Daveigh continued. "My mother took care of him and nursed his body back to health, but the one thing that did not return to health was his mind. You see, he'd seen so many horrific things that even a glimpse of a broadsword would turn him into a madman. He would run and hide. This was when the de Winter war machine was at its weakest point, and it was my father's younger brother, Olivier, who commanded the army because my father was incapable. It took time for my father to recover, and eventually he did, and he was able to take the field again. My father died on the field of battle in Normandy about fifteen years ago. The point is that I can see the same symptoms in you, Bric, that my father suffered from. You were not sick today; you suffered from a bout of panic, the same panic my father had from time to time."

By this point, Bric was standing in tense silence. But he didn't want to admit anything because he didn't believe what Daveigh was suggesting. He hadn't panicked like a weakling; it simply wasn't possible. He was the High Warrior, and there wasn't a weak bone in his body.

"I did not panic, my lord," he said firmly. "I am not sure what happened, but it will not happen again. This I vow."

Daveigh looked at him. "There is no shame in this, Bric," he insisted. "Sometimes, it happens. Men have more than they can take on the field of battle and it happens. With you, I believe the moment the arrow struck you was when you realized you are not immortal. Knowing that does not make you weak in and of itself, but how you handle that knowledge is where the men are separated from the fools. Running away as you did today, that is what a weakling would do, and I know you are not weak. You are right when you say it will not happen again; it *cannot*. The de Winter army must believe you are as fearless as you have always been, because the moment they start doubting your strength is the moment you are no longer any good to me."

Bric knew that; God, he knew that. He knew that the respect of the army was hard fought and easily lost. If he lost it, there would be nothing left. He would no longer be de Winter's High Warrior. The mere thought of losing everything he'd worked so hard for made his palms sweat.

"I understand, my lord," he said. "As I said, it will not happen again."

Daveigh's gaze lingered on him for a moment. "You *do* know there are rumors about that you are not the same man you were before your injury."

"I do."

"When I see how you are with the new recruits, it is easy to believe you are not the same man. The Bric MacRohan before his injury was a harsh, sometimes brutal taskmaster, yet you were always fair. That is why the men loved you so. The man I have seen training these new recruits as of late is more of a nursemaid than a master. Everyone is seeing it, Bric."

Bric sighed heavily. "Then what would you have me do? What do you *want* me to do? I am doing my best, Daveigh."

It was rare that Bric called Daveigh by his given name, but that was the type of relationship they shared. They were not simply liege and servant; they were friends and kin, as well. Daveigh moved in his direction, his manner subdued.

"I want you to leave Narborough for a time," he said quietly. "The men know you are still recovering from your injury, so it will be a simple thing to tell them that you need rest. Go to Bedingfeld Manor in the countryside with your wife and stay there until you feel as if you can watch an arrow fly again without coming apart at the seams. You have a new wife, Bric; enjoy her, rest, and relax. Take the time away and recover yourself. I need my High Warrior in top form and if you must take a rest to do that, then so be it."

It wasn't a bad idea, in fact. Before his injury, Bric had been thinking of asking Daveigh for a lesser post and his own command so that Eiselle could have a home of her own. And he knew Bedingfeld; it was like heaven out there in the countryside. A fortified manor with a small lake and a beautiful garden from what he remembered. A perfect place to take his new wife so they could spend some time alone, and perhaps he could overcome the urge to run when he saw an arrow. In truth, he has scared himself with that reaction because it hadn't been something he'd been able to control.

Perhaps Daveigh was right.

The High Warrior needed to regain his form.

"Very well," he said after a moment. "If you believe that is best, then I will go."

Daveigh was relieved that he wasn't going to have a fight on his hands. He went to Bric and put his hand on the man's shoulder.

"I respect you more for agreeing to go," he said. "Had you fought me on this, I would have believed you to be in denial that there may be a problem. But I truly do not believe there is any shame in this, Bric. My father went through it. Many men go through it. I know there is talk of a weak heart or of dishonorable behavior when something like this occurs, but I do not believe it is either. A man's mind is a vast and mysterious thing, and there are times when even the best of us must deal with something we cannot control."

Bric appreciated that Daveigh was being understanding over something that Bric didn't even understand himself. What he felt wasn't something he could put into words.

"Mayhap I can use some time away," he finally said. "In truth, before all of this happened, I was going to ask you if you could station me at Roxham or Wissington so that Eiselle could have her own home. Here, she is one of Keeva's women, but at one of the lesser castles, she could run it how she saw fit."

Daveigh nodded. "Every woman wants her own home," he said, trying to make it seem like it was a good thing for Bric to leave Narborough. "Go to Bedingfeld for a time and if you like it, you can remain there. If not, I will move you to one of the other castles. Go where you like, Bric. You may choose."

This way, it wasn't like Daveigh was sending Bric away for his mental health. It was more a mutual decision, so Bric could heal completely and get control of his nerves, and Bric appreciated that.

It left him his dignity.

In truth, he felt better than he had in weeks. He felt there was hope for him to return to the man he once was. He had no idea what was happening to him and an understanding liege helped tremendously. With time away, he could sort himself out and deal with whatever was happening. But just as he and Daveigh were heading towards the table where the maps were, so they could take a look at all of the de Winter properties where Bric and Eiselle could go, Mylo suddenly appeared in the doorway.

"My lord," he said, somewhat breathlessly, as he had run all the way from the main gatehouse. "We have a rider from Castle Acre. The French have amassed and are attacking both the town and castle. De Warenne begs us for help, my lord."

It was unwelcome news, but not entirely surprising. Daveigh looked at Bric, who had a stony expression on his face. In fact, it was unreadable, like a marble statue. It was the face of a man who had confronted war many times, a man who knew his duty no matter how he personally felt. As of this moment, Bric MacRohan was still in command of the de Winter army and Bric's gaze lingered on Daveigh for a moment longer before turning to Mylo.

"You and Pearce shall muster the army," he said. "And we will bring the new recruits. There is no better time for them to gain experience than in an actual battle, so make sure they are mustered. I will join you shortly."

Mylo nodded and fled. Bric began to follow, moving swiftly, but a word from Daveigh stopped him.

"Bric," he said quietly, firmly. "You do not have to…"

Bric cut him off. "There is a war to fight, my lord, and the de Winter army has been summoned," he said, turning to look at him. "Unless you tell me I am no longer in command of the army, then my place is at its head. *Am* I still in command?"

As Daveigh looked at him, it seemed like the old Bric to him – immovable, fearless, ruthless. Sending the man into battle, given how his manner had been over the past several weeks, was against his better judgment, but Daveigh couldn't in good conscience hold him back. Bric was a knight; he had been for most of his life.

He needed to do what he did best, or die trying.

"Aye," Daveigh said. "You are still in command."

Bric's gaze lingered on him a moment before heading out of the solar, following Mylo's trail out of the keep.

When he was gone, Daveigh stood there a moment, wondering if he'd made the right decision. He was still standing there when Keeva entered the chamber, her eyes wide with concern.

"What's it all about, Daveigh?" she asked. "Why are Mylo and Bric running?"

Daveigh didn't even know where to start. He didn't want to tell Keeva about Bric's mental state, fearful that she wouldn't understand. Keeva was a wonderful woman, and he loved her dearly, but she didn't quite understand what fighting men went through. She'd never faced a battle herself; not even a siege. Therefore, he wasn't going to tell her about Bric because he didn't want her scolding the man for being a weakling. There were some things that Daveigh was apt to keep to himself.

"A rider from Castle Acre," he said. "Sounds as if the French are going after the town and de Warenne has asked for help. I'm off to see the messenger myself to find out what is going on; meanwhile, Bric and Mylo are mustering the army. Can you please keep the women and children inside the keep? The last thing we need is Eiselle wandering into the outer bailey or, worse, that little beast Eddie running amok while men are being assembled."

Keeva nodded swiftly; she knew what needed to be done, as she'd been through this procedure many times. "I will," she said. "Is that all you need me to do?"

"That is all, love. I will return when I know more."

Quickly, he quit the keep, heading out into an outer bailey that was starting to roll with the chaos of men, driven by a big Irish knight with a voice that carried across mountains.

A big Irish knight who would soon be facing the challenge of his life.

CHAPTER FOURTEEN

T HE MULTITUDE OF torches that lit up the night sky was an eerie sight. There was something uneasy about the brilliant fire that fought off the night, a night so black that it was as if looking into the face of Satan.

At least, that's what Eiselle thought as she stood at the gatehouse leading from the inner bailey into the outer bailey, watching the army as it prepared to move out.

There was something uneasy about this entire night.

Earlier, she'd been sewing on one of Bric's tunics in their chamber when Keeva had come to tell her about the call for help from Castle Acre, sixteen miles to the east. It belonged to the powerful Earls of Surrey, the de Warenne family, and it was a mighty and strategic castle with property that butted up against the de Winter lands. De Winter and de Warenne were close allies, so there was never any question about answering the summons.

De Winter would answer the call.

At first, Eiselle had been understandably concerned for Bric. After what had happened earlier that day, she was worried that he was heading into battle and wasn't yet ready for such a thing. But she didn't share that concern with Keeva, instead keeping it to herself, and following an afternoon of sewing on her husband's tunics, she could no longer keep her focus. As night fell, she wandered out of the keep and right to the mouth of the outer bailey, watching the activity and hoping for a glimpse of her husband.

Everything seemed business as usual. She remembered how the

army was methodically mustered from the first time she had witnessed it, when they were departing for Holdingham. Wagons were brought out, horses were groomed and saddled, and the quartermasters were thorough in the supplies they brought with them. Everything was moving smoothly and, in the middle of it, she could hear Bric's voice, bellowing to the men, as Mylo and Pearce made sure the new recruits were properly outfitted for the coming battle march.

As she caught a sighting of Bric now and again as he moved in and out of the herd of men, she could also see Manducor out in the organized chaos. He seemed to be helping, too, mostly with the infantry, and Eiselle was coming to think that the man might never return to his church.

The drunk, smelly priest had transformed over the past several weeks; he didn't drink as much, although he still ate to excess and farted when he pleased, and he spent more time with Weetley, the surgeon, helping the man with his patients, and generally finding other things to do. Whether or not he'd been invited to stay, he was finding a place for himself at Narborough.

It seemed to Eiselle that the man had reclaimed something in himself – perhaps it was self-worth, or a sense of purpose. It was difficult to know. All she knew was that Daveigh permitted him to stay as long as he made himself useful. Perhaps he simply felt more at home at Narborough than he did serving his parish. Whatever the reason, Manducor was starting to become a fixture at Narborough and Eiselle wasn't displeased. He had a wisdom about him that she found comforting. Oddly enough, the man was coming to be something of a friend.

So, Eiselle stood and watched as the men went about their duties, feeling the chill as the night began to deepen. As she stood there and watched, she began to hear voices behind her and turned to the keep in time to see Mylo emerge from the entry with Angela in tow, carrying a wailing Edward.

"But he just wants to be with you!" Angela was saying as she virtually ran after her husband. "He wants to see the soldiers and the army. If he is to be a knight like his father, what is the harm of you taking him with you as you go about your duties?"

Mylo was beyond frustrated. He came to a halt and turned to his wife. "I have explained this to you several times, so I will do it once more and let this be the end of it," he said. "It is too dangerous for him out there with the army and I do not have time to watch him. Moreover, it is late and he should be in bed."

Angela frowned. "I think you are being very cruel to your son."

Mylo had no patience for her. "He is too young, Angela. When he is older, mayhap I will take him with me, but right now, he is far too young. He would want to get down and run, and if he does that, he will be killed. Someone will run him over and it would be all your fault."

Angela gasped, offended by his words. Although Eiselle was genuinely not trying to listen to their argument, it was difficult because they were standing so close to her. When Angela realized Eiselle was listening, she quickly turned back for the keep with the crying baby in her arms. As she ran off, Mylo resumed his walk towards the outer bailey and caught sight of Eiselle as he did so. He smiled weakly.

"She wants me to take the baby with me," he said. "It is not safe."

Eiselle nodded. "I agree with you," she said. "But when he is older, then you must take him with you so that he may learn from you."

Mylo shrugged. "I hope he will outgrow this screaming he does," he said. "I hope I can undo the damage that his mother has done."

Eiselle smiled. "He is young, still. I am sure he will outgrow his tantrums."

Mylo gave her a nod that suggested it might be possible. "Mayhap," he said. "Now, if you will excuse me, Lady MacRohan, I have duties to attend to or your husband will have my hide."

Eiselle waved him off, watching him head out into the group of men who were now starting to form loose ranks as the knights whipped them into shape. It seemed to her that they were preparing to move out soon and the worry she felt for her husband began to increase. She'd been fighting it off all day, but now that their departure was approaching, it was coming on with a vengeance. Her nervous stomach, something she'd hardly suffered from since her arrival to Narborough, was beginning to make itself known and she could already feel the gas bubbles popping up, reminding her of her worrisome spirit.

Worried, indeed, for Bric.

But she remained at the smaller gatehouse, vigilantly watching the army and ignoring both the chill of the evening and her upset stomach. She stood there as the sun set, and the air turned damp and cold, still watching everything, still seeing Bric on occasion. She was starting to live for those glimpses, seeing flashes of the man she was so deeply in love with. It was the only thing she cared about. As she stood there, shivering in the darkness, someone came up behind her and put a heavy shawl over her shoulders.

"I thought you might need this," Keeva said, smiling at Eiselle when the woman looked at her in surprise. "It is a cold night."

Eiselle pulled the shawl tight. "It is," she said. "Thank you for the wrap. I can feel the dampness in the air."

Keeva, who was warmly dressed against the night, glanced up at the sky. "There is always dampness in the air because of our closeness to the river," she said. "Even in the summer, we will have misty mornings over the land. I have a feeling we may see a misty morning tomorrow."

Eiselle's gaze was on the army. "But they will move out regardless of the mist, won't they?"

Keeva nodded. "They will move out no matter what the weather is like."

So much for hoping that fog would delay the army and, consequently, Bric's departure. Eiselle tried not to appear too disappointed about it.

"I do not know how you have become accustomed to this," she said after a moment. "Your husband leaves for battle and yet you appear so calm. I wonder if I shall ever feel so calm."

Keeva put her hand on Eiselle's arm. "I may appear calm, but the truth is that I am just as anxious as you are," she said. "Daveigh is all I have. If he does not return, I do not know what I shall do or where I shall go."

Eiselle looked at her. "I am sure that Daveigh is well-protected by the knights," she assured her. "And Narborough is your home. If something… well, if something happened, surely you would remain here, as is your right. Why would you even think to leave?"

Keeva shrugged. "Narborough is the crown jewel in the Honor of Narborough, and with it goes the title of Baron Cressingham," she said. "All of this would go to the next Baron Cressingham, who would be Daveigh's younger half-brother, Grayson. He has only seen fourteen years, but he is already a fine young man. I know that Grayson would permit me to remain here if I wished it, but it is more than that. Daveigh is my heart and my soul, Eiselle. When I say he is all that I have, I mean that he is the life that beats within me. I could not lose that, much as you could not lose Bric."

Eiselle understood the passion of her statement. "I almost did," she said quietly. "Our life together was almost over before it began. I am concerned for him returning to battle so soon."

Keeva could see the stress in her fine features. "I know you are worried for Bric, lass," she said quietly. "I have heard the rumors, too. We all have. But Bric descends from the High Kings of Ireland, and he is a warrior of legend. You must not worry over him. He will come home to you."

Eiselle wasn't comforted by her words. Dashiell had told her the last time the army had left for battle that Bric would come home to her, and he had – as a casualty. Therefore, Keeva's words had no real meaning to her but she didn't say so. She simply nodded her head.

"I am coming to see that worrying for Bric serves no purpose," she said. "I do believe it displeases him if he knows I am worried for him, so I try not to show it. But watching him ride off to battle and not feel sick to my stomach is going to take practice. The one and only time I watched him ride away was when he returned to me injured."

Keeva squeezed her arm. "It was not usual, I assure you," she said.

"I have been watching Bric ride off to battle for many years and that was the first time he has returned injured. Have faith that it will be the *only* time."

Those words bore some comfort to Eiselle, and she smiled bravely at Keeva, who put her arms around her and hugged her. The two of them had bonded quite a bit over the past several months and had become great friends. As they stood there, watching and waiting, Bric suddenly appeared.

Instead of losing himself in the men as he'd been doing all day, he was heading in their direction. Keeva had to let go of Eiselle or risk being pulled along with her when she ran out to greet him.

Eiselle had no real intention of embracing her husband as she ran to him. He was coming towards her so it seemed natural that she should go to him. But he suddenly opened his arms to her, something he'd never done before, and it seemed to Eiselle that he wanted to embrace her. Therefore, she threw herself into his arms when she came within range and he lifted her up from the ground, holding her tightly.

"That's my lass," he murmured into her hair. "I could no longer stay away. You have been watching me for a very long time."

Eiselle loosened her grip, enough to look him in the face. "Untrue," she said. "I have not been watching you at all."

"Then who have you been watching?"

"Mylo."

He scowled. "Again?"

Eiselle laughed and tightened her grip around his neck, kissing him on the cheek. "I am jesting with you," she whispered, kissing him again. "I would never watch another man. You are the only man in the world worth watching."

Bric set her to her feet, his heart full of the warmth from her words. "You always know the right thing to say to me," he said, taking her hand in his big mitt. "All is forgiven, *mo chroí*."

Eiselle's eyes twinkled at him as he led her back towards the keep, passing Keeva as they went. Keeva was smilingly openly at Bric, a gesture he thought was rather taunting, so he ignored her for the most part. Keeva already knew how happy he was, and how it was because of her bullying tactics he was so happy, but he didn't want to inflate the woman's pride by acknowledging it. He heard her laugh as he walked by.

But Eiselle had eyes only for Bric as they headed into the keep, unaware of Keeva's taunts. "Can I help you pack your things?" she asked. "If I had known what to pack for you, I would have already done so."

He squeezed her hand as they approached the keep entry. "I appreciate the offer," he said, "but you need not trouble yourself. I can pack for myself."

Her face fell. "But I would like to help you and it would save you time," she said. "Shouldn't a wife pack for her husband?"

He paused, seeing how very much she wanted to help. He thought it rather adorable. "Very well," he said. "If you would truly like to pack my things, I will show you what I need."

Eiselle was eager. "I know I cannot help you with your weapons, but I can help you with clothing and provisions and your bedroll."

They entered the keep, passing into the torch-lit innards. "Indeed, you can," he said. "I will show you all you need to know so that the next time, you may help me with it."

Eiselle was thrilled. Bric took her up to their chamber and pulled out his saddlebags, which he now kept in their chamber as opposed to the armory or his former chamber. He'd moved everything he owned into this room, now his permanent residence, and he spent some time showing her everything he packed when he left on campaign – dry clothing, his oiled cloak, a sewing kit to repair whatever he might tear, small strips of leather with any number of purposes, jerky, a shaving kit, and other small but important things.

He was a patient teacher and Eiselle soaked it up, memorizing everything and the order in which he placed them in his saddlebags. But he was nearing the end of everything he needed and Eiselle still hadn't seen one particular item that she knew he would want to bring.

"What about your talisman?" she asked. "Won't you take that, also?"

Bric reached down into the tunic he was wearing and produced it, hanging around his neck. "I always keep it on me," he said. "You need never worry about that."

Eiselle admired the piece for a moment. "Please do not ever give it to me again. Promise?"

He gave her a lopsided smile. "If you insist."

She nodded. "I do."

He winked at her before returning his attention to his saddlebags, making sure he had everything with him. Meanwhile, Eiselle moved over to the table near their bed, to the embroidered box that contained her sewing kit. Opening the box, she pulled something forth, something she kept enclosed in her hand, and returned to him. Bric noticed that she was trying to keep something from him.

"What do you have?" he asked.

She lifted her shoulders, hesitantly. "It may be silly of me to ask, but would you like to take something of me with you? A keepsake, I mean. Should you want to think of me once in a while on your travels."

A smile played on his lips. "I always think about you, every moment of every day," he said. "What did you wish to give me?"

Eiselle finally held up her hand, holding out what she'd been concealing from him. It was a necklace, with a chain made of braided fabric and at the very end was a carefully-looped bunch of dark hair tied up tightly with the same fabric that made the chain. The smile faded from Bric's face as he took it from her, inspecting it, and Eiselle spoke before he could ask her the obvious question.

"It is the only thing I have to give you that is part of me," she said. "It is a lock of my hair. I did not have a chain or anything solid to put it on, so the fabric is from the dress I wore when we were married. I am sure you do not recall it, but it was the dress that had belonged to Keeva's sister. She gave me permission to take some of the fabric from the seams and make this necklace out of it. If you do not wish to wear it, then I completely understand, but I wanted to give you something that meant something to me. Mayhap it will mean something to you, too."

Bric stared at it. Well did he remember the pale green garment she had worn, the dress Eiselle had been so careful with. He could see that she'd cut three slender scraps and braided them together to create the necklace, which was tied off at the ends with a lock of her hair.

Bric wasn't a man of great sentiment. Or, at least he never thought he was. He always thought himself rather hardened to emotion, but the introduction of Eiselle had changed that opinion dramatically. He'd grown up in a family of warriors, and had fostered at a very young age, so all he'd ever really known was the seriousness and dedication of the knighthood. Emotions were crippling things, and he had an old master, the same one who had given him the talisman, who had tried to beat all of the emotion out of him.

That was why he had been so puzzled when he'd run from the arrow. He experienced something he'd never experienced before – genuine fear. He never thought himself capable of such emotion, but it was clear that whatever his old master had tried to beat out of him hadn't entirely fled.

Bric was a man of feeling.

Which was why his throat felt tight as he looked at the necklace Eiselle had made him. It was difficult for him to put his emotions into words.

"I have never in my life received anything so valuable," he said after a moment. "Your hair… and this dress that I remember you looking so beautiful in… this is the most precious thing I own, Eiselle. To thank you for this doesn't seem enough."

Eiselle hadn't been entirely sure how Bric would have felt about received such a gift and she was deeply pleased that he seemed thrilled by it.

"You like it?" she asked. "Truly?"

He nodded as he continued to look at it. "Truly."

"I hope that when you look at it, you remember how much I love you. And how much I want you to come home safely."

He looked at her, his silver gaze lingering on her before putting the necklace over his head and tucking it down his tunic, making sure it was close to his heart. Then, he reached out and cupped her face, kissing her so sweetly that Eiselle's head began to swim. The man's kisses were warm, soft, and delicious, and Eiselle put her arms around his neck, pulling him close as his kisses gained in intensity. Before she realized it, he had backed her into the wall as his mouth moved over the tender skin of her neck.

It was natural for him to touch her, to taste her, so his hands and mouth had a mind of their own. He couldn't even stop himself from pulling at the ties on her surcoat, loosening it just enough so he could pull it down over her shoulders and expose her breasts. He was never content with just a kiss from her; it had to be all of her. He feasted on her nipples as her garment bunched up around her waist, and his hands snaked underneath her skirt.

Eiselle was his plaything. She offered no resistance as his hands stroked her thighs, and finally the tender junction between her legs. She groaned as he slipped his fingers into her, so highly aroused that she climaxed twice before he turned her around, braced her hands against the wall, and flipped up her skirts. Untying his breeches, he lowered them to his knees as he thrust into her from behind.

Eiselle gasped with the pleasure of it as he joined his body with hers, surrendering to the primal mating rhythm. Not a day passed that they didn't make love at least once, but more often than not it was more than once, and Eiselle's body was deeply in tune with Bric's needs. She let him do whatever he wanted to do, and when she asked how she could pleasure him, he'd taken the time to show her how to use her mouth to make him groan.

But there wasn't time for that tonight; Bric had her where he wanted her and knowing how little time they had left, he branded his wife as only he was capable. When he felt her tremors begin again, he permitted his own release, spilling his hot seed deep into her womb. But even when it was finished and they'd both found their pleasure, he remained joined to her, holding her against him, memorizing the moment for the lonely nights to come, of which there would probably be many.

He missed her already.

"Is this part of the packing process?"

Bric heard her softly-uttered question and he began to laugh, so hard that by the time he and Eiselle uncoupled and she was pulling up her bodice, he was literally crying with laughter. He didn't let her finish dressing before he was throwing his arms around her, squeezing her tightly as he kissed the side of her head.

"It will be from now on," he said. "As long as I have breath left in my body, by God, it *will* be."

"Good. I like that part of it."

He released her, his eyes warm upon her. "So do I," he said. "I love you, Lady MacRohan. You are more than my heart could have ever hoped for."

His words had her heart aflutter. Coming from a man who often couldn't find the right words, when he did find them, they were glorious.

"And I love you. With all that I am, I do."

He kissed her again, enjoying the moment of warmth and passion and humor between them. Never had his heart been so full. As Eiselle quickly finished with the ties on her surcoat, Bric fastened his breeches and turned back to the bed with the saddlebags on it.

From that point on, little was spoken between them. They had said everything that needed saying, so when Bric carried his saddlebags out of the chamber a short time later, he held on to Eiselle tightly, soaking in their last few moments together. Never in his life had he not wanted to attend a battle but, at the moment, he would have been much happier to remain with his wife.

But he had little choice. He walked with Eiselle out of the keep and to the smaller gatehouse that separated the outer bailey from the inner bailey, and there he left her. A gentle kiss, and a few whispered words of love, and he left her standing there, watching him head out into the coal-black night with a lock of her hair nestled snuggly against his heart.

When Bric kissed his talisman as the army left Narborough, as was usual for him, he also kissed the bunch of silken dark hair that smelled faintly of roses. Now, he had both good luck charms with him.

He *was* immortal.

CHAPTER FIFTEEN

THE FRENCH HAD no intention of leaving Castle Acre.

French scouts had been out in the countryside as the army from Narborough approached from the north, so by the time the de Winter troops were on the outskirts, the French had set up a second line and were ready for them.

It was a nasty battle from the start.

The French army had scavenged nearly everything of value out of the village of Castle Acre, leaving burning homes and dead peasants in their wake. They stole horses and livestock, even dogs. The de Winter army could hear the screaming from the villagers, but they were blocked from helping by the line of French who were intent to chase them away. The de Winter war machine, however, would not be chased away; Bric ordered his archers to unleash, and as the French rebels began to retreat back into the burning village, the de Winter army charged after them.

But the French soon fragmented, meaning the de Winter army also had to fragment in order to chase them down, and there were pockets of brutal fighting in the village and near the gatehouse of Castle Acre. The castle wasn't a main residence for the Earl of Surrey, but it was strategic, and the earl stationed about five hundred men to protect both the castle and the village, but it wasn't nearly enough against the one thousand Frenchmen who wanted to steal the castle and destroy the village.

As soon as the army made headway into the village, Daveigh headed to the castle with a contingent of bodyguards to speak with the garrison commander while Bric took charge of the fighting. He sent Mylo to the east, Pearce to the west, while he and the main body of the army plowed right down the middle of the town. The streets were narrow, the alleys dark and dangerous, and half of the town was burning by the time Bric and his men began to gain the upper hand against the enemy.

But it was the French army's fault that they began to lose ground. Since they'd stolen so much, they weren't moving very swiftly and the de Winter troops were able to take back horses, cows, and other livestock that had been stolen. There was a livery near the gatehouse of the castle, one with a big corral, and the de Winter army began stashing the reclaimed livestock there. It began to fill up with frightened horses and cows, a few calves, and many goats, one of which tried to ram those who were attempting to help it. It was a rare humorous moment as Bric watched two of his soldiers get mowed down by a very angry Billy goat as they were trying to lead the creature to safety.

And the fight went on long into the day.

As Keeva had predicted, there was some mist hanging heavy over the land as the sun rose, a mist that didn't quite burn off even in midday. Mylo returned from the east after several hours of fighting to report that he'd either chased away or killed the French factions he'd been fighting against, but at the same time a report came from the west that the French were moving on the Castle Acre Priory, a large monastic enclave west of the castle. Bric shifted his manpower over to the priory, and there was heavy fighting in the fields all around it.

It was clear very early how badly the French wanted Castle Acre. It was not only a rich castle, but minimally staffed for such a large place because of its somewhat remote situation. Even though the location was out of the normal paths of travel, it was still strategic because it was near the mouth of the River Ouse, and the port city of King's Lynn, and although the Honor of Narborough controlled the river into the heart of England, Castle Acre sat in a position to control near the river. If the French took it, they could permit French ships to dock in the river, bringing more men and supplies.

At least, that was what Bric assumed their intentions were. It would be a terrible situation for Narborough and its neighbor to the north, Castle Rising, to have a French outpost so close. Castle Acre was under threat of becoming a French lair and Bric wasn't going to allow that to happen. In truth, it was a much more serious situation than he'd originally thought and even though he didn't have the military support that he'd had at Holdingham, he was under the belief that he could hold the line at Castle Acre and beat the French back.

The High Warrior would not fail.

Surprisingly, the new recruits had done a good job at fighting the French. Bric had taken about half of them with him, and the rest of them were divided up between Pearce and Mylo. The first hour into the fight, Bric was screaming at the men as he used to before his injury. He even knocked a head or two when they didn't listen to him fast enough.

For the seasoned de Winter troops, it did them good to see Bric back to his old form. This was the High Warrior they knew, the man who wouldn't hesitate to insult you if you deserved it, but would also kill for you if need be. Seeing Bric return to the man they once knew was a huge boost for the de Winter army and as the day dragged into night, they fought with a vengeance.

The battle continued as a moonless sky unfolded. The priory was lit up with torches, from every window it seemed, casting rays of light into the darkness beyond. The de Winter army had created something of a barrier around the priory, preventing the French from getting close even though some of them had run off into the nearby woods only to emerge with a battering ram. They used the battering ram to push aside de Winter men, who retaliated by trying to take the battering ram away from them.

It had been quite a struggle, with the de Winter men finally emerging the victors, and Bric watched it all from astride his big war horse. Liath had been unmuzzled at the start of the battle and, even now, he snapped at men who came too close or used his big hooves to knock them down. Bric was quite certain the horse had killed at least one man by kicking him with his powerful rear legs. The horse was intelligent, experienced, and mean, something Bric adored in the beast.

For the first time in a very long while, Bric felt like he was finally back to his top form. Whatever had happened with his panic attack back at Narborough, he was feeling as if he had overcome it. He was too strong to let something so foolish take him down. With Liath beneath him, and with his beloved sword in-hand, it was an unstoppable combination and Bric felt as if he could take on the entire world.

As the fighting went on around him, Bric remained at the door to the priory to cut down any French who managed to make it through the line of de Winter men in the distance. Two massive oak and iron doors were shut and bolted from the inside, and Bric remained in front of the doors and beneath the great Norman arch of the entry. He'd been here before, a few times, and was awed every time at the sheer size and scope of the priory. It was truly a massive place. As he remained in place, watching the pockets of fighting and guarding the door with a couple of hundred men that would not be moved, Pearce thundered up on his war horse.

"Well?" Bric demanded. "What is the status of the battle?"

Pearce tipped his helm back and wiped at the sweat that was rolling into his eyes. "The fire in the town has stopped for the most part," he said. "When we drew the fighting over to the priory, the soldiers from the castle emerged to help put it out. They also rounded up the villagers, and most of them are now in the castle for safety."

Bric moved Liath out from the doorway, looking over towards the village. It was a black outline against the dark sky and he couldn't see much, but he could see that the castle was lit up with pinpricks of light, torches burning in the darkness.

"That is good news," he said. "What about the livestock?"

"I think we were able to get back most, if not all, of it. The soldiers moved everything back into the castle for safe keeping."

Bric was pleased to hear that the villagers and their livestock were at least safe from the French. "That is good news," he said. "The French were more determined than I thought they would be."

Pearce finished wiping his eyes and put his helm back on. "Indeed," he said. He, too, could see the pockets of fighting. "They want the priory badly."

Bric glanced back at the towering structure. "You know why, don't you?"

"Because it's there? Because they can?"

Bric chuckled. "Nay," he said. "This is a Cluniac establishment, meaning the monks here are loyal to the Abbot of Cluny in France. They are loyal to a French abbot and our French friends out there must feel that this is something that belongs to them. I am sure they thought it would be an easy thing to seize the priory."

Understanding dawned with Pearce. "Now it makes sense," he said. "I had not realized that about Castle Acre Priory."

Bric nodded. "Now you know," he said. "But the monks want no part of these rebels, so I imagine this is a rather strange situation for them. They are on English soil, and depend on the English for protection, but they are loyal to the French dioses."

It was an odd situation, indeed. Leaving Pearce by the door, Bric headed out to the clusters of fighting to get a look of the situation for himself, hoping to make short work of the French that were still resisting. He'd done some serious damage in town against the enemy, but now that they were out in the open, he intended to do more damage.

The High Warrior was on the prowl.

Unsheathing his enormous broadsword, the one with the serrated edge, he began stalking the individual groups, coming up behind the unsuspecting French soldiers and lobbing off a head or two. God, he felt powerful when he did that. It was his favorite thing to do in battle. When word started getting around about the English knight who was beheading men, some of the French began to flee. Mylo, who had been fighting off a particularly vicious group, threw caution to the wind and began going for the neck like Bric was.

Soon enough, the fighting began to break up as the French began to retreat. The River Nar ran just to the south of the priory, and Bric watched Mylo rush down to the river because there was some heavy fighting going on down there. He lost sight of Mylo because it was so dark, so he returned to his duties of cleaning up the field of battle by dispatching any remaining fighting.

More often than not, men would simply scatter when they saw him coming, and sometimes they would scatter in the direction of the river. Bric wasn't entirely sure how many men were down by the river now, so he thought to take a look. If there was more fighting going on, then he would hasten to disband it. It was so dark down there, however, that he took some of the soldiers away from the priory entrance and had them carry torches down towards the river so he could see what was happening.

What he saw unfold was disturbing.

The French had regrouped down by the river and were fighting the de Winter army furiously. When Bric saw this, he bellowed to the men near the priory, telling them to pass the word to send every available man down to the river. In a rush, the English were coming, all of them rushing down to the river to engage the French who were being stubborn.

The River Nar was a wide body of water, but not very deep at all, and the foliage around it was quite heavy, making everything seem darker than it was. Bric charged into the foliage, swinging his sword when he was certain he was swinging it at an enemy. His horse, however, was snapping at anything that moved, French or English.

Unfortunately, the near total darkness in the river made fighting chaotic and dangerous. Bric could only really see occasional movement, and the grunting of men, and the torches brought by the English soldiers didn't illuminate much at all. At one point, Bric stopped swinging his sword, fearful he was going to kill one of his own men. He resorted to kicking and punching mostly, or knocking the heads he could see. It was as much as he could do considering he couldn't see anything, nor could anyone else. It was fighting in total darkness, a deadly situation.

Light came unexpectedly when soldiers with torches suddenly appeared in the area that Bric was fighting in and he saw that he was right in the middle of the stream, with mostly French soldiers around him. When the French saw the big English knight with the bloodied blade, they began to run, and Bric tried to catch them before they could get away. But just as he was turning to charge after them, he heard someone yell behind him.

"Bric! Behind you!"

Bric heard Mylo's voice in a panic. An attack was imminent and Bric could feel something off to his right, like the breeze when something rushed by, and the water splashed heavily next to him. He heard a growl, saw the flash of a blade, and ducked low on his horse, hoping to miss the weapon that was flying out at him.

His sense of survival kicked in; determined to defend himself, Bric brought up his sword to counter, or even kill, the man attacking him. He heard a grunt of pain a split second before he brought his sword around and plunged it into the neck and shoulder of the man who had suddenly appeared next to him. He could see the body in the darkness, but nothing more, and at this moment, anything in the darkness was his enemy.

He wasn't going to go down without a fight.

But he noticed too late that man next to him was on a horse. There was also another man between them, on foot. The man on foot fell into the river, as did the man on the horse, but Bric couldn't tell what had happened. He couldn't see anything. He began screaming for light and a soldier with a torch rushed into the area and the foliage, the water, lit up with a golden glow. Bric looked down to see a dead Frenchman lying in the water and Mylo lying on top of him with his head half-cut off.

Horror seized him.

Bric leapt from his horse, into the freezing water, screaming for the soldier with the torch to come closer. Falling to his knees in the bloodied, cold water, he pulled Mylo up, seeing the wound in the man's shoulder and neck and knowing he had put it there. God help him, he knew. He could see how easily the sword had cut the flesh, something his serrated blade did easily. It was made for lobbing off heads.

"Oh, God," he breathed. "Oh, God, no... Mylo? Can you hear me?"

Mylo was ghostly pale, with blood pouring from his neck and shoulder. His eyes opened at the sound of Bric's voice.

"He... he was going to kill you," he murmured. "I... had to... stop..."

"Stop what?" Bric demanded, his voice cracking. "What happened?"

"I... put myself between you and... you could not see him. I had to stop him."

I had to stop him. The confusion, the horror Bric experience was now transforming into something unspeakable as the situation became evident. The warrior who had never shown emotion in his life on the field of battle was feeling a rush of it as he realized what had happened.

He'd killed his own man, who had been trying to save him.

"Sweet God," he gasped. "Mylo, you yelled a warning. I could not see in the dark and I thought you were the man coming to kill me. I did not know it was you!"

Mylo tried to swallow, to breathe, but everything was cut. He was bleeding out all over Bric, his bright red blood seeping into the man's tunic.

"I... know..." he rasped. "Not... your fault, Bric. You did not know it was... me..."

With that, he breathed his last. Bric stared at him, unable to comprehend what he had done. The fighting around him had died down, but he didn't notice. At that moment, all he saw in the entire world was his knight in his arms.

The man he had killed.

The sound that came out of him next was something every man in the de Winter army would remember for the rest of their lives.

"*No!*"

It was a scream that reverberated off of the priory, startling the monks who were hanging out the windows, watching the battle dwindle. But down in that heavily-foliaged river, Bric held Mylo against him and wept as he'd never wept in his life. He cried for the life he took, for the man he loved who had sacrificed himself to protect him, and for a young son who would never know his father.

He wept until he could weep no more.

As he sat there in the river with Mylo's cooling body against him, he noticed perhaps the only thing he would have noticed under the circumstances. Somehow in the fighting, in the twisting and the turning, his talisman had managed to escape from underneath his hauberk and he could see it outlined beneath his tunic. As he looked at it, the words inscribed on it suddenly came to mind.

A maiorem caritatum nemo habet.

Greater love hath no man than he lay down his life for his friends.

That was what Mylo had done. He'd laid down his life so that Bric could live, and he felt painfully unworthy of those words. Without hesitation, Bric yanked off his helm, his hauberk, and pulled off the talisman. He put it over Mylo's head, thinking that Mylo was much more deserving of the talisman than he was.

He'd made the greatest sacrifice of all.

Pearce, who had come upon the shocking scene of Bric and Mylo in the middle of the river, ran to the castle to tell Daveigh what had happened. Daveigh flew away from the castle in a panic, determined to get to Bric and Mylo to see for himself what a devastated Pearce had told him. His heart was in his throat, tears in his eyes, as dozens of his soldiers ran with him, lighting the way through the darkness.

When he finally reached the scene, the carnage was horrific. Daveigh entered the river only to see it running red with blood, and the dead and dying littering both the river and the river bank. It was so bloody that it was as if every man there had been through a meat grinder, and he plunged feet-first into the river, running to the spot where Bric held Mylo, both of them half-submerged in the freezing water.

When Daveigh saw what had happened, he wept, too.

Oh, God… it was hell.

But it only grew worse as the night went on. Bric wouldn't move and he wouldn't let anyone take Mylo away from him. He simply sat in that freezing river and held the knight who had tried to save his life. That was all Bric could comprehend, and as morning began to dawn over the meadows and lands of Norfolk, Bric finally picked himself up out of that water and carried Mylo to the shore.

But he didn't stop there.

With the dead knight in his arms, Bric began to walk. It was as if he couldn't even function, his mind devoid of reason. All he knew was that he'd cut down his own knight, and his mind simply couldn't accept it. He wouldn't let the man go, and he wouldn't mount his horse to ride back to Narborough.

All he did was walk.

All the way back to Narborough.

The army, seeing that their High Warrior was devastated beyond words, simply walked with him. Not one man mounted his horse, and not one man spoke a single word. Bric was walking home, and so would they.

They would escort him and Mylo home.

It was a tragic and poignant sight.

As Bric carried Mylo down the road, heading west as the sun rose, it was an agonizing reminder of the fragility of life. What the French couldn't accomplish in a day and a night of vicious fighting, and what dozens of armies over the past twenty years couldn't do, a single stroke from a serrated broadsword managed to achieve.

The High Warrior was finally broken.

CHAPTER SIXTEEN

T HE MORNING AFTER Bric had left with the army, Eiselle had awoken with a belly ache. Given that her belly was usually quite sensitive, she didn't give it much thought. She tried to eat bread and cheese to soothe it, but that didn't seem to help too much. The cook had made porridge, so she had a little of that with honey, and that seemed to settle her belly right down.

At least it did for a little while. When nightfall came around, she was nauseous again and ate a big bowl of porridge to ease it. She never mentioned her upset stomach to Keeva, or Zara for that matter, because she thought it was because she was worried for Bric. She didn't want the women to think she was being foolish and not brave. If she was to be the wife of the High Warrior, then she was going to have to come to grips with the man going off to war.

It was easier said than done.

Two days after the army departed for Castle Acre, Eiselle awoke to more nausea. She wasn't feeling well at all and began to think that she must have eaten something that made her ill. But she rose from bed, burping and uncomfortable, and proceeded to wash with warmed water and dress in a pretty blue garment that her mother had made for her. In the warmer weather, the fabric was light, so it was an excellent choice on this day. Even though there was some dew in the fields, she could tell that the day was to be a warm one simply because of the morning temperatures.

She had much to do on this day, and that was intentional. She found that as long as she was busy, she had less time to worry. She had started a new dress for Keeva using a gorgeous silk fabric that Keeva had purchased in Cambridge, and she was hoping to get a good deal finished on the dress. In fact, Eiselle was earning something of a reputation as a master seamstress around Narborough and in addition to the several dresses she'd made for Keeva, she'd also made two for Zara. She'd even instructed some of the servants on the techniques she knew for sewing, so now she had an army of seamstresses to help her.

In truth, Eiselle had never been happier. She was married to a man she loved dearly and life at Narborough was pleasant and lovely. She had a great friend in Keeva, and in Zara, and she would have been happy to include Angela in that group if the woman ever stopped being a hermit. Eiselle was hoping that someday the woman would realize that she wasn't doing her son any favors by permitting him to be such a terror, and would understand that any criticism had been meant to help her. Not that Eiselle was an expert in children, but even she knew that children needed some discipline.

As the day progressed, she began to feel better, a condition that was spurred on when the old cook gave her fresh currant bread with honey. The bread made her belly full and very happy. Retreating to the ladies' solar, which still reminded her very much of Bric since it had been his former chamber, she settled down with the crimson silk and stitched careful, tiny stitches into the bodice. It was exacting work, because silk was difficult to work with, so she was patient with it. It was a perfect project to pass the time and pretend she wasn't thinking about Bric every moment of the day.

"Ah!" Manducor was suddenly standing in the solar door. "Here I find you, Lady MacRohan."

Eiselle looked up from her stitching. "And I am sure you are surprised."

Manducor grinned, his teeth yellowed with age. "Your movements are predictable," he said. "If you are not in the hall or with Lady de Winter, then here you shall be."

Eiselle couldn't talk and stitch carefully at the same time. She set the garment in her lap. "So you have found me," she said. "What can I do for you today?"

His old eyes twinkled at her. "Nothing," he said innocently. "But I may be able to do something for you."

"What?"

"It is possible I have seen a de Winter rider at the main gatehouse," he said. "It is also possible that it is advance word that the army is returning."

Eiselle wouldn't let herself become too excited. "And it is equally possible that it is not," she said. "The army only left three days ago."

Manducor stepped into the chamber, eyeing the pitcher of wine on a table against the wall. He had a talent for finding the wine pitcher in any room he entered.

"Aye, they did," he agreed. "But Lady de Winter has been called to the gatehouse. The odds are in our favor that the army is returning and she is being told."

So much for Eiselle not becoming too excited. A smile flickered on her lips. "I suppose the battle wasn't too far away, was it?"

Manducor shook his head. "It was not. Castle Acre is only sixteen miles away, so whatever happened must have happened quickly."

Eiselle was encouraged by that. "Why did you not go with the army?" she asked. "Keeva said that Daveigh invited you to go. You are a former knight, after all. Why should you not go and fight?"

Manducor shook his head. "It was a very long time ago," he said. "I no longer possess any mail or weapons. Besides, I would probably cut someone's head off if I tried. Nay, lass, that is a past life for me."

"Then mayhap you should ask Bric to practice with you. I am sure he would."

Manducor poured himself some of the wine he'd been eyeing. Lifting the cup to his lips, he drank deeply.

"I am too old, Lady MacRohan," he told her. "I would prefer to remain here, away from battle, and then help when I am needed. I am quite versatile, in fact – I can help Weetley with the sick or injured, and

I can also perform a mass or a blessing. I think that makes me a rather indispensable figure here."

He sounded full of himself and Eiselle grinned, turning back to her sewing. "Tell that to Daveigh, not me," she said. "He has let you remain this long, so I do not see why he would not permit you to be a permanent resident."

"That is my intention, madam."

"You like Narborough that much?"

"Let's just say that I feel useful here. I feel as if I belong."

Eiselle chuckled, shaking her head at the priest who refused to leave a good thing when he saw it. But she didn't mind; she liked Manducor and she'd come to appreciate his wisdom. She considered him a friend.

"Then if you feel as if you belong, sit down and tell me some stories," she said. "You can keep me company whilst I sew on Lady de Winter's gown."

Manducor was more than happy to plant his fat backside onto the nearest chair, making sure to stay within arm's length of the wine pitcher.

"It will be my pleasure, Lady MacRohan," he said. "What kind of stories would you like to hear?"

"Something with humor. Or even adventure."

"How about bloody adventures?"

She made a face. "Don't you dare!"

Manducor snorted. "No blood?"

"No blood!"

He grunted. "You have no sense of fun," he said. He took another long drink of wine. "Humor and adventure, eh? Then let me tell you about my early days when I fostered. I come from a fine family, you know. One of the best in England."

"Who?"

He cast her a quirky expression. "I will not tell you. You will have to wonder about that the rest of your life."

She cocked an eyebrow. "Well, *you* brought it up."

"So I did.

Eiselle had to laugh at the man who was being both petulant and evasive on a subject he had introduced. She turned back to her sewing again.

"Tell me," she said. "Where did you foster?"

"Okehampton Castle," he said. "Seat of the de Courtenay family. Have you heard of them?"

Eiselle shook her head. "I have not," she confessed. "Are you sure you won't tell me your family name?"

"Mayhap someday. My family controls much of the northern Welsh Marches."

"Are you Welsh, then?"

"I am English to the bone, lass."

Eiselle didn't ask any more questions. It seemed that Manducor didn't want to discuss his family, only his life experiences. He told of a mother who was reluctant to let him foster, so he wasn't able to leave his family until he was much older than most boys. He felt that held him back, but he also met his wife whilst he was fostering, when he'd seen ten years and four, or so he told Eiselle, and he spoke mostly of his wife as a young girl, a ward of his liege. She was a lovely creature and he had been very much enamored with her.

It was a pleasant conversation on a pleasant day, hardly foreshadowing what was to come. Eiselle's first hint of the darkness she was about to face came when Keeva entered the solar. She didn't look at Eiselle; instead, her focus went to Manducor.

"Leave us," she said quietly. "Go to the gatehouse and seek the sergeant in command, Roget. He will instruct you."

Manducor immediately stood up, shuffling from the room as Eiselle looked at Keeva curiously. "What is the matter?" she asked. "Has he done something wrong?"

Keeva shook her head. She seemed subdued, unable to look Eiselle in the eye as she went to her and took her hand.

"Put the sewing aside," she said quietly. "I must speak with you."

Eiselle didn't like the tone in her voice and her nervous stomach began to quiver. "You seem distressed. Has something...?" Her eyes suddenly widened and all of the color drained out of her face. "Dear God... Manducor told me of the rider at the gatehouse. Something has happened to Bric!"

Keeva grabbed hold of the woman before she could bolt from her chair. "Nay," she said firmly. "Eiselle, Bric is not injured. But the rider has been sent ahead from the army, who is on its way back to Narborough. Bric is well, but something terrible has happened."

Eiselle was so relieved that her husband was unharmed that she was starting to feel lightheaded. "What has happened, Keeva?" she begged softly. "What did the messenger say?"

Keeva's eyes began to fill with tears but she fought them, struggling to maintain her composure. "My husband sent the messenger ahead of the returning army, so what I am to tell you has come from him," she said. "There were many French rebels at Castle Acre and they tried to seize both the castle and the priory. The fighting was fierce, and they fought into the night. You remember last night, Eiselle. There was no moon."

Eiselle nodded, now greatly concerned for what was to come. "It was as black as ink," she said. "Only the stars were visible."

Keeva swallowed the lump in her throat. "Imagine fighting in that darkness," she said. "Imagine not being able to see ally or enemy. But our men had to fight in the darkness because the French would not surrender. It was very dark and dangerous, and in the course of the battle, Bric accidentally killed Mylo."

Eiselle's hands flew to her mouth in horror. "Nay!" she gasped. "It is not possible!"

Keeva nodded. "I am afraid it is," she said. "According to the messenger, a French knight tried to kill Bric, but Mylo put himself in harm's way in order to save Bric. Because it was so dark, Bric did not see that it was Mylo and killed him, thinking he was the enemy."

Tears flooded Eiselle's eyes and she blinked, sending them cascading down her face. As she started to weep, Keeva gave her firm shake.

"Nay," she hissed. "You will not weep. It is not your right. I must still tell Angela that her husband is dead, and it is not your right to weep. Do you understand me?"

Eiselle did. She realized that everything Keeva said was correct and, very quickly, she stilled her tears. She wiped at her cheeks furiously, struggling to reclaim her composure.

"I am sorry," she said. "It... it will not happen again. You are correct – it is not my right."

Keeva could see the pain in her eyes and she felt for the woman. Mostly, she felt for her because of what she would soon be dealing with as her husband returned home.

"You must be strong, Eiselle," she murmured. "Bric needs your strength. I did not tell you the rest of the message – Bric is carrying Mylo back to Narborough, but not on horseback. He is walking the entire way with Mylo in his arms and when he gets here, it will be up to us to separate him from Mylo's body. I cannot pretend to know what is going through Bric's mind right now, but surely he is suffering greatly. The army knows this and that is why they are walking with him. They are all walking back to Narborough because Bric is."

Eiselle stared at her in shock and horror. It was true she had not spent her life around knights, and she didn't entirely know the bond they shared, but she could only imagine how strong it must be. These were men who spent their lives defending each other, fighting with each other, and a bond like that must have been one of the strongest of all bonds.

The army is walking with him. Only men who had great love for Bric would do such a thing, supporting him in this horrible moment. It was such a touching thing to do, men united in tragedy. It was then that Eiselle realized, more than ever, that it wasn't her right to grieve the situation. That right belonged solely to Bric, Angela, and the de Winter army.

All of them, united in grief.

"Poor Bric," Eiselle finally breathed. "Tell me what to do, Keeva. Tell me what to do for him and I shall do it."

Keeva was pleased to see that Eiselle was showing her strength. The woman had been forced to show a great deal of strength since her marriage to Bric, so she wasn't surprise. In fact, she hadn't really expected anything less. Keeva let go of her hands and stood up, touching her cheek affectionately.

"I must go to Angela," she said softly. "She must know of Mylo's passing. You will go to the gatehouse and wait for Bric. When he comes, you will tell him that he must give over Mylo's body to be tended. Daveigh said that no one has been able to convince Bric to release Mylo, so it must be you. He must listen to you. Be firm, but be kind. Be understanding. But do what you must to force Bric to release Mylo. Once he does, you must bring Bric to your chamber and keep him there. Daveigh fears that Bric has suffered some kind of breakdown and we must make sure Bric is safe above all."

It was a good deal to absorb but Eiselle forced herself to understand and to agree. It seemed to her that Bric had survived the battle, but only physically. The death of Mylo had cut him deep, but just how deep remained to be seen. Truth be told, Eiselle had seen Bric at his weak points. She knew the best way to handle him was with love and patience.

At least, she hoped that would work.

There was little choice.

As Keeva went to find Angela, Eiselle left the keep and headed for the gatehouse. It was mid-afternoon on a fine summer day, and she shielded her eyes from the sun as she crossed from the inner bailey and into the vast outer bailey, noting the group of men gathered by the main gatehouse.

There were soldiers everywhere and she normally stayed away from the outer bailey and, in particular, the gatehouse. So as she drew near the imposing two-storied structure, she naturally slowed her pace, seemingly uncertain about her place in the grand scheme of things. But

Keeva had told her to come to the gatehouse, so here she was. As she drew near the collection of men, one man in particular approached her.

"Lady MacRohan," the man addressed her formally. "My name is Roget. I am in command of the gatehouse when the army is away."

Eiselle looked at the man; he was tall, rather thin, and walked with a limp. "My lord," she said. "Lady de Winter told me to wait for my husband at the gatehouse."

Roget nodded, the strain on his features apparent. "Aye, my lady," he said. "Did... she tell you why?"

"She did."

"Then you know that he is carrying a dead man."

Eiselle had understood that, but it hadn't been in the forefront of her mind. Now, Roget had put it rather bluntly and the mere thought made her queasy stomach feel even more queasy.

"I have been told," she said. "Lady de Winter has told me that I must ask my husband to release Mylo. That is why I have come."

Roget simply nodded, the distress on his features evident. He indicated for her to follow him and she did, beneath the enormous gatehouse until they were outside of it, gazing at the road beyond that was clear for a quarter of a mile before disappearing into the trees.

The lands surrounding Narborough were lush and green because of the river, and across the road, Eiselle could see fields of summer flowers blowing in the gentle breeze that came from the east. The gatehouse of Narborough was at an angle, so it faced northeast, while the road that led up to it came from the east, passed by, and then continued on to the west towards the river.

Like most of the men at Narborough, she now stood outside of the gatehouse, looking down the road the led off to the east because the soldiers were looking in that direction. Roget stood beside her, his gaze also on the road leading east.

It seemed to Eiselle that everyone around her was tense with apprehension, knowing what was approaching and fearful to see it. Truth be told, Eiselle was fearful, too, but she had taken to heart what Keeva had told her – it wasn't her right to grieve. She had to do whatever necessary to help her husband, who was evidently in a terrible state. But much like the men around her, all she could do was wait for him to come.

It was like waiting for a hammer to drop.

"How far away is the army?" she asked Roget.

The old soldier's focus was on the road. "Not too far away, according to the messenger," he said. "We should start seeing them shortly."

Eiselle didn't know if she felt better or worse about that. The tension from the army was beginning to affect her, filtering into her veins no matter how hard she tried to shake it off. The wind was picking up a bit, lifting her hair, swirling around her and whistling. It only served to enhance the uneasy atmosphere they were all facing.

Waiting and watching for something they'd prefer not to see.

As they stood there, Eiselle heard some commotion off to her right, turning to see Manducor run through the gatehouse, a bundle of material in his arms. He headed straight for Roget.

"I found this," he said to the man, holding up what appeared to be a horse blanket, dusty with straw. "Will this do?"

Roget nodded. "It will do fine," he said quietly. "If MacRohan hasn't covered up the body…"

His gaze trailed over to Eiselle, standing a few feet away. Manducor caught sight of her and immediately understood the implications.

"The women must be spared," he muttered, handing the blanket over to Roget. "Lady de Chevington must not see her husband in that state."

As Roget took the blanket, Manducor headed over to Eiselle. She watched him approach.

"They told you what happened?" she asked him.

Manducor nodded. "They did. It is very unfortunate."

Eiselle's gaze lingered on him a moment, to perhaps decipher what he truly thought about the situation, before returning her attention to the road.

"I am not sure what to think about any of this," she said. "I have never been around armies or knights prior to my marriage and I cannot help but feel I have trespassed into a situation that I have no right to be part of."

Manducor looked at her. "Why would you say that?"

Eiselle was struggling with emotions that were trying very hard to bubble up. "Bric had his life her at Narborough before I came. These men he fought with... they are part of the brotherhood that is Narborough. Then Bric married me and, although he loves me and I love him, I feel wholly unworthy to be part of this tragedy. He killed his knight and I understand that is terrible, indeed, but who am I to comfort him? I know nothing. I am stupid when it comes to what he must be feeling."

Manducor understood. "By virtue of your marriage to MacRohan, you are involved more deeply than most," he said quietly. "Eiselle, I know you are frightened and, God knows, you have faced a great deal of tribulation since you married Bric. It is too much to ask of any woman. But let me see if I can explain what has happened in words you can understand – men that fight and die together form a bond that goes beyond blood. Do you have a sister? A brother?"

Eiselle shook her head. "Nay."

"But you have a mother and father that are still living?"

"Aye."

"Then imagine if you accidentally killed your mother. Can you imagine the grief and guilt you would feel for such a thing?"

"I believe I can."

"Then that is what your husband is feeling, only worse. All you need to know is he probably feels grief and guilt badly enough that it will eat him alive if he lets it."

"Then what must I do to help him?"

Manducor sighed faintly. "All I can tell you is to be gentle with him, and to be understanding," she said. "Do not tell him that he will feel better someday. Do not tell him that everything will be all right. Do not tell him stories to try and take his mind off of what has happened. Hold him when he weeps, feed him when he cannot eat, and simply be there to listen to him should he need to speak. That is the only advice I can give you."

It didn't sound as if she could do very much at all. "But I feel so… useless. I do not know if I can be any help to him."

Manducor put a big hand on her shoulder. "Simply being with him, every second of every day, will be enough. He must know that you will never leave him, lass. Can you do that?"

"Of course I can," she said. "But will you please do something for me?"

"If I can."

Eiselle looked at him, tears glimmering in her eyes. "Pray for him," she whispered. "Mayhap God will finally talk to you and He will tell you how we can help him."

Manducor simply nodded, patting her on the shoulder gently before dropping his hand. As they stood there, one of the sentries on the wall shouted, and men began to take up the cry that the army was on the approach.

That cry was like a scream to Eiselle. It seemed to run right through her, making her entire body feel as if she'd been struck by lightning. Everything tingled. Her nervous stomach began doing flips as she labored to remain calm. *You must be calm for Bric*, she told herself. *No matter what he looks like or how he behaves, you must be strong for him!*

God, she didn't want to fail him.

The activity on the walls grew as, far down the straight stretch of road, they could see men appear. They looked like little specks, dots with legs, all of them moving. In the distance, they could also see horses, but they had no riders. They were being led by their masters, all of them walking down the road towards Narborough, all of them feeling the summer heat as the temperatures on this day had remained elevated. It was enough to cause a man to sweat as he stood in the sun, watching and waiting, and Eiselle saw Roget as the man began to walk down the road, quickly, carrying the horse blanket with him that

Manducor had brought him.

Somewhere down the road, Roget disappeared into the gang of men and horses that was approaching. Eiselle took a few steps away from Manducor, lifting her hand to her eyes to shield them from the sun, straining to catch a glimpse of her husband as he carried his dead comrade home.

And then, she saw him.

She saw a man walking down the center of the road at a distance, carrying a burden which, as the man drew closer, appeared to be a body. Hypnotized by the sight, Eiselle took a few more steps down the road and away from the gatehouse, struggling to make the figure out clearly. She saw the pale blond hair before she ever saw any features, knowing that it was her husband and that he was, indeed, carrying a body in his arms. Considering Mylo had been a well-built man, to carry his body those sixteen miles back from Castle Acre was enough to put a strain on even the strongest man.

But her heart was breaking at the sight. The closer he came, the bigger the lump in her throat. She blinked rapidly, chasing off the tears, thinking she'd never in her life seen anything so horrible and tragic. Her dear, poor husband was carrying his brother-in-arms all the way home.

It was the saddest thing she'd ever seen.

The group grew closer and she could make out the features on Bric's face. He looked dazed to her, his entire face red with sweat and exhaustion. The warm temperatures weren't helping. She could see Daveigh and Pearce walking beside Bric, and she saw clearly when Daveigh took the horse blanket from Roget and tried to cover Mylo with it. But Bric wouldn't let him; for whatever reason, Bric didn't want Mylo to be covered up.

And they drew closer. Eiselle caught a glimpse of Mylo's pasty-white form and she could see the caked blood and gore all along the left side of the man's neck, shoulder, and head. When she realized his head was flopping back and forth because it had been nearly cut loose, she stopped looking at him. Fighting down the vomit, her eyes fixed on Bric's face and that was where they remained. When he came within about twenty feet of her, she walked out to meet him.

But Bric wasn't looking at her; he really wasn't looking at anyone. He was simply looking ahead. Eiselle looked quickly to the faces around him, to Daveigh and Pearce, and other soldiers who were walking with him in solidarity. They all appeared so stricken and shattered.

But rather than feel stricken and shattered herself, Eiselle realized she had to do something. Keeva had told her that it was up to her to separate Bric from Mylo, and that was exactly what she intended to do. An entire army was watching her husband crumble and, God willing, they weren't going to see anymore. She would protect Bric from their pity and even judgment if it was the last thing she did.

It was time for her to show her worth.

"Bric?" she said, walking right up to him and cutting off his path. When he came to an unsteady halt and looked at her, she smiled timidly. "Bric? You are home now, my love. You made it home."

Bric looked at her with an expression that could only be described as hollow. It was as if the man was completely hollow. But he recognized her; the silver eyes shifted when he looked at her as if realization dawned. Then his features tightened.

"I did this," he said hoarsely. "I killed him."

He sounded so very pathetic, his voice raspy and breathless, as if a thousand knives were scraping up his innards and coming out of his mouth. Eiselle felt his pain and it was an effort not to react.

Be strong!

"It was an accident," she said softly, moving towards him slowly. "You did not mean to kill him. It was an accident."

Bric watched her as she came closer and closer, finally putting her hands on his left one, the one that was holding Mylo around the shoulders. When she touched him, he inhaled sharply, drawing in an unsteady breath. It was like her touch awoke something in him, breaking him out of the daze he'd been in.

228

"He sacrificed himself for me," he said, speaking to her as if they were the only two people in the entire world. "He told me to watch my back, but it was so dark... so dark... I felt a man next to me and believed it to be the enemy. But it was Mylo. I cut him down, Eiselle. I killed him."

Eiselle could see that something wasn't right with him. The man had reached the breaking point and all she could think of was getting him inside the keep and away from his men. Bric needed peace, quiet, and privacy to work through whatever was happening to him. Her sense of protectiveness towards the man came on strong.

"It was an accident," she said again. "You must not blame yourself. Now, you must let the men take him away because he needs to see Angela. She is waiting for him and you must let him go. You have taken great care of him and I know he would be appreciative, but now you must let him go. Please, Bric... let him go."

She began pulling at his fingers, trying to force him to release his grip. Swamped with temporary madness and indecision, Bric hesitated.

"Please, my love," Eiselle said softly, reassuringly. "Please let him go. It is time."

Bric resisted a moment longer before finally allowing her to move his hand. Swiftly, Pearce and several other men swooped in to remove Mylo from his arms as Daveigh threw the horse blanket over the corpse to shield it from the world. As this was happening, Eiselle put her arms around Bric and began pulling him towards the gatehouse.

"Come with me," she said softly, steadily. "Come inside with me. You must rest now."

He was walking stiffly, being separated from Mylo and not at all sure he wanted to be. "But... but Mylo..."

"Mylo will be well tended, I promise," Eiselle assured him, looking to Manducor and silently pleading for his help. "Mylo will be taken care of and now we must take care of you. It was a long walk from Castle Acre and you must rest now. Come along, Bric."

Manducor came up behind them, walking on Bric's other side. He didn't try to touch the man, but merely walked alongside him should he be needed. Right now, Lady MacRohan was doing an excellent job of tending her husband, but it was a sight that was shocking even for a seasoned man like Manducor.

Seeing MacRohan carry his dead colleague home was one of the most tragic sights Manducor had ever seen. He should have been shocked by it but, in truth, he wasn't. MacRohan's brush with death had changed him, as most were aware, and it was a fragile man who had returned to battle far sooner than he should have.

Bric MacRohan was strong, stronger than any man alive, but slaying his fellow knight, accidental though it might be, had pushed him beyond his endurance. The fragile man had cracked, and the results were before them.

It was devastating.

So, Manducor followed the pair as they headed into the keep. He thought they might lose MacRohan when Lady de Chevington and her terrible son came bolting from the keep, with Lady de Chevington screaming and Lady de Winter running after her. But Eiselle kept a tight grip on Bric and wouldn't let him follow Angela even though he tried. He tried to call after her, to tell her that he was sorry, but Eiselle put her hands on his face and made him turn away. Then, she pleaded with Manducor to physically help her and he did, coming alongside MacRohan and taking one of the man's arms to pull him into the keep.

But they all heard Angela screaming and weeping over the body of her husband.

It was a sound none of them would ever forget.

CHAPTER SEVENTEEN

"How is he feeling?"

The softly-uttered question came from Daveigh.

Standing outside of Bric and Eiselle's chamber in the dark and cool corridor, the question was directed at Eiselle. Keeva was sitting with Bric because Daveigh had wanted to speak with Eiselle, who hadn't left her husband's side since his return to Narborough two days before. She'd remained with him every second and, even now, she was nervous to be away from him.

Her manner was edgy.

"He is sleeping," Eiselle said. "Weetley prescribed wine with poppy in it, so every time he has awoken, I have forced him to drink it. Weetley says it is best right now to make him sleep."

Daveigh grunted miserably. "God," he muttered. "So the man has been kept sedated."

"He must recover, my lord. Sleep will surely help."

Daveigh wasn't so sure that was true, but he couldn't dwell on that. Decisions had to be made. He'd been agonizing over the situation since it happened, devastated at the loss of two of his knights. All of Narborough was in mourning.

"Eiselle, we must speak," he said, running his fingers through his dark hair in a weary gesture. "After Bric's injury and before the battle at Castle Acre, Bric and I discussed sending him to Bedingfeld Manor to rest and recover. He seemed quite agreeable to going and now I believe it is more important than ever. You must get the man away from Narborough so he can recover his wits, and his emotions, and Bedingfeld is a perfect place for this. It is simply not healthy for him to remain here."

Eiselle remembered her conversation with Bric where they had discussed going to a lesser de Winter castle so she could have a keep of her own, but she didn't know about the discussion regarding Bedingfeld. At this point, she was going to have to trust Daveigh to do what was right for Bric, so she simply nodded.

"Whatever you feel is best, my lord," she said. "All he has done is sleep for two days, so I have not spoken to him about it, but if you believe it best, then we will go."

Daveigh nodded. "Good," he said. "I will have horses and wagons prepared, and you can depart on the morrow. I will send fifty men with you, and servants, and will make all necessary preparations, so you needn't worry about anything."

"I will not."

Daveigh gazed at the woman in the darkness of the corridor; there was still a good deal more on his mind, things he felt that he needed to say. "You must know how much anguish I feel over the situation," he said, lowering his voice. "Bric is my rock, the greatest knight in my arsenal. I feel as if the heart of the de Winter army has been ripped out with Mylo's death and Bric's... illness. You cannot know how terrible I feel about all of this. I simply want him to get better."

Eiselle smiled weakly. "As do I," she said. "And he will. Rest is all he needs, I am certain of it. He will come back, better than before."

Daveigh wasn't so sure. Although he had seen his own father suffer with battle fatigue, it hadn't been as bad as what Bric was suffering. At least his father hadn't killed a friend. He wasn't entirely sure there would be any coming back from it, but he wouldn't dispute Eiselle, who had been as steady as the northern star throughout the ordeal. The timid, quiet woman who had married the fearsome Irish knight had transformed into something powerful. He couldn't help but feel both respect and pity for the woman.

"Let us hope so," he murmured. "Meanwhile, I will make the arrangements for your departure to Bedingfeld."

"Thank you," Eiselle said. As Daveigh turned to leave, she stopped him. "If Bric asks, where is Mylo? He has already asked for him when he woke briefly, but I did not answer him. At some point, I must tell him something when he is lucid and it is my fear that he may want to attend the man's funeral mass, or at least go to the man's grave."

Daveigh began shaking his head before she'd even finished speaking. "That would be a terrible idea," he said. "That would throw the man right back to that horrific moment and he would never heal from it. Angela has taken Mylo back to his home of Chevington, in Suffolk, and he will be buried in the church of his ancestors. Bric cannot do anything more for the man and he must understand that. It is over."

Eiselle simply nodded, for Daveigh seemed agitated and despondent over the whole thing. She could see how much the situation pained him. As she turned for the door to her chamber, Daveigh spoke again.

"Did you know that he put his talisman around Mylo's neck?" he asked. When Eiselle turned to him, shocked, he nodded his head. "I, too, was surprised by it. Do you know what is inscribed on it?"

Eiselle pictured the fine metal cross in her mind's eye. "He showed it to me, once," she said. "It says 'Greater love hath no man than he lay down his life for his friends'."

Daveigh appeared particularly saddened as she spoke the words, those poignant words that every soldier lived and breathed. Words that meant so much to any man who had ever lifted a weapon, Daveigh included.

"He said that Mylo deserved it," he said quietly. "I have never seen Bric without that talisman, and for him to give it to Mylo... it was a sacrifice on his part. That talisman means a great deal to Bric."

Eiselle hadn't even realized what Bric had done. He'd given her the talisman, once, to comfort her, and she had given it back and made him promise never to give it to her again. But she hadn't made him promise never to give it to anyone else. Knowing how much it meant to him, she was overwhelmed with the sadness of it, too.

"I know it does," she said. "But he must have felt very strongly if he gave it to Mylo. Being responsible for his death, I suppose it was the only thing he *could* give him, something that was so close to his heart. I hope Angela permits him to be buried with it."

"I asked her if she would and she agreed. She doesn't blame Bric, you know. I found that surprising."

"As do I. But I am glad."

Daveigh simply nodded as he headed down the corridor, with the unhappy duty of sending his High Warrior away from Narborough looming ahead of him. Eiselle watched the man go, noting his slumped shoulders and damp spirit. That wasn't the Daveigh de Winter she had come to know.

Mylo's death and Bric's breakdown was affecting them all.

Retreating back into the chamber, Eiselle shut the door softly behind her. As she stretched her back out, stiff from sitting for so long next to her sleeping husband, she heard Keeva speak.

"Why not try and sleep, Eiselle?" she murmured. "I will sit with Bric while you do. Certainly, you have not slept much."

Eiselle grinned. "Is it that obvious?"

Keeva smiled in return. "You are a lovely lass, with or without sleep," she said. "But you do look tired."

Eiselle stood at the foot of the bed, looking at her husband, who was breathing heavily and steadily as a result of the poppy potion. Her smile faded.

"It does not matter how I feel," she said. "All that matters is Bric. Daveigh is going to send us to Bedingfeld Manor. He says Bric needs to go away from Narborough."

Keeva already knew that. She and Daveigh had discussed it the night before. Her husband wasn't sleeping well, either, thinking he was responsible for all of this. It was his army, after all, and Bric and Mylo were his knights. He'd let them fight in the dark when he could have just as easily called a retreat simply for safety's sake. But he'd let them fight and Mylo's death had been the result.

But it was more than that with Daveigh. His guilt over Bric's mental state ran deep. It had been against his better judgement to allow Bric to go to Castle Acre, especially when he knew how mentally unstable the man was after his injury, but he'd let him go just the same. It wasn't as if Bric had given him any choice, but Daveigh knew he shouldn't have let him go.

That decision was going to cost him.

But Keeva didn't say anything about that. What Daveigh felt was only between them, and she would not share it. Much like Eiselle, she didn't want her husband's weaknesses or doubts to be known.

"Bedingfeld is a beautiful place," she said. "It is deep in the country and has a lovely garden and a pond. It will be an excellent place for Bric to rest and regain his health."

Eiselle moved to the other side of the bed, opposite Keeva, and put a gentle hand on Bric's forehead. He wasn't warm, or ill, simply exhausted, and the poppy was having a strong effect on him. As long as he was sleeping, he wasn't miserable, so Eiselle was glad for small mercies.

"I hope so," she sighed. "I do believe I will take Manducor with me. He seems to know much about knights, and men, and he will be of assistance."

Keeva thought on the smelly priest who had made himself a fixture at Narborough, whether or not they wanted him there. She snorted softly.

"Then if he is going, I shall make sure to send double the provisions," she said. "And double the wine."

Eiselle chuckled. "Aye, you'd better," she said. But quickly, she sobered. "Keeva, you have been around knights your entire life, have you not?"

Keeva nodded, her thoughts turning towards her youth, her childhood. "Aye."

"Have you ever seen anything like this? What Bric is going through, I mean."

Keeva sighed faintly. "Aye," she said. "But warriors do not speak of such things. Men who suffer from this keep it to themselves, like a dark shame. We do not speak of it."

Eiselle's brow furrowed. "But why?" she asked. "I do not understand why it is a shameful thing. Men like Bric… he is the strongest man I know, but he is also just a man. That means he has the weaknesses of a man. Why is it shameful when these weaknesses become evident?"

Keeva could see she didn't quite understand. In truth, Keeva wasn't even sure she understood. "Because men like Bric are perfect," she said softly. "Perfect warriors who inspire the armies. Men look to knights like Bric and they have faith in their strength. When that strength falls, they all fall."

"I do not believe that. It does not seem fair."

"Fair or not, it is the truth," Keeva said. "I come from a family of warriors that believes in this ideal of the perfect warrior, and Bric is part of that family. That means he has had a good deal to live up to. He has two younger brothers, Brendan and Ryan, and they are both just like Bric. They all fostered in England, as Bric did, but only Bric actually serves in England."

Eiselle was interested in anything that had to do with her husband's background. "He did not tell me that he fostered in England," she said, "but he did tell me of his brothers."

Keeva sat back in her chair, thinking of her big, loud Irish family that she missed so much.

"Our family is from Munster," she said. "In fact, our family is descended from the High Kings of Munster, but Munster is a region with a great deal of English influence. English lords have properties there and, long ago, my ancestor knew it was better to ally with England than fight to the death. He wanted peace for his people, so he agreed to allow some of his young men to foster in England and learn English ways. Bric fostered in the finest houses, you know – Bowes Castle in Durham – before returning to Ireland to share what he'd learned with other Irish warriors. When I was betrothed to Daveigh, he came with me, back to England where he already had many friends. Bric's bond with his English counterparts runs deep."

Eiselle was looking at Bric's sleeping face as Keeva spoke. "Friends," she murmured. An idea was coming to her as she thought on Keeva's story. "My cousin, Dash, adores Bric. He speaks very highly of him. Keeva… if I write down some notes, can you pen Dash a missive and have it delivered to Ramsbury Castle right away?"

Keeva nodded. "Of course, love. Why?"

Eiselle was on the verge of a plan that was lifting her spirits the more she thought on it. She'd expressed her concern to Manducor about not having lived with knights, about not knowing what they were going through. But even if she didn't, there were men who loved Bric and knew exactly what he was going through. Perhaps men willing to help him.

Men who might come to Bedingfeld.

"Because you have given me an idea," she said. "You said that Bric has many friends. He has men who love him. I know you said that men who suffer as Bric is suffering do not speak of it, but I cannot believe his friends would not want to help him. Dash, for example. I cannot believe he would judge Bric for suffering so."

Keeva knew Dashiell and his reputation as a fine, fair knight. "I cannot believe he would, either."

Eiselle lifted her hands. "Then who better to help Bric through this terrible state than those friends who adore him?" she said. "Surely Dash will know what to do, because with God as my witness, I certainly do not. Mayhap, instead of hiding Bric's situation, we should ask for help. I ask you to write to Dash immediately and ask him to come to Bedingfeld Manor."

Keeva appeared rather encouraged by the suggestion. "Do you think he will?"

Eiselle was feeling increasing excitement over her idea, thinking that finally there might be some genuine hope for Bric. Perhaps Dashiell would give him the understanding and guidance he needed.

"I do," she said firmly. "If Bric is suffering, he will want to help. I know it."

As Eiselle rushed over to the table that held Bric's writing kit so she could scratch out a few notes, Keeva thought that her suggestion was a very good one. Eiselle could give Bric all of the love and support he could ever need, but it might not be enough. Only a man who understood battle and sacrifice might truly be able to get to the core of Bric's issues, and Keeva knew for a fact that there were many men who owed Bric their very lives.

Men who would be willing to help.

Daveigh couldn't help because he was too close to the problem. Pearce now had his hands full with the command of the de Winter war machine, so he couldn't help, either. Therefore, the logical solution was to seek those men who knew Bric, and loved him, and would be willing to do anything to help him.

Perhaps there was hope, after all.

For the first time in days, Keeva began to feel some relief.

The next morning when Eiselle and a groggy Bric were loaded in to a fortified carriage for the trip to Bedingfeld, Keeva sent a rider with her missive straight to Ramsbury Castle in Wiltshire. The recipient of that missive, Dashiell du Reims, was one man who literally owed Bric his life.

Help would soon be on the way.

CHAPTER EIGHTEEN

Bedingfeld Manor
13 miles southeast of Narborough Castle

B IRDS WERE SINGING.
And they were damned loud.

Bric had no idea how long he'd been laying there, listening to the birds screaming outside of his window. When he rolled onto his side to actually look at the window, it wasn't something he recognized at first. It wasn't the window from his chamber at Narborough and as his gaze moved around the room, he realized he wasn't even at Narborough. He was somewhere else.

Slowly, he sat up.

"So the sleeping giant awakens," Eiselle said softly. "Good morn to you, my love."

Bric heard Eiselle's voice, turning to see her sitting over by a rather elaborate hearth that was burning gently. The hearth was set into a brick wall that was as tall as a tree. In fact, the entire chamber itself was huge, as was the bed Bric was lying in. It had four huge posts, one on each corner, and a canopy overhead with heavy brocade curtains.

Bric looked around, muddled by the opulent surroundings. This definitely wasn't their tiny chamber at Narborough. Rubbing his eyes, he felt as if he'd been asleep for a thousand years.

"Am I truly awake?" he asked.

"You are."

"Where are we? This is not our chamber."

Eiselle had been sewing on something that she set aside as she stood up from her chair. With a smile on her lips, she made her way over to the bed.

"We are someplace safe," she said. "How do you feel?"

Bric blinked his eyes. "I do not know yet," he said. "*Where* are we?"

"Bedingfeld Manor."

Recognition dawned. Bric looked around again, gaining his bearings. He didn't feel quite so confused now. "I see," he said. "I should have recognized those windows."

He was referring to the elaborate windows with the diamond-shaped mullions, a unique feature. Eiselle leaned over and kissed him on the head.

"Not to worry," she said. "We have all the time in the world to become acquainted with this place. It's really quite beautiful, at least what I've seen of it."

Bric reached up and pulled her down to him, and Eiselle slid into his embrace easily. But it wasn't any embrace; it seemed powerful and tense. When she tried to move, he wouldn't let her. He just held on to her, tightly.

"How long has it been?" he whispered.

Eiselle wasn't sure what he meant. "Since when?"

"Since..." He couldn't finish. He abruptly let her go, raking his fingers through his closely cropped hair. "I do not know. That sounds foolish, but I truly do not know."

Eiselle sat down on the bed next to him, watching him struggle. Although he seemed more lucid than he had the last time they'd spoken, only time would tell just how coherent he really was. She proceeded carefully.

"What is your last memory?" she asked gently. "Let us start there."

He shook his head. "I cannot," he muttered. "I do not want to think."

Eiselle didn't push him. "Then don't," she said. "Lie there and think of nothing more than the shape of the windows, if it pleases you. I shall be here if you need me."

She stood up from the bed with the intention of returning to her sewing, but she didn't get very far. His hand shot out, grasping her by the wrist so she couldn't move away. When Eiselle turned to look at him, questioningly, he simply sat there, staring off into space.

"Do not leave me," he whispered.

Slowly, Eiselle sat back down, but he kept his grip on her as if afraid she was going to get away. He kept staring off into the room, not focused on anything in particular, but it was clear that his mind was working. After a moment, he released her wrist.

"Mayhap… mayhap I should speak of it," he muttered. "It is not as if I can run from it."

Eiselle didn't want him to think he was under any pressure to talk of his feelings. "You do not need to speak of it now if you do not wish to. There is all the time in the…"

He cut her off, but it wasn't harshly. "Nay," he said, more firmly. "I… I must speak. I feel as if my head is about to burst."

"Then speak. I will listen. What do you remember?"

Bric thought hard, trying to collect thoughts that were as tangled as cobwebs. "I remember the battle at Castle Acre," he said as the day of the battle started coming back to him. "It was a good day, Eiselle. I was strong and the men were strong. I felt… I felt fine, as I normally do in battle. I was killing and men were dying, so it was a good day for me. We chased the French away from the village and they ended up by the priory. That is where… is where…"

He abruptly faded off and Eiselle reached out and took his hand, squeezing it tightly. "That is where?"

He looked like he was growing nervous because he swallowed hard. His manner seemed uneasy.

"That is where night fell, and we found ourselves in a fight down by the river," he continued. "It was a dark night, darker than I have ever seen, and the fight became dangerous. I even stopped swinging my sword, fearful I was going to strike down my own men. And then… then I heard Mylo shouting to me."

"What did he say?"

"He told me to watch my back," he said. The hand Eiselle was holding was beginning to shake. "It was too dark for me to see anything, but I could feel men beside me, struggling. There was a fight going on right next to me. I saw the flash of a blade in the darkness, and was certain I was about to be killed, so I had no choice but to strike out in self-defense. But then the torches were brought in and I saw that it was Mylo I had cut down. God help me… it was Mylo."

He lowered his head and Eiselle lifted the hand she was holding, kissing it. "Bric, it was not your fault," she insisted softly. "You did not know it was Mylo. How could you?"

He was hanging his head now, looking at her hands as she held on to his scarred fingers. "That was what he said," he muttered. A lone tear dropped onto their tangle of hands. "He said it was not my fault."

"You were able to speak with him?"

"He lived for a brief time. He told me that he had put himself between me and the man attempting to kill me. He sacrificed himself so that I might live."

Eiselle was starting to tear up because she could hear the anguish in his voice. More than that, she now knew what had truly happened between Bric and Mylo, and it was too tragic for words. But it wasn't her right to cry; she knew that. Bric was the one in need of comfort, and not her, no matter how badly she hurt for him.

Reaching up, she gently caressed his stubbled cheek, wiping away his tears.

"Bric," she said, quietly but firmly. "I know you are devastated, my love. I cannot pretend to know how you feel, but I can only think to say one thing to you – if the situation was reversed, and it had been Mylo who cut you down under the same circumstances, would it have been his fault?"

Bric drew in a long, unsteady breath before releasing it all in a heavy rush. He simply sat there, holding her hand, pondering her words.

"Nay," he said after a moment, his voice trembling. "He would not have known it was me, as I did not know it was him. There is no one to blame. Even so, I cannot shake the guilt, Eiselle. I killed a man who was trying to protect me."

"He laid his life down for you, just as you would have done for him had the situation been different."

"That is true. I would have. I would gladly give my life now for his."

Eiselle almost said something selfish, that she was glad Bric hadn't given his life for Mylo, but she bit her tongue. It was not her place to say such a thing, even if she did think it.

"Daveigh told me that you gave him your talisman," she said. "That was a generous thing to do, Bric. I am sure it would have meant a great deal to Mylo."

Bric could only nod. Then, he began to search around his neck, hunting for something beneath the smelly tunic he wore. He was still in much of the clothing he'd worn for the battle because, not wanting to disturb him too much, Eiselle had only stripped him down to the breeches and tunic he wore beneath his mail. But he quickly found what he was looking for, pulling out the keepsake that Eiselle had given him.

"The talisman belongs to Mylo, but this belongs to me," he whispered, looking at it. "It is the most valuable thing I own."

Eiselle smiled. "And *you* are the most valuable thing I own," she said. "Daveigh sent us to Bedingfeld because you must regain your strength. Being wounded as you were, and then suffering through Mylo's death, has earned you some time to rest, Bric. You have been through too much as of late. Even the strongest of men must rest."

Bric looked at her with eyes that didn't seem to glisten as they usually did. The Bric MacRohan she had married was a sharp man with a sharp mind, fearless in every way. But the man that looked back at her now… it wasn't the same man.

He seemed empty.

"What I have endured as of late is something I have never had to endure," he said. "It as if I do not even know my own mind any longer.

I woke up in a room I did not recognize but what is even more frightening is that I do not remember how I got here. You asked me what I remember, and I have told you everything I can recall. I also remember carrying Mylo in my arms after I killed him… and now I am here. Bleeding Christ, I am surely losing my mind. What is happening to me?"

It was a plea and Eiselle felt it carve through her like a dagger. She didn't know what to say because Manducor had warned her against tell him that the world would be well again, or trying to make his concerns not sound so serious.

The man was seeking answers she could not give.

Therefore, she did the only thing she could think of – she threw her arms around his head and neck, embracing him tightly. She had never had to fight off tears so strongly as she had to at this moment.

He was breaking her heart.

"Nothing has happened to you," she said hoarsely. "You simply need rest and I shall make sure you get it. You shall rest and then you shall be ready to take on the world again, I swear it. You *are* the High Warrior, Bric. You are the strongest man in all of England and you must never doubt that, not for a moment."

His big arms went around her, holding her so tightly that he was squeezing the breath from her.

"I do not know who I am any longer," he whispered.

Eiselle kissed the top of his head, holding him close. "*I* know who you are," she whispered fiercely. "You are my husband and I love you very much. Now, can you do something for me?"

"If I can."

"Can you eat something? You've not eaten in days and if you are going to regain your strength, then you must eat. Please?"

He didn't say anything for a moment. He simply held her tightly, his face buried in her bosom. When he finally spoke, it was muffled against her flesh.

"If you wish it," he said.

Eiselle kissed his head again and released her grip on his head. "It would make me happy," she said. "Stay in bed. I shall send for food right now."

She kissed him on the lips before bolting from the bed and rushing to the chamber door, pulling it open. They were on the top floor of Bedingfeld and right outside the door was a landing and a small servant's alcove. The servants had been told by Daveigh to stay close to Lady MacRohan in case she needed anything, so both a male and female servant were nearby, prepared to move when Lady MacRohan sent them down to the kitchen for food. She also asked for hot water so she could clean Bric of the battlefield grime, and the gore on his skin that she was certain had been left by Mylo.

If she was going to help him, and tend to him, then it would start now.

As the servants fled for the kitchens, Eiselle shut the door and turned to Bric, still sitting on the bed.

"Food is coming," she said, smiling at his pale face. "You shall eat and then you shall sleep again, and mayhap tomorrow, I shall escort you on a walk outside. The gardens are truly lovely, though I only had a brief glimpse of them when we arrived."

He looked at her, his lovely little wife with her beautiful dark hair pulled into a bun at the nape of her neck. The guilt he felt, that was his constant companion, began to shift as he gazed into her sweet face.

"*Mo chroí,*" he said after a moment. "You married a man only to take care of him constantly. That is no life for you."

Her smile vanished. "You will not say that again," she said sternly. "I have the exact life that I want with the man I want. My life is perfect."

He sighed faintly. "You are not married to a man. You are married to a weakling."

He looked away from her as he said it, but she moved around the bed so he couldn't avoid looking at her. When he tried to turn away again, she put her hands on his face, forcing him to meet her eye.

"I am married to the man I love," she whispered. "You are the High

Warrior, Bric. You will always be the High Warrior. You do not have a weak bone in your body. You are simply tired."

Bric closed his eyes because he could no longer look at her. "I am broken."

He sounded so grieved, so very torn and shattered. Eiselle wasn't sure what more she could say to the man. She knew he was upset and it was an effort for her not to become upset, too, because his words hurt. She didn't like to see him so down on himself, his usual confidence destroyed.

That was perhaps the worst part.

"Broken or weak, you are still my husband," she said. "If you are trying to scare me into leaving you, I will not do it. I do not scare easily."

Bric stared at her a moment before breaking into a crooked smile. "I do not imagine that you do," he said. "You have proven to be quite formidable, Lady MacRohan. You are a fine tribute to a man who does not deserve you."

It did her heart good to see him smile, if only for a moment. Her hands were still on his cheeks and she kissed him, a sweet and lingering gesture.

"Do not tell me how wonderful I am because it will go to my head," she said, watching him smile yet again. "Whether or not you like it, I am here to stay. I am not leaving you, not ever, so you had better come to terms with it. Please do not ever try to discourage me again because next time, I might have to punch you in the face."

Bric started laughing, a raspy sound that was like music to Eiselle's ears. It was good to hear him laugh. She put her arms around him again and kissed him just as there was a knock on the door. Moving quickly to the panel, Eiselle opened it up to the servants bearing food and hot water.

As it turned out, Bric was very hungry and ate everything on the tray. Once he was finished with his meal, he permitted Eiselle to strip him and wash him down with hot water and soap that smelled of flowers, but he really didn't care. Her attention, and her warm touch, was the best medicine in the world for him at that moment.

When he slept again, it was with Eiselle in his arms.

Two days later

"WE HAVE FOLLOWERS."

"I know."

It was Bric who had uttered those words, words of observation as he and Eiselle walked in the garden of Bedingfeld on a bright summer morning. The garden was truly a delight, surrounded by tall stone walls, with every imaginable flowering plant and vine contained within. Several servants tended the garden constantly, and it showed – it was a marvel to see, and Eiselle had to stop every few feet and smell a bloom. Bric walked along beside her, dressed simply in a tunic and breeches, following his wife as she marveled at the glorious flowers.

But he'd seen movement out of the corner of his eye when they'd first entered the garden. They'd come in through the main gate but there was also a smaller gate in the southern wall that paralleled the brook that ran through Bedingfeld's property and fed the moat that surrounded the manor house. That smaller gate had opened, and then shut, and then he'd seen the top of someone's head as they moved amongst the bushes, trying to stay out of sight. First one head and then two.

Bric was curious, but Eiselle wasn't paying much attention. She was more interested in the flowers. As she paused by a stalk of foxgloves that was taller than she was, Bric casually looked over his shoulder in time to see two little faces peeking out at him from a bush several feet away. When they saw that the big knight was looking at them, they quickly disappeared. Bushes shook as they moved away, and Bric was certain he heard laughter.

Children's laughter.

"They are giggling," he said. "Our stalkers are giggling."

Eiselle stood up from having been bent over a smaller variety of foxgloves. "I heard," she said. "I do not know who they are, but I am sure we will discover it soon enough."

She was casual about something that had Bric's curiosity. Perhaps it was the observant knight in him. As he watched the stalkers move through some bushes over near the wall, the main gate suddenly swung open again, spilling forth Manducor. When Bric realized that it was the priest, he shook his head in a gesture of disapproval.

"What are you doing here?" he asked, though he didn't sound entirely displeased. "My wife and I came to Bedingfeld for a rest and we do not need an audience."

Manducor sensed that Bric was jesting with him, at least for the most part. He was sure there was some part of the man who genuinely wanted to be alone with his wife, but Manducor couldn't stay away any longer. He'd spent the past few days staying clear of Bric and Eiselle, simply to give them time alone, and keeping busy around the manor house, at least as much as he could.

But when he saw Eiselle and Bric head to the garden on this bright morning, he wanted to see for himself how Bric was feeling. He'd not seen Eiselle enough to have a decent conversation with her, as she had remained in the master's chamber with Bric since their arrival, so now was his chance to sate his curiosity.

"My lord, I promise I will not be a burden," he said. "But I thought I would come in case I could be of service. You may want a man to play games with, you know. There is a chess set in the hall and I shall be more than willing to challenge you for supremacy."

Bric eyed the man as he came near. "Chess," he muttered. "I've not played that in years."

"Good," Manducor said firmly. "Then I shall triumph over you."

"I did not say I'd forgotten how to play, old man. Be careful who you challenge."

Manducor grinned. "I am very bold now, but ask me again when we actually start playing. You frighten me, MacRohan."

Bric couldn't help but snort at the man. "If that is true, then you are the only one."

His smile rapidly faded as he turned away, wandering in the direction of a stone sundial in the middle of the garden. Manducor and Eiselle exchanged glances, hearing the struggle in Bric's voice again. Eiselle sensed that perhaps this time, Bric didn't want to hear her tell him how great he still was or how much she loved him. He'd been hearing that enough. Perhaps this time, he needed to hear something from another man, someone who, perhaps, understood more of what he was going through.

It was time for Manducor to earn his keep.

Manducor understood Eiselle's pleading expression, though he was hesitant. He wasn't a peer of MacRohan's, but he had been a knight, once. He understood the profession. As Eiselle pretended to turn back to the flowers, Manducor followed Bric as the man wandered towards the sundial.

"Have you thought about what there is for you if you do not return to the knighthood?" he asked, watching Bric turn to look at him. "I did not and look what became of me. You are better than me, MacRohan, a thousand-fold. What would you do if you were not a knight?"

Bric's brow furrowed. "Who says I will no longer be a knight?"

Manducor shrugged. "No one," he said. "But it must have crossed your mind."

Bric's gaze lingered on him a moment before turning back to the sundial. It seemed to be leaning to him, so he kicked at it, trying to level it.

"It has not crossed my mind," he said. "There is nothing else for me. I was raised as a knight and it is what I know."

"Then you *will* return to the battlefield."

Bric sighed sharply. "I am sure I will, at some point."

"Then why do you say no one is afraid of you?"

Bric was becoming more agitated as he moved the sundial around.

"I do not wish to discuss this with you."

Manducor didn't want to upset the man; he was simply trying to get him to think a little. "Do you remember when we first met?"

"Regretfully, I do."

"You slapped me and called me a drunkard."

"Your point being?"

Manducor grinned as he leaned in Bric's direction. "You do not even have to try to be frightening, MacRohan," he muttered. "All you need do is look at a man and he is terrified. You have that gift and it is not something everyone has. Even now, the gift is apparent. It is not something you will ever lose, no matter how damaged your confidence."

With that, he turned away, heading towards the smaller garden gate, looking at the flowers as he went.

Bric watched him go, realizing that, in some very small way, he felt better. He was still capable of frightening Manducor, so that had to be a boost to his pride. He remembered slapping the man around when they'd first met and, strangely, he felt rather sorry he had. But not sorry enough to tell him.

As Manducor headed out of the gate, Bric caught movement off to his left again, seeing that the bushes were moving once more. There was so much lush undergrowth in the garden that it was easy for his stalkers to conceal themselves. He was growing more curious now so he moved away from the sundial, his focus on the shuddering bushes several feet away. It was some kind of a yellow flower bush and since he didn't know a flower from a weed, all he knew was that it was a big bush with big, yellow blooms. But it was shaking so hard that some of the yellow petals were falling off. Just as he neared the bush, a young boy jumped out at him.

"Halt!" the child cried, holding a small switch in his right hand. "You may not pass!"

Dutifully, Bric came to a halt. The boy couldn't have been more than four or five years in age, dressed in simple peasant clothing, but having a fairly fierce expression for a servant. He was brave, this one. Behind him, a little girl with golden curls bolted out of the bushes and ran for the wall of the garden, pressing herself against the stone beneath a creeping vine of purple flowers as if fearful of Bric.

"Who are you?" Bric asked the lad. "What are you doing here?"

The boy swished the stick back and forth, quickly enough to make it sing. "I am Sir Royce," he declared. "You are the wicked knight and I must vanish you!"

"Do you mean vanquish?"

"Nay!" the child barked. "Vanish! You must go!"

Bric put a hand up to his face, hiding the smile that threatened. "I see," he said. "Tell me, Sir Royce – where do you live?"

Royce pointed at the manor house, briefly, with his stick before returning it to a defensive position. "There," he said. "Now, will you fight me?"

"I will not."

Royce lost his aggressiveness. The stick came down and he frowned. "But why not?"

Before Bric could answer, he heard a voice behind him.

"I agree – why not?"

He turned to see Eiselle standing behind him, grinning. Lifting her hand, she extended a stick to him about the same size as the one the little boy held.

"Well?" she said. "You have been challenged, MacRohan. Since when do you refuse a challenge?"

Bric looked at her. Then, he looked at the stick. Suddenly, his heart began to pound and his palms began to sweat. He was coming to feel agitated and angry, something he didn't like in the least. He didn't want to be angry and agitated at Eiselle, but he couldn't help himself. At that moment, all he wanted to do was run.

He couldn't get away fast enough.

"I won't do it," he muttered.

Turning on his heel, he blew past her, knocking the stick out of her hand as he went. It was an accident; he hadn't meant to do it, but he'd been moving so swiftly that he'd recklessly hit it.

But it was a small stick and even as it popped out of Eiselle's grip, it hardly made a sound. Truthfully, she didn't even care – she was more concerned about Bric as he practically ran away. She watched him go, her smile fading, feeling bad that she'd tried to coerce him into something he wasn't willing to do. It had only been a game, from her perspective, and she thought it might do him good. But Bric hadn't viewed it as a game at all. Perhaps in that little boy's stick, he saw another sword.

He saw a battle.

He wasn't ready to fight.

Eiselle thought that he simply needed some time to be alone. She had been with him every second of every day since his injury, the only time that they were separated being when he had gone to Castle Acre. Perhaps, in this instance, the man just needed some time away from her, to ponder his thoughts and clear his mind without her constant presence. The thought brought tears to her eyes, thinking that maybe she'd been too attentive, and now pushing him to do something he clearly wasn't ready to do. Playing with a child, even with a pretend-sword, had upset him.

She had upset him.

As the main gate slammed when Bric passed through it, Eiselle didn't follow. She made her way over to a stone bench that was lodged near the smaller gate, one that was situated beneath the shade of a big poplar tree.

As young Royce and his curly-haired playmate found excitement elsewhere, Eiselle plopped down on the stone bench and wept.

CHAPTER NINETEEN

Ramsbury Castle
Wiltshire

D ASHIELL WAS SITTING in the very large solar of Ramsbury Castle, one used by the Dukes of Savernake for generations. Presently, it belonged to the current duke, Bentley de Vaston, and the man was seated at one end of a very large, cluttered table whilst Dashiell was seated at the other.

Dogs milled about the solar, looking for any scraps of food left over from the night before, while two servants tried to unblock the hearth that was billowing clouds of smoke into the chamber.

But Dashiell and Bentley weren't paying attention to the distractions; they were both working on tasks, with Bentley scribing a missive to William Marshal and Dashiell studying a map that showed the entire southern portion of England. He was studying it with a purpose because the day before, they'd received a message from William Marshal that was about to shape the course of their next few months.

Another battle was on the horizon.

It would seem the rebels, still reeling from the defeat at Lincoln, had moved south and were starting to converge near Dover in Kent, shores that could easily receive supply ships from France. It was serious news because it meant they weren't defeated, or even finished as far as that went. It meant the French intended to stay. As Dashiell studied the map and the roads that would become the Savernake army's path into Kent, another figure entered the solar.

Enormous, with dark blond hair and eyes of the clearest blue, Sir

Sean de Lara was the man who had brought the news of the rebel movements from William Marshal. Sean was part of the de Lara family, the Lords of the Trilateral castles along the Welsh Marches, but Sean's status in the annals of England's politics went far beyond being a mere member of a prestigious family.

He was one of William Marshal's most trusted spies.

A spy who had been placed with King John for many years, earning the king's trust and becoming the man known as *Lord of the Shadows* – the bodyguard for the king, whom all men feared. Sean had earned himself a terrible reputation during his tenure as John's bodyguard, becoming known as someone who would do anything the king told him to do – kill, abduct, or anything else that came from John's twisted mind.

It had been a horrific assignment for the moral and ethical de Lara, who'd had to put all of that aside in order to earn that terrible reputation so he could spy on the king for William Marshal. The information he'd killed, begged, or stolen to obtain had saved the rebel cause against John too many times to count. His position had been invaluable and he knew it, but the personal cost to him had been great.

Sean de Lara had become a monster.

But that monster had been slain two years ago when his true identity had been discovered and he'd nearly been killed by John's assassins because of it. Yet, for a man as strong and seasoned as de Lara, it hadn't ended him. He'd come back into William Marshal's fold as the Marshal's greatest spy and advisor, only now he was actually working with those he was allied with rather than pretending he was against them.

"So you have finally decided to rise this morning," Dashiell said as the man approached the table. "You've become lazy in your old age."

Sean snorted. "And you've become foolish in yours," he returned. "It was not you who rode forty-three miles yesterday. I have earned my rest, du Reims."

Dashiell pulled up a stool for the man. "So you have," he said. "Bent is writing a missive to Marshal as we speak, but I did not ask you last night how soon you will be returning to the Marshal. Will you be leaving today so that you may take the missive with you?"

Sean sat down on the stool but not before sending the nearest man-servant for food and drink. He grunted wearily as he planted his backside on the wooden seat, his gaze moving to the map Dashiell had laid out on the table.

"Nay," he said. "I only stopped at Ramsbury because I was on my way home to see my wife. I've not seen her or my children in two months, so the Marshal gave me permission to see them before I am tied down to the army in Kent. God's Bones, I would like for this to be the last time for a very long while. I am tired of spending all of my time with the army while my children grow up."

Dashiell understood his position. With his own wife pregnant with their first child, leaving her now did not thrill him. "My wife is due to deliver our child in the next month," he said. "I do not wish to be with the army in Kent, fighting off the damnable French, when my son is born."

"Hopefully, you will not be.'"

"Tell me of your children, Sean. We've not had a chance to talk about them."

Sean smiled faintly, a big dimple carving into his left cheek. "I have three girls," he said. "The twins, Lorica and Lorelle, are the eldest. They were barely a year old when my third daughter was born. Her name is Evangeline and she is a holy terror. Had she been a boy, she would have made a magnificent knight."

Dashiell grinned. "Three girls," he said, lifting eyebrows. "Thank God you have the de Lara wealth to support the dowries you will need."

Sean couldn't disagree. "If you have a son, then we must speak. Evie will need a husband someday."

Dashiell looked at him in disbelief. "Marry my son to the Holy Terror? You must be mad."

"I will pay you handsomely."

Dashiell started to laugh. "Then I may consider it," he said. "But we have time enough to discuss it later. Right now, I am more concerned about moving my army into Kent. So the Marshal is very sure that Prince Louis is bringing over a fleet from his father?"

Sean sobered as he looked at the map. "Aye," he said. "We have intercepted messages between Louis and his father. There is a fleet coming, supported by French nobles, and unless we want a massive war on English soil, we are calling all English warlords to Kent and to ensure that fleet never makes it to the shore. This is serious, Dash. I cannot stress it enough."

It was a gloomy situation they were facing. Dashiell shook his head, disappointed.

"After the battle at Lincoln, I thought the Marshal was negotiating with Louis for peace," he said. "What happened?"

Sean's expression turned bitter. "They simply could not come to an agreement," he said. "Louis has too many stipulations, too many men he wants pardoned or, worse still, given lands in England. The Marshal has denied him most of his demands, and Louis has resolved to fight on. We only recently received news about the incoming fleet and we suspect it will be docking somewhere at or near Dover."

Dashiell was looking at the map, which included most of Kent and Dover. "I was very much hoping Lincoln would be the last of it," he said. "It seems as if we've not even seen the worst of it yet if Louis is waiting for a fleet to support him. That means new and fresh men, Sean. Our warlords are exhausted from years of heavy fighting."

Sean knew that. "We will have to take a last stand at Dover," he muttered. "It was a chance we took inviting the French over in the first place to help us defeat John, but we have a new king and no longer any need for French support. Still, Louis cannot understand that. He wants what we have promised him and I cannot say that I blame him, but promising him the throne of England was done in desperation. We are no longer desperate and we must push the French away once and for all. If we do not, I fear we will lose our country."

It was a terrifying thought. Bentley was listening now; he had a new son, and a new position as the Duke of Savernake, and he didn't want to risk any of that. Bentley was a good man and the Savernake dukedom was in good hands after he married the heiress last year. The more he heard the conversation between Sean and Dashiell, the more concerned he became.

"Has the Marshal put out a call to everyone, Sean?" he asked from across the table. "I cannot imagine that he would not summon every warlord in England."

Sean looked to the young and handsome duke. "Everyone, my lord," he said. "The de Lohr brothers, Worcester and Canterbury, are already in Kent, heading for Dover, as is Arundel and nearly everyone else from the south of England. It takes longer, of course, to send word to the far reaches of the country, which is why he asked me to stop at Ramsbury. He would like to see Savernake's army move out within the week."

Dashiell was looking at Bentley; the two were close friends and had served together for many years. If they couldn't read each other's minds these days, then they were close to it. Dashiell said what Bentley was thinking.

"We shall be ready," he said quietly. "Have you sent word to East Anglia and Norfolk? My father should be mobilizing his army, and Norfolk has de Winter at its head. You must have their strength."

Before Sean could reply, a Savernake soldier appeared in the doorway of the solar, knocking on the doorjamb in the open portal.

"My lord?" the soldier said. "Beg pardon for interrupting, but we received a missive from Narborough Castle. It is for Dashiell."

Dashiell stood up and went to the door. "Speaking of de Winter," he said ironically. He took the missive and sent the soldier away, breaking the seal as he headed back to the table. "It is probably from Bric, wanting to know when our army is departing for Kent. Surely they have already been informed."

The seal came away and Dashiell reclaimed his seat next to Sean as he started to read. Bentley turned back to his missive and Sean accepted the food brought to him by the manservant. He plowed into the warmed-over beef and gravy, with big hunks of bread to sop up the juices. In fact, he was so involved in his meal, and Bentley was so focused on his missive, that neither one of them noticed the expression on Dashiell's face as he read the missive twice. When he finally finished, he lowered the missive to the table and simply stared at it.

"Oh, God..." he finally muttered. "I cannot believe it."

Bentley didn't look up from his missive. "What?"

"Bric is in trouble."

That prompted Bentley to look at him. "What do you mean? What has he done?"

Dashiell shook his head, picking the missive up and handing it over to Bentley. "You misunderstand," he said. "Read it. This missive comes from Lady de Winter and she says Bric has suffered a breakdown, of both the spirit and the mind. Eiselle has asked for my help."

By this time, Sean was looking up from his food. "Bric?" he repeated. "Bric MacRohan?"

Dashiell nodded, his expression tense with concern. "You would not know this, but Bric married my cousin last month," he said. "He suffered a serious injury shortly after their marriage in the battle at Holdingham Castle. According to Lady de Winter, the injury turned Bric into a timid man, but he went to battle against French rebels at Castle Acre recently and in the heat of battle, accidentally killed one of his own men. Lady de Winter says that Bric is unable to function any longer and that my cousin requests that I come to Bedingfeld Manor in Norfolk immediately."

Sean stopped chewing. "*MacRohan?*" he said again, as if he didn't believe it. "This cannot be the same Bric MacRohan I know."

"I am afraid it is."

"But... it is simply not possible."

Dashiell was nearly ill with distress. "Possible or not, I am sure Lady de Winter would not lie about the situation."

Bentley read the missive twice before setting it down. He, too, appeared greatly distressed. "My God," he breathed. "He cut down one of his own men. I wonder who it was?"

Dashiell shrugged. "Does it matter? I can only imagine how I would feel if I cut you down, or any other warrior close to me. God, it must have destroyed Bric completely for him to lose sight of his duty like this. Honestly, I am in shock by all of this."

Bentley was, too. He looked down at the missive as if more of an explanation would be contained within those words, something that gave a catastrophic reason behind Bric's collapse. But all he could see was desperation in Lady de Winter's careful writing, speaking of a man they all knew.

But it was like she was speaking of another man entirely.

"There is no denying we have seen lesser knights fold under the stress of battle," Bentley said. "It is not uncommon. But it certainly does not happen to men as fearless and powerful as Bric MacRohan."

Dashiell could only shake his head. "Well, *something* has happened to him, or Lady de Winter would not have sent this missive," he said. "Were it not for Bric, I would not be alive, and you, Bent, would not be the Duke of Savernake. He has made all things possible for us and we owe him everything."

"Truer words were never spoken, Dash."

As Dashiell nodded firmly to Bentley's statement, Sean spoke. "Bric and I have seen a few battles together," he said. "I do not know him as well as you two do, but I consider him a friend. Hearing this greatly disturbs me. Men like MacRohan do not break."

Dashiell sighed faintly, thinking of the last time he saw Bric as he'd been recuperating from his battle injury. "The last time I saw him was after he'd been badly wounded," he said. "He'd been weak but alive, and certain nothing to indicate he was... disturbed. But he had passed into unconsciousness and I left before he recovered. Still... sometimes the strongest men cannot bend, and when stress becomes too great, they simply shatter. I have seen it before, as Bent has said. Mayhap Bric was so strong that when he finally felt weakness as others do, mayhap... mayhap it was simply enough to destroy him."

The mood of the chamber was full of gloom. Each man was lost to his thoughts of Bric MacRohan, evidently weakened beyond his endurance. It simply didn't seem possible, to any of them, coming from a man such as Bric. But Dashiell knew there was only one thing to do.

"I must go to him," he finally said, standing up from his stool. "Bent, I will have Aston muster the army to move to Kent. But I must attend Bric and I will have to meet you in Kent at some point."

"Wait," Bentley stood up, too. "I agree that Aston can handle the army, which is why I am going with you. You said it yourself – I owe Bric my very happiness. If he is in trouble, then I will do all I can to help."

Aston Summerlin was Dashiell's second in command at Ramsbury, a knight who was quite capable, as they were suggesting. Therefore, the army could still move out as the Marshal had requested. But Dashiell and now Bentley would not be moving out with the army.

They had something more important to attend to, and Dashiell accepted Bentley's help without argument.

"Sean," Dashiell turned to the man next to him. "I know you wanted to return home to see your wife, but Bent and I should leave immediately. Could you possibly put off your departure until tomorrow to aid Aston as he assembles the army? He may require your assistance and I would consider it a personal favor."

Sean shook his head, rising to his feet. "I am going with you," he said. "Bric has been a paragon of power for the cause of England in every battle I have ever fought with the man. If he is in trouble, then mayhap you will need my assistance more than Aston will. I have seen men crumble under the pressure of battle and it is not a sight for the faint of heart. I know what it is like to be so badly wounded that you are certain death will claim you. I know what it feels like to struggle to return from such an injury, thinking that you will never be the same again. Let me come, Dash; I may be of some use to MacRohan."

Dashiell was genuinely touched by Sean's offer. There was no more noble or dedicated man in all of England as far as Dashiell was concerned, knowing Sean's past as he did. He was a man of great experience and great worth. That he should want to help Bric, too, spoke volumes to the man's generosity.

"Of course you may come," he said after a moment. "But what of your wife? I would imagine we will spend some time at Bedingfeld and you may not be able to return to her before we head for Kent."

Sean grunted, regretfully. "The Marshal wants his armies in Kent in the next few weeks," he said. "We will have very little time as it is, so it was not like I was going to have a good deal of time to spend with my wife. But this... this is important and she would understand that. Bric is in command of the de Winter war machine, and as powerful as it is, it will not be nearly as strong without him at the helm. Do you get my meaning?"

Dashiell did. "We must put a sword in Bric's hand again."

"It sounds heartless, but when men suffer such as Bric is evidently suffering, the longer they are allowed to wallow in their depression, the more likely that they will never wield a sword again."

"Then the sooner we help him regain what he has lost, the better for us all."

"We need him in Kent, Dash. A man like MacRohan is irreplaceable. We must help him find himself again."

It did sound heartless, but it was also true. They needed Bric's power and command presence against the French, in perhaps the final battle to end all battles as they had been suffering through since King John and his warlords splintered into separate factions. If William Marshal thought the battle at Dover was going to be enormous, then chances were, it would be. It would also be decisive.

They needed a man of Bric's caliber to help win that fight.

"Then we go to help him for his own sake," Dashiell said with some finality in his tone. "But we also help him for England's sake as well."

Sean simply nodded. It was something they all knew. Their reasons for going to Bric's aid were altruistic, but they were also self-serving. Without Bric in the battle, somehow, they would be diminished as a whole, so it was imperative to get Bric back on his feet. It was imperative to fight off the demons that had the man in their grips and put that broadsword back in his hand so he could do what he was born to do.

He wasn't called the High Warrior without reason.

CHAPTER TWENTY

Bedingfeld Manor
One week later

THE FIRE IN the hearth snapped quietly as Eiselle, Bric, and Manducor sat in the hall of Bedingfeld Manor.

It was after sup on a lazy summer evening, and the doors of the manse were open to let the cooling breeze flow through the house. The day had been a warm one, and the fire was more for light than for warmth. Servants had brought in banks of tallow candles that now shed their yellow glow around the room, casting away the darkness of the coming night.

Bric and Manducor sat on opposite ends of a small table near the hearth, a vicious game of chess between them. This was their second game, even though they had been playing most of the week, but the first game took two days before Bric had finally triumphed, and this game was nearing the end with Bric inching towards victory yet again.

Manducor was beside himself because of it. As Bric had quickly come to learn, the man was a poor loser. He groaned, grunted, cursed, and tried to cheat his way to victory, but Bric watched him closely and was able to tell when he tried to do anything unseemly. This thoroughly upset Manducor, who denied cheating to the point of nearly throwing a punch at Bric for the intimation. But he wasn't foolish; he'd tangled with Bric before and knew the man's strength, so not even in the spirit of friendly competition would he try and strike the man.

For certain, he would lose more than just the game.

As Bric sat silently and stoically, studying the game board for his next move while Manducor drank more wine and farted to break Bric's concentration, Eiselle sat over by the hearth and sewed on the interior for a heavy robe she had been making for Bric, one she'd been working on since before he left for Castle Acre. She had the leather pieces for the exterior of the robe, tanned and softened by the tanner at Narborough, and now she was stitching together the fine interior that was made of brown wool with a silk pattern sewn into the back of it.

As she worked, her ears were attuned to the men playing chess, fighting off a grin when Manducor would make a spectacle out of himself. In truth, she'd been watching their relationship for the better part of a week and she was pleased to see that Bric was at least willing to do something other than stare aimlessly from a window. He'd done that the day after their first walk in the garden, when she'd tried to coerce him into engaging the servant boy and Bric had run off as a result. She'd come into the manse later to find him sitting in their chamber, simply staring out of the window. It took her some time to realize he'd been staring at the garden, watching her the entire time.

He'd apologized to her for snapping at her, and she'd forgiven him on the spot. In truth, she'd forgiven him before he'd even asked for forgiveness, but she still didn't think it was a good idea for her to cling to him day in and day out. Certainly, she wanted to be there if he needed her, but she worried that her constant hovering presence would both annoy and cripple him.

And that was where Manducor came in.

In speaking briefly to the priest, she explained her fears, thinking that Bric would need the company of a man more than ever. A man who understood what he was going through. Manducor didn't exactly understand Bric's demons, but he knew the man needed someone to give him a sense of worth and respect. Perhaps, it would even help him regain his confidence. That was why he played chess with him, or backgammon on occasion, resolved to let Bric win when the truth was that Bric was winning regardless. It was something that had put a smile on Bric's face, much to Eiselle's delight.

And there was something more she hoped might put a smile on his face, although she wasn't quite sure how to tell him. The nausea she'd been feeling in the mornings and sometimes in the evening had been constant, and growing worse, and even with Bric's breakdown, he still made love to her every night, telling her how very much he loved her. It began to occur to Eiselle that she hadn't suffered through her menses since her arrival to Narborough, which had been several weeks earlier.

With her upset belly and tender breasts, Eiselle was thinking that, perhaps, she might have conceived. In speaking to one of the older female servants that had come with her from Narborough, the woman convinced her that she was, indeed, pregnant.

It was a secret Eiselle had been holding in for an entire day. She and Bric had never discussed children and given the fact that his nerves were frayed, she wasn't sure the news would be well-met. But she quickly decided that the man had to know because it wasn't something she'd be able to keep a secret forever. At some point, he was going to figure it out, especially the way he liked to make love to her, so a rounded belly wouldn't escape his notice.

The man had to know.

But she would tell him later, in the privacy of their bedchamber, because he was enjoying himself with Manducor at the moment. She continued to sit by the fire and sew, glancing up at him every so often. When their eyes met, he would wink at her and she would smile in return. She loved the man so much she couldn't put it into words, and she knew he felt the same way. She just wanted to see him well again and although she'd never been one to pray very much, she was coming to pray daily that Bric would find his sense of self again.

He was too great a man not to.

Eiselle was just putting the final stitches in part of the silk pattern when someone appeared beside her. Looking to her right, she saw that it was young Royce, or Sir Royce as he had introduced himself. She'd learned that the child who had challenged Bric to a duel with sticks was the son of a woman who worked in the kitchen. His father, she'd been told, had died the previous year of a fever.

Eiselle had discovered that when she'd asked about the boy, and evidently he wasn't supposed to be in the garden when the lord and lady were present, so he'd been punished as a result. All week, his mother had kept him to the kitchens, so Eiselle was surprised to see the lad standing beside her with a wooden plate laden with something baked. She smiled at him but the smell of baked goods hit her in the nose and with her strange stomach as of late, she immediately felt nauseous.

"Goodness," she said, trying to lean away from the tray of delights. "What did you bring me?"

Royce didn't seem particularly pleased to be forced into servitude. "My mam says I should give these to you, my lady."

Slightly confused, Eiselle looked over her shoulder to the door that led into the kitchen and saw Royce's mother standing there, smiling encouragingly. Assuming she was trying to teach her son how to be a proper servant, Eiselle played along.

"They look... delicious," she said. "What are they?"

Royce sighed heavily, as if he wished he was anywhere but offering food to the lady. "Mam made them," he said. "They have oats and... and honey... and... and currants. Mam says to eat them."

Eiselle took one of the little cakes simply to appease the child, but she had no intention of eating it. Even looking at it was making her stomach roll. She pointed to Bric.

"Go and ask Sir Bric if he wants a cake," she said. "Go ahead."

Turning towards Bric, Royce shuffled his way across the floor. When Manducor saw him approach, he reached out to take more than one cake but Royce quickly pulled the tray away.

"Nay," he said. "Not you. The lord."

Eiselle started to giggle, turning her face away when Manducor looked at her in outrage. Bric, however, smiled faintly and with some approval.

"As it should be," he said. "I should always be served first before this hairy boar."

Royce held the plate up to him. "Mam says to eat them."

Bric cocked eyebrow. "She does, does she?" he said. Then, he inspected the small cakes, selecting one. But he didn't eat it right away and Royce looked at him with some worry, so he forced himself to take a bite. "Delicious. Thank your mam for sending these to me."

Royce nodded, but he didn't leave. He simply stood there, watching Bric eat the honey cake. There was wonderment and awe in his expression, much as there had been in the garden when they'd first met. Royce was clearly enamored with Bric.

"Are you a knight?" he finally asked.

Bric was still chewing. "I am."

"I want to be a knight."

Bric swallowed his bite and looked at the child. Clearly, the boy had no concept of the knighthood, or how men achieved such things. But he remembered from the first time he'd met Royce how the child had been pretending to hold him off with a stick. But to Royce, it had been the biggest broadsword in the land. He'd even challenged Bric to a fight, which didn't go particularly well in the child's favor.

As Bric gazed at the little boy, he felt himself softening, just a little. He'd never been around children much, leaving the training for squires and pages to the knights with more patience, but that didn't mean he didn't feel some compassion for a very small servant boy who had no idea of the way of the world. In fact, he envied the child for his innocent view of the world. For Bric, that innocence was long gone, with disillusion and doubt taking its place.

He longed for those days when nothing in the world bothered him.

He wondered if he'd ever know them again.

"Are you sure you want to be a knight?" he asked after a moment. "Why not follow your father? What does he do?"

The child made a face of distaste. "He tends the garden," he said. "I do not want to tend the garden. I want to fight!"

Bric lifted his eyebrows. "That is a fine goal, but it takes training and discipline," he said. "The knighthood is only for the sons of noblemen, I am afraid. Tending a garden is not so bad."

Royce frowned. "But I am strong," he pointed out, holding up an arm to show Bric his muscle as the tray of cakes wobbled dangerously. "I would make a good knight."

"I am sure you would, but I am afraid it will not be possible," Bric said. "But when you are old enough, and if your father allows it, I am sure Lord de Winter would permit you to be a soldier for the de Winter army. You would still get to fight."

"Can I have a sword?"

"You can, indeed."

That seemed to give Royce a good deal of hope and he smiled brightly at the idea. But Royce's mother, realizing that her son was making a nuisance out of himself, rushed forward to collect her bold son. Royce saw her coming and began to run. The platter with the cakes tumbled to the ground.

"Nay!" he said as he ran away from his mother. "I do not want to go! *Nay!*"

Royce's mother was beside herself with embarrassment. Before she realized it, her son had taken her on a chase twice around the hall as Eiselle, Bric, and Manducor watched with varied levels of amusement and annoyance. When the child started to make the third round, Manducor stuck out his foot and the little boy went sprawling.

"There," Manducor said quite casually as he turned back to the chess board. "That solves that."

Bric looked at the poor lad who was now being hauled up by his mother. As the woman apologized profusely whilst dragging her son away, the child reached out and pinched Manducor on the arm. As Manducor howled and lifted his hand to hit the boy, Bric burst into laughter and stopped him.

"Nay," he said. "Do not strike him. He is bold and fearless. You'll not retaliate."

Manducor was fuming, but he had his satisfaction when Royce's mother swatted the child's behind as she pulled him into the kitchen.

"Ha!" he said as he heard the boy scream. "I have my vengeance!"

The problem was that Bric could hear the crying, too, and for some reason it upset him. He didn't want to see the child's spirit crushed because he rather liked a spirited child, a servant boy who didn't understand he had limitations. It was only when one grew up and understood the world at large, and the frailty of life, did limitations become apparent. Nay, he didn't like hearing the lad cry one bit.

He turned to Eiselle.

"*Mo chroí*," he said softly. "Will you please see to the lad? He should not be punished. I do not want to hear him cry."

Eiselle smiled at her husband and his tender heart when it came to a crying boy. From the hardened man she had first met, it was a little surprising. But it gave her hope that, indeed, he might be pleased that in a few months, he, too, would have a boy, if God was willing. Putting her sewing aside, she stood up and headed towards the kitchen where she could hear the lad weeping in the distance.

For whatever reason, she felt somewhat woozy after standing up. Perhaps she had stood up too quickly. Whatever the case, she thought she could simply walk it off but the closer she drew to the kitchen door, the stranger she felt. Her head began to swim and spots danced before her eyes, and the last thing she remembered was reaching the door leading into the kitchen and trying to brace herself against it.

And then... nothing.

SHADOWS WERE DANCING on the wall of the darkened chamber when Eiselle opened her eyes again.

It took her a moment to realize she was in her bed as the familiar surroundings came into view. She rolled onto her back, immediately feeling a stabbing pain on the side of her head. She winced as her hand flew to her scalp, only to feel a lump.

"Ouch," she muttered.

Bric was suddenly in her line of sight. "Ah," he said softly. "You have awakened. How do you feel?"

Eiselle blinked up at him. "I do not know," she said. "What happened?"

He smiled at her. "You fainted."

Eiselle seemed shocked. "I did? Are you certain?"

Bric chuckled. "Do you remember how you got here?"

She looked around a little. "Nay."

"Then you fainted. I brought you here." His smile faded as he sat down on the bed beside her, putting an enormous hand on her forehead. "You gave me quite a scare, love. Can I get you anything? Wine? Something to eat? Mayhap you need to eat something. God only knows, you've been tending to me like an angel and have not taken care of yourself."

She waved him off. "God, no," she mumbled. "Nothing to eat."

The way she said it concerned him. "Why? Are you ill?"

Are you ill? Eiselle hear his words and she almost denied them but, as she thought about it, there was perhaps no better time to tell the man he was to be a father. Perhaps that was why she had fainted in the first place; her body had been doing strange things as of late, with pains where she'd never had pains before and something terrible happening to her belly that made her feel like she was burping up fire.

No better time than the present.

"I am not ill," she said quietly. "My belly has simply been upset as of late."

"More upset than usual?"

She eyed him. "What do you mean by that?"

He fought off a grin. "I know your stomach pains you from time to time," he said. "Sometimes you belch louder than I do. It is a prideful talent, Wife."

She tried to scowl but ended up laughing. "I cannot help it," she insisted. "Besides – it is unseemly to discuss such things."

"I have never discussed it with anyone but you."

"See that you don't." Eiselle watched him snicker, thinking that it was good to see him laugh, even if it was at her expense. "Be serious, Bric. I must speak with you."

He wasn't catching on to her solemn tone. "About your stomach?"

"In a way. It is upset for a reason."

"What reason?"

"We are going to have a child."

That stopped his giggles in an instant and the smile vanished from his face unnaturally fast. He just stared at her for a moment before his eyebrows lifted in a deliberate motion.

"We *are*?" he asked in a strangely low tone.

Eiselle nodded, though she couldn't tell if he was happy or enraged about it. Her nervous stomach began to do flips.

"We are," she said quietly.

As Eiselle looked at him anxiously, Bric couldn't quite catch his breath. The room began to rock to the point where he had to stand up from the bed, holding on to the bedposts for support. His mind was whirling with something he'd honestly never thought about even though, in hindsight, it was stupid that he hadn't. He'd been bedding his wife daily, sometimes twice a day, and taking delight in her supple body as he'd spilled his seed into her, again and again.

Of course she was pregnant; his powerful Irish seed had taken root. It shouldn't have been a great surprise.

But it was.

Whirling to face her, Bric could see that she was verging on tears, concerned with his reaction. Or perhaps it was because she didn't want to bear a child. Perhaps she was afraid. In any case, now he wasn't sure how to react even though his momentary surprise was about to turn into a joyous explosion.

"Bleeding Christ," he finally breathed. "Eiselle..."

"You're not happy!" she said, bursting into tears.

He was back on the bed in an instant, his hands on her arms as she covered her face. "I am," he insisted. "With God as my witness, I am. It is simply that I wasn't expecting to hear the news. Are *you* happy?"

Eiselle's hands came away from her face as she looked up at him, the tears miraculously fading. "I… I think so," she said. "It is difficult to be happy when I do not feel very well. But I am happy if you are happy."

He just looked at her, the silver eyes glimmering with warmth and hope and the light of a thousand dreams for the future. Then, he started to laugh, pulling her up against him and holding her so tightly that she burped when he squeezed too hard. That made him laugh even louder.

"Oh, *mo chroí*," he murmured. "My heart. My dearest, sweetest heart. Am I happy? Aye, I am. I truly am. A son, Eiselle. We shall have a son and he shall be the greatest knight the world has ever seen."

Eiselle had her arms around his neck, holding him tightly as she realized that he wasn't upset by this at all. She felt a huge amount of relief.

"It could be a lass," she said. "I have no way of controlling such things."

He released her from his grip so he could look her in the eye. A big hand came up to cup her face. "It will be a son," he said with quiet authority. "God and I are not terribly close, but I intend to have a talk with the man. Our child *will* be a boy, Eiselle."

There was no convincing him otherwise so Eiselle simply smiled at him and he kissed her, twice, before laughing low in his throat and throwing his arms around her again. She could literally feel his giddiness and it made her feel comforted, safe, and loved.

His joy was contagious.

But as he celebrated, Eiselle inevitably thought of Keeva, who had only suffered loss after loss of pregnancy. She and Keeva were dear friends and she was certain the woman would be happy for her, but it still hurt her heart to know that Keeva would be wounded deep-down that the pregnancy was not her own. It wasn't strange that she should think of Keeva at a time like this since Keeva had often shared her childless trials with her.

"I have been thinking," she finally said.

He was still holding her tightly. "About what?"

She sighed faintly. "Keeva," she said. "She is my friend, Bric. I am concerned that our joy will hurt her somehow. All of these years with Daveigh and she has wanted a child so badly. How will we tell her of that we are to have a child, so soon after our marriage?"

Bric released her from his embrace. He wasn't unsympathetic, but he certainly wasn't going to let the thought run his joy.

"Keeva is a strong woman," he said. "She has suffered many disappointments, but we cannot keep the news from her simply to spare her. She will be hurt if we do *not* tell her."

Eiselle knew that. "I am sure you are correct," she said. "She will be happy for us in spite of her personal feelings, I know. She is giving that way."

"She is."

"Mayhap we will give our son the name of her father to honor her. She is your cousin, after all."

Bric cocked an eyebrow, that imperious eyebrow Eiselle has seen back in the days before his injury. She was quite happy to see it now.

"My son will have the name *I* choose for him," he said firmly. "But… I am sure he will have several names, not the least of which will be my father's name, mayhap Daveigh's name, your father's name, and God only knows who else. Our son will have twenty names by the time we christen him."

Eiselle giggled, thinking of a baby with a name longer than he was. Bric kissed her on the cheek before standing up, his mind full of thoughts of a strong son. It was joy beyond measure.

"This summer season has been… difficult for me," he said, his gazing turning to the window and the night outside. He could hear the night birds singing. "It is hard for me to admit that, but it is the truth. Other than our marriage, it has been the most difficult time of my life. But this… *this* brings me happiness as you cannot imagine, Eiselle. *You* bring me happiness."

Eiselle sat up in bed, feeling well enough to stand up. "Do you remember what you told me before you left for Castle Acre? You told me that I was more than your heart could have ever hoped for. You are more than my heart could have ever hoped for, too, Bric. I am so proud that our son will have you for his father, and you can teach him everything you know to ensure that he grows into a fine man."

"Your faith in me is everything. I hope that I can live up to it."

He didn't say anything more than that. Bric's smile faded because, inadvertently, she'd reminded him about his duties as a father, to teach his son what he knew. To teach him about being a knight, and all of the strengths and nuances that went along with the profession.

Two months ago, he would have been eager to teach his son about being a knight, but as he thought on it, he could only feel anxiety and uncertainty. Was he even capable of teaching his son about being a knight? With everything he'd been through as of late, he wasn't even sure he could ever pick up a sword again. Eiselle had tried to coerce him into picking up a stick to mock-fight with a child, and he couldn't do it.

What made him think he could ever touch a sword again?

It was something he didn't want to voice to Eiselle. She'd married a knight, the High Warrior, and not a weakling who couldn't even stomach looking at a blade. He was terrified she was going to think less of him if, after their sojourn to Bedingfeld, he still wasn't capable of resuming his duties. But for his son, he badly wanted to.

He simply wasn't sure if he could.

As he stood there and struggled with his inner turmoil, Eiselle wandered up to him and he put his arm around her, kissing her on the top of the head as they gazed out over the garden to the east. It was dark, but torches along the wall of the manse lit up some of the night, and they could see a glimpse of the garden, dark and shadowed beneath the sliver moon. Bric pulled her close against him, feeling her in the curve of his torso, wanting more than anything to make her proud of him.

Never in his life had he ever suffered such self-doubt.

It was completely alien to him, and ever had been since the odd pangs of nerves and fear had started to pull at him when he'd healed from his injury. The first time he'd gone out to work with the men, as light as that had been, had been the first time he'd ever felt afraid that he'd might be injured again. It was that fear of his own mortality that he couldn't seem to shake, something he'd never before considered.

But it also occurred to him why.

He had a wife he didn't want to leave.

For the knight who had been a polished professional his entire life, the introduction of emotion, as much as he loved Eiselle, had been the beginning of his downfall. Now, with a child, he wondered if he wasn't going to crumble completely. He wanted to stay with his family, not leave them. He didn't want to die like Mylo had.

God help him, that was the core of his problem.

He didn't want to die.

Sweeping Eiselle into his arms, he carried her back to their bed, losing himself in the passion that overcame him so easily when it came to her, the woman he loved with all his heart.

Tonight belonged to them.

CHAPTER TWENTY-ONE

SOMEONE WAS KNOCKING on the chamber door.

Bric heard it and his knightly instincts had him instantly awake, reaching for a broadsword that he no longer kept beside his bed. But that was habit. Glancing to the oil-cloth covered windows, he could see that it was barely dawn. There was a tiny bit of light poking through in what promised to be another lovely summer day.

Climbing out of bed carefully, as not to awake Eiselle, he made his way over to the door. He was nude, so he didn't open it. Instead, he hissed through the crack.

"Who comes?" he muttered.

"My lord, some men have arrived for you," Manducor said. "They are in the hall."

Bric sighed heavily, glancing at Eiselle, who stirred with the raised voices. "Who is it?"

"I do not know. They simply told me to fetch you."

"Are they armed?"

"They are knights."

"Then find me a broadsword before I go down into the hall."

Manducor must have wandered off to do what he was told because Bric didn't hear a reply. Frustrated that he'd been woken so early, and the least bit curious as to who was in the hall, he found his breeches and a tunic, pulling both on. He also pulled his boots on, tying them off before quietly opening the door and slipping from the chamber.

The landing outside was dark, but there was a doorway ahead of him that opened out onto the gallery above the hall. He fully intended to have a look at the men who had come to see him before he went down to confront them.

As he moved into the gallery, Manducor came up behind him, a weapon in hand, but Bric wouldn't take it. He just wanted it at the ready should he be forced to defend himself and his wife. In a life or death situation, that was the only way he was going to pick up a weapon again. But what he saw in the gallery wasn't a threat at all. A grin crossed his lips as he quickly turned and headed down the spiral stairs.

Entering the darkened hall where the servants were just building the fire, Bric saw the three men over near the hearth where Royce's mother was giving them all warmed wine to drink. Bric could see the steam wafting up from the cups in the chill of the room.

"Lock up the women and the silver," Bric said, watching the men turn and look at him. "Someone must have left the door unlocked and now we are overrun."

Bentley laughed as Dashiell headed right to Bric, reaching out to cup the man's face between his two big hands.

"You ugly wretch," he muttered, his eyes glittering with warmth. "The last time I saw you, you had a hole in your chest. God be praised that you survived it."

Bric smiled in return. "I did, indeed," he said. When Dashiell dropped his hands, Bric caught sight of Bentley approaching. "Lord de Vaston, I am surprised and pleased to see you. What brings you both to the wilds of Norfolk?"

Before Bentley could answer, the third figure came into focus and Bric's eyes widened when he realized who it was.

"De Lara?" he gasped. "Bleeding Christ, do my eyes deceive me? It is really you?"

Sean shook his head, a smile playing on his lips. "It is," he said. "It has been a while, MacRohan. But Dash is right; you are still ugly."

Bric was truly astonished to see the legendary Sean de Lara in his hall. "Fortunately, my wife does not think so," he said. "She is sleeping, but I will send for her right away. She will want to see you all."

Sean held up a hand. "No need to wake the woman," he said. "We will be here for a day or two, I would imagine, so there will be plenty of time for us to tell your wife what a terrible mistake she made when she married the likes of you. In truth, when Dash told me you'd married his cousin, I could hardly believe it. I did not think the High Warrior to be the marrying kind."

Bric shrugged. "Nor did I," he said, looking at Dashiell. "It was not as if I had a choice. Dash was going to force me into marriage whether or not I wanted to, so I am happy to say that it has been more than agreeable for me."

"Then you have discovered a whole new life other than warfare?"

Bric's smile faded somewhat. "A whole new life, indeed. It has been... soul-changing. Much has happened."

The mood suddenly changed, turning into something vaguely uneasy. The reason for their visit was like a cloud over their heads, something that could not be ignored any longer. Rather than continue to good-naturedly insult one another, the purpose behind their appearance had to be spoken of. Sean glanced at Dashiell, who took the lead.

"So we have heard," Dashiell said quietly. "Bric, you should know that we have come on Lady de Winter's summons. She said that you have suffered greatly as of late and that you are not yourself. We came to help."

Bric's smile disappeared and he suddenly felt quite embarrassed. He loved these men, and respected them greatly, and he didn't want them to think he was some sort of weakling.

"While I appreciate your kindness, I do not need help," he said with forced bravery. "I am fine. Just seeing you fortifies my heart. A day of feasting and conversation with you three will heal whatever ails me."

"It is more than that."

The words came from the darkened hall entry and the four of them turned to see Eiselle standing in the shadows. Clad in a deep blue robe, with her dark hair slightly mussed and braided over one shoulder, she was astonishingly beautiful. Not one man in the room didn't think so. But as she came into the hall, the light from the hearth hit her face. She was looking at her husband.

"Forgive me, my love, but I cannot let you pretend nothing is wrong," she said. "And Keeva did not send for Dash. I did. I asked her to send him to Bedingfeld because whatever has happened with you, whatever pain and distress you feel, I fear I cannot help you. I fear that only men who understand the strains of the knighthood will understand and I pray that it is through them you find yourself again. Be angry with me if you must, but I did it because I love you. I want simply want you to be well again."

Bric was looking at her with a mixture of frustration and sorrow. His terrible secret was out, courtesy of his wife, and he couldn't decide just how he felt about her interference.

"Eiselle, it was not necessary," he said after a moment.

He was going to try and talk his way out of this; Eiselle could see it. Even if he was too embarrassed to admit the truth, Eiselle wasn't. She turned to Dashiell.

"After his injury, there were rumors at Narborough that his brush with death had changed him," she said. "Keeva saw it, and Daveigh saw it. Daveigh said that Bric became a nursemaid to the men rather than the master they needed. If that wasn't bad enough, he went with the army to defend Castle Acre from a French raid and accidentally killed Mylo de Chevington."

By this time, Bric was hanging his head, but he didn't stop her. Nothing she said was untrue. But hearing his failure from her sweet lips did something to him; it made him feel so very ashamed. Reaching out a hand, he grasped her by the arm to beg her to silence herself, but it was all he could muster. He could do no more because he knew, deep down, that she was trying to help him.

"Eiselle, please..." he whispered.

Eiselle's eyes were filling with tears because she knew this was something profoundly painful for them both. She felt she was spilling

KATHRYN LE VEQUE

all of Bric's deep and dark secrets, but they were secrets meant to be known by those who loved him. Men who could help him, and if they were to help him, they had to know everything.

"They were fighting in the dark at Castle Acre," she went on, her lower lip trembling. "Mylo saw a man go after Bric, but Bric did not see this. Mylo put himself between Bric and the French knight in order to save my husband, but Bric didn't realize it was Mylo. He thought he was about to be killed and struck out in the darkness. After Mylo died, Bric carried him back the sixteen miles to Narborough. He walked the entire way and the army walked with him. After that... after that, he was incoherent. It was as if killing Mylo had broken him. We kept him sedated with a poppy potion and brought him here, hoping the rest would do him good, but he needs more than that. Please... help him if you can. He is the most powerful and wonderful man I have ever known. I beg you... help him."

Her voice cracked with the last few words and tears spilled over. Quickly, she wiped at her face, struggling with her composure, but Bric pulled her against him and wrapped his big arms around her. Eiselle began to weep, painful sobs, as Bric simply held her.

It was a heartbreaking moment for Dashiell, Bentley, and Sean to watch. In fact, Dashiell had to swallow away the lump in his throat. The missive Lady de Winter sent suggested things were bad, but he couldn't have imagined just how bad they were or the exact circumstances. He glanced at Bentley, who was greatly distressed at the scene, and then at Sean, who only had sadness in his eyes. After a moment, Dashiell went over to Bric and Eiselle, in their tight embrace, and put his hand on Bric's head.

"That is why we have come," he said hoarsely. "I owe you my very life, Bric. There is nothing I would not do for you and I swear, I will do all I can to help you through whatever ails you. You saved my life once and now, I am going to save yours."

Bric simply nodded his head, still holding fast to Eiselle. "I am grateful," he whispered. "My wife is grateful. Let me return her to our chamber and then I will come back to the hall and we may... speak on things."

"Take your time," Dashiell said. "We will be down here when you are ready."

Bric could only nod. Dashiell patted him on the head before dropping his hand, watching with great sorrow as Bric escorted the weeping Eiselle back across the hall and up the spiral stairs. When the pair was out of sight, he turned to the men standing behind him.

Bentley was pale with sorrow while Sean seemed to have a deeply intense look about him. Both of them were shocked by what they'd seen, reacting to it in different ways. Dashiell sighed heavily.

"We have work to do, good men," he said. "Whatever happens, we do not leave here without restoring Bric to the man he was."

Bentley shook his head. "We do not have all the time in the world, Dash. God, I wish we did."

Dashiell looked at him. "Whenever you think that we do not have enough time, remember that you owe him your dukedom. Do you have time for that?"

Bentley threw up his hands and turned away, knowing he was resigned to helping Bric no matter how long it took. Even if William Marshal himself had to come and pull them away, still, they wouldn't go without Bric.

Without the man being the confident warrior they knew him to be.

As Bentley wandered back over towards the hearth, Sean was prepared to speak. He'd spent the past several minutes observing something he'd never thought he'd see, and he was as distressed as Dashiell and Bentley were.

But unlike Dashiell and Bentley, he'd been through a time in his life where he'd nearly been killed and he, too, had struggled to come back from it. In that respect, he very much understood what Bric was going through because he'd gone through it, too.

Aye, he understood the man's position well.

"Two years ago, I was nearly killed when the allies marched on the

Tower of London," he said. "I know you were both a part of that siege, but what you may not know is my role in the event. You know of my past with John, so I will not repeat it, but my mission when the rebels were closing in on London was to assure the fall of the Tower of London."

Dashiell came closer to him as he spoke. "I remember that siege," he said. "That was a very difficult and bloody event. Bric was there, too, you know. The de Winter army was one of the first armies to breach the castle."

Sean remembered that particularly dark and terrible night. "At that point, my identity as a spy had been discovered, so the king sent his assassins after me," he said. "They set up on me near the White Tower and they managed to badly wound me, in the chest and in the groin. As I lay there, I was certain that I was dying and I cannot describe what that awareness does to a man. There is an odd sense of peace but there is also a profound sense of disappointment. I had just married my wife, you see, and the thought of not living the rest of my life with her damaged me in a way that is difficult to describe. Only by God's mercy did I heal, but to this day I carry a sense of gratitude – gratitude that I was given a second chance. Bric must be instilled with that sense of gratitude, too. Right now, all he knows is that he almost died, and it frightened him. That is a heavy burden for a fearless man to bear."

Dashiell and Bentley were listening intently. "Then what do you suggest?" Dashiell asked. "Shall we speak to him? Pray with him? How do we instill this gratitude in him?"

Sean smiled thinly. "The man has to understand that he will not break," he said. "When his wife described his timidity following his injury, I understood that completely. I do not believe he is broken so much as he may be at a crossroads. To move forward is a path of no return, of a man who will live timidly the rest of his life. But to go back means he can reclaim what he was. Therefore, we work him until he can hardly stand, and while we are working him, one of us will rush out at him with a broadsword so that he must defend himself. We must revive that killer instinct in him, the one that cost Mylo de Chevington his life."

It seemed rather extreme. "Are you serious?" Dashiell said. "We must wear the man out and shock him in order to help him?"

Sean nodded. "Do not forget; I have been through this myself. I could be wrong, but Bric has two issues as I see it – not only is he living in fear of dying, but because of what happened with Mylo, he has suppressed the killer instinct that is stronger in him than in any man I have ever seen. Instill the gratitude, coax forth that killer instinct, and I do believe he will be restored."

It sounded logical enough, coming from the wise de Lara, a man who had seen and experienced so much in his lifetime. In truth, Dashiell and Bentley had no choice but to agree with him, for they had no better answers. Neither one of them had ever suffered from battle fatigue, but Sean had.

He knew what he was talking about, and they had to trust him.

"Then it is fortuitous that you came with us to Bedingfeld," Dashiell said. "How do we begin?"

Sean lifted his big shoulders. "There is no better time to begin than now," he said. "When Bric comes down from settling his wife, tell him to find his gloves. The man is going outside with us."

With that, he headed towards the kitchen, but Dashiell stopped him. "Where are you going?"

Sean was pulling tight his own gloves. "To the wood pile," he said. "We are going to chop wood, cut down trees, and any other heavy labor we can force Bric into. Have Savernake get his sword and follow us. When Bric least expects it, Lord de Vaston is going to come at him like a runaway ale cart."

Dashiell lifted his eyebrows in surprise, turning to look at Bentley, who didn't seem quite agreeable to Sean's suggestion.

"And do what?" Bentley asked.

"Attack him."

Bentley's eyebrows lifted. "Have you seen Bric when he is enraged?"

he demanded. "The man could knock down a castle single-handedly. I do not want my head cut off!"

Sean simply grinned. "We must hope he tries."

Bentley was horrified. "If he kills me, I will come back to haunt you both, I swear it."

Sean chuckled. "Don't you see?" he asked. "The last time Bric was charged by a fellow knight, he killed the man. You must prove to him that it was an accident."

"How?"

"By living."

With that, he continued on through the kitchen, disappearing out of the door that led to the kitchen yard beyond. When he faded from sight, Dashiell turned to Bentley.

"You always thought you were a better knight than I am," he jested. "Now is your chance to prove it."

Bentley didn't find it the last bit funny. "Did I say I wanted to help? I have changed my mind."

"Too late."

Bentley wasn't really serious, but Dashiell was. They had come to do a job and they were damned well going to do it.

"I AM SORRY, Bric," Eiselle wept. "I did not tell you I sent for Dash because I feared you would be angry. I only asked him to come because I love you."

Bric was trying to calm her down as he pulled off her blue robe, guiding her towards their bed.

"I know," he said patiently. "And I love you. I am not angry, I promise."

Eiselle wasn't convinced. She sat on the bed, wiping the tears and mucus on her face until Bric found a handkerchief and gave it to her so she could blow her nose. As she wiped off her face, she looked up at him with eyes that wouldn't seem to stop watering.

"I hope you mean that," she said, "because I would never do anything to make you angry, Bric, but I fear that you need more help than a simple rest in the country can give. I know that Dash and those men will help you."

Bric sighed faintly as he pushed her down onto the mattress, forcing her to lie down. "We shall see," he said quietly. "It is difficult to know how to fix a problem when you are unsure what that problem is."

Eiselle allowed him to push her down and cover her with the blanket. "At least you are willing to discuss it," she said. "That takes a brave man and I am proud of you. No matter what, I am proud of you, Bric. Surely you must know that."

He smiled, somewhat modestly. "Mayhap I do, but it is good to hear you say it."

Eiselle reached up, touching his stubbled cheek. "Then you will let them help you?"

His smile faded and he averted his gaze. "As you said, I am willing to discuss it," he said. Then, he kissed her hand and stood up. "I would have you rest now while I tend to our visitors. I do not want you straining yourself, Eiselle. You must take care of yourself and my son."

She put her hand on her belly, instinctively. "Do not worry, for we are well," she said. "I will stay to the manse while you are doing what needs to be done. I have much that will keep me busy."

He bent over and kissed her on the head before quitting the chamber. Heading back down the spiral stairs, he could see that there was more light in the manse now that the sun had risen. The early morning sun was streaming in from the east, sending pillars of yellow light through the eastern-facing window. By the time he entered the hall, there were great streams of illumination filling the room, brightening it greatly, and he could clearly see Dashiell and Bentley over near the hearth.

Royce's mother had brought forth bread, butter, and fruit from the kitchen. Dashiell was stuffing bread into his mouth and Bentley was smearing the stewed fruit on his bread, taking a bite as he noticed Bric approaching.

"Join us?" he asked, mouth full.

But Bric shook his head. "Nay," he said. "Only weaklings and women eat a morning meal. Where is de Lara?"

His insult sounded very much like the Bric of old, something that gave both Dashiell and Bentley hope that, somewhere beneath that beaten façade, the Bric they knew was waiting to be unleashed again.

"He is out in the kitchen yard, waiting for us," Dashiell said as he swallowed the bite in his mouth. "He says to tell you to bring your gloves."

Bric looked at Dashiell in surprise. "Gloves?" he repeated. "What for?"

"You shall find out."

Bric was both intrigued and wary of such a declaration, but he dutifully hunted down his gloves and went out into the kitchen yard where Sean and a sleepy-looking Manducor were waiting for him.

As Bric found out shortly, he had good reason to be on his guard.

CHAPTER TWENTY-TWO

"**F**ASTER, FASTER!"

As Manducor watched from afar, Dashiell was bellowing at Bric, urging him on in a heated race to see who could chop through a six-inch-thick oak log faster. It was Bric and Dashiell against Bentley and Sean, and at the moment, Sean and Bric were in a dead-heat, pounding away with axes against oak logs that were nearly as hard as stone.

Beneath the summer sun, Bric was sweating buckets. He was stripped down to his breeches and boots, as were Dashiell and Sean, all of them straining under the sun, struggling to beat one another in a race of strength that had been taking place for almost two hours.

Bric and Sean would chop away at logs until they split in two, and then quickly put another log up for Bentley and Dashiell to cut away at. It was a matter of pride now as the men labored against each other. Dashiell was like a wagon master, whipping his beasts as he bellowed at Bric, telling him that Sean was about to win so Bric would hit the wood harder and faster. Then, when the tides would turn and it was Dashiell's time to chop, Bric turned into the Irish master knight that the de Winter army had feared and loved for years. He would insult and shout at Dashiell until the man wanted to throw a punch at him.

But that Irish master was the glimpse the men were hoping to see.

Truthfully, Dashiell feared what would happen to him if he didn't beat Bentley, so he chopped wood harder and faster than he had in years, finally beating Bentley by a significant margin. When he quickly put another log back on the stump for Bric to chop, he stood back and cheered the man on as the High Warrior pounded on the wood with the ax that was quickly growing dull from such use. After chopping through twenty-four fairly large pieces of oak between the four of them, the men finally called a rest and everyone dropped what they were doing.

Bentley collapsed onto his backside in the dirt as Sean and Dashiell leaned up against the side of the manse. Bric was the only man standing without support, his shoulders red-kissed by the summer sun and the freckles on his skin even more pronounced than ever. But the purple scar on the left side of his torso was also pronounced, giving Dashiell, Sean, and Bentley a glimpse at the wound that nearly killed him. Sean finally pointed at it.

"So that was your injury," he said.

Bric, panting and wiping sweat from his brow, looked down at his torso and nodded. "That is the hole a French bastard put in me," he said. "It was a heavy arrow, one used to take down horses and boars and the like. It happened to hit me instead."

Sean shook his head in wonder. "It is truly a miracle that you survived," he said. "But you *did* survive, Bric. Can you not feel the joy of life right now, competing with your friends and losing to me?"

They all laughed, especially Bric. "You did *not* best me, de Lara," he said. "You may be a man of legend, but I am a man of strength. *Is mise an laoch ard.*"

Sean smirked. "And what does that mean in your terrible language?"

"It means that I am the High Warrior. You cannot best me."

"Ah," Sean said. "You have not lost your arrogance. That is good. That tells me the knight inside of you is alive and well."

Bric wasn't sure how to respond to that. While he was considering his reply, he didn't see Bentley getting to his feet and casually moving over towards the corner of the manse where he'd propped up two broadswords. As Sean kept Bric's attention, Bentley handed Dashiell a sword as he moved around behind Bric, keeping his broadsword behind his back should Bric see him. When Bentley finally moved into position and nodded his head, Dashiell suddenly shouted.

"Bric!" he boomed. "Behind you!"

Bric startled as he'd never startled in his life. *Behind you!* God, those words… those terrible words… and suddenly, he was back in the dark river of Castle Acre Priory, and Mylo was yelling at him because a French knight was about to take his head off. His heart leapt into his throat and a bolt of terror raced through him, but it was also a bolt of rage.

Pure, unadulterated rage.

From the corner of his eye, he could see Dashiell tossing a broadsword at him and he deftly caught it, purely a reflex, before spinning around to see Bentley charging at him, sword held high.

The rage took over at that point. Bentley had been a high-caliber knight long before he'd been the Duke of Savernake, but he was no match for an enraged Bric. Bric brought his sword down to bear on top of Bentley, who was literally staggered by the blow. Just as he rolled to his left so that he could come back in for another strike, Bric lashed out a big boot and caught the man on the side of the knee. As Bentley went down in pain, Bric tossed the broadsword aside and threw a fist into Bentley's jaw.

The man went sprawling.

But Bric wasn't finished. He was going in for the kill. He hadn't take two steps when Sean rushed up behind him and grabbed him around the chest, pulling him back as Dashiell moved in to protect Bentley, who was only half-conscious. Unfortunately, Sean was having a difficult time, even with his size and strength, restraining Bric.

"Easy, Bric," he said steadily. "No harm done. We were simply testing your reflexes and I am happy to say that your knightly traits are still there. You are still as deadly as you ever were."

A test. That made the whole thing even worse. When Bric realized what they had done, he yanked himself from Sean's grasp, still furious and shaken. His face was red and sweaty, and he began to pace, keeping away from Sean and Dashiell and now Bentley, who was starting to come around. They were all looking at him with concern but perhaps even a ray of hope. Yet, Bric dashed all of that.

"Mylo shouted those same words to me at Castle Acre when we were fighting," he said, his lips white because he was so angry. "He shouted those exact words and when I turned around, I killed him. Damn you for taking me back to that time I have been trying so hard to forget."

Bentley was just sitting up, shaking off the bells, but he heard Bric's angry words. He looked up at Dashiell, whose expression was stoic – but only marginally. It was clear by the tick in his jaw that he was deeply regretful.

"We did not know, Bric," Dashiell said quietly. "You know we would have never used that tactic had we known. I am sorry you are so angry. As Sean said, you still have your knightly instincts. Those have not gone away. Mayhap we have clumsily proved that to you, but it is true."

Bric stood back, flexing his big fists, his features taut with rage. Bentley was climbing to his feet at this point, pulled up by Dashiell, and Bric's focus seemed to be on the man he'd just punched in the jaw.

So many things were going through Bric's mind. He knew his friends had only been trying to help, but their poor choice of words and tactics had caused him to relive the moment he'd killed Mylo. The terror of that moment was all he could seem to feel, and his heart was still pounding from the excitement of it.

But this time, things had gone markedly different.

Bentley was alive.

As Bric looked at Bentley, he realized the man had survived not only his surprise, but his rage. He hadn't been cut down as Mylo had. In truth, it was daylight and he could see much better than he had on the night in question, but he'd been moving so quickly that light wouldn't have made any difference. Bric could see that now. Even if he had been able to see Mylo, because he had been moving so fast and everything was in such close proximity, he probably would have killed him, anyway. Nothing could have been done to spare him.

In realizing that, Bric's anger began to fade.

Perhaps his clumsy friends had helped him, after all.

Taking a deep breath, he made his way over to Bentley, who took a step back when he realized Bric was heading towards him, perhaps to throw another punch. But he stood his ground after that, watching as Bric came up on him. He found himself looking the man in the face, wondering if he was going to get a tongue lashing or worse. But what Bric did next surprised them all.

Bric put his arms around Bentley and squeezed the man so tightly that Bentley was getting the air squeezed right out of him. The tears flowed from Bric's eyes as he whispered over and over:

"You are alive. I did not kill you; you *are* alive."

Bentley put his arms around Bric, too, in a brotherly gesture. "Aye, Bric," he said. "I am alive. I am sorry if I startled you, but I am alive. You did not kill me."

It was Bric's acknowledgement that he knew they had only staged the attack to help him. Perhaps they even had. Dashiell watched the scene with a smile on his lips, a smile of relief and, indeed, a great deal of hope. He looked at Sean, who had the same expression. The man they so admired, the one they'd come to help, was capable of *being* helped.

There was optimism.

Bric held on to Bentley for a few moments longer before finally releasing the man, quickly wiping the tears from his face, embarrassed with his reaction. But in a small way, he felt better somehow.

"I would call you all idiots, but to do so would mean insulting a duke," he said. "Suffice it to say that I apologize for my outburst. I know you were only trying to help. I suppose my biggest fear has been shaming myself in front of men I so deeply respect. I hope I have not done that – yet."

Sean went to pick up the broadsword that Bric had tossed aside.

"There is nothing to be ashamed of," he said. "Two years ago, I was like you. I'd just suffered a terrible injury at the hands of John's assassins and should have died. Yet, I did not. I have come back, stronger than before, and you shall come back as well, Bric. It is only a matter of time. With help, your confidence will return. You will cast out those demons that haunt you."

Bric knew of Sean's past, the Lord of the Shadows who had been England's greatest spy. That was why he respected the man so much – he'd gone head-to-head with King John and had lived to tell the tale. Not many men could say the same.

"I am glad you think so because, at the moment, I am not so sure," he said. "I can use a sword, of course, but it does not feel natural in my hand any longer. It feels like something I am allergic to."

"You were not allergic to it when you struck me with it," Bentley said. "You used it as you have always used it. And you had better feed me well tonight if I am to forget about that blow to the jaw."

Bric smiled weakly. "I will ply you with wine in the hope that you will forget a mere knight struck you."

Bentley shook his head. "You are not a 'mere' knight, Bric," he said. "You are *the* knight. I have the bruise to prove it."

As everyone laughed softly, Sean went to Bric and put his hand on the man's neck. "Now," he said. "If you feel like continuing, then we have work to do. But do not be surprised if you are attacked again by a man wielding a broadsword. It may happen again, some time."

Bric now understood what they were doing; trying to work the fear out of him and in doing so, help him regain his confidence. He'd told Eiselle in a low moment that he didn't know who he was any longer but, at this moment, he was starting to recognize himself again, the knight who had taken a beating ever since his injury.

But he still had a long way to go.

"Then I suppose I shall have to accept it," he said. "Are we finished chopping wood? I am growing bored."

Sean cocked his head. "We are finished if you choose to submit to my victory."

"I do *not* choose to submit to your victory."

"Then we are not finished."

The wood chopping, the yelling, and the camaraderie went on the rest of the day.

Three days later

"HE IS FUNCTIONING much better," Manducor said as he watched Eiselle fuss around the smaller feasting table in the hall of Bedingfeld. "I have been watching him and his companions for four days now and he seems to be getting much better. Yesterday, they had him participate in a mock sword fight and he beat de Lara right into the ground. There seems to be an anger in him when he fights, my lady. Such... anger."

Eiselle was making sure everything on the table was nicely set for the evening feast. Bedingfeld had apple and pear orchards, and she'd gone out with Royce and a few of the servants today to pick apples and cut off some of the branches so that the table had a lovely decoration of apples and green-leafed branches. Her mother used to decorate their table so, and she thought it rather fresh and festive.

But Manducor's words worried her. She had not really known her husband before his injury, so she could only base her knowledge of him on her experiences since their marriage. He didn't seem like an angry man to her, simply overwrought and exhausted at times, so his anger wasn't something she was familiar with.

"Mayhap they are working him too hard," she finally said. "Mayhap he is angry because his friends are pushing him so."

Manducor could only shrug. "They are pushing him so that he will recover," he reminded her. "That is what you want, isn't it?"

"Of course it is."

"Then mayhap the anger he feels is at himself."

Eiselle looked up from the table. "Why would you say that?"

Manducor reached out and took one of the apples from her careful decoration, taking a big bite out of it. As he spoke, pieces of apple went flying from his lips.

"Bric is a man of strength," he said. "That is all he knows. To lose that strength would make him very angry at himself, so this is a way of displaying that anger. But I would not worry; mayhap it is all part of the process of restoring him to what he was before."

Eiselle believed his words because they made sense to her. "I hope so," she said. Then, he stole another apple and she found herself wishing he'd go away from her pretty table. "Why are you not out there with the men? Why are you in here with me?"

Manducor averted his gaze, chomping down on his second apple. "They do not need an old man in the way," he said. "You have four of the finest knights I have ever seen out in your garden, Lady MacRohan. Not just any knights; you even have a duke. Who am I? A knight who laid down his sword to become a priest. I am not worthy to be with the likes of them."

Eiselle replaced the apple he'd taken with another one in her basket. "You are very worthy," she said. "Whether or not you realize it, you have been a great help to both Bric and me. You have a great deal of wisdom. But I must ask you something."

"Anything, my lady."

"Are you ever going to tell me your real name?"

He snorted, taking the last bite of the apple and tossing the core into the hearth. "I am Jesus Christ," he said, throwing up his arms. "I am John the Baptist, the Apostle Paul, and Charlemagne. I am every man."

Eiselle chuckled at him. "You are impossible," she said. But quickly, she sobered. "Do you remember when you and I used to have discussions about God speaking?"

Manducor nodded. "I do."

She looked at him. "Has He spoken to you about Bric?" she asked. "Surely, I would have thought God would speak to you about something so important."

Manducor pondered her words. "I think, mayhap, we are looking at this all wrong," he said. "We are waiting for God to use words. But when those three knights arrived to help Bric, mayhap that was God speaking in actions. He sent those men here to help. Did you ever think of it that way?"

Eiselle hadn't, but she liked the idea. "I had the missive sent to Dash."

"And Dash came and brought his friends," he pointed out. "You did not ask for that, so mayhap God is speaking through de Lara and de Vaston."

Eiselle was comforted by his words. Perhaps God had been speaking all along but she had been listening for the wrong sign.

It was certainly something to consider.

Manducor turned to leave the hall, perhaps to go and watch the knights he'd been shadowing since they arrived. He'd never actively participated in what they were doing, as he said, but he'd been watching them closely and reporting back to Eiselle.

Eiselle, too, had kept a low profile since the arrival of Dashiell and the others, not wanting to be a distraction or a crutch to Bric, who seemed to be genuinely responding to what they were doing. His mood seemed better, and although his hands bled from the work and his body was sore at night, he seemed to be enjoying it immensely and that was all she could hope for. He *did* seem better and Eiselle could not have been more pleased.

In fact, she was so very happy the he seemed to be returning to normal, much more like the man she'd met on the day she'd arrived at Narborough. Not that she didn't love the man he'd become. In truth, she loved his weaker moments with her, the moments he would let his emotions run free. But in order for Bric to be healthy, he had to return to the man he'd been before the madness started.

She was starting to see that, little by little.

Leaving her half-dressed table, she followed Manducor as he headed up the spiral stairs. She knew he was going to the chamber with the windows that overlooked the garden, and she wanted to see what her husband was taking part in on this fine day because, in truth, they could hear the shouting all the way in the hall. Whatever it was must have been exciting.

Once Eiselle and Manducor peered from the windows overlooking the garden to see the activity below, it was something that immediately brought a smile to Eiselle's lips. Someone had set up four targets against the western wall of the garden, targets that consisted of hay from the stables that had been bundled up with rope. She could see that they'd taken charcoal from the ashes of a fire and had drawn targets on the hay bundles, dark enough so they could be seen from a good distance away.

Then, standing over against the eastern wall of the garden, she could see the four knights, all lined up. They had longbows and arrows in their hands and as she watched, she could see Bric and Sean arguing over the fact that Sean had a crossbow that he wanted to use, when everyone else had traditional longbows. Sean finally surrendered the crossbow and picked up the same bow that the others hand. Using arrows that Dashiell and Sean had brought with them, they all lined up, aimed at the targets, and fired.

Eiselle heard cheering as the knights rushed across the garden to see who came the closest to their targets and Manducor pointed out young Royce as he stood along the southern wall of the garden, jumping up and down excitedly.

The sight of the servant boy gave Eiselle an idea; if young Royce could watch from inside the garden, then she wanted to watch at close range, too. It was true that she'd been purposely staying out of the way as of late, but in watching her handsome husband and his friends, she couldn't stay away any longer. She very much wanted to see them up close.

Departing the chamber with Manducor on her heels, she rushed back the way she'd come, heading out of the rear door of the manse and onward to the walled garden where all of the excitement was happening.

Excitement, today, that she intended to be part of.

UNAWARE THAT HIS audience in the manse was coming to take a closer look, Bric was standing by the targets he'd helped build, noting that he, Dashiell, and Sean had hit their targets while Bentley had been slightly off. While Bentley was out of the competition at that point, humiliated in a good-natured sort of way, Bric, Dashiell, and Sean began arguing over who had come closest to the very center of the target.

It was Sean who had started the argument because, in truth, it was a ploy to distract Bric. As the men argued and pointed, Bentley went to collect the broadsword that they'd been carrying around for four days, attacking Bric with it intermittently, and watching the man's reaction to the surprise attacks.

After the first attack, when Bric had become so angry and then had broken down and wept, the High Warrior's reactions were quickly improving. Sometimes it was Bentley doing the charge, sometimes it was Dashiell, and once it was Sean, an attack that had turned into a fist fight when Bric disarmed Sean and had furiously thrown a punch.

But there had been no animosity, even when Sean ended up with a bloodied nose. They'd all laughed in the end, and hugged one another, and everything had been fine between them. It was all part of the healing process for a man who had done much healing as of late.

But he had also become wise to their tricks, very quickly.

Therefore, when Bentley came up behind Bric with a broadsword leveled at him, Bric was ready. He caught the movement out of the corner of his eye, ripped the arrow from its target, and then moved swiftly away from Bentley's sword to come up beside the man, grab his hair, and hold the arrowhead as his throat.

Instantly compromised, Bentley dropped the sword, but Bric held the sharp arrowhead at his throat a few seconds longer before breaking down into laughter and releasing the man. Rubbing his scalp where Bric had grabbed his hair, Bentley held up a hand.

"I am not doing this again," he said. "The last three times, I've had my hair grabbed or my knees kicked out. I refuse to be pummeled any longer."

As he turned to pick up the sword that had been dropped, Dashiell snorted. "That is the only reason we brought you along," he said. "It certainly was not because you could hit a target with an arrow."

Bentley scowled. "I can still hit your eye with my fist."

Dashiell shrugged. "And it is your right to do so, Savernake."

It was Dashiell acknowledging the hierarchy that hadn't existed until last year between them. Before that, Bentley had been his subordinate, but marrying the heiress to the Savernake dukedom had changed the dynamics somewhat. Still, they were great friends, and Dashiell showed Bentley all of the respect he'd ever shown the former duke. That was never in question. But the knightly camaraderie hadn't changed between them.

Bentley chuckled at Dashiell to let him know there wasn't, and never would be, any animosity. Taking the sword in-hand, he headed over to the stone bench to set it down as Royce, excited more than his little mind could adequately handle, came rushing up to the knights as they began to pull their arrows out of the hay targets.

"I saw you, my lord!" he said as he jumped up and down. "You shot the arrows!"

Bric looked over at the child; Royce had been something of their shadow for the past few days, but he'd stayed well out of sight most of the time. Today was the first day he'd actually come into the area where they were, into the garden this time, and Bric frowned at the boy.

"Aye, I shot the arrow," he said. "What are you doing in the garden? Your mother will be cross with you."

Royce's features flickered with concern, meaning he knew very well that he wasn't supposed to be here, but his excitement had overruled his fear of punishment.

"But I want to fight," he said. "You said I could be a soldier. Can I shoot the arrow, too?"

Bric had to admit that the bold little servant boy was growing on him. "Mayhap later," he said. "We are busy at the moment, but mayhap when we are finished. Until then, you can do a job for us."

Royce began jumping up and down again. "I will do it! I will do it!"

"You do not even know what it is yet."

Royce stopped jumping and just grinned, a gap-toothed smile that had Bric chuckling at the lad. The child certainly was enthusiastic, for anything at all when it came to the knights and combat.

"When we are finished shooting the arrows, it will be your job to carefully remove them and bring them back to me," Bric said. "Do not break them. Can you do that?"

Royce nodded eagerly and ran straight to the targets as if to stand there and wait for the arrows to come. But Bric waved a big arm at him.

"If you stand there, you are going to be hit with the arrows," he said. Then he pointed to the southern wall. "Go and stand there. Do not move until I tell you to."

Wildly, with arms and legs flying, Royce raced over to the wall and stood there, but he was not still. He was bouncing around with excitement, and Bric had to shake his head with humor. He'd never thought about children as being adorable before, but if he did, the boy was all that.

"Who *is* that?" Sean asked.

Bric glanced at him to see that his focus was on Royce. "That is a servant boy who very badly wants to fight for de Winter," he said. "His name is Royce and he will not take 'no' for an answer."

Sean, having twin daughters who were slightly younger than Royce, seemed to have some patience for the child. He didn't order him away or snap; he simply shrugged and turned back to his work. The knights finished gathering their arrows and returned to the spot where they'd been firing at their targets. Resuming their positions and taking aim, another volley of arrows flew to their marks.

In truth, it was an exercise that was helping Bric a great deal. *Fire, collect arrows. Fire, collect arrows.* It was repetition in the strictest sense of the word. They'd been doing it most of the morning because, yesterday, Bric had spoken of the arrow that had wounded him and it was Sean and Dashiell's impression that arrows in general were making Bric nervous these days. This morning when the men had come out to continue their work, Bric had seen the hay bunches set up with targets, and they'd been firing arrows at them since early morning.

The first two volleys had been difficult for Bric. His palms had sweated, and his heart had pounded, but as the day continued and they fired off round after round, the sweaty palms eventually faded, and his heart rate had returned to normal. The repetition of it had calmed him down and the competition of it turned the act of a firing arrow into something that wasn't so terrifying. Certainly, arrows were still deadly, but the more he used the bow and arrow, the more he began to put the weapon into perspective.

An arrow had nearly killed him, but he wasn't going to let that disturb him any longer.

He was slowly regaining control.

After firing off their last arrows, Bric whistled between his teeth, loudly, to get Royce's attention. When the boy looked at him, he motioned to the targets, and the child raced over and began yanking out the arrows, or at least the ones he could reach. Bric turned away from the boy to examine his longbow, which was starting to splinter. This was a longbow that was kept in the small armory at the manse for protection, and he inspected the split closely as Dashiell came up next to him.

"What is the trouble?" Dashiell asked.

Bric sighed, with some frustration. "These longbows have been in the armory for quite some time and it is clear that no one has maintained them. This one is starting to split under the stress. You had better check the other longbows as well."

Dashiell did just that. He and Bentley began pouring over the bows while Sean headed out to the targets to help Royce collect the arrows that were taller than his reach. The boy had already toppled one hay bundle trying to reach the arrows at the top, so Sean went out to assist him. The young servant boy was thrilled to see yet another knight and even at a distance, Bric could hear the boy telling Sean how much he wanted to fight. It made him smile, something Dashiell noticed.

"Why are you grinning, Bric?" Dashiell asked. "What is so funny about a splintered longbow?"

Bric shook his head, looking to the west side of the garden where Royce was evidently showing Sean his moves with a stick he'd picked up off the ground, the same moves he'd tried to show Bric the first day they'd met.

"I am not smiling at a broken longbow," he said. "I can hear the servant boy from here. He was very excited to see me on my first day here, also, and told me how he wanted to be a knight. I wonder if my own son shall be so eager to follow in my footsteps."

Dashiell's gaze moved to the far end of the garden where Sean pretended to seriously watch Royce as the child demonstrated his skill.

"Your son will have the greatest teacher in all of England in his father," he said. "In fact, I will send my own son to you for training."

Bric looked at him, a somewhat surprised expression on his face. "You would...?" He stopped, swallowed, and then started again. "Even after all of this, you would still send your son to me for training?"

Dashiell nodded without hesitation. "Bric, you worry overly," he said. "You seem to think that we are all ashamed of you, but the truth is that our respect for you has not changed. All men falter from time to time; it is part of a man's nature, I think. But you are so damned perfect that when you faltered, it was completely unnatural and you thought the entire world had caved in. But it hasn't, you know. Don't you see? You are still as great as you ever were. Greater, even, because you are working to overcome something that could have destroyed you. But you did not let it. That is the mark of a true man."

Of everything that had been said and done over the past four days,

Dashiell's words of faith, in stressing how he would gladly send his son to Bric for training, bolstered Bric more than anything ever had. Dashiell believed in him. In fact, all of these men believed in him or else they would not have come. Bric never felt the bonds of brotherhood, or of friendship, more strongly than he did at that moment.

"You deserve the credit, not me," he said quietly. "My wife was right to send word to you, Dash. I do not know if I could have done this without you."

Dashiell patted him on the shoulder. "You could have," he said. "It just would not have been nearly as fun. We have had a good time at your expense, Bric. But it was worth it."

Bric chuckled softly. "I *do* feel better," he said. "I feel as if I can face myself again. I can hold a sword again and I can shoot a longbow again without my palms sweating. That is progress."

"It is, indeed."

"I suppose I shall know for certain when I next find myself in battle."

Dashiell looked at him, thinking that now might be a good time to tell him about William Marshal's directive to England's armies. But he didn't get the words out of his mouth before Eiselle suddenly appeared, and Manducor along with her. After that, Bric was righteously distracted.

As well the man should have been. His lovely wife had just entered the garden and she was all he could see. Clad in a pale blue dress made from a light fabric to combat the warmer temperatures of summer, she looked radiant and rosy-cheeked as she headed straight for her husband. Bric handed the longbow over to Dashiell to go and greet her.

"Lady MacRohan," he said as he reached out to take her hand, bringing it to his lips for a gentle kiss. "To what do we owe the honor of your visit?"

Eiselle positively glowed at her husband. "We could see you practicing with your longbows from the window," she said. "I also saw Royce cheering you on, so I thought if he can come out here and not be chased away, mayhap I can come out here, too. May we watch?"

Bric kissed her hand again. "Of course you may," he said. "But I do not think we shall be practicing with the longbows anymore today. Mine has a crack in it and I do not think the others will be able to stand up to the strain, so we are going to find something else to do. But whatever it is, you may watch."

Eiselle beamed, wrapping her arms around his big bicep. "More wood chopping?"

"God, no."

"More lugging around those very big tree stumps?"

Bric made a face, glancing over at Bentley and Sean, who were coming over to join them. "Those damnable stumps have my eternal ire," he said. "Moving those things around the stable yard nearly broke my back. Whose stupid idea was that, anyway?"

Bentley and Dashiell laughed as Sean spoke up. "Are you calling me stupid?"

Bric cocked an eyebrow. "Not you; simply your idea to drag those tree stumps all over the place."

"It was a test of strength, Bric."

"I do not need to test my strength. I know how strong I am."

Sean's eyes narrowed threateningly. "As do I," he said. "I shall tell your wife to make the next garment she sews for you a dress because, clearly, you need one. You complain just like a woman."

Bric started to laugh. "Bleeding Christ, you're a vicious beast."

"And don't you forget it."

By that time, they were all laughing. Eiselle could see the easy camaraderie between the men and it did her heart good to see Bric's good mood. The man was quite humorous when he wanted to be, and she was coming to see a side of him she hadn't really seen before. All she'd seen was the serious side of him, the sad side of him, and the sweet side of him on occasion. But this side was quite bristly, in a funny sort of way.

"It *is* getting rather warm," she said, looking up into the bright blue sky and shielding her eyes from the sun. "Why not come into the manse? It is cooler inside and the cook has made some cider. It will be delicious on this warm day."

Bric thought some time with his wife would be a good idea, but Sean, ever the task-master, shook his head.

"We are not finished yet," he said, "but I will look forward to sampling the cider come this evening, Lady MacRohan. Your husband has more things to accomplish before he can rest for the night."

Bric sighed with great frustration. "Accomplish what?" he demanded. "More tree-moving? Or do you wish for me to find rocks in the fields and then build you a house with them? What more could we possibly have to do today, Sean?"

Sean fought off a grin. "You care complaining like an old woman again, MacRohan."

"*Taispeánfaidh mé mo chuid liathróid duit má chreideann tú sin.*"

"Stop it with your devil's tongue already. What in the hell does that mean?

"It means that I will show you my ballocks if you really believe I am an old woman."

Sean burst out laughing and Eiselle pulled away from Bric, covering her ears. "Bric!" she gasped. "How crude!"

Bric looked at his wife, suddenly very contrite. "I am sorry, my dearest," he said. "But no man will call me an old woman, most especially in front of my wife."

Eiselle shook her head at him but she couldn't quite summon the serious face necessary to convey her disapproval at so boorish an insult. She grinned, slapping her hand over her mouth, as she turned for the manse.

"I am going inside where we do not speak of such things," she said. "Leave the vulgarity out here, for if it comes inside, I may have to beat it to death."

"Aye, my lady."

"I mean what I say, MacRohan. Not in my house."

"I swear to you, I will never again be so rude in front of you."

His eyes were glimmering with mirth as he spoke, properly remorseful, and Eiselle thought it was one of his more charming moments. He was being quite sweet and contrite, but there was a flirt in the air as he said it, something she'd never quite experienced from the man. She rather liked it. She was just about to say so when one of the old house servants suddenly entered the garden.

The servant was a very old man with fine, white hair. It would fly around his head and look like a cloud. Everyone turned to the poor old man, who seemed terribly nervous in the presence of so many fighting men. Serving in the quiet manse as he was, he wasn't used to the boisterous knights.

"Forgive me for interrupting, m'lord," he said, pointing a gnarled finger in the general direction of the front of the manse. "Lord de Winter has arrived. He has asked for ye."

The warm mood that had been present only moments earlier vanished. Bric's brow furrowed in surprise.

"Daveigh?" he repeated. "*Here*?"

The old man nodded. "He is in the hall, m'lord. He has asked for ye and the lady."

Eiselle looked at Bric, who looked at her with equal astonishment. As Eiselle turned for the manse in a rush, Bric turned to his friends.

"I cannot imagine why he has come," he said, "but you will all come with me. He will want to see you."

With that, he turned for the manse as well, and Bentley immediately followed. But Dashiell and Sean hung back, collecting the arrows, and the longbows, lingering behind because they had something to say about de Winter's unexpected visit. The arrival of Daveigh de Winter wasn't coincidental, they were certain.

It was all starting to fall into place.

"De Winter must have received word from the Marshal," Dashiell said quietly. "That must we why he has come. He has to move the de Winter army south and he will want to see if Bric can manage it."

Sean nodded. "Truthfully, we could not have remained at Bedingfeld much longer," he muttered, picking up the last longbow. "You know that as well as I do. We have been here four days, Dash. At some point, we were going to have to tell Bric about the Marshal's order and convince him to go with us."

Dashiell nodded reluctantly as they began to head towards the manse. "Indeed," he said. "But de Winter should tell Bric about the orders to move into Kent, and if he doesn't, then we shall have tell Bric tonight, especially with de Winter here. If Daveigh has not been told what is happening, then you must tell him. The de Winter army must move south immediately."

Sean knew that. They passed from the walled garden, seeing the manse looming in front of them. With all of the brotherhood and warmth, games and serious work that had gone on over the past four days, time had moved swiftly but Sean felt as if Bric had made tremendous progress. He was strong, that one, so strong that nothing short of God Himself could keep him down.

"I have every faith that Bric can lead the army," he said as the door to the manse loomed before them. "Do you?"

Dashiell nodded. "I have seen the old Bric before me," he said quietly. "But he said it best – sword play and target practice is one thing, but he has yet to face an actual battle."

"And what do you think will happen when he does?"

They came to the open door, hearing voices inside as Bric greeted his liege. Dashiell came to a halt, facing Sean.

"I think Bric will lead the charge as he always does," he muttered seriously. "And if he does not, we will be there to carry him. Whatever happens, I will not let him fail."

"Nor will I."

The situation was settled. Dashiell and Sean entered Bedingfeld to greet Daveigh, but the agreement between them – to keep Bric from failing – was set in stone. They never said another word about it.

They didn't have to.

Bric MacRohan would succeed, no matter what.

CHAPTER TWENTY-THREE

"**G**OD'S BONES," DAVEIGH gasped. "Du Reims is here, too? And de Lara? I am overwhelmed."

Already, Daveigh was moving forward to greet them properly. He shook their hands, a customary greeting that had evolved over the centuries to ensure that no man was carrying a weapon to harm the other but, in this case, it was a greeting of genuine friendship and warmth. Daveigh shook Dashiell's hand but when he came to Sean, he held the man's hand just a few moments longer.

"I have not seen you in over a year," he said, smiling at him. "It is good to see you again, Sean. You are looking far better than you did the last time I saw you. You were still recovering from your terrible wound."

Sean nodded, hoping that Bric had heard Daveigh's comment. "Indeed," he agreed. "It took me some time to recover from that but I did, indeed, recover. I am better than before."

Daveigh chuckled. "I would agree with that," he said. "I'd forgotten how physically formidable you were, but given your reputation when you shadowed John, I should not have forgotten that at all. I think I remember running from you on occasion, years ago, when our paths had the potential of crossing."

It was Sean's turn to grin. "I hope you run from me no longer, my lord."

Daveigh shook his head. "Never," he insisted. His gaze moved over to Dashiell again, and then to Bentley, and it was clear that he was curious about their presence. "I suppose I should ask why you have all come, but I can guess. Meanwhile, let us sit and be comfortable while Lady MacRohan shows us her hospitality."

Eiselle had already sent servants running for some of the cider she had tried to entice the knights with. As the five men took seats around the feasting table, Manducor was on his knees before the hearth, stoking it into a blaze while the servants had their hands full bringing out food and drink for the lords around the table. Eiselle was caught up in the rush until Bric reached out, grasped her by the wrist, and pulled her to sit next to him.

"Not you," he said. "You will sit with us. I do not want you rushing about and tiring yourself."

Eiselle shook her head at him. "I am fine," she said. "Stop worrying."

"I cannot help it. It is my duty to worry over you. I do not want you fainting again."

She patted him on the cheek to reassure him that she felt fine, indeed. But Dashiell, who was sitting on her other side, heard the conversation and he turned to Eiselle with concern.

"Fainting?" he repeated. "Did you faint?"

"I am fine," she said in a tone that suggested she didn't want to discuss it. "My husband worries overly."

But Bric spoke up. "I do *not* worry overly," he said. "You must take care of yourself and my son. I'll not have you falling to the ground simply because you exhausted yourself. I am going to make sure you rest until he is born even if I have to sit on you to keep you down."

Dashiell's eyebrows flew up in surprise. "A son?" he said. "Selly, are you –?"

He didn't finish because it was unseemly for a man to speak of pregnancy to a woman not his wife, not even if the woman was his cousin. But he knew what he heard, and Eiselle smiled to confirm it.

"Aye," she said. "Did Bric not tell you? We are to have a child in the spring."

Dashiell looked at Bric in outrage. "Nay, he did not tell me!" he said, sounding angry until he put his arms around Eiselle and gave her a warm hug. "I am thrilled, truly. That is the most wonderful news."

By this time, everyone at the table had heard what they were speaking of and hearty congratulations went all around. Daveigh seemed particularly thrilled, going so far as to actually hug Eiselle in his glee. It was a joyful start to Daveigh's surprise visit and, through it all, Eiselle kept watch on the man's expression to see if she could see any disappointment there, for the same reason she was sensitive to Keeva's reaction to their news.

But she sensed nothing from Daveigh that could be interpreted as sad, and she was grateful. She genuinely liked the man and she was pleased that the news hadn't upset him. In fact, when the cider came, passed around by Manducor who made sure to take the jug for himself when everyone was served, Daveigh insisted on proposing a toast to the unborn MacRohan son.

"I would like to wish Eiselle and Bric the greatest of happiness with this blessed event," he said, lifting his cup high. "To the coming MacRohan – may strong arms hold you, may caring hearts tend you, and may God's blessing await you at every step."

The men around the table lifted their cups to Eiselle and Bric, drinking deeply of the strong cider. Bentley actually choked on it briefly, for it was much stronger than he'd anticipated. Daveigh, too, coughed a few times but that didn't stop him from taking another long drink.

"Delicious," he said. Then he set the cup down and looked at Bric. "Tell me – have you decided where Little Daveigh will foster? Are you thinking of sending him to Ireland to be with your father for a time?"

Bric fought off a grin. "Little *Daveigh*?"

"Of course. What else would you name him?"

Bric started to chuckle, looking at Eiselle, who merely shook her head in resignation. "I was thinking on calling him something other than Daveigh," he said. "My old master, the one who gave me my talisman, was named Conor. I have always thought to name a son, if I ever had one, Conor."

"A fine name," Daveigh said. "But it is very Irish."

"My son will be half-Irish."

Daveigh simply shrugged and took another drink of the cider, coughing as he choked it down. "I suppose naming your son is your prerogative," he said. "But any child named Daveigh would be sure to receive an inheritance, just so you know."

Bric stood his ground. "And it would be an honor, indeed," he said. "Would you do the same thing for a child that was not named for you, yet was your godson?"

Daveigh looked at him in surprise. "My godson?"

"Aye. My son will bear the name of Conor and Daveigh de Winter, Baron Cressingham, will be his godfather. When he is baptized, will you stand with him?"

Daveigh grew very serious. In fact, he may have had a tear or two in his eyes. "With all my heart, I will," he said, suddenly very emotional, whereas moments before he had been in a jovial mood. "Do you mean it, Bric?"

"I never say anything I do not mean. Although I have not discussed it with my wife, I am sure she agrees with me. We would be honored."

Daveigh was truly touched. He looked at Eiselle, who nodded her head, and then he was overcome with emotion.

"I… I do not know what to say, Bric," he said, putting his hand over his heart. "You do me the honor. I am overjoyed."

Bric could see how overwhelmed the man was. Then, he looked around the table, at the knights who had worked so hard with him for the past few days, and the gratitude he felt was beyond measure.

It was the gratitude that Sean had spoken of once, something he'd never spoken of to Bric but, in truth, he didn't need to. Bric had found that gratitude on his own. He was grateful for his life – and those who loved him, and it showed.

"My son shall bear the name of Shane Dashiell Bentley Sean de Gael MacRohan," he said quietly. "As I said, I've not discussed any of this with my wife, so I hope she agrees, but that is what I should like to name him."

Eiselle, who had been choking up watching Daveigh's reaction, turned to the table of knights. "I think it is a wonderful name," she said. "For what you have all done for Bric these past few days, I am happy to honor you so."

The knights lifted their cups to her in thanks. The day, so far, had been full of much to celebrate. Bentley was just setting his cup down when he spoke.

"Will you keep the name MacRohan, then?" he asked Bric. "Is it not Irish tradition for the sons to bear the surnames of their fathers?"

Bric nodded. "My father's name is Rohan," he said. "My brothers and I all bear the surname of MacRohan, meaning 'of Rohan'. But I think I will stop that tradition because it is not something the English follow. My son will be half-English, after all, with the bloodlines of the Earls of East Anglia. MacRohan will become our family name from now on."

He looked at Eiselle, who was smiling openly at him, and kissed her on the forehead. The joy between them at this moment was immeasurable. Putting an arm around the woman and pulling her against him, his focus moved to Daveigh.

"But I am sure you did not come to discuss family names and baptisms, Daveigh," he said. "I am assuming there is a reason behind your visit?"

Daveigh's smile faded as he shifted from the news of his soon-to-be-born godson to the reason for his appearance at Bedingfeld.

"There is," he said. He seemed serious as he collected his thoughts, scattered by the news of Eiselle's pregnancy. "Bric, I know you came to Bedingfeld for a rest and I must say that you look much better than you did when you left Narborough."

Bric glanced at the knights sitting at the table. "I am," he said, "thanks to these men. Did Keeva tell you that she sent word to Dash on behalf of my wife?"

"She did."

"Then you must know why they are here."

Daveigh shrugged. "I can only assume," he said. "They came to help you."

"They did."

"You *do* look better."

Bric could see that Daveigh wasn't quite sure how to ask him just how *much* better he was feeling and he assumed it was because Daveigh had need of him. The last time Bric had gone to battle for Daveigh, he hadn't been ready for it, but Daveigh had let him go anyway. He understood the reluctance on Daveigh's part – the man didn't want to make the same mistake twice, putting a man into battle who was not mentally prepared for such a thing.

"I *am* better," Bric assured him quietly. "Sean and Dash and Bentley have been here for four days. In that time, they have done everything in their power to snap me out of whatever horror has its claws in me. As shameful as it is for me to speak of it, we must – you saw me, Daveigh. You saw how I was after Mylo's death. I cannot explain how I felt at that time because I truly do not remember much. I remember the fight at Castle Acre Priory and I remember holding Mylo in my arms as he died, but after that... I do not remember anything until I woke up here, at Bedingfeld."

Daveigh was listening to him with much regret. "I am so sorry, Bric," he said after a moment. "I let you go to Castle Acre and you were not ready for it. I should have known that by the way you were acting after your wound healed. I should have known you were not the same man. It is my fault that Mylo's death affected you so. It should have never happened."

Bric could see, in that moment, that Daveigh was assuming much guilt for Mylo's passing, almost as much as Bric had. But with what he'd learned over the past several days with Sean and Dashiell and Bentley, he had come to see that what had happened had been a terrible accident and nothing more.

"It was not your fault," he said. "I suppose I knew there was something amiss with me, but I did not want to admit it. I lied to you when I said I was capable of going into battle because I knew I wasn't. But what happened with Mylo... you cannot imagine the learning and the healing that has gone on with Sean and Dash and Bentley. I realize that all of this has taken place in a short amount of time but, for me, it has been a small eternity. From sunrise to sunset, we have worked ourselves into exhaustion. We have chopped wood and fired arrows until our fingers were bleeding. I have felt more alive than I have in months, with their help, and I have come to see that the circumstances with Mylo were simply an accident. Looking at the situation one hundred different ways, the conclusion is always the same – Mylo put himself in harm's way to save me. It was his sacrifice. And I feel that if I continue to mourn his loss, and not honor his actions, somehow it diminishes what he did. Does that make sense?"

Daveigh nodded, a smile playing on his lips. "It does," he said. "It makes perfect sense."

Bric looked at his friends around the table, men who were gazing back at him with approval in their eyes. He gestured to the group.

"And these foolish, brave, wonderful men," he said. "They came here to fix me or die trying. I cannot say that I am the same man I was before the injury, but I do not think I should like to be. That man was hollow somehow. He pretended he was as strong as an ox and as immortal as stone, but he wasn't. That strong façade encased a man with a hollow heart."

"And now?" Daveigh asked quietly.

Bric looked at him. "And now he is as full and solid as he has never been in his life," he said. "I cannot say that I am not ever going to feel fear again, for I am sure that I will, at some point. But I shall not think of the fear; I shall only think of my duty, to myself and to my wife, and to men who have shown me what is to be strong and honorable and noble every minute of the day. Thanks to them, I *am* healing, Daveigh. I will be better than I ever was."

Daveigh could feel the sincerity. Before the battle at Castle Acre, he'd had doubts about Bric. But at this moment, he had no doubts whatsoever because Bric believed what he was telling him; Daveigh could see that. If Bric believed it, then it would be so.

There was no doubt in Daveigh's mind.

"That is good to hear," he said. "Because now I must bring about the reason for my visit. I received a missive from William Marshal, Bric. It would seem that a French fleet, full of supplies and men, is due to land in Dover and the armies of England must be there to greet them. We have been ordered to move the army south, into Kent, immediately, and I came to see if you were at all ready to face such a responsibility. I thought that I was hoping beyond hope that you would be ready, but after listening to you, I am willing to believe that my hope is a real one."

Bric wasn't surprised to hear about the missive from William Marshal. In fact, he felt drawn to the news, because the battle with the French had been part of his life for a few years now. His reaction was calm because this kind of news was perfectly normal in his world.

In fact, that's how the news made him feel – *normal.*

"That makes sense," he said. "After the French fought so zealously at Castle Acre, stealing cattle and trying to pilfer supplies, it was a tell-tale sign as to how badly supplied the French army is right now. Where is Prince Louis?"

"In London," Sean answered quietly. When Bric looked at him, surprise in his features, Sean nodded faintly. "I was with William when he received word about the coming French fleet. In fact, I was at Ramsbury Castle telling Dashiell and Lord de Vaston about the summons from the Marshal when they received the missive about you."

Bric's eyebrows rose. "And you came to Bedingfeld?" he said, astonished. "But why? You should be moving your armies into Kent at this very moment."

Sean's eyes glittered. "You were more important, Bric," he said. "There is not one man around this table that does not owe you something. Were it not for you, Dashiell would not be alive, and

Bentley would not be the Duke of Savernake. If there is a battle, you will lead it, and if there are men to be killed, you will always lead the charge. You are the High Warrior and without you, our armies are somehow diminished. You mean a great many things to a great many people, and when we received word that you needed help, there was nothing more important for us to do. There will always be French to fight, or armies to move, but there will never be another Bric MacRohan."

Bric was both embarrassed and touched by Sean's words. "I am just a knight," he finally said. "I am one of many."

"You are one of a kind," Dashiell spoke up, answering for Sean. "The truth is this – and mayhap we are being selfish about it – but we did not want to face this battle without you. You have been fighting against tyranny for as many years as I have, and that is a long time, indeed. Who else but the big Irish knight with the silver eyes, who lobs off the heads of his enemies, can strike fear into the hearts of the French? You are more valuable than you know, Bric, to all of us, and I am thankful to God that Sean was able to come to Bedingfeld with us because he understands what you have been doing through. You needed a man who understood your fears, and he did. I am coming to think that God sent him to Ramsbury at the right time, knowing we would be receiving the missive about you. If we have not fixed you, then I hope we have at least helped you along the way to reclaiming who you once were."

Bric realized that he was fighting off a lump in his throat. "You have," he said hoarsely. "And you have my eternal thanks. As I said, I will never be the man I was before but, somehow, I do believe I shall be better. The world is different than it was before my injury and before Mylo's death, but that is a good thing. I have learned something about myself."

"What is that? Dashiell asked.

Bric looked at Eiselle, who was gazing at him with utter adoration. He smiled at her. "That I am stronger than I thought I was," he said. "And I have friends to whom I am very grateful. But most of all, I learned that the love of a good woman is stronger than anything on this earth. With Eiselle by my side, I could take on the devil himself and win."

Every man at the table understood that because every man at the table had a wife they were madly in love with. It was Daveigh who finally asked the fateful question.

"Pearce is mustering the army as we speak, Bric," he said with some hesitation. "I would like you leading it, but if you cannot, I must hear it from you. And I will not fault you for it. But you must be honest with me and not tell me what I want to hear. Tell me what *you* feel, Bric."

Bric's gaze lingered on the man. Then, he looked around the table, seeing the expressions of his friends – expressions of hope, of encouragement, but of truth. Always, of truth. He didn't want to disappoint them but, in the same breath, he knew that whatever his answer was, they would understand. He didn't feel pressured; he felt their love and support, no matter what.

Then, he looked at Eiselle. She was looking at him in much the same way his friends were – with hope, encouragement, and support. But glimmering in her pale eyes, he could also see a love that ran deeper than the ocean. It was a love that embraced him, filled him, and touched him like nothing else ever had. He was strong, and he was invincible, but the love he shared with Eiselle was stronger than all the men in all the world, now and forever more. It was that love that gave him the confidence to do his duty and to be the knight he was born to be.

It was time to reclaim who he was.

"I will lead the army," he finally said. "And the French will be very sorry they ever came to England."

Everyone heard him, but he was looking at Eiselle as if she were the only person in the room. Eiselle, too, was gazing into his eyes as if nothing else on earth existed.

"I am so proud of you," she whispered. "You are fierce, and you are mighty, and who else but you can lead the de Winter army to victory? It will be your shining moment."

He put a hand up, cupping her sweet face. "Nay," he murmured. "*This* is my shining moment. With you."

As Eiselle wrapped her arms around his neck and hugged him tightly, the men around the table grinned at each other. Bric was the strongest man they knew and he was proving it now. He'd worked hard, they'd all worked hard, and the end result was a man who had managed to find some of what he'd lost. He wasn't perfect yet, but he would be. He wasn't the man he was before the injury but, as Bric had said, he didn't want to be.

He wanted to be better.

The next day, Eiselle, Bric, Manducor, and Daveigh returned to Narborough while Sean, Dashiell, and Bentley headed out to rendez-vous with their own armies, all of whom were heading across England to converge in Kent where the French fleet would have quite a welcoming committee. It was the build up to something big, as Sean had stated, a battle that would perhaps decide the future of England herself.

When Bric rode out of Narborough at the head of the de Winter army two days later, it was as a proud and strong man who held his head high. He felt as confident as he looked. The sight of him bolstered the de Winter men, men who had seen him at his lowest not long before, but his transformation had been astonishing. Not one man disbelieved that the High Warrior hadn't returned to lead them all to victory, and they had faith in the man whose well-established reputation long outweighed whatever brief failing he might have had.

They had to believe.

As Bric departed from the gray-stoned castle, his last sight was of his wife, standing by the gatehouse, and waving to him. No tears, no weeping, simply complete faith and confidence that he would return to her. She had even packed for him. But the one thing she didn't need to pack for him was strung around his neck, the lock of dark hair with a pale-green fabric chain that he kept close to his heart.

The talisman that would be with him in this life, and beyond.

CHAPTER TWENTY-FOUR

October

"DO YOU REMEMBER this lad, Eiselle?" Keeva asked. "The major-domo from Bedingfeld seems to think you do."

In the great hall of Narborough on an unseasonably warm October day, Eiselle found herself looking at Royce. The child was dirty and red-eyed, indicative of his emotional state, and simply by looking at him, Eiselle could see that something terrible had happened.

"We met during our stay at Bedingfeld," she said, going to the child and peering at him with concern. "Royce? What has happened, lad? Why are you here?"

Royce's lower lip began to tremble, and he wiped at his eyes, smearing more dirt across his face. "He... he was going to take me to the priests," he said, pointing to the cloud-haired old servant from Bedingfeld. "I don't want to go! I want to fight and Sir Bric said I could be a soldier!"

The old man didn't have much patience for the boy. "He's a found-ling now, m'lady," he said, stress in his tone. "His mother was killed when a cow kicked her last month, and we've no use for a foundling at Bedingfeld. I am taking him to the priests at St. John's in King's Lynn. I have heard they have a foundling's home, but he insisted on coming to Narborough to see you first. I am sorry if this angers you, m'lady, but he would not go quietly until I brought him here."

Now, the boy's red face was starting to make some sense. It was a sad turn of events for young Royce. Still, Eiselle wasn't sure what to say. It wasn't as if she could take on the burden of the child. She had a child of her own on the way and the pregnancy was exhausting her, so she knew she wasn't capable of watching after a lively little boy.

Still, looking into that sad little face, she knew she couldn't send him to the priests. She'd heard horrible things about foundling's homes and she couldn't subject Royce to such terrible treatment. That sweet little boy who only wanted to fight.

Torn, she put a hand on his shoulder.

"I am sorry about your mother, Royce," she said. "Do you not have relatives anywhere? A grandmother, mayhap?"

Royce shrugged. "I don't know."

"Not even an aunt or an uncle?"

Again, Royce shrugged, still wiping his eyes furiously of the tears that wouldn't seem to stop. "Can't I stay with you?" he begged. "I will be no trouble, my lady, I promise. My mam told me to be good, and I will be. I will be good for you."

The plea from the child was weakening Eiselle but she seriously wondered what Bric would say if she chose to accept responsibility. As she pondered the problem, she glanced up and saw Manducor sitting at the end of the feasting table, eating what was possibly his fifth or sixth meal of the day. He was a man who had no responsibilities whatsoever, and as she watched the man eat, a thought occurred to her.

She turned back to Royce.

"You and the majordomo will sit down and wait for me," she said, looking to the harried majordomo. "Sit at the end of the feasting table and I shall have food brought out to you. Lady de Winter, may I have a word with you?"

Keeva followed her to the far end of the feasting table where Manducor was chewing loudly on bread and cheese. He was also drinking his fill of wine, burping loudly, something he was trying to cut down on because the sound of it, and the frequency, made Eiselle sick to her stomach these days. Any burp had her gagging so, as she approached, Manducor turned his head and struggled not to burp loudly in her presence.

"What is it, Eiselle?" Keeva asked. "How well do you know the lad?"

Eiselle paused at the head of the table, making sure to include Manducor in the conversation. "All I know of the child was that he was sweet and helpful when Bric and I stayed at Bedingfeld," she said. "But the child had more interaction with Bric because he very much wants to be a knight. I believe Manducor had some interaction with him, too."

Manducor looked down the table where the skinny little lad was sitting rather sadly. "That little monster," he grunted. "I know him. He is the devil."

Eiselle pursed her lips wryly. "He is *not* the devil," she said. "Bric seems to think well of him."

"He pinched me."

"You deserved it. You tripped him."

Manducor didn't reply, mostly because she was right, but he let her know his displeasure by emitting a burp that made her frown. All the while, Keeva was listening closely, looking at the boy every so often as he sat with his head lowered.

"So... what does he want?" Keeva finally asked. "Does he want to stay here? He is far too young to be used in any capacity as a servant."

"He is the *devil!*" Manducor hissed.

Eiselle shushed the man sternly before answering Keeva. "I feel a great deal of pity for the child," she said. "He should not be sent to the priests at the foundling's home. If someone can simply watch over him and make sure he is fed and taken care of, I am sure that when he is a little older, he will make a fine servant or even a soldier. He is very bright."

She was looking at Manducor when she said it, who immediately took her meaning. "Nay!" he boomed, standing up. "I will *not* be that devil's keeper."

Both Eiselle and Keeva put their hands up to silence him. "Be still," Keeva hissed. "You do nothing else around here except eat my food and drink my wine, and once in a great while you decide to help Weetley with his patients. But even so, I would not entrust a child to you. With your appetite, you would probably make a stew out of him."

Manducor knew better than to snap back at Lady de Winter, so he simply lowered his head and sank back into his seat, returning to his wine and ignoring the women standing near him.

But his reaction was a disappointment to Eiselle. In truth, she had been hoping that Manducor might offer to mentor the boy and see to him, but that was not to be. Keeva was right; he didn't do much at Narborough other than eat and drink, and look after Eiselle on occasion because he felt some fatherly obligation towards her, but that was the limit of his service. Perhaps it was for the best that he refused to look after Royce; she wasn't at all sure the man had the patience to deal with a child, and especially not a child he carried a grudge against. Without Manducor as an option, she looked to Keeva.

"Bric seems to think something of the child, but I cannot accept such responsibility without his consent," she said. "Besides, we have our own child coming in the spring and I must focus on my baby."

Keeva nodded seriously. "That is true."

"But you have no such obligations, Keeva. What about you?"

Keeva looked at her in shock. "Me?"

Eiselle smiled faintly. "*You*," she said. "As I said, Royce is a bright child and I found him sweet and eager. Look at him; he is not un-handsome. He is well-formed and I am sure he will be stronger with a regular diet. I am quite sure he would become a fine young man under your strong and steady hand."

Keeva grunted hesitantly. "Eiselle, I cannot. He is a servant."

"That makes no difference, does it?"

"What in the world will Daveigh say?"

Eiselle grasped her gently by the arm. "He is just a little boy, Keeva," she said. "Tiny, even, and his only choice will be to go to the foundling's home where the priests will probably starve him and work him to the bone. I could not live with myself knowing he was being abused like that, and given that you are a kind and caring person, I do not believe you could allow the child of one of your servants to be mistreated."

Keeva was staring at the young boy, shocked by Eiselle's suggestion. But the more she looked at the child, the more she could feel herself considering it. *A little boy*, Eiselle had said. That was true – he was quite small for his age. The obvious consideration was that such a child could replace the children she never had, but Keeva couldn't go that far. No one could replace what she had lost. But could she take care of the boy? Of course she could. Could she nurture him and ensure he grew up obedient and strong? Absolutely.

Eiselle seemed to think well of the lad and it was true what she'd said – that foundling's homes could often be brutal places. To send the boy there would be condemning him to a terrible life. Perhaps Keeva was getting soft in her old age, but she found herself relenting to Eiselle's suggestion.

Perhaps she could, indeed, help a lost little boy.

"Very well," she said. "I am not sure what Daveigh will think about all of this, but I can watch over the boy and make sure he is taken care of. I will tell the majordomo to leave him here."

With that, she headed over to the end of the table where food was just being brought around to the hungry child and the old man. Eiselle watched, her heart happy, as Keeva began talking to the pair. Eiselle knew that Royce would be in very good hands.

As Keeva took Royce by the hand and led him away, Eiselle felt proud of herself. What could have been a terrible circumstance had ended up for the better, and she was satisfied. She was about to leave the hall and return to her chamber when she heard Manducor's voice behind her.

"So the little devil has a keeper now," he said. "When Lady Angela left with her husband, God rest his soul, she took her little monster with her. Now you have brought another monster into Narborough."

Eiselle looked at him. "I could not permit him to go to the foundling's home," she said simply. "I thought you would make the generous decision to watch over him, but it seems as if you have no generosity."

With that, she stuck her tongue out at him and Manducor snorted.

"The boy and I would not get on," he said. "It would be like water and fire."

"You do not know that. Besides... I think Narborough is missing something without Eddie's screams echoing off the walls. It will do us all good to have a child about, as Keeva's ward."

Manducor simply lifted his shoulders. "She will cool the fire in him, to be sure," he said. "She is a fearsome lady. Besides... I do not need a child to watch over, but she does. She has not had her own children, but I have."

Eiselle heard the sadness in his tone when he spoke. Or perhaps it was simply resignation – a man resigned to his past. He wasn't one to mention his children, or even speak of personal things, not even his identity, which truthfully drove Eiselle mad with curiosity. Manducor kept himself quite removed personally from everyone, including Eiselle and Bric. The smelly priest with the penchant for farting had attached himself to them, as an advisor or a companion or even simply an annoying presence, and when Bric had been struggling with his battle fatigue, Manducor had been with him constantly.

To Eiselle, that meant that the man was nearly part of their family and she knew almost nothing about him. As he sat at the feasting table with a distant look in his eye, perhaps thinking on the children he had lost, Eiselle sat down across the table from him.

"You have much to offer a child," she said. "What about *my* child? When he comes, will you simply ignore him?"

Manducor looked to his wine, unable to meet her eye. "Mayhap," he mumbled into his cup. "He will probably be a devil, too."

Eiselle fought off a smile as her hand instinctively moved to her gently rounded belly. She was only four months along, but her belly was growing nicely and she was certain she could feel the baby kick from time to time.

"He will not," she insisted. "With Bric as his father, would you truly think such a thing?"

Manducor chuckled, setting his cup down. "I would not," he said.

"Bric would not allow it."

"Nay, he would not. But I do want to ask you something."

Manducor cocked a bushy eyebrow. "Nay, I will *not* be his godfather. He already has one in de Winter."

She shook her head. "It was not that," she said. "But there is something else I have been thinking on. Whether or not you realize it, I have known you as long as I have known my husband. You performed our marriage mass and when Bric was suffering with his loss of confidence, you were always there to speak to him if he needed help. You are annoying, and quite disgusting at times, but you have also meant a good deal to Bric and me. It is for that reason that I should like this child to bear your name as one of his own, but I refuse to name my child Manducor. Won't you tell me your real name so that I may honor you?"

Manducor stared at her, startled by her request. He wasn't quite sure how to react, or what to say, and he'd spent so many years denying anyone who wanted to know his identity that to think of revealing it left a bad taste upon his tongue.

"I do not need to be honored," he said after a moment. "You provide me with food and drink and, on occasion, pleasant companionship. You do not need to add my name to the long list of names you intend to saddle your son with. I do not belong with the others."

That wasn't the answer Eiselle wanted but it was the one she had expected. "Then you offend me," she said. "You offend Bric by not allowing us to show you what you have meant to us. I have spent the past four months coming to know you and while I have seen a man of uncanny wisdom, I have also seen a man who is selfish and careless. And now you offend me by denying my wish to give my son your name."

She was building up a righteous rage and Manducor stood up, moving away from the table because he didn't want to get into a verbal confrontation with her. The woman was pregnant, and her moods had been volatile, so it was best to simply leave her and let her stew.

But even as Manducor moved away from the table, he was hesitant to leave completely. He had grown fond of Eiselle, and of Bric, and in truth, they were the only real family he had, even if he had practically forced himself upon them. The knight who tried to drown him when they first met, and the lady who had been so very timid at the beginning of her marriage to the big Irish knight had grown into people who were everything Manducor had ever wanted to be.

In fact, he saw much of his own wife in Eiselle and perhaps that was why he'd grown fond of the woman. His wife had been sweet, and soft, and he'd adored her deeply. Losing her and their children had left him empty inside, and he'd been empty all of these years until meeting Bric and Eiselle.

Now, they had a child on the way, a child Eiselle wanted to bear his name. She had been wrong; Manducor wasn't honoring her by allowing her to use his name. She had honored *him* simply by asking.

Perhaps it was time for him to open himself up to people he genuinely cared about. It wasn't as if he'd ever given them any choice; he'd latched on to them the moment he'd come to Narborough and even though they could have chased him away, they hadn't. They'd permitted him to stay, and his life was the better for it. He'd taken about ten steps away from the table before coming to a halt, turning slowly, and retracing his steps all the way back.

Eiselle was sitting there, looking at him with a displeased expression. He sat back down again, facing her.

"You must understand that I ceased to become the man I had been born as the moment I joined the priesthood," he said quietly. "You ask for my name... I do not even know who that man is any longer."

Eiselle knew this was a difficult discussion for him. "If I can piece together what you have told me about your past, you were a man who loved his wife and children," she said. "You are a very wise man, Manducor. You have been a comforting presence for both Bric and me. Please let me honor you by giving my child your name."

He could see that she was sincere and, in truth, he was very humbled by her request. After a moment, he sighed faintly. "I told you that you would not believe what my real name was."

"What is it?"

"Robert."

Eiselle smiled. "Why would I not believe that?" she said. "It is a lovely name and will go well with the multitude of other names we have already selected for our son."

Manducor was surprised that she hadn't pushed him for his full name, including his surname. Because she hadn't pushed, he would show her the respect of telling her. Somehow, there was a sense of relief in that confessional.

"I am the bastard son of the Earl of Norfolk," he said quietly. "I was christened Robert Bigod and I fostered in the best homes my father could arrange. My wife was a member of the de Vere family. We had everything – wealth, some prestige – everything. And I lost it all in two days when my wife and two children died of a fever. I have said that the priests of St. Margaret's found me in the gutter and gave me a life in the priesthood, but that's not quite true. My father sent them for me because he could no longer be troubled by a son who had allowed himself to become so crippled with grief. That was many years ago and I have not spoken of it since. But... may I ask a favor?"

Eiselle was quite astonished by his confession, but she nodded. "Of course."

Manducor took a deep breath. "Instead of naming your child for me, would you name him for the son I lost? His name was Rhys. It would give me much comfort to know that my son's memory will live through your child."

Eiselle blinked away the tears now. "That is a beautiful sentiment," she said. "I am sure Bric will agree with me. I would be honored to name my son after yours."

Manducor simply nodded, the moment perhaps a little too emotional for his taste. Forcing a smile at Eiselle, he stood up from the table again and headed off somewhere, perhaps to reconcile himself to the fact that he'd just confessed information he'd kept long buried. Speaking it made it real again, and there were bittersweet memories in that.

Eiselle remained at the table, thinking of Manducor, from a fine Norfolk family, but so destroyed by the death of his family that to this day he wasn't quite able to speak of it. As she sat there, pondering the lovely name of Rhys Bigod, Zara came rushing into the hall.

"Eiselle!" she gasped. "The army is returning! You must come quickly!"

Startled by the cry, Eiselle stood up from the table and scurried in Zara's direction. "Now?" she asked excitedly. "Did you see them?"

Zara shook her head. "Nay," she said, grabbing Eiselle's hand. "But the sentries are announcing their approach. You must come!"

Eiselle took a deep breath and allowed Zara to drag her along. She didn't move too quickly, knowing she wasn't allowed into the outer bailey with the army arriving. But it was more than that – the last time the army returned, Bric had arrived holding a dead knight. Before that, he'd returned to her wounded. She'd never known her husband to return from a battle intact and that realization had her walking slower and slower.

Zara was trying to pull her along, but Eiselle simply didn't want to move very fast, her anxiety growing by leaps and bounds. She knew this moment would come; she'd prayed for it. But now, she found herself wholly unprepared. As was usual, her nervous stomach started to lurch, creating a miserable symphony in her gut. Zara finally gave up dragging her along and let her go, running out into the outer bailey just as the gates were beginning to crank open.

But Eiselle didn't follow her. Now, she could hardly breathe.

Standing in the small gatehouse that bridged the gap between the inner and outer bailey, she watched the sentries on the wall call out to each other, shouts that indicated what they were seeing in the distance. Someone was holding up fingers to indicate the number of knights that could be seen and Eiselle couldn't quite see just how many fingers were being held up, so she began to pray.

Furiously and passionately, she began to pray that Bric would return to her this time, unharmed in any fashion. It was a prayer she'd muttered many times over the past few months, but never more fervently than she did now.

Please, God... let Bric return to me whole!

Near the big gatehouse, she could see Manducor milling about, talking to the guards. Zara was trying to run out to greet Pearce on the road beyond, but the gatehouse sergeant wouldn't let her go. Eiselle ended up leaning against the inner wall because her knees were shaking so that she couldn't seem to stand still. As she continued to watch and wait, Keeva came up beside her.

"They did not send word ahead as they usually do," she said quietly.

Eiselle turned to look at her. "Does that mean something terrible?"

"Nay, lass. It doesn't mean anything at all."

Eiselle couldn't decide if she felt better or worse about that. "The last time Bric returned..." She couldn't even finish the sentence. Taking a deep breath, she tried to distract herself. "Where is Royce? I thought for certain he would want watch the army return."

Keeva shook her head. "The lad was exhausted," she said. "I put him to bed and he was asleep before I even left the room. There will be more armies for him to watch in the future."

Eiselle reached out and took her by the hand, giving it a squeeze. "He is very fortunate to have you. You were very kind to take responsibility of him."

Keeva wasn't going to admit that, already, she felt rather maternal towards the child, so she simply smiled, perhaps an embarrassed little gesture, and returned her gaze to the distant gatehouse.

"I cannot tell you how many times I have watched the de Winter army return," she said. "It seems like thousands of times, but I know it is not so. And every time, I feel like it is the first time. I am anxious to see my husband. That is all that matters to me."

Eiselle's smile faded as she, too, returned her focus to the gatehouse. "Bric was strong when he left," she said. "He seemed at peace with returning to battle, but I have worried every day that in spite of his assurances, he was not ready."

"I know," Keeva said softly. "But you must trust that everything is well, Eiselle. You cannot have any doubt. When Bric returns, no matter what you feel... you must be strong for him, in any case."

Eiselle was struggling not to let her imagination run wild. "I will be whatever he needs me to be," she whispered. "But I pray that he returns to me as well and whole as when he left."

It was a prayer spoken by every wife, of every fighting man, throughout time. Keeva understood the prayer well, for it was the very same prayer she uttered.

Time passed as the two women stood together, listening to the sentries shout at each other. Men gathered in the gatehouse, watching the road beyond and, soon enough, they began to disband as the first of the de Winter army began to pass beneath the gatehouse.

Two knights were leading a group of hundreds of infantry and when Keeva recognized Daveigh, she let out a little cry. Suddenly, she was rushing past Eiselle and into the bailey, running to her husband, who brought his weary steed to a halt. He dismounted just as Keeva rushed up to him, and she fell into his arms.

It was a beautiful reunion, one that had Eiselle smiling. Daveigh was home safe and she was glad. Over towards the stables, the second knight came to a halt and Zara was standing beside her husband's horse when he dismounted. Pearce handed his horse off to a stable servant before kissing Zara chastely on the head. Leaving his wife standing there, he headed in Eiselle's direction.

But Eiselle didn't notice. She was watching the bulk of the army as it poured in through the gate, now with wagon after wagon of supplies and weapons. She was watching for Bric and fighting off the panic that threatened because he hadn't appeared yet. She was so wrapped up in the watching for signs of her husband that when Pearce approached her and removed his helm, she still didn't notice him. She only noticed when he started speaking.

"Lady MacRohan," he said. "I am sure you will hear this from other men, but I wanted you to hear it from me first."

Eiselle looked at him; she didn't like his words. They sent fear into her veins, and the panic she'd been fighting off was threatening to explode.

"Where is my husband?" she asked tremulously.

Pearce turned to glance at the army as it continued to enter through the gates. "He is back with the wounded." When he saw the color drain from her face, he shook his head quickly. "Nay, my lady – he is not wounded himself. He is traveling with them to bring them comfort. He has been telling them stories of Irish glory nearly the entire trip home, trying to distract them from their pain and suffering."

Eiselle felt such relief that she was weak with it. Leaning against the gatehouse wall for support, she labored to reclaim her composure. "Thank God," she breathed. "Thank God he is safe."

"He is, indeed."

He started to turn away, but she stopped him. "Pearce, how was he?" she asked. "What I mean is… did the Bric of old return? Was he the man you have always known? Or was he… was he…?"

She couldn't finish, but Pearce knew what she meant. He smiled faintly at her as he recalled the campaign they'd endured the past several weeks.

"You needn't worry," he told her quietly. "Lady MacRohan, your husband is a hero. Not only did he lead the army against the French prince who had arrived to intercept his fleet, but he saved Daveigh's life as well. Somehow, Daveigh got separated from his infantry and the French targeted him with their knights. Had Bric and Dashiell not risked themselves to save him, Daveigh would not be here. I have fought with Bric for many years, Eiselle, and I can honestly say that I have never seen him greater than he was on that day. It was nothing short of legendary."

Eiselle looked at him in awe. "Then... then he was well? He did not falter?"

Pearce shook his head firmly. "He fought as strongly as I have ever seen him."

With that, he turned away and headed back to the incoming army, with Zara trailing after him. As he walked off, Daveigh and Keeva approached. Daveigh has a big gash on his face, and looked exhausted, but he was alive. As he came near, Eiselle called out to him.

"Welcome home, my lord," she said. "Were the armies victorious, then?"

Daveigh had his arm around Keeva's shoulder as his wife held on to him, tears on her cheeks. "Aye," he said. "We were victorious. There were two battles, in truth, one at sea with the French fleet, and one on the land with Prince Louis' army. We triumphed in both battles, thank God. But I would not be standing here were it not for Bric."

The anxiety and panic that had filled Eiselle not moments before had been replaced by pride and joy so strong that she felt as if her heart were about to burst from her chest.

"Pearce told me," she said. "I am glad he was there for you when you needed him."

Daveigh nodded wearily. "As am I," he said. Then, he sighed heavily, looking at his wife who was shaken up by the story of his near death. "I cannot describe how Bric fought. I can only tell you that I have never seen anything like it. Some of the greatest armies were present – de Burgh, Marshal, de Braose, de Lohr, Lincoln, de Lara, de Wolfe, Savernake... so many great armies. But no one stood out more than Bric. The battle he fought is one for the ages. I heard someone describe him as heroic, and he truly was. In fact, his actions reminded us of that talisman he used to wear, the one he gave to Mylo."

Eiselle cocked her head curiously. "Why?"

Daveigh's eyes grew moist. "Because of what was etched on it," he said. "*Greater love hath no man than he lay down his life for his friends.* Bric was willing to do that, without thought but, in the end, he did not have to. He saved me as well as himself. But that kind of selflessness… that is worthy of only men of legend, of which Bric is one."

Eiselle simply smiled at him, watching as Keeva urged her husband towards the keep. She watched them go, returning her attention to the outer bailey only to see that Bric had arrived.

He was astride his fat dappled war horse, Liath, surrounded by wagons that were bringing the wounded in. Even though Eiselle knew she should remain out of the way of the men and animals, once her eyes beheld her husband, there was no holding her back. She began to walk towards him, her gaze fixed on him as if they were the only two people in the bailey.

Around her, dust kicked up, men shouted, and animals rumbled, but Eiselle's focus never moved from the man astride the gray steed. When Bric caught sight of her, he leapt from his horse as if there were nothing else in the world more important than greeting his wife.

Nothing more important than her in the whole world.

They came together in a clash of linen and armor, and Eiselle threw her arms around his neck, hugging him tightly even though she was encumbered by mail and metal between them.

"Bric," she breathed. "You have returned to me. Thank God you have returned!"

Bric couldn't speak because of the lump in his throat. He had imagined this moment for the past sixty-nine days. It had been that long since he'd seen his wife and as he held her, it was all he could do not to break down.

"Aye," he said hoarsely. "I have returned to you. Did you truly have any doubt?"

Carefully, he set her to her feet, but Eiselle wouldn't let go of him, nor would he let go of her. The moment was too joyful for them to release one another.

"Nay," Eiselle said, looking into his tired, stubbled face. "I did not have any doubts at all. How do you feel?"

"Better than I ever have."

"Swear it?"

"I swear."

She looked him over. "This is the first time you have ever returned to me the same way you left me – whole and healthy."

Bric smiled. "And it will not be the last time for this happy circumstance, I promise."

"I will hold you to it," she said, touching his bristly face. "I have heard rumors that the High Warrior was in top form on this campaign."

He gave her a lopsided smile. "Have you been speaking to my most ardent admirers already?"

Eiselle giggled. "Pearce and Daveigh told me what you did," she said. "They said you saved Daveigh from French knights and to say that I am proud of you is putting it mildly."

Bric was surprisingly modest. "I did what I had to do."

"Of course you did, but it sounds like it was a very great feat."

His eyes glittered at her, perhaps remembering that moment in time when he thought he might not make it back to her. The odds had been against him as he and Dashiell had pulled Daveigh from the fire.

But it hadn't damaged him. It had only made him stronger.

"It was simply part of a larger battle," he said. "But Daveigh is alive and that is all that matters. It could have very easily gone differently."

"But because of you, it did not," Eiselle insisted gently. "You are a hero, Bric. You are *my* hero."

Bric's response was to kiss her, deeply, right in the middle of the bailey and with the entire de Winter army as a witness. He had been so careful with his public displays of affection for Eiselle but, at this moment, he would demonstrate his love for his wife and he didn't care who saw it. If the whole of Narborough Castle didn't already know he was madly in love with the woman, then they were all deaf and blind.

He finally released her from his kiss, but not from his embrace. As Eiselle watched, he pulled out the talisman that she had made for him and held it up between them.

"This is what did it," he said, kissing the talisman before kissing her again. "I had this next to my heart the entire time, reminding me of the true power of a knight. I cannot explain it except to say that I have spent my life on the field of battle, and what drove me was my own ambition and sense of honor. It was what carried me to victory so many times. But in those victories, I always felt I was missing something. I never knew what that was until I fell in love with you."

She stroked his face sweetly. "What did you discover?"

He sighed, trying to find the right words. "With the battle at Holdingham, I knew I felt something for you, but I wasn't sure what. When I realized what it was, I felt crippled by it. Frightened, because I did not want to die. I did not want to leave you. When Mylo fell at Castle Acre, I was confused and broken. You know this. And I leaned on my love for you, like a crutch. It held me up. But in fighting at Sandwich and at Dover, I came to realize that the power of love is stronger than anything I've ever known. Whatever I was missing before in my hollow victories of the past has been filled by you. Here I am, holding you, telling you of my victory, and the only thing that matters is that you are proud of me. That is the greatest glory I could ever receive."

His words touched Eiselle more than she could have ever imagined. He was home, he was safe, and he was a better man than he had ever been. It was all she could ask for.

"And that glory is yours, forever," she whispered. "You will always have my love, and my pride in you is without measure. Even at your lowest point, I told you that you were the strongest, most wonderful man I know, and now as you taste victory again, you are still the strongest and most wonderful man I know. Nothing you can do will every change that."

Bric looked at her, feeling the love pour forth, and he basked in it. The accolades from his men, from his liege, meant little compared to the accolades from his wife.

The one he never wanted.

Thank God he'd been wrong.

"I love you, Lady MacRohan," he murmured. "Now and forever, I love and worship you."

Eiselle wrapped her arms around his neck again, never to let him go.

"And I love you," she whispered. "You are more than my heart could have ever hoped for."

Bric heard his words, repeated in her sweet voice. There was so much meaning in those words, to the both of them. He kissed her again, smack in the middle of the bailey with everyone watching.

And he didn't care a lick.

The High Warrior had finally come home.

EPILOGUE

The Ides of March
Year of our Lord 1218 A.D.

BRIC WAS FEELING so much anxiety that his hands were actually hurting. So was his chest. He couldn't sit for very long and when standing, he simply walked in circles.

That's what he was doing at the moment.

He was pacing the edges of Narborough's hall, hands behind his back, seemingly lost in thought. But he had a shadow; right beside him, Royce was pacing as well, hands behind his back and mimicking every move Bric made. When Bric would stop and look at the child, the child would stop and look up at him. Bric would sigh heavily and resume his pacing with Royce right beside him.

Bric and his little shadow.

"You are going to pace a trench right into the floor, Bric," Daveigh said from his seat at the feasting table. "Come and sit. Have some wine. Relax."

But Bric shook his head. "I cannot," he said as he continued his pacing. Then, he came to halt near the hearth. "Does it always take this long?"

Daveigh grinned, looking at Pearce and Manducor, who were sitting at the table with him. As he shrugged and took a drink of his wine, Manducor spoke up.

"It can take days or hours," he said. "My children took hours."

Bric sighed again, heavily, but it was a gesture of impatience as well as concern. "Her pains started this afternoon," he said. "It is well into

336

the night now. Surely something can be done to hurry it along."

"I am sure Weetley is doing all he can, Bric," Daveigh said. "You must be patient."

But Bric didn't want to be patient. He wanted to see his son and he wanted his wife to come through unharmed. That was perhaps what was frightening him most – if his son did not survive the birth, he could bear it. It would be devastating, but he would recover. But if Eiselle did not survive, then his world would be ended.

There would be nothing more for him.

He glanced at Manducor as he resumed his pacing, thinking of the man's dead family. He didn't want to become Manducor, a man who was still trying to find his place in the world after he lost everything. But he knew he couldn't go on without Eiselle, so what would be left for him? But he shook himself, fighting off the morbid thoughts, praying to a God he didn't speak to very much that his wife would survive childbirth. As he made another round about the room with Royce beside him, Keeva suddenly appeared.

Having come down the spiral stairs from the chamber Bric and Eiselle shared, Keeva had on an apron and her hair was pulled back, tied behind her head. The front of the apron had faint bloodstains on it, indicative of the work she had been doing. When Bric saw her, he practically ran to her.

"Well?" he demanded. "Has my son arrived?"

Keeva shook her head, reaching out to take his hand. "You must come with me."

Bric felt a stab of fear as he'd never felt in his life. "Why?" he breathed. "What is wrong?"

Keeva shooed Royce away when the boy tried to follow, sending him back to sit with Daveigh. She pulled Bric into the stairwell before speaking.

"We need your help," she said quietly. "Your son is turned around in Eiselle's womb and cannot be born without help."

Bric felt lightheaded. "What does that mean?"

"It means that you must hold your wife steady while Weetley tries to turn the baby around, so that he comes head-first."

They had reached the top of the stairs and Bric came to a halt. When Keeva turned to him, she could see the tears in his eyes. He was absolutely terrified.

"God, no," he breathed. "My wife…"

Keeva tugged on his hand, pulling him along. It was like towing a barge. "Eiselle is in good spirits," she said. "She is not in terrible distress, but the babe must be turned."

Bric struggled to calm himself. "Will it hurt her?"

Keeva pulled him all the way to the door, pausing before she opened it. "I am sure it will not be pleasant, which is why we need you to hold her steady." She put a hand on Bric's cheek to comfort him. "You must be brave, MacRohan. Your wife needs your strength, not your fear. If you show any measure of it, I will throw you out of the window. Is this in any way unclear?"

He swallowed. "It is clear."

"Good."

With that, Keeva opened the door into the chamber Bric was so familiar with. It smelled strongly of peppermint, thought to ward off the evil tidings of childbirth, and as he stepped into the chamber, his gaze immediately found his wife.

Eiselle was sitting on a birthing chair near the hearth. She looked weary, her face sweaty and her beautiful hair pulled away from her face, but her expression lightened when she saw her husband. Bric went to her, choked up with emotion in spite of Keeva's threat. He went to his knees next to the chair, wrapping his arms around her shoulders and pulling her head to his lips for a tender kiss.

"How do you feel, *mo chroí*?" he asked softly. "Keeva tells me that our son is being difficult."

Eiselle put her hand on his face, chuckling. "Do not look so worried," she said. "Weetley simply needs to turn him so that he is facing the right way."

She was being incredibly brave, far braver than he was. Bric nodded, unable to speak because he was genuinely trying not to weep. He was as frightened as he had ever been in his life and trying very hard not to show it.

"Then I will help however I can," he said, sounding surprisingly calm. "I am anxious to meet Conor."

Eiselle smiled. "As am I," she said. "He will be here soon, I am certain. You needn't worry."

"I won't."

That was as much of a greeting as Keeva would allow. Things needed to happen and they needed to happen quickly, and there was no time for sentiment, not if this baby was going to be born any time soon. She began waving her hands at Bric.

"Get in behind her and put her your arms around her shoulders," she said. "You must hold her as still as you can while we attempt to turn the baby."

Bric summoned his courage. For the fearless warrior, this was something of a very new experience for him, but he did as he was told. As he stood up and moved to the back of the chair, Weetley flipped up the bottom of Eiselle's shift, revealing her enormous belly. Truth be told, Bric was well-acquainted with that belly, for he had slept with it nightly for the past several months, and his lip prints were all over it as a result of speaking to his son on a regular basis.

All he could see was Eiselle's belly and her legs as they rested on a chair that was made for childbirth. He really couldn't see anything else, which was fine with him. He didn't want to see the birthing process in the least, mysterious and terrifying thing that it was. As he knelt down behind the chair and wrapped his arms around Eiselle, pulling her into his powerful embrace, Weetley began greasing up Eiselle's belly.

From that point, Bric didn't want to see anymore. He held on to his wife as he felt her body jerked around by whatever Weetley was doing. Eiselle grunted and gasped, but she never emitted anything more than that. With all of the buffeting going on, it must have surely been excruciating, but she never cried out or wept. She simply held on to Bric's arms as he held tightly to her. Bric's face was pressed into her back, eyes closed as he held on and prayed.

More greasing and more turning. Bric could hear Weetley and Keeva as they worked in tandem to move the child. Zara and a female servant stood behind them, ensuring they had enough pig fat to grease up Eiselle's belly, and ensuring Weetley had everything he needed in order to ensure the safe and healthy delivery. More grunting and groaning from his wife and Bric was ready to explode but, mercifully, it came to a halt before he could.

"The child is turned as much as we can move him, my lady," Weetley said in his thin, high-pitched voice. "With your next pain, you must push as hard as you can."

Eiselle was breathing heavily from the pain of trying to turn her child around. For Bric's sake, she'd kept as quiet as she could because the pain was more than she had anticipated.

"I will," she gasped. Turning her head, she whispered to her husband. "Do not let me go, Bric. Hold me tightly."

It sounded like a plea to him, and a frightened one. Tears popped out of Bric's eyes, wetting the back of her shift where he had his face pressed against her.

"I will not let you go, I swear it," he said hoarsely. "I will not leave you."

That seemed to give Eiselle a great deal of comfort. When her next pain came, as they were very close together now, she was able to bear down and push with all her might. With every pain she would push again, as hard as she could, as Weetley and Keeva encouraged her.

But it seemed to Bric that Eiselle had been pushing for quite some time with little results. His arms were around her shoulders and he could feel her entire body tensing up every time she pushed. It was agonizing to feel her work so hard for something that was very slow in happening. But through it all, she maintained her composure, grunting and even growling as she pushed almost angrily sometimes. Just when

Bric thought he was surely going to lose his composure, Keeva gave a shout.

"I see him, Eiselle!" she cried. "Push very hard the next time, sweetheart. *Push!*"

Eiselle did. Summoning her dwindling strength one last time, she gave a big push when the next pain came and, suddenly, the baby dropped out right into Weetley's waiting hands.

Relief was almost instant, and Eiselle collapsed against the back of the chair, against Bric, breathing heavily.

"Is he well?" she demanded. "Keeva, is he well? Why is he not crying?"

A thin wail pierced the air and Eiselle burst into happy, exhausted tears, as did her husband. He was holding her so tightly that she could barely breathe, but Eiselle could feel Bric behind her, weeping into her back. She patted the arms that were locked around her.

"He is well," she assured Bric, as if he was the one needing comfort. "Do you hear him? He is well."

Bric lifted his head from where it had been pressed between Eiselle's shoulder blades. His cheeks were damp but there was a huge smile on his face as he kissed Eiselle's cheek over and over. Meanwhile, Keeva took the baby from Weetley as the man tended to the afterbirth and held the child up for the exhausted and elated parents.

"Look at him," she said joyfully. "Look how big he is!"

Eiselle and Bric got their first glimpse of the fat, lusty baby, now screaming loudly in the warmth of the room. It was, indeed, a boy, as they could see, and Eiselle held out her arms for him.

"Give him to me," she begged. "Oh, please give him to me."

Keeva complied, handing the child over to his eager mother, standing back as Eiselle carefully cradled the squirming infant against her breast. Overwhelmed with the first touch of her son, Eiselle started weeping again.

"Look," she sobbed, holding up his little fist. "He is so perfect. Look at his hands, Bric."

Bric was hovering over the pair, his eyes alight with wonder. "I cannot believe he is finally here," he said. Gently, he put his enormous hand on the baby's head, dwarfing it. "Eiselle, he is beautiful. Absolutely beautiful."

He kissed his wife again as she cradled the baby, both of them watching their newborn son with wonderment. For all of the anticipation they had felt towards this moment, nothing could do it justice. Bric felt as if he'd been born anew the moment his son had made his way into the world, because every hope and dream he'd ever had for his child somehow became a reality. A strong son to follow in his footsteps and a wife who had come through the birth unscathed.

He had so very much to be grateful for.

"He already looks like you," Eiselle said. "Look at his ears – they have a little point on them like yours do."

Bric smiled at the sight. "Blame my father," he said. "He has those ears, too."

"I think they are beautiful ears."

He laughed softly, putting timid fingers on those tiny baby ears. "He *is* perfect," he said, kissing Eiselle on the cheek. "Like you. Thank you, *mo chroí*. From the bottom of my heart, thank you."

Eiselle tore her gaze away from the baby, looking up at Bric and accepting his tender kisses of gratitude and adoration. But Keeva was lingering just behind them, interrupting their tender moment, although she was loathed to do it.

"Let me take the baby," she said. "He must be cleaned up and swaddled, and mother must be returned to her bed. Let me take care of them, Bric. You have done your duty."

Bric looked crestfallen. "But I want to stay."

Keeva shook her head, pulling him away from Eiselle and the baby. "You may return in time," she said. "But we must clean Eiselle up and put her to bed. She needs to rest now. You must go and tell the men that you now have a fine, strong son. You have received the greatest gift this night, Bric, and I am happy for you. So very happy."

Even in the midst of his own delight, Bric took time for Keeva, realizing this was a moment she had always wanted to experience but never would. He kissed her on the cheek to thank her for everything she had done, leaving her with a smile as he headed down to the great hall to inform his friends that, indeed, his son had been born this night.

Conor Dashiell Bentley Sean Rhys de Gael MacRohan had finally made his grand entrance. And, no... he'd never considered shortening the name, not once.

There was much joy at Narborough that night as the birth of the High Warrior's son spread among the men, and Bric brought out eight barrels of fine ale he'd purchased just for the occasion. As the night went on, men toasted the newest MacRohan son, offering their congratulations to the new father who prowled the grounds of Narborough that night as his wife slept, spending time with his men and drinking to Conor's good health.

Towards the early morning, he finally returned to his chamber, fairly drunk, to find Eiselle awake, breastfeeding their son as Keeva stood by to lend a hand. But Keeva departed once Bric entered, leaving the new family alone, and Bric lay down on the bed beside his wife, his head on her shoulder as he watched her feed their son for the first time. If there was a heaven, he knew he'd found it.

It was the best moment of his life.

The little boy with the name longer than he was would go on to do great and heroic things, mentored by a father who had become a legend in his own time.

The High Warrior was, indeed, immortal.

❧ THE END ❧

Bric and Eiselle's children:

Conor

Avaleen

Corey

Quinn

Kevin

Kira

For more information on other series and family groups, as well as a list of all of Kathryn's novels, please visit her website at www. kathrynleveque.com.

ABOUT KATHRYN LE VEQUE

Medieval Just Got Real.

KATHRYN LE VEQUE is a USA TODAY Bestselling author, an Amazon All-Star author, and a #1 bestselling, award-winning, multi-published author in Medieval Historical Romance and Historical Fiction. She has been featured in the NEW YORK TIMES and on USA TODAY's HEA blog. In March 2015, Kathryn was the featured cover story for the March issue of InD'Tale Magazine, the premier Indie author magazine. She was also a quadruple nominee (a record!) for the prestigious RONE awards for 2015.

Kathryn's Medieval Romance novels have been called 'detailed', 'highly romantic', and 'character-rich'. She crafts great adventures of love, battles, passion, and romance in the High Middle Ages. More than that, she writes for both women AND men – an unusual crossover for a romance author – and Kathryn has many male readers who enjoy her stories because of the male perspective, the action, and the adventure.

On October 29, 2015, Amazon launched Kathryn's Kindle Worlds Fan Fiction site WORLD OF DE WOLFE PACK. Please visit Kindle Worlds for Kathryn Le Veque's World of de Wolfe Pack and find many action-packed adventures written by some of the top authors in their genre using Kathryn's characters from the de Wolfe Pack series. As Kindle World's FIRST Historical Romance fan fiction world, Kathryn Le Veque's World of de Wolfe Pack will contain all of the great story-telling you have come to expect.

Kathryn loves to hear from her readers. Please find Kathryn on Facebook at Kathryn Le Veque, Author, or join her on Twitter @kathrynleveque, and don't forget to visit her website and sign up for her blog at www.kathrynleveque.com.

Please follow Kathryn on Bookbub for the latest releases and sales: bookbub.com/authors/kathryn-le-veque.

Made in the USA
Middletown, DE
26 June 2018